NEVER HAVE I EVER

NEVER HAVE I EVER

stories

Isabel Yap

Small Beer Press
Easthampton, MA

This is a work of fiction. All characters and events portrayed in this book are either fictitious or used fictitiously.

Small Beer Press
150 Pleasant Street #306
Easthampton, MA 01027
smallbeerpress.com
weightlessbooks.com
bookmoonbooks.com
info@smallbeerpress.com

Distributed to the trade by Consortium.

Library of Congress Cataloging-in-Publication Data

Names: Yap, Isabel, 1990- author.
Title: Never have I ever : stories / Isabel Yap.
Description: First edition. | Easthampton, MA : Small Beer Press, [2021] |
Summary: "Spells and stories, urban legends and immigrant tales: the magic in Isabel Yap's debut collection jumps right off the page, from the joy in her new novella, "A Spell for Foolish Hearts" to the terrifying tension of the urban legend "Have You Heard the One About Anamaria Marquez.""-- Provided by publisher.
Identifiers: LCCN 2020049102 | ISBN 9781618731821 (paperback) | ISBN 9781618731838 (ebook)
Subjects: LCGFT: Short stories.
Classification: LCC PR9550.9.Y37 N48 2021 | DDC 823/.92--dc23
LC record available at https://lccn.loc.gov/2020049102

First edition 1 2 3 4 5 6 7 8 9

Set in Centaur MT. Titles in Goudy Old Style.
Printed on 30% PCR recycled paper by the Versa Press in East Peoria, IL.

For Mommy, Lolo, and Carlo Santiago:
you taught me how I want to live

Contents

You've denied the hunger for so long that when you transform tonight, it hurts more than usual. You twist all the way round, feel your insides slosh and snap as you detach. Your wings pierce your skin as you leave your lower half completely. A sharp pain rips through your guts, compounding the hunger. Drifting toward the open window, you carefully unfurl your wings. It's an effort not to make a sound.

You're a small girl, but it's a small room, and though your boyfriend is snoring you can't risk being caught. You look back at him, remembering how he'd breathed your name a few hours ago, pouring sweat as you arched beneath him—*Kaye, baby, please.* You wonder if he'll say it that way when you eventually leave.

The half you've left behind is tucked in shadow: gray, muted pink where your intestines show through. The oversized shirt you're wearing hides the worst of the guts that hang from your torso as you glide into the sticky night air. You suck in a deep breath as the living bodies of your housing complex flood your senses. A girl sobs in her bedroom while her father hammers at the door. A pair of elderly foreigners lie in each other's arms. A stray dog licks its balls outside the iron gates while a security guard dozes in his cramped sitting room.

Manila is a city that sleeps only fitfully, and you love it and hate it for that reason.

The first thing taught at the Bakersfield Good Girl Reformation Retreat is the pledge: "I'm a good girl. A good girl for a good world. And while I know it is not always easy to be good, I promise to at least try." The girls are made to repeat this three times at orientation, and one girl seems moved enough to shout "Amen!" at the end. Or she could be mocking it; Sara can't tell. The girls on either side of her are listless, mouthing the pledge without care or conviction. One scratches her knee then digs underneath her fingernails, puckering and unpuckering her mouth like a goldfish. Sara suspects she's wearing a similar expression. She frowns and squints at the clear blue California sky, the same one from the home she was just forced to leave.

Afterwards they're herded onto the field for physical exercises and split into groups. Sara's group starts running. She quits on the second lap out of five, short of breath and thinking *nope, not worth it.* She jogs off the field and is trying to disappear someplace when Captain Suzy, who is in charge of PE, catches sight of her. Captain Suzy frowns and starts heading for her, except the flag football team erupts in a hair-snatching free-for-all. Captain Suzy surges into the brawl and flings girls away from each other, so that by the end mud and grass is strewn everywhere and more than one girl has fainted from the heat.

Later, Sara learns the fight was because of a butterfly knife that someone had snuck in and stupidly showed off. Lots of girls wanted it.

They're given Exploration time after lunch, with the stern reminder that they have to be prepared for Group Sharing (4:30 PM), followed by Journals (6 PM) in their respective rooms before

Dinner (7 PM). After leaving the dining hall, Sara surveys the abandoned schoolhouse where all Good Girls are forced to stay. It's mostly dusty classrooms with chalkboards. Tiny white bugs swirl in every sunbeam. Most chairs and tables are child-sized, and colored mats cover the floor. A mesh-wire fence circles the entire yard, and past it, a tall rusted gate. Beyond them lie endless fields, roasting under the sun. The fence is too tall to climb, and Sara is neither agile nor motivated. She heads back to her room and decides to Explore her bed.

There are meals all over the Metro, so many routes to explore. You've mapped them out over years and months of nightly travels: countless delicacies, different treats for different moods. The only difference is your start point, your end point. You never last more than a few months in the same place. You always need to find someone new to take you in—to believe you're human, just like them.

Tonight your hunger is confusing. You don't know what you want, what will satiate you. You decide to start upscale and work your way down, so you veer towards the part of the city with its lights still on.

Music pulses loudly from a club. Three high school girls totter out on four-inch heels, standing awkwardly on the carpet to avoid the potholed road. One of them is holding a phone to her ear. A car comes up; a maid hops out of the front seat and opens the door for the girls, and they climb in, unsteady from lack of practice or too many vodka Sprites. You think about dancing, about what it's like to occupy the skin of a beautiful party girl, something you can do with ease—slipping into a bar with confidence, slipping out with someone's fingers twined in yours, ready to point at the stars and laugh then lean in close for a kiss.

They can never smell the blood and sputum underneath the liquor in your breath. Humans make up wonderfully intricate rituals, pretend to have such control—but they easily devolve into animal longing, just heartbeats flaring in their cage of skin and bones.

Something is knocking at Sara's door. A monster of some kind, an overgrown baby bleeding from the chest. Its clawed fist is tapping in a way that's supposed to be quiet, almost polite—then Sara realizes she's asleep and scrambles out of bed.

She opens the door. It swings into the hallway and bumps into the girl standing there. "Sorry," Sara says. Her shirt is soaked in sweat.

"No worries. I'm Kaye! Nice to meet you." The girl's hand is cold and dry in Sara's gross sticky one.

"Sara," Sara says. "So I guess we're roommates?"

"Yep," Kaye says. She is petite and *gorgeous,* with shiny black hair and flawless honey-colored skin. Asian, but Sara can't guess which. She wears an easy, friendly grin as she wheels in her luggage. She stops to note which bed Sara has occupied, then throws her backpack onto the empty one.

Sara shuts the door and sits on her bed. She picks up her regulation Pen + Diary in a halfhearted effort to prep for Group Sharing, but ends up watching Kaye unpack instead. Kaye unzips her overstuffed luggage, displaying piles of neatly folded clothes and small colorful snacks: *Sweet Corn, Salt and Vinegar Chips, Boy Bawang.* Notebooks and papers are wedged between socks and shoes in plastic bags. Kaye fishes out a pair of slippers and slaps them on the floor triumphantly.

"So what's your deal?" Sara asks, as Kaye peels off her shoes and socks and sticks her feet into the slippers.

"I eat fetuses," Kaye replies. "If I feel like it, I eat organs too."

Sara frowns and shuts her notebook. Kaye doesn't elaborate, and starts sorting clothes on her bed. Sara leans forward so that she can better inspect Kaye's luggage. There are stickers all over it. One says *Fragile;* another says *Delta Airlines;* three are written in Chinese characters; two read *Wow! Philippines.* They're faded, the edges picked off as if someone with long fingernails was extremely bored.

"You came from abroad?"

"A few months ago." She opens a pack of chips and holds it out to Sara. Sara peers in; they look like shriveled corn kernels. She shakes her head.

"So you were flown all the way out here to stop eating babies," Sara repeats. Her gut churns, and a voice in her brain goes *no, no, no.*

"*Unborn* babies," Kaye clarifies. "But it's not like I can help it." She starts laying out her clothes on the bed, methodically. "I would tell you what they call me, but you wouldn't be able to pronounce it anyway."

"Try me," Sara says.

Kaye smirks and rips out a page from her regulation Diary, then scribbles something on it. She holds it up for Sara to read.

"Manananggal?" Sara tries.

Kaye collapses onto her bed laughing.

The sky is outlined by skyscrapers, some still in construction. A half-finished high-rise condo is fenced off with boards bearing the image of the newest starlet. She's wearing a red dress, hair fetchingly arranged over one shoulder, glass of champagne in hand. The flowery script next to her head reads: *Where luxury and comfort reside.*

The giant open-air shopping complex next to it is almost empty. A few cafes remain lit, although the chairs inside are turned up. A barkada of young professionals staggers back to the parking lot, high on caffeine and the adrenaline of overwork. They are laughing louder than the silence calls for. One man swears he will kill their boss the following morning.

You like these declarations. They can only be made at this hour—witching hour, *your* hour. You like them because they're not true.

❁

The Group Sharing discussion leader is named Apple. Sara ends up on her right, legs curled on the pink-and-orange mat. Apple greets everyone with a giant smile, then takes attendance. There are five girls in the sharing group, including Kaye. Apple begins by saying how happy she is that everyone has come to the Good Girl Reformation Retreat, where all girls are expected to be supportive and encouraging in their journey toward goodness.

"In order to get to know one another better, I would like each of you to tell the group which particular circumstances brought you here. There is no need to be shy or secretive about it. While we know it is not always easy to be good, we are now at Retreat, and we are going to try."

Tamika, seated on Apple's left, starts: she knifed her last boyfriend in the ribs. Trang has a habit of setting small fires because they are very pretty. Lena stalked her favorite lab teacher and sent threatening messages to his wife. Dana doesn't say anything, but she pulls up her shirt and shows everyone a scar that cuts across her extremely toned belly. Sara notices Kaye looking at the pinkish flesh marring Dana's brown skin with a sad smile.

"You have to tell us, Dana," Apple insists. Dana says, "It hurt," and that's all she can be persuaded to say.

"Maybe next time then," Apple says, with too much hope. "And you, Kaye?"

"I was brought to the US to marry someone," Kaye says, the perfect mix of defiant and ashamed. Someone gasps. Sara's mouth drops open, but Kaye doesn't notice, and adds: "I'm not as young as I look." She gives a tiny, tired grin, before proceeding to tell them about the drug bust at her husband's place, her illegal papers, how no one will pay for her flight back to Manila. How the US government took matters into its own hands, and sent her here. How she's homesick and rattled and maybe it's for the best that her husband of two months OD'ed, but really mostly she's glad to be here, it seems safe. Everyone nods solemnly, and Dana reaches out and holds Kaye's shoulder, briefly.

Liar, Sara thinks, but no, this is the truth. Of course this is the truth, and Kaye was just messing with her. Kaye was just having a little fun.

Then suddenly Apple says, "Sara? What about you, Sara?"

"I—" Sara says, and wonders how she can explain.

Manila's gated communities, home to the rich and famous, swanky as fuck. You flap past some consulates, flags drooping from their balconies, but you're not interested in foreign food today. You sweep closer, lower, appreciating the distinct features of each house: angels cut into columns, black iron gates with gold accents, circular drive-ways sweeping up to meticulously lit front doors. Gardens over-flowing with gumamela blossoms and palm trees. All the houses are humming with electricity, air-conditioners running at full blast. The humans moving inside them are less electric: house-helpers clearing leftover party dishes, children stuck on their game consoles, everyone else asleep. It's all boring boring boring until you smell tears—so much sorrow in the saline—from the odd modest house, a little decrepit for the neighborhood. The sound of sniffling is amplified. You stop and circle the air with interest.

Sara explains it like this:

"It started after I dropped my sister's baby. Nobody knew if the baby would be okay. Then the baby *was* okay, after they'd checked it out at the doctors 'cause everyone was convinced that the bruise was some kind of tumor. I was just playing with it. I just wanted to hold it for a little while. So anyway after that, I was forbidden to touch the baby. That was okay. I could deal with that.

"The problem was, I started always thinking about babies. Because a baby is this terrible, fragile thing, you know? And so many things can happen to it. I just kept theorizing: if you keep pushing your thumb into its head, won't your thumb actually sink into its brain? Or if you hold it upside down for too long—like those dads on TV, you know, always swinging their babies around?—like, maybe all the blood fills up its little brain and it gets a mini-baby-stroke. It got so bad that whenever I saw a baby, any baby, I got the sense that, like—me being alive—like it could cause that baby to die. Them or me, you know, and why the hell should it be me?

"So I started thinking I should fix that. I started looking out of windows and thinking I'm better off—you know—*out there.* Like when I'm in a moving car. Or when I'm in the fourth-floor corridor of my school building. I get this sense that I can jump out and all the babies in the world will be saved. I kept trying, but something would always stop me, and when they asked me what my problem was—you see how hard it is to explain? So I would tell them—I want to fly. That's all I could say. I want to fly."

She *is* pregnant, the private-school princess in her immaculate bedroom. The tiny thing growing inside her is incredibly fresh—six or seven weeks old—and she's just found out, or just admitted it to herself. She doesn't know what to do. She's composing an email to her boyfriend, or maybe her best friend. She types in quick bursts, interspersed with falling on her bed and beating her pillow with impassioned fists. You imagine the taste of her child in your mouth; you consider sucking it up and sparing her the agony of waking tomorrow. Wouldn't that be a mercy to this child? Not having to live with the shame of bearing her own, so young, and her parents so disappointed, and her schoolmates so ready to talk shit about her?

You settle on the roof, testing the tiles, positioning yourself above her bedroom.

Then she starts playing a Taylor Swift song. It's blaring from her iTunes and she is wailing on the bed, and suddenly it's so hilarious that you can't bear to end it. Besides, you don't want to wait for her to fall asleep. She might not fall asleep at all.

You sigh, take off again, and decide that it's time for a change of scenery.

"So that's your story," Sara says that night, eyes gazing into the pitch darkness. (Lights out at 9, 9 is so early, do they think anyone can *actually* sleep at 9?) "Mail-order bride. Drugs. Gross old man. That sounds really terrible, but that . . . makes more sense."

"That's why I'm here, but only *you* know the truth about me," Kaye says, an undercurrent of laughter in her voice. She sits up in bed, looks across at Sara, and Sara's only imagining the weird light reflecting in her irises. "Hey Sara, I'm glad the baby was okay, by the way. It wasn't your fault you were careless. Well I mean, it kind of is, but can anyone really blame you? Babies are such fragile things. I don't know why you girls keep having them."

"Says the baby-eater," Sara says, with what she hopes is humor, but she's exhausted and suddenly imagining a baby tumbling down the stairs.

"You don't believe me, do you?" Kaye laces her arms across her knees. "That's okay. I only told you because I thought maybe you wouldn't—haha. If you *did* believe me you probably wouldn't like me, and I'd have to say it's in my nature, and then we'd fight, and god I'd have to leave again, when I'm not even hungry yet. When I've got nowhere to go."

"You're weird," Sara says, because clearly Kaye is more messed up than she lets on.

Kaye laughs. There's so much laughter in her, it surprises Sara. Kaye crosses the room and sits on the opposite end of Sara's bed—so quickly, suddenly she's there and Sara sits up and draws her knees back reflexively. She should be freaked out, but after weeks of being treated like broken glass back home, in school—this proximity is not entirely unwelcome. Everyone sidestepping the baby issue, Dad and Mom hissing about suicide treatment in the kitchen after dinner, her meager friends suddenly evaporating.

A person who treats her like she's real? It's an odd relief. Kaye leans closer. She smells nice, and her eyes crinkle.

"Tell me about your home," Kaye says.

You head for a shantytown: homes made of hollow blocks, roofs of corrugated metal. It's hardly a mile from the fancy neighborhood. The nearby river is peaceful, although the banks are still torn up from the last typhoon. From a distance you can already smell people, piss, dogs with festering sores, wet grass, shit, washing detergent. The earth is always damp here, soaking up rain, and the proximity of the houses makes everything feel warmer, more alive.

They do this nightly talking thing a lot, exchanging stories, doodling on each other's Diaries then laughing and ripping out the pages. Then shushing each other. There's no TV and no nail polish and no ovens to bake brownies in—only these, their words, their memories.

Sara finds herself in Kaye's beloved Manila: garish colors everywhere, clogged highways, grimy naked children running next to spotless cars, in which the bourgeoisie sit with a driver, a maid, sometimes a bodyguard. Sara doesn't have much to say about her own suburban neighborhood in Pleasanton, but Kaye seems fascinated by America anyway, so Sara tries. She explains the difference between Democrats and Republicans, and the nuances of California slang: *Hella bomb,* they repeat. *Hella sick.*

Kaye describes the parts of the body she likes best—she eats the fetus pretty much whole because it's the tastiest ("I take it down my throat, and, uh . . . it's a little hard to explain,"), then the heart, liver, stomach. Kidneys are surprising flavorful. It must be the bile.

When she talks about her monster self Sara just holds the thought apart from her brain. It's too weird. It's almost funny, how earnest Kaye is about it.

Sara recounts her sister's wedding in Vegas, which they couldn't really afford, but it was cool to act touristy and kitschy, posing next to the unsexy French maids in the Paris Hotel casino. It was stupid, and that's what made it fun.

You count the number of warm bodies in each house you pass, considering the possible damage. Family of four, six, another six, three (absent father), four (absent mother), five (including grandmother). That one won't manage if you eat the mother, because Lola is sickly and Tatay beats the children. Interesting drama, but you seem to be craving something else. Entrails won't do tonight—you want a baby.

You're enchanted by the amount of closeness you find in many homes: sweaty couples pressed together, children crowded on either side, useless electric fans whirring. It's love and hunger bound up in acceptance, minute joys punctuated by a mostly typical dissatisfaction, the longing for something better, some way out of this.

They're not exactly unhappy, despite everything. You think you understand that.

Very lightly, you settle on a gray roof with a gaping hole in the corner. You look down at the man and woman tangled and snoring on a bed, their two-year-old squashed between them. The scent of fresh mangoes is just enough to entice you. There's only so much time left to properly enjoy your meal, so after a brief consideration you open your mouth and let your tongue slip through the ceiling.

The Retreat is all routines. After the first day, it's only variations on a theme, and it gets harder to remember when they started, although that's what the Diaries are for. Sara isn't too worried. It must be expensive to run the retreat. Girls come in batches, sponsored by donations, desperate family or community members, and government money; they can't stay forever. Three weeks, she figures. Four. In the meantime: free food, thirty other girls that are just as fucked up as she is, and even the daily exercise is starting to become manageable.

She figures things out. The cooks are on rotation, and the one every third day actually makes edible food. If you wake up at 5 there's still hot water left in the showers. It's okay to walk quickly instead of running during laps, as long as you finish all five. Apple expects you to write at least a paragraph in your diary every day, or else you'll have to do a long-ass recap at the end of the week. If only there was more to say.

Most girls stay in their rooms during off hours. If the retreat is for repentance, Sara's not sure how effective it is. At night she can usually hear sobbing down the hall, or hard objects (Bodies? Heads?) smacking against the walls (Sex? Fights? A mix?). Girls who act out are given warnings and punishments. There are no field trips, but they do painting and basket weaving, and learn an alarming number of songs in different languages. If not for the fact that someone always showed up for music class with a burst lip and a black eye, it would almost be like summer camp. Even the Captains turn nicer, only harsh when someone gripes about exercise or doesn't finish her tossed greens.

Still, despite the moderated peace, restlessness is starting to build beneath the monotony. Someone claims that on their last day the teachers will clear out, and they're going to gas the place, kill all the girls. It's a stupid claim, but it has its effects.

"What the fuck are we doing here?" becomes a common question, a chant: in between tooth-brushing, or eating soft-but-actually-hard rolls, or making honest-to-god charm bracelets.

Sara asks it, herself, sprawled out on her bed. *It's Going to be Okay!* is the motivational statement Apple has assigned them this week. It's pretty weak, as far as encouragement goes. "What the fuck are we doing here?"

She doesn't really expect an answer, but Kaye says, "Learning to be good girls. Right?"

"Well when do we get to say *okay already,* I get it, I'm good?"

Kaye shrugs. "What are you going to do when you get out of here, anyway?"

Sara doesn't answer, but she pictures it: going back, holding up her nephew triumphantly, the mediocre joy of normalcy after so much exposure to other people's shit. So she's thought about killing herself and has a weird thing about babies. She's never actually *hurt* anyone. *I'm not like these girls,* she thinks, and it makes her feel both proud and disgusted. Then she sees herself climbing onto a balcony, feeling the salt edge of the wind, wondering if there's still a part of her that wants to leave everything.

"Hey Sara. Were you serious about wanting to fly?"

Sara feels jolted. Kaye's eyes are opaque on hers.

"What do you mean?" Her heartbeat quickens. Kaye smiles and looks out their window.

"You get to decide. Are you going to be good when you leave here? Are you going to turn out all right? You could, you know. *You* could. There's no need to stop trying." She stands and stretches, then clasps her hands over her stomach meaningfully. "But not me. I don't get to pick. I never get to say *I'm good.* I can try, but I'm powerless against my hunger. I mean, we all need to eat sometimes, right?"

Sara swallows. Her saliva sticks in her throat. She isn't afraid of Kaye. Kaye is her friend. Her gorgeous, crazy, baby-eating, compulsively lying friend.

Kaye crosses the room, lightning quick, until she is standing before Sara. The setting sun turns her face a weird shade of orange. She crouches down so that she's level with Sara, stretched on her bed.

"You know," she says, face contorting, like she's holding back tears. "I'm getting hungry. I'm going to need to feed soon. Promise me something. We're friends, right, Sara?"

Sara pauses, maybe too long, before nodding. Then, to increase her conviction: "Yeah. Of course."

"When I feed—promise me that you won't care. You can just—sleep. It doesn't really change anything. I've always been this way, you know? And all you girls—" she shakes her head, stops herself. "You do that for me, I'll let you fly for one night. It's nicer here than in Manila. It's cooler." She pats the top of Sara's head. Which is funny, because she's shorter than Sara.

"What do you think?" she asks. "I *can* fly, you know. I'm pretty fucking great at it."

Sara thinks of falling, of landing on the pavement and hearing her shoulder shatter, seeing her own blood streak out past her vision. Her mother sobbing by her bed at the hospital, saying *I can't do this anymore, honey. It has to stop.* And after being released, how she'd had no idea, how the van had come one day, and in a haze of antidepressants she'd stepped onboard. She'd come here.

If Kaye could fly—hold her, dance her through the air—she'd be able to see. If it's safe to go back. If she's tired of being this way, at least for now.

But more than that, Kaye wants her to pretend everything's fine. She can do that. She's had a lot of practice.

She reaches up and puts her hand on top of Kaye's, not feeling scared or threatened or awed. Just tired. Bonesucked tired. She squeezes Kaye's hand and says, "Okay."

Your tongue settles on her stomach, and you start feeding, sucking greedily. You're starving, and it tastes so fucking delicious. The woman squirms, and the child next to her utters a short, soft moan. You don't want this. You do.

Sara wakes up sweating. It's sometime past midnight? It's too early. She needs to go back to sleep. She shuts her eyes. The sound of her breathing is too loud. She decides to get a glass of water and stumbles out of bed, bumping into something in the middle of the floor. She falls backwards, landing on her ass.

The window is open, the metal fastenings they installed after some girl attempted escape somehow undone. A cloudy moonbeam streams through it, illuminating the lower half of Kaye's torso and her legs, her feet still in their slippers. It is standing erect, perfectly immobile, like someone sliced a girl in half and left it there for fun. The insides are shimmering, grisly, unreal.

Sara crawls back under her sheets and goes to sleep. Sometime later something slides in next to her, nudging for space on her pillow. Something wraps its arms around Sara and puts its forehead against the small of Sara's back. Sara smells blood mixed with the faint tinge of—mango?—and after a moment's hesitation, she holds those arms against her. The back of her shirt grows damp with what might be tears.

When you're finished, when you've shriveled up everything inside her stomach so that your own is full, you spool your tongue back into your mouth and breathe deeply. The horizon tells you that you have about an hour before the sun rises. That's just enough time to head home, rejoin your lower half, shuffle back into bed. Good girls don't get caught with babies in their bellies; good girls don't lie; good girls don't sneak out wearing only their boyfriends' shirts.

You know what you are; you know what you aren't.

In their twentieth session, Apple says they've all been exceedingly Good Girls, and they're going to be moving on the following week. The girls have demonstrated that they've absorbed the values of the retreat and are ready to rejoin the good world. Once Admin gets their paperwork done, the Captains do their sign-offs, and the discussion leaders file their reports—the girls will be free.

"You get to go back home," Kaye says while they're packing.

"So do you," Sara says, but she's suddenly not sure.

Kaye flashes her teeth, feral. "I told you, girl, I don't have one. I go where the wind takes me!" She flings out her arms, dramatically, and flops backwards on her bed. "This was nice," she says. "Even when it sucked it was okay. I should hang out with girls more. They don't want as much from you as guys do. I can stay full for longer! Girls are like fiber."

Sara doesn't like the wistful tone in Kaye's voice. Sara doesn't like how her own heart squeezes, or how lonely she feels. How afraid she is of going home to find—but no, it'll be okay. She's different now. She's going to do better.

You get to decide, Kaye said. It's not that easy. But she can try. Some girls will break their promises, lose their homes, keep on rattling against the gates, biting and sobbing and breathing. Sara, if she wants to, can change.

Kaye rolls over on her bed, arm covering her eyes. She lifts it to peer at Sara. "I still owe you. How about tonight?"

You've never detached with someone watching. You're so fascinated by her gaze on you that you hardly notice the pain. Sara's big blue eyes are an excellent mirror—how there are stringy bits when you twist off, how the way your spine tears from sinew is fluid, almost graceful. Your shirt is short this time so she sees your entrails hanging out, nearly glowing with all the slick against them.

To her credit, Sara doesn't vomit. You move slowly over to the window, keeping your wings folded, and undo the latches with your knifelike fingers. You drift out and motion for her to stand on the desk. She climbs up, shakily, and says, "Can you really carry me?"

You like to think your smile, at least, is familiar—even if the pointed tongue between your teeth isn't.

"Yeah," you say. "Trust me." This is you: this is your life, the strength that fills you as you fly, feed, move on. Spanning provinces, cities, countries, continents. Finding new homes to leave, new bodies to keep you warm when you're not hungry, new strangers to suck dry when you are. And you'll keep doing this, as long as you can make it back in time. Before the sun rises, or someone finds the parts you've left behind—something must always be left behind.

This is how you survive.

Sara will get to go home. You'll just have to find a new one.

"You ready?" The trees are crowding out most of the wind, but you can still taste the breeze, drifting over the dormitories where so many girls are sleeping like wolves, retreating from the world. Just waiting to bare their fangs.

Sara nods. You can't read her expression—like she's about to scream or laugh or cry. You squeeze her hand as hard as you can without hurting her, and spread your wings.

A Cup of Salt Tears

Someone once told Makino that women in grief are more beautiful. *So I must be the most beautiful woman in the world right now,* she thinks, as she shucks off her boots and leaves them by the door. The warm air of the onsen's changing room makes her skin tingle. She slips off her stockings, skirt, and blouse; folds her underwear and tucks her glasses into her clean clothes; picks up her bucket of toiletries, and enters the washing area. The thick, hot air is difficult to breathe. She lifts a stool from the stack by the door, walks to her favorite spot, and squats down, resting for a few beats.

Kappa kapparatta.

Kappa rappa kapparatta.

She holds the shower nozzle and douses herself in warm water, trying to get the smell of sickness off her skin.

Tottechitteta.

She soaps and shampoos with great deliberation, repeating the rhyme in her head: *kappa snatched; kappa snatched a trumpet. The trumpet blares.* It is welcome nonsense, an empty refrain to keep her mind clear. She rinses off, running her fingers through her sopping hair, before standing and padding over to the edge of the hot bath. It is a blessing this onsen keeps late hours; she can only come once she knows Tetsuya's doctors won't call her. She tests the water with one foot, shuddering at the heat, then slips in completely.

No one else ever comes to witness her grief, her pale lips and sallow skin. Once upon a time, looking at her might have been a privilege; she spent some years smiling within the pages of *Cancam* and *Vivi,* touting crystal-encrusted fingernails and perfectly glossed lips. She never graced a cover, but she did spend a few weeks on the posters for *Liz Lisa* in Shibuya 109. It was different after she got married and left Tokyo, of course. She and Tetsuya decided to move back to her hometown. Rent was cheaper, and there were good jobs for doctors like him. She quickly found work at the bakery, selling melon pan and croissants. Occasionally they visited her mother, who, wanting little else from life, had grown sweet and mellow with age. Makino thought she understood that well; she had been quite content, until Tetsuya fell ill.

She wades to her favorite corner of the bath and sinks down until only her head is above the water. She squeezes her eyes shut. *How long will he live,* she thinks, *How long will we live together?*

She hears a soft splash and opens her eyes. Someone has entered the tub, and seems to be approaching her. She sinks deeper, letting the water cover her upper lip. As the figure nears, she sees its features through the mist: the green flesh, the webbed hands, the sara—the little bowl that forms the top of its head—filled with water that wobbles as it moves. It does not smell of rotting fish at all. Instead, it smells like a river, wet and earthy. Alive. Some things are different: it is more man-sized than child-sized, it has flesh over its ribs; but otherwise it looks just as she always imagined.

"Good evening," the kappa says. The words spill out of its beak, smoothly liquid.

Makino does not scream. She does not move. Instead she looks at the closest edge of the bath, measuring how long her backside will be exposed if she runs. She won't make it. She presses against the cold tile and thinks, *Tetsuya needs me,* thinks, *No, that's a lie, I can't even help him.* Her fear dissipates, replaced by helplessness, a brittle calm.

"This is the women's bath," she says. "The men's bath is on the other side."

"Am I a man?"

She hears the ripples of laughter in its voice, and feels indignant, feels ashamed.

"No. Are you going to eat me?"

"Why should I eat you, when you are dear to me?" Its round black eyes glimmer at her in earnest.

The water seems to turn from hot to scalding, and she stands upright, flushed and dizzy. "I don't know who you are!" she shouts. "Go away!"

"But you do know me. You fell into the river and I buoyed you to safety. You fell into the river and I kissed your hair."

"That wasn't you," she says, but she never did find out who it was. She thinks about certain death; thinks, *Is it any different from how I live now?* It can't possibly know this about her, can't see the holes that Tetsuya's illness has pierced through her; but then, what *does* it know?

"I would not lie to you," it says, shaking its head. The water in its sara sloshes gently. "Don't be afraid. I won't touch you if you don't wish me to."

"And why not?" She lifts her chin.

"Because I love you, Makino."

She reads to Tetsuya from the book on her lap, even when she knows he isn't listening. He stares out the window with glassy eyes, tracing the movements of invisible birds. The falling snow is delicate, not white so much as the ghost of white, the color of his skin. Tetsuya never liked fairytales much, but she indulges herself, because the days are long, and she hates hospitals. The only things she can bear to read are the stories of her childhood, walls of words that keep back the tide of desperation when Tetsuya turns to her and says, "Excuse me, but I would like to rest now."

It's still better than the times when he jerks and lifts his head, eyes crowding with tears, and says, "I'm so sorry, Makino." Then he attempts to stand, to raise himself from the bed, but of course he can't, and she must rush over and put her hand on his knee to keep him from moving, she must kiss his forehead and each of his wet eyes and tell him, "No, it's all right, it's all right." There is a cadence to the words that makes her almost believe them.

Tetsuya is twelve years her senior. They met just before she started her modeling career. He was not handsome. There was something monkeylike about his features, and his upper lip formed a strange peak over his lower lip. But he was gentle, careful; a doctor-in-training with the longest, most beautiful fingers she has ever seen. He was a guest at the home of her tea ceremony sensei. When she handed the cup to him, he cradled her fingers in his for a moment, so that her skin was trapped between his hands and the hot ceramic. When he raised the drink to his lips, his eyes kept darting to her face, though she pretended not to notice by busying herself with the next cup.

He thanked her then as he does now, shyly, one stranger to another.

She has barely settled in the bath when it appears.

"You've come back," it says.

She shrugs. Her shoulders bob out of the water. As a girl Makino was often chided for her precociousness by all except her mother, who held her own odd beliefs. Whenever they visited a temple, Makino would whisper to the statues, hoping they would give her some sign they existed—a wink, maybe, or a small utterance. Some kind of blessing. She did this even in Tokyo DisneySea, to the statue of Rajah the Tiger, the pet of her beloved Princess Jasmine. There was a period in her life when she wanted nothing more than to be a Disney Princess.

It figures, of course, that the only yōkai that ever speaks to her is a kappa. The tips of its dark hair trail in the water, and its beaklike mouth is half-open in an expression she cannot name. The ceiling lights float gently in the water of its sara.

She does not speak, but it does not go away. It seems content to watch her. *Can't you leave me here, with my grief?*

"Why do you love me?" she asks at last.

It blinks slowly at her, pale green lids sliding over its eyes. She tries not to shudder, and fails.

"Your hips are pale like the moon, yet move like the curves of ink on parchment. Your eyes are broken and delicate and your hands are empty." It drifts closer. "Your hair is hair I've kissed before; I do not forget the hair of women I love."

I am an ugly woman now, she thinks, but looking at its gaze, she doesn't believe that. Instead she says, "Kappa don't save people. They drown them."

"Not I," it says.

Makino does not remember drowning in the river. She does not remember any of those days spent in bed. Her mother told her afterwards that a policeman saved her, or it might have been the grocer's son, or a teacher from the nearby elementary school. It was a different story each time. It was only after she was rescued that they finally patched the broken portion of the bridge. But that was so many years ago, a legend of her childhood that was smeared clear by time, whitewashed by age. She told Tetsuya about it once, arms wrapped around his back, one leg between his thighs. He kissed her knuckles and told her she was lucky, it was a good thing she didn't die then, so that he could meet her and marry her and make love to her, the most beautiful girl in the world.

She blinks back tears and holds her tongue.

"I will tell you a fairytale," the kappa says, "because I know you love fairytales. A girl falls into a river—"

"Stop," she says. "I don't want to hear it." She holds out her hands, to keep it from moving closer. "My husband is dying."

Tetsuya is asleep during her next visit. She cradles his hand in hers, running her thumb over his bony fingers—so wizened now, unable to heal anyone. She recalls the first time she noticed her love for him. She was making koicha, tea to be shared among close companions, under her teacher's watchful gaze. Tetsuya wasn't even present, but she found herself thinking of his teeth, his strange nervous laughter, the last time he took her out for dinner. The rainbow lights of Roppongi made zebra stripes across his skin, but he never dared kiss her, not even when she turned as the train was coming, looking at him expectantly. He never dared look her in the eye, not until she told him she would like to see him again, fingers resting on his sleeve.

She looked down at the tea she was whisking and thought, *This tastes like earth, like the bone marrow of beautiful spirits, like the first love I've yet to have. It is green like the color of spring leaves and my mother's favorite skirt and the skin of a kappa. I'm in love with him.* She whisked the tea too forcefully, some of it splashing over the edge of the cup.

"Makino!" her sensei cried.

She stood, heart drumming in her chest, bowed, apologized, bowed again. The tea had formed a butterfly-shaped splotch on the tatami mats.

Tetsuya's sudden moan jolts her from her thoughts—a broken sound that sets her heart beating as it did that moment, long ago. She spreads her palm over his brow.

Does a kappa grant wishes? Is it a water god? Will it grant my wish, if I let it touch me? Will I let it touch me?

She gives Tetusya's forehead a kiss. "Don't leave me before the New Year," she says. She really means *don't leave me.*

❁

This time, it appears while she's soaping her body.

It asks if it can wash her hair.

She remains crouched on her stool. The suggestion of touch makes her tremble, but she keeps her voice even. "Why should I let you?"

"Because you are dear to me."

"That isn't true," she says. "I do know about you. You rape women and eat organs and trick people to get their shirikodama, and I'm not giving you that, I'm not going to let you stick your hand up my ass. I don't want to die. And Tetsuya needs me."

"What if I tell you I need you? What if I could give you what you want? What if I," it looks down at the water, and for a moment, in the rising mist, it looks like Tetsuya, when she first met him. Hesitant and wondering and clearly thinking of her. Monkeylike, but somehow pleasing to her eyes. "What if I could love you like him?"

"You're not him," she says. Yet when it reaches out to touch her, she does not flinch. Its fingers in her hair are long and slim and make her stomach curl, and she only stops holding her breath when it pulls away.

The grocery is full of winter specials: Christmas cakes, discounted vegetables for nabe hotpot, imported hot chocolate mixes. After Christmas is over, these shelves will be rapidly cleared and filled with New Year specials instead, different foods for osechi-ryōri. Her mother was always meticulous about a good New Year's meal: herring roe for prosperity, sweet potatoes for wealth, black soybeans for health, giant shrimp for longevity. They're only food, however; not spells, not magic. She ignores the bright display and walks to the fresh vegetables, looking for things to add to her curry.

She's almost finished when she sees the pile of cucumbers, and ghostlike, over it, the kitchen of her childhood. Mother stands next to her, back curved in concentration. She is carving Makino's name into a cucumber's skin with a toothpick. "We'll throw this in the river," Mother says, "so that the kappa won't eat you."

"Does the kappa only appear in the river, Mother? And why would the kappa want to eat me?"

"Because it likes the flesh of young children, it likes the flesh of beautiful girls. You must do this every year, and every time you move. And don't let them touch you, darling. I am telling you this for you are often silly, and they are cruel; do not let them touch you."

"But what if it does touch me, Mother?"

"Then you are a foolish girl, and you cannot blame me if it eats up everything inside you."

Young Makino rubs the end of the cucumber.

Is there no way to befriend them, Mother? But she doesn't say those words, she merely thinks them, as her mother digs out the last stroke, the tail end of *no* in *Ma-ki-no.*

She frowns at the display, or perhaps at the memory. *If I throw a cucumber in the hot spring it will merely be cooked,* she thinks. She buys a few anyway. At home, she hesitates, and then picks one up and scratches in Tetsuya's name with a knife. She drops it into the river while biking to work the following morning. The rest of them she slices and eats with chilled yogurt.

When it appears next it is close enough that if it reached out it could touch her, but it stays in place.

"Shall I recite some poetry for you?"

She shakes her head. She thinks, *The skins we inhabit and the things we long to do inside them, why are they so different?*

"I don't even know your name," she says.

The way its beak cracks open looks almost like a smile. "I have many. Which would please you?"

"The true one."

It is quiet for a moment, then it says, "I will give you the name I gave the rice farmer's wife, and the shogun's daughter, and the lady that died on the eve of the firebombs."

"Women you have loved?" Her own voice irritates her, thin and breathless in the steam-filled air.

"Women who have called me Kawataro," it says. "Women who would have drowned, had I not saved them and brought them back to life."

"Kawataro," she says, tears prickling at the corner of her eyes. "Kawataro, why did you save me?"

"Kindness is always worth saving."

"Why do you say I am kind?"

It tips its head, the water inside sloshing precariously. It seems to be saying, *Will you prove me wrong?*

She swallows, lightheaded, full of nothing. Her pulse simmers in her ears. She crosses the distance between them and presses herself against its hard body, kisses its hard little mouth. Its hands, when they come up to stroke her back, are like ice in the boiling water.

Kawataro does not appear in the onsen the next time she visits. There are two foreigners sitting in the bath, smiling at her nervously, aware of their own intrusion. The blonde woman, who is quite lovely, chats with Makino in halting Japanese about how cold it is in winter, how there is nothing more delightful than a warm soak, or at least that's what Makino thinks she is saying. Makino smiles back politely, and does not think about the feeling rising in her stomach—a strange hunger, a low ache, a sharp and painful relief.

This is not a fairytale, Makino knows, and she is no princess, and the moon hanging in the sky is only a moon, not a jewel hanging on a queen's neck, not the spun silk on a weaver's loom. The man she loves is dying, snowfall is filling her ears, and she is going to come apart unless somebody saves him.

The bakery closes for the winter holiday, the last set of customers buying all the cakes on Christmas Eve. Rui comes over as Makino is removing her apron. "Mizuki-san. Thank you for working hard today." She bows. "I'll be leaving now."

"Thank you for working hard today," Makino echoes. She's not the owner, but she is the eldest of the staff, the one who looks least attractive in their puffy, fluffy uniforms. Rui and Ayaka are college students; Yurina and Kaori are young wives, working while they decide whether they want children. Makino gets along with them well enough, but recently their nubile bodies make her tired and restless.

She never had her own children—a fact that Tetsuya mourned, then forgave, because he had a kind heart, because he knew her own was broken. She used to console herself by thinking it was a blessing, that she could keep her slim figure, but even that turned out to be a lie.

Rui twists her fingers in her pleated skirt, hesitating. Makino braces herself for the question, but it never comes, because the bell over the door rings and a skinny, well-dressed boy steps in. Rui's face breaks into a smile, the smile of someone deeply in love. "Just a minute," she calls to the boy. He nods and brings out his phone, tapping away. She turns back to Makino and dips her head again.

"Enjoy yourself," Makino says, with a smile.

"Thank you very much. Merry Christmas," Rui answers. Makino envies her; hates her, briefly, without any real heat. Rui whips off her apron, picks up her bag, and runs to the boy. They stride together into the snowy evening.

That night, the foreigners are gone, and Kawataro is back. It tells her about the shogun's daughter. How she would stand in the river and wait for him, her robes gathered around one fist. How her child, when it was born, was green, and how she drowned it in the river, sobbing, before anyone else could find it. How Kawataro had stroked her hair and kissed her cheeks and—Makino doesn't believe this part—how it had grieved for its child, their child, floating down the river.

"And what happened?" Makino says, trailing one finger idly along Kawataro's shoulders. They are sitting together on the edge of the tub, their knees barely visible in the water.

Kawataro's tongue darts over its beak. Makino thinks about having that tongue in her mouth, tasting the minerals of the bathwater in her throat. She thinks about what it means to be held in a monster's arms, what it means to hold a monster. Kappa nappa katta, kappa nappa ippa katta.

Am I the leaf he has bought with sweet words, one leaf of many?

Kawataro turns to her, face solemn as it says, "She drowned herself."

It could not save her, perhaps; or didn't care to, by then? Makino thinks about the shogun's daughter: her bloated body sailing through the water, her face blank in the moonlight, the edges of her skin torn by river dwellers. She thinks of Kawataro watching her float away, head bent, the water in its sara shimmering under the stars.

Katte kitte kutta.

Will I be bought, cut, consumed?

She presses her damp forehead against Kawataro's sleek green shoulder. *Have I already been?*

"How will this story end?" she asks.

It squeezes her knee with its webbed hand, then slips off the ledge into the water, waiting for her to follow. She does.

She spends Christmas Day in the hospital, alternately napping, reading to Tetsuya, and exchanging pleasantries with the doctors and nurses who come to visit. She leans as close as she can to him, as if proximity might leech the pain from his body, everything that makes him ache, makes him forget. It won't work, she knows. She doesn't have that kind of power over him, over anyone. Perhaps the closest she has come to such power is during sex.

The first time she and Tetsuya made love he'd been tender, just as she imagined, his fingers trembling as he undid the hooks of her bra. She cupped his chin and kissed his jaw and ground her hips against his, trying to let him know she wanted this, he didn't need to be afraid. He gripped her hips and she wrapped her legs around him, licking a wet line from his neck to his ear. He carried her to the bed, collapsing so that they landed in a tangled pile, desperately grappling with the remainders of each other's clothing. His breath was ragged as he moved slowly inside her, and she tried not to cry out, afraid of how much she wanted him, how much she wanted him to want her.

On his lips that night her name was a blessing: the chant of monks, the magic spells all fairytales rest on.

Now he stirs, and his eyes open. He says her name with a strange grace, a searching wonder, as if how they came to know each other is a mystery. "Makino?"

"Yes, my darling?"

His breath, rising up to her, is the stale breath of the dying.

"So that's where you are," he says at last. He gropes for her hand and holds it. "You're there, after all. That's good." He pauses, for too long, and when she looks at him she sees he has fallen asleep once more.

The next time they meet, they spend several minutes soaking together in silence.

She breaks it without preamble. "Kawataro, why do you love me?" Her words are spoken without coyness or fear or fury.

"A woman in grief is a beautiful one," it answers.

"That's not enough."

Kawataro's eyes are two black stones in a waterfall of mist. It is a long time before it finally speaks.

"Four girls," it says. "Four girls drowned in three villages, before they fixed the broken parts in the bridges over the river. My river." It extends its hand and touches the space between her breasts, exerting the barest hint of pressure. Her body tenses, but she keeps silent, immobile. "You were the fifth. You were the only one who accepted my hand when I stretched it out. You," it says, "were the only one who let me lay my hands upon you."

The memory breaks over her, unreal, so that she almost feels like Kawataro has cast a spell on her—forged it out of dreams and warped imaginings. The terrible rain. The realization that she couldn't swim. The way the riverbank swelled, impenetrable as death. How she sliced her hand open on a tree root, trying desperately to grab on to something. How she had seen the webbed hand stretched towards her, looked at the gnarled monkey face, sobbed as she clung for her life, river water and tears and rain mingled on her cheeks. How it tipped its head down and let something fall into her gaping, gurgling mouth, to save her.

"I was a stupid little girl," she says. "I could have drowned then, to spare myself this." She laughs, shocking herself; the sound bounces limply against the tiles.

Kawataro looks away.

"You are breaking my heart, Makino."

"You have no heart to break," she says, in order to hurt it; yet she also wants to be near it, wants it to tell her stories, wants its cold body to temper the heat of the water.

It looks to the left, to the right, and it takes a moment for her to realize that it is shaking its head. Then in one swift motion it wraps its arms around her and squeezes, hard, and Makino remembers how kappa like to wrestle, how they can force the life out of horses and cattle by sheer strength. "I could drain you," it says, hissing into her ear. "I could take you apart, if that would help. I could take everything inside you and leave nothing but a hollow shell of your skin. I do not forget kindness, but I will let you forget yours, if it will please you."

Yes, she thinks, and in the same heartbeat, *but no, not like this.*

She pushes against it, and it releases her. She takes several steps back and lifts her head, appraising.

"Will you heal my husband?" she asks.

"Will you love me?" it asks.

The first time she fell in love with Tetsuya, she was making tea. The first time she fell in love, she was drowning in a river.

"I already do."

Kawataro looks at her with its eyes narrowed in something like sadness, if a monster's face could be sad. It bows its head slightly, and she sees the water inside it—everything that gives it strength—sparkling, reflecting nothing but the misted air.

"Come here," it says, quiet and tender. "Come, my darling Makino, and let me wash your back."

Tetsuya drinks the water from Kawataro's sara.

Tetsuya lives.

The doctors cannot stop saying what a miracle it is. They spend New Year's Eve together, eating the osechi-ryōri Makino prepared. They wear their traditional attire and visit the temple at midnight, and afterwards they watch the sunrise, holding each other's cold hands.

It is still winter, but some stores have already cleared space for their special spring bargains. Makino mouths a rhyme as she sets aside ingredients for dinner. Tetsuya passes her and kisses her cheek, thoughtlessly. He is on his way to the park for his afternoon walk.

"I'm leaving now," he says.

"Come back safely," she answers. She feels just as much affection for Tetsuya as she did before, but nothing else. Some days her hollowness frightens her. Most days she has learned to live with it.

When the door shuts behind him, she spends some moments in the kitchen, silently folding one hand over the other. She decides to take a walk. Perhaps after the walk she will visit her mother. She puts a cucumber and a paring knife into her bag and heads out. By now the cold has become bearable, like the empty feeling in her chest. She follows the river towards the bridge where she once nearly lost her life.

In the middle of the bridge she stands and looks down at the water. She has been saved twice now by the same monster. Twice is more than enough. With a delicate hand, she carves the character for love on the cucumber, her eyes blurring, clearing. She leans over the bridge and lets the cucumber fall.

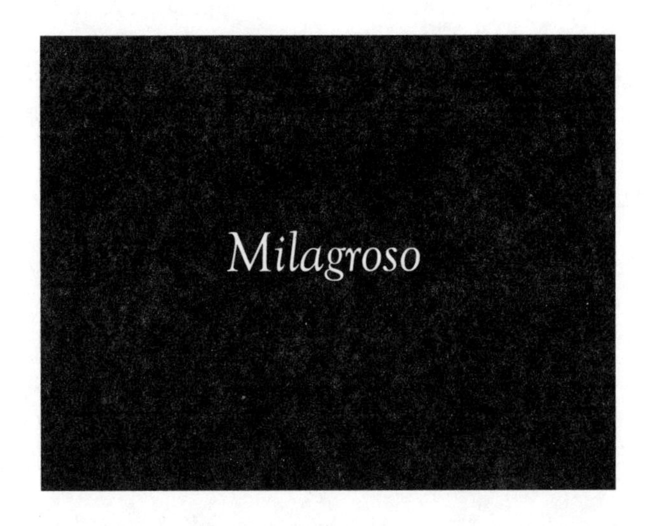

It's late afternoon on the eve of the Pahiyas Festival when Marty finally drives into Lucban. The streets are filled with people congregating outside their houses, stringing up fruits and vegetables shaped into chandeliers. Entire roofs are covered in kiping, leaf-shaped rice wafers, their colors flared to dazzling by the slowly setting sun. Someone has tacked poster paper all over the preschool wall, and children with paint smeared on their cheeks are making trees full of hand-shaped leaves. Vendors have already set up shop, prepping for the onslaught of tourists.

Most side streets are blocked, so Marty has to drive through the town center, which is the usual explosion of propaganda—posters of the mayor and councilors alternate with banners for washing detergents, Coca-Cola, Granny Goose Chips, and the latest summer-special, *MangoMazings—exactly like the real thing!* Marty ignores these as he navigates the still-familiar streets. They didn't leave Manila for this.

They left Manila to see a miracle.

Inez is stirring awake, though she keeps her eyes shut. She groans, shifts, and slaps her thigh, impatiently. In the rearview mirror, Marty can see Mariah's head snapping back and forth to match the car's rhythm, her mouth hanging open. JR is also asleep; the seat belt is tight across his hunched chest, making him look smaller than he is. Sunlight beams through the car, shading half his face yellow.

"Is this Lucban, hon?" Inez has finally stopped forcing sleep. She yawns and stretches her arms.

"Yep." Marty tries to sound more awake and cheerful than he feels.

Inez looks out the window. "How colorful," she says, as they drive past a house with a giant Ronald McDonald stationed by the doorway, waving his hands. Her tone makes everything seem gray.

Marty stands by the door, wiping his palms on his shorts. Looking up, he sees five strings of kiping dangling from the second-floor balcony. Even their ratty papier-mâché carabao is out, gazing forlornly at the street with its one remaining eye.

Inez is looking for a spot with better reception; he can hear her muttering in the distance. The kids are unloading their luggage.

"Tao po," Marty calls. When no one replies, he enters, heading for the living room. "Manong? Mang Kikoy? You there?"

He hears a door creak open, then the slap of slippers as Mang Kikoy shuffles into view. His skin is wrinkled and brown as tree bark. The mole on his cheek has grown even more colossal, but otherwise he is the same old Mang Kikoy who has maintained this house, Marty's ancestral home, since forever.

"Boy? Is that you?"

"Yes, manong."

"Just in time, just in time. Where is your family?"

"Outside," Marty says, feeling a twinge of guilt. It's been a little too long, perhaps, a little too late—but once he married Inez, and they had Mariah, he'd felt compelled to remain in Manila. He liked his job at San Miguel Corp., and he always believed that Lucban was near enough that they could visit anytime. As a result, they never did. To ignore these thoughts, he asks, "I noticed the décor. Are we part of the procession this year?"

"No, but I thought it might be good to decorate the house anyway. You never know."

Mariah materializes at Marty's elbow, dragging her duffel bag. "Dad, it's so *hot,*" she says, fanning herself.

Mang Kikoy beams at her and moves forward to take her bag.

"Please don't—it's heavy." Marty turns to his daughter. "Mariah, this is your Manong Kikoy. Show him you can carry your own bag, please."

"Hello po," she says, straining for politeness as she lugs her bag towards the stairs.

"Hello, hija." Mang Kikoy grins wider as she slouches past. His teeth are a gray, sickly color. "Well, Boy, I must go back outside; the kiping is cooking. Let's talk again later."

"Sure," he says. Mang Kikoy has already turned to go when JR rushes past, arms held stiffly away from his body, making fighter-jet noises.

"*Wee-oop! Wee-oop!*" he yells. "I'm attacking you! Propeller BLAST!"

He makes swiping motions at Mang Kikoy, who laughs. "So this is your little kulilit. Has he ever tasted a miracle before?"

Marty's throat dries. He swallows. He doesn't ask, *Is it true, manong? Is it real?* He doesn't say, *It's not right, who knows what eating those things can do.* Instead he puts a hand on JR's head, to stop him from airplane-ing, and says, "No, never."

Dinner is at Aling Merrigold's. Inez fusses over their clothes and hair, and asks Marty *twice* whether they shouldn't have brought some pasalubong from Manila. The children are sleepy, already bored. Marty promises that tomorrow will be more fun.

On the way to dinner they walk past increasingly extravagant houses. One has a robo-rooster attached to its roof, where it *cacaws* ear-splittingly every minute. Another has *The Last Supper* rendered on its walls, made with colored straw and palm leaves. Still another bears the mayor's face, fashioned out of kiping, all across the roof. Two giant animatronic carabaos are lowing by the main door, while a life-sized San Isidro stands on a rotating platform. He holds a spade in one hand and a sheaf of corn in the other.

"Farmer Jesus!" JR exclaims.

"That's not Jesus, you idiot." Mariah snaps a picture with her phone. "Who's this, Dad? I want to tag it properly."

"San Isidro Labrador. Patron saint of farmers and peasants."

"That's Mang Delfin's house," Mang Kikoy adds. "This year, the procession goes through this road, and he's determined to win. He's got a pretty good chance, don't you think?"

Marty nods, although the house speaks for itself. The Pahiyas Festival has always been a chance to show off one's home, but now the stakes are even higher. These homeowners want to be chosen for the miracle. They want to boast of a natural harvest, and have jealous neighbors beg them for a taste.

Aling Merrigold's house at the far end of the main street is simpler, though she has deployed her trademark rose pattern that no one has been able to copy. Vivid fuchsias and yellows adorn the typically drab white walls. She welcomes each of them in by smelling their cheeks.

"Martino!" she coos. "I haven't seen you since you were a young man! But how *old* you look now!" In a softer tone that everyone still hears, she adds, "You've grown quite the belly!"

"Thank you for having us," Marty says. "You look healthy as always."

She laughs with delight then swats him on the shoulder, the flab of her arms jiggling.

"This is Inez, my wife," Marty says.

"Well, but you look so very young for Martino!"

"Oh, not at all," Inez demurs.

"And what do you do, Inez?"

"I'm a merchandiser for Rustan's." She tips her chin up, just a fraction.

"*Wonderful*," Aling Merrigold says.

"And these are my children." Mariah and JR give her halfhearted hellos, and she smacks her lips at them.

"And Mang Kikoy, of course, how good to see you," Aling Merrigold says. Mang Kikoy smiles, then shuffles off to eat with the rest of her household staff. She leads Marty and his family to the dining room, babbling the whole time: "I can't believe it's been four years since your father died. I spent *lots* of time with him after your mama died, you know. And he did talk about you such a lot—how he was so proud of you, and how he missed you so much! But then I can't blame you, my dear; it's so hard to get time off with the economy like this, no? And then you have these two children. So healthy!" She beams at the kids. "So healthy! You feed them well! Do you get plenty of free food from San Miguel? You still work there, di ba?"

"Yes. He was recently promoted to Procurement Manager," Inez says. "Extra vacation time is one of the perks, so we were finally able to take this trip."

"Is that *so*?" Aling Merrigold draws a dramatic breath. "Well, I'm not really surprised. When San Miguel created that breakthrough formula for the Perfect Pork—*wow*. I said to myself, *This is it, this is the future!* And you know, I was right. I mean, the lechon we're having tomorrow . . . and you *will* eat here tomorrow. I *insist*. After all the events, of course. My balcony has a great view of the fireworks! . . . What was I saying? Oh yes, tomorrow's lechon is Perfect Pork, which truly *is* perfect."

"I'm very glad to hear that," Marty says.

They walk past a sliding door into the air-conditioned dining room. Aling Merrigold gestures for them to sit. "This dinner is mostly from San Miguel, as well—the roasted chicken is, for sure. This is your Spam, and I think the bangus relleno is yours, too. Pero the cake is from Gardenia. And the chicken cordon bleu is by Universal Robina, because I'm sorry, their cheese is better than yours, you know? Anyway, let's eat."

She says grace, and they dig in.

Marty takes a bite of the roasted chicken. It's delicious. He feels a swell of pride. He helped *make* these things. Not directly—that was the research team's job—but he handled most of the exports and imports that provided the raw materials for their meats. After the lockout with China he had shifted grudgingly to more expensive vendors in Vietnam, only to realize that their bio-plasticine millet (BPM) adhered to flavorants more easily, and could be molded into more convincing shapes. Chicken and tuna, in particular, could be replicated using Vietnamese BPM for a cheaper unit cost, and San Miguel was quickly able to launch a new line of canned goods, labeled: *More nutritious. Extra-delicious!*

People still say it doesn't beat the real thing, but Marty thinks it comes pretty damn close. They've finally reached an era when neither Mariah nor JR will incur a health risk from their diet; when people don't need to fret about foodborne illnesses; when it's conceivable, if the government gets its shit together, for people below the poverty line to have three meals a day.

"Has the Department of Health decided on a budget for its feeding program yet?" Aling Merrigold asks.

"No," Marty says. "I hear they're working on it."

Aling Merrigold rolls her eyes. "They're always working on it." She takes a sip of Coke. "Still, I can't pretend I'm thinking about anything except tomorrow. You haven't seen it live, but the moment when San Isidro makes his choice and the produce becomes—you know, natural—it's *wow*. Talagang *wow*."

The news reporters said the same thing, when the first miracle happened during Pahiyas three years ago. No one believed the sensational coverage on *TV Patrol* at first, but then the owners of the winning house started selling chunks of food as proof: a bite of real corn, a handful of real green beans, a cluster of real juicy grapes. The reporters showed the old church's statue of San Isidro in the town square, surrounded by people bursting into tears as they bit into their first unsafe food in years. It was ridiculous. Marty remembers thinking, *Why is everyone so hung up on this? Why is everyone freaking out?*

He remembers thinking, *It can't be a miracle, because we've already INVENTED the miracle.*

What are you doing here, then? something inside him asks. He recalls the twist in his gut, the saliva filling his mouth, as he watched an old woman nibble on a real banana, weeping wretchedly.

This is home, another voice that sounds more like him insists. *I just wanted to see the fiesta. I wanted the kids to see.*

He pauses over his next forkful. "You don't think it's—you know, a hoax, or something?"

"Ay naku, no, never! You'll understand when you see it," Aling Merrigold says. "You don't even need to taste it. It's the smell, the color, the everything. I mean, the mayor tried to keep it from spreading, played it up as airbrush and fake imports, but there's no denying it. Really, how long naman can you lie without shame? Last year, I shelled out for a few pieces of camote—that's my favorite, you know?—and when I ate it, Diyos ko, it was so good."

"I see." Marty licks his lips. "Well, it'll be fun to watch."

Aling Merrigold nods and swallows a spoonful of milkfish relleno. Marty watches her, satisfied. It doesn't matter that the milkfish is made of the same thing as the chicken, the rice, the vegetables. They look different, taste different, and have the same high nutritional content. They're better for everyone.

Mass the following morning is at 6:00 a.m., which causes much groaning. They manage to make it through the church doors in time for the second reading. The priest is particularly zealous, exhorting everyone to give thanks for their gathering together as one community, and for the bountiful harvest that San Isidro—"and our sponsors San Miguel Corp., Universal Robina, Golden Arches, and Monde Nissin"—have provided. The people of Lucban are restless, beaming at each other as they exchange signs of peace. Only the image of San Isidro remains calm, already primed in a float for the beauty-pageant winner to carry him in later.

After mass there are a few hours left before the procession, so they decide to explore the town. Stalls selling woven buri hats, fans, handbags, and little straw birds are interspersed with old ladies on fold-out stools, hawking rice cakes and empanadas. Inez haggles over a bundle of hats. Mariah picks out keychains for her friends. JR drops the buko juice he's slurping and it bursts on the concrete, leaving a slushy puddle that nobody minds. Inez *tsk*s, and Mariah wonders loudly when the procession will start. They each have a serving of pancit habhab on banana leaves.

Marty remembers not caring much about the actual Pahiyas Festival as a child. He was more interested in the preparations leading up to it. He would squat next to Mang Kikoy as the old man ground soaked rice, until it was pale and liquid as milk. Mang Kikoy would stir the wet rice, divide it into shallow buckets, then mix in the coloring: blue and yellow to make apple green, red and blue to make dark pink. Then he would dip a large kabal leaf in the mixture, as a mold for the kiping, and hang it so that the excess coloring dripped. To finish he would cook them over a charcoal grill, while Marty ate the rejected attempts and recited random facts he had learned at school.

Marty didn't watch the kiping preparation yesterday. Something about the BPM Mang Kikoy was using instead of rice made Marty feel weird. It might have been misplaced nostalgia, and he knew that was a useless feeling.

JR, however, had watched and reported to Marty after: about how he had eaten some of the leftovers and they tasted kind of funny, kind of like nothing, but Mang Kikoy said it was made of rice so that was probably normal, right, Dad?

"Kiping has no taste," Marty said, laughing. "I mean, rice itself has barely any flavor."

"But Mang Kikoy said the real foods in the fiesta taste awesome, and if I can eat a fruit or veggie from the winning house tomorrow, I'll understand what he means!"

"Oh, did he say that? Those things are really expensive. And they'll probably make your tummy ache. Or make your teeth gray, like Mang Kikoy's!" Marty rumpled JR's hair, so that JR squirmed. "Don't know if you'll get to taste any of that, anak."

"I will," JR said. "I'm gonna grab some with my stretchy arms—SHEEE-OW!" He whipped his arms wildly. "And then I can tell all the kids in my class, and they'll be jealous, because they've never eaten yummy real food and they never *will!*" He chuckled, evil and gleeful, and robotically walked away to heckle his sister.

Marty remembers the great glass houses they passed on their way to Lucban, lining the fields stretched beneath Mt. Banahaw. Piles of corn and rice, endless rows of pineapple and root crop, stewing in their meticulously engineered domes, more delicious than nature could ever make them. Simply *more* than God could ever make them.

The procession begins at 1:00 p.m. with the local policemen leading the marching band through the streets. The crowd surges from the town center. Those who live along the procession route peer out from windows and balconies, waving at onlookers. An ABS-CBN TV crew starts their segment. People in bright red shirts bearing the Universal Robina logo hover near the cameras, holding up signs that say *Don't Eat the Miracle Food—It's Poison! You Could Die!*

Marty frowns at their lack of respect for the festivities, even as he recalls his last meeting, where the Procurement Division Head had raised her eyebrows at his vacation request. ("For Lucban?"—and when Marty nodded, how she cleared her throat and averted her eyes.) Ignoring this, he gestures for his family to follow, and heads for the middle of the parade. JR complains that he can't see, so Marty hoists him onto his shoulders. They walk on, keeping to the edges of the crowd. The higantes come after the band: giant, cartoony replicas of the president, the kagawad, a schoolgirl, a farmer. A carabao—live this time—follows, pulling a cart full of waving children. Unlike the animatronic version, this carabao plods silently on, martyr-like. It is trailed by girls with feathered headpieces and dresses in garish colors, shimmying to a syncopated drumbeat.

The priest from morning mass scoops water out of a bucket and sprinkles everyone with it. Behind him walk the beauty-pageant entrants, led by the newly crowned Miss Lucban and her escort, standing on a float, carrying San Isidro between them. Marty is transfixed by the face of the saint—how it looks tired and drawn in the middle of the crowd, rocked to and fro by the music. The parade is pushing, pulsing from all sides; Marty presses onward, checking that Inez and Mariah are still following. The band has gone through its traditional repertoire and is now playing the Top 40. Everyone sings along—some droning, some with effort. Marty moves faster so that he can keep pace with San Isidro, but it's difficult. He feels crazed, dehydrated, but he's determined to witness the so-called miracle, determined not to care.

"Dad," JR says, "Dad, hurry up, we're going to miss the selection!"

Marty tries to walk more quickly, but the crowd keeps him at bay, measuring his pace. The people proceed down the street in a blare of noise and sound and color, getting more raucous as they approach the fancier homes. At some point the fiesta-goers begin to stop in front of each house, and lift San Isidro above the crowd, holding him there for a few moments. Each time this happens the procession holds its breath, then bursts into cheering when nothing changes. Marty is starting to get exhausted. He brings JR down and clutches his hand. JR beams up at him, infected by the delight of the crowd. Marty smiles back, as best as he can through the heat and confusion and the sudden shower of confetti and kiping raining from the house they are passing.

They're drawing closer to Mang Delfin's house, with the animatronic carabaos and giant replica of the mayor's face. The frenzy and expectation heightens each time San Isidro is raised, but there is also a sense of inevitability, because only one house can win, and everyone seems to know which house it is. Someone starts chanting: "Mang Delfin! Mang Delfin!" The marching band launches into the current chart-topper. People are headbanging and wiggling and not-quite-accidentally grinding each other.

Marty realizes they're not going to see anything if they stay where they are. Ducking into a side street, he skirts past former neighbors' houses. He counts the walls before turning back onto the main road, right at the cross street between Mang Delfin and Aling Sheila's house. They have a perfect view of the proceedings: the crowd is amassing in the home right before this one, breathing a collective "Ooooh!" as San Isidro is raised, then bursting into laughter when nothing happens, and he is lowered once more.

JR jumps up and down. "It's going to be this one! It's going to be this one!"

Marty's heart races. He squeezes JR's hand, and gazes at the façade of Mang Delfin's house: up close, he can see potato-faced people pieced from squash and taro, with string-bean-and-okra hair; intricate butterflies made of rambutan and longgan; long, sweeping bunches of banana mingled with kiping. The mooing of the fake carabaos is incredibly loud. If there's any house that can feed the whole town, it's this one.

But what's wrong with this food? he thinks. *Isn't this worth giving thanks for? What more do people want?*

"Mang Delfin! Mang Delfin! Yaaaay!" The crowd whoops as it reaches its destination. Everyone quiets down enough so that the band can start a drumroll. Miss Lucban and her escort slowly, tenderly lift San Isidro up to face the house. Marty is magnetized, again, by the saint's face: its severely rosy cheeks and sleepy eyebrows, the stiff golden halo behind his head. He can't tell if San Isidro wears a look of benevolence, or of agony.

"Real food! Real food! Real veggies, real fruit!" JR hasn't stopped jumping or chanting. Marty fights the urge to tell him to shut up.

"Oh my god," Inez says. "This is actually so exciting!"

Mariah, who has whipped out her phone to record everything, says, "The signal here sucks!"

The hush continues. As the crowd watches, the statue of San Isidro—now facing its life-sized twin, in front of Mang Delfin's house—lifts its wooden arm, the one holding the sheaf of corn, in a rigid salute. His face remains frozen, but for one instant, his eyes seem *alive*—and even though they aren't directed at Marty, his belly churns and his eyes water. A child in the crowd bursts into tears.

Then: an explosion of smell and color. The house is suddenly unable to bear its own weight, and several ornaments come loose from the ceiling and balcony, falling on the crowd below. Potatoes and bananas roll off the shingles, detach from the windows; tufts of kiping billow out and descend on everyone's heads. Marty sees this in slow-motion. Each fruit and vegetable is more alive, the smell so intoxicating Marty nearly vomits. He lets go of JR's hand to cover his mouth, and JR immediately lunges for the food. Inez shrieks and darts forward as a squash-face starts to come loose from the wall. She tries to catch it in one of her new hats, shouting, "What are you doing, Marts? Grab some! Hurry!"

Everyone is frantically scooping. Mariah has her mouth full of something. "Oh my *god*," she says. "Oh my god, it tastes totally different!"

Marty looks back at where the procession had been neatly standing, and it's all gone—San Isidro has disappeared, swallowed by a swarm of flailing limbs. Someone—Mang Delfin?—roars over the noise, "This is my house! Those are mine! Stop! Stop!"

"There's enough for everyone, you greedy ass!" someone shouts back. The cheer that follows quickly dissolves into grunting as people climb over each other.

Marty comes into focus. "JR!" he calls frantically. "JR? JR!"

His little boy could be trampled. His little boy could get LBM, salmonella, stomach cancer. That food should never touch his lips.

Inez is still filling her hats; Mariah is helping her. Marty tries to enter the writhing mass of fiesta-goers. An elbow bashes him on the cheek, a knee catches his ribs. Someone to his left retches. The stench of body odor and puke overpowers the sweet fragrance of the fruits.

"JR!" He keeps shouting.

"Dad!"

JR squeezes his way towards him, reaching over two women grappling with a knot of bitter gourd. Marty manages to grab JR under the armpits, lifting then hauling him toward a side street. He takes deep breaths, trying to clear his head, and through a haze of nausea he sees JR's giant grin. JR is clutching a swollen banana in his fist: a banana full of bruises, green at the base, just like the ones Marty used to eat as a child, nothing like the ones they now grow. "Dad! I got one! Can I eat it?"

Marty feels sick, overwhelmed, like too many eyes are on him. He reaches out, grabs the banana, and peels it without thinking. JR watches him, wide-eyed. Marty has no idea what he's going to do—hold it out to his child and let him eat it? Eat it himself, because it looks so goddamn delicious? Thank God, San Isidro, for a miracle? Cry for his manmade miracles, so much nothing when held to the light of day, to a pair of tired eyes in a wooden face?

"Yes," he says. "Go ahead," he says, his mouth already tasting the sweetness, craving it—the truth of a miracle, too bitter to swallow—"But don't, no, you shouldn't, it isn't safe, it isn't right," he says, and he is suddenly crying, and JR looks at him with an expression that edges bewilderment and terror. In his closed fist the banana has been mashed to a pulp.

A Spell for Foolish Hearts

The Rulebook for Witches had over 300 entries, but Aunt Gemma stressed only three:

1. Tend to your jar of blackberries.
2. Beware men's hearts; never let them be your master.
3. The shape of things can be deceptive.

She'd copied them by hand on card stock, drawn a row of hearts and stars as a border, then tucked it into the front cover of the Rulebook, which she sent Patrick for his eleventh birthday. He read it all the way through twice, wondering if he should tell Mom and Dad. It was weird, the wondering. Why shouldn't he tell them? Aunt Gemma never said it was a secret, and it didn't seem prohibited per witch laws because he carried the book around in plain sight.

Once, over breakfast, Mom asked him, "What are you reading?"

He answered: "The Rulebook for Witches." She smiled fondly, because her son was a bookworm and she probably thought this was a Harry Potter spin-off.

Gradually Patrick understood, without wanting to, that he was afraid of telling them because they'd either not believe it, or it would upset them. There would be something inherently *wrong* in the revelation that Patrick was a witch. Both those reactions would hurt, because he *was* a witch. He'd been doing spells for years, he just didn't know they were spells until Aunt Gemma sent him the book. Magic thrummed in his veins, sparking off him in small gestures: in the words he'd mutter under his breath, in the look he'd give a wailing toddler in the food court—*don't do that*—so that they'd snap their mouths shut and stare at him, affronted. He already knew that few people could do magic, but it didn't make you all-powerful. It was rare, but only in the sense that being really good at instruments or sports was rare. It could be used or not, and you could develop it or not. It could be noticed or ignored.

The longing to tell his parents swelled. He felt as if there was a jar of water balanced on his head, whenever they were around. The worst was the hope: that Mom might say, "Oh, don't worry, I'm that way too," carelessly waving a hand to revive the dead herbs by the kitchen sink. Or Dad might admit that he wasn't afraid of cats, he just didn't like hearing their thoughts.

When he finally told them, Mom cried: quiet tears, running down her cheeks, the lack of drama highlighting how *truly* sad it made her. Dad turned away and muttered something under his breath.

"Are you sure?" Mom asked.

Patrick nodded.

"I should've known," Mom sniffled. "It runs in my side of the family. Mother had it, and so did Gemma, but I thought it might be thinned out between me and your dad. *Dammit,* Gemma should have *asked* me first."

"One of my cousins has it too," Dad said sheepishly. Mom said, "Alan!"

They started arguing, while Patrick sat on his hands and marveled at his shame. He should've kept his mouth shut. At least he wasn't crying.

Mom blew her nose and said, "No it's *not* something he can go to a doctor for—"

"It's not a big deal," Patrick blurted. He felt awful.

His parents looked at him.

"I mean, no one really needs to know, and I'm not—I've never, like, shown it off. Most people don't notice magic, unless they're looking. It'll be fine."

"You mean you won't . . ." Mom paused, considering her words. "You won't be a witch?"

"I," Patrick said, faltering. That seemed impossible to answer. "I'll, uh. Try."

That conversation was sixteen years ago, though some mornings, halfway through coffee #1, Patrick recalled it with crystal precision. He wondered what he could have said instead. *Yes* would be wrong; *no* was inaccurate. Eleven-year-old Patrick had done his best. There weren't massive consequences, either. Sometimes you needed to get the bad feelings out of your system, cry and argue, and plod on.

They rarely spoke of his witchcraft after that. Patrick continued to work minor spells because he couldn't *not*, but being a witch didn't spell his doom. He didn't run away from home, quit school, or launch a drug cartel like maybe his parents feared. He went to college and got his degree (in Physics, on a whim, with a minor in Design). Patrick felt he was doing a decent job of adulting. He had work as a UX/UI/Marketing Designer at a "fast growing, VC-backed start-up" (air-quotes not because these statements were untrue, but because they were so typical), and an apartment in San Francisco (tiny, out in the Richmond, but it was all he needed). He knew where to get quarters for laundry. He paid off his credit card every month.

His only witchy activity was the part-time work at the Mission Spell Shop, just off Valencia street, mostly because Myrtle was a sweetheart who let him tinker with ingredients. They donated some of their proceeds to a nearby shelter program, which served both magical and non-magical folks alike. It was nice to stay tangentially connected to the Bay Area magic scene, even if most people were hobbyists like him. Rent was too high, magic too impractical; there were much more lucrative ways to spend one's time.

The Rulebook he kept on his nightstand, the notecard on his refrigerator. Sometimes he wondered if maybe he'd taken those rules too seriously. Number one he'd followed faithfully, after mother gave him his blackberry jar ("I have no idea what it's for, but I kept it anyway, upon Grandma's orders, so you might as well have it"). He didn't exactly *tend* it. He just wiped dust off the lid every few months. Number three seemed fairly obvious, less a witch rule than common sense, though he suspected it might hold some deeper meaning about fae or humanesque glamours.

Number two he'd never had experience with, because he'd never been in a relationship.

Patrick didn't know how to be in one. He wasn't *dissatisfied* with being single—most days he didn't even think of it. Now that he was on the other side of twenty-five, it seemed unlikely to change, unless he had one of those movielike encounters in an airport or a party (he didn't go to parties). He'd been on a dating app for all of three days before deciding it was too stressful and deleting his account.

He wasn't sure how to feel about being single. He wasn't sure he *felt* much about it. It was sad in this remote way, like an acquaintance's tragedy. He could empathize with it . . . to a degree. On the other hand, he was certain that he'd saved himself a lot of personal drama by never falling for anyone. He didn't even know how to fall for someone. The concept was mysterious. Did you *choose* to be attracted? Did you pluck someone from your environment and decide to attach feelings to them? If all of media was to be believed, he was highly unusual in this regard, but it didn't exactly bother him. He'd never even had a real crush—besides Ben Whishaw, he was really into Ben Whishaw. But Ben Whishaw was a celebrity and taken, so.

Sometimes Kat, who ran Product Marketing at his start-up, tried to cure his remarkable lack of dating by inviting him to go dancing in the Castro. Kat was very concerned for Patrick's happiness, which was sometimes exhausting, but he liked Kat a lot so he didn't mind. He thought life would probably be a lot easier if he and Kat could be a couple. Kat was sweet and took excellent care of him, and they could have had a very happy life together. Only he wasn't into women, and she wasn't into long-term relationships. Kat was the only person at work who knew about the witch thing *and* the gay thing, and Patrick intended to keep it that way.

Monday. There was a boy with hair made of starlight in the elevator. He blinked luminous gray eyes at Patrick as he stepped inside, and parted bow-shaped lips to say, "Thank god! I was starting to think I'd have to take the stairs the whole way."

Patrick was halfway through a Starbucks white chocolate mocha, which he only indulged in on days that started out not-good. His hair was not-good that morning, his face was not-good. He had mystery sniffles, and he'd overslept. He flinched, but it was only a *mental* flinch—a jolt of feeling that ran through him, so unexpected he barely had the composure to say "Er, hi." He blinked. The boy's hair wasn't starlight, just a bleached platinum that really *shouldn't* have worked. He wore a stud earring and a dangling earring in one lobe like a K-pop star, a dark blue button-down under a tailored jacket with elbow patches, and new-looking Cole Haans. "What floor?" he asked.

"Sixth. I didn't realize the elevator needed a card reader. I'm surprised no one else came in! Is everyone here fit enough to take the stairs?"

"It's health awareness month," Patrick said, and tapped his card on the reader. "It's also a little . . . early, for most people." Only weirdoes like Patrick came in at 8:30.

When Patrick didn't press any other button, Starboy said, "Well, seems like we're headed to the same place!"

"Marquet?" Their core product was a platform for quantifying the impact of various Marketing activities across the funnel; one of the cofounders had thought the name incredibly clever. Most employees disagreed but were resigned.

"Yeah!" Starboy says. "I start today. Product team. I'm Karl." He stuck his hand out, and Patrick shook it.

"Karl, like the fog?"

"What?"

Awkward. The elevator doors slid open. "Oh. It's a Twitter account. Karl-the-Fog. Haha."

"*Ohhh.* Yeah, it's Karl with a K."

"I'm Patrick," he said, trying not to feel like an idiot. "I'm on the Design Team. Um. I would take you to HR, but I'm not sure she's in yet. Do you, uh, want some coffee?"

"Coffee would be great."

They walked into the kitchen, where Melody was starting to unpack the weekly Costco delivery. "Hey! Another newbie today? You guys are *multiplying!*" As she and Karl started chatting, Patrick busied himself making coffee for the earlybirds. He pictured his blackberry jar to calm down. He felt ridiculous. Starboy—Karl—was not even his type. That *hair,* for one thing. Patrick had never known what a crush was like, and if this was it, it was a bad idea. He was a firm believer in keeping work and personal life separate. That shit was messy, and if there was one thing Patrick did not like, it was messy shit. Plus he didn't really believe in things like attraction at first sight, even if those *were* awfully nice Cole Haans.

Karl was good at his job: efficient and communicative, confident but not controlling. The first product Karl and Patrick collaborated on was a long-awaited v2 feature release spurred by vicious Tweets from angry users (#marquit). Patrick initially felt sorry for Karl; he'd been given a shitty project, shipping something that already fostered negative sentiment. But Karl had risen to the task admirably, translating all that user fury into clear pain points that Patrick could actually design solutions for. They'd sat in a brainstorming session together for half a day, and at the end of it they had three options to show the rest of the team. Patrick had actually been *excited* to get back to his desk and prototype. It was the good kind of start-up rush. Talking to Karl, picking his brain, felt easy.

Karl was also super friendly. By the end of week one everyone knew his name, which was rare given how many newbies started each week. He and Kat got along amazingly; they quickly established weekly lunch dates, which made Patrick slightly jealous (of whom, he wasn't sure). Kat, being Kat, looped Patrick in, so he found himself spending a lot more time with Karl than expected. Before he knew it his Slack convo with Karl was a minefield of gifs, they regularly ate lunch together, and he'd spent more than a couple nights in a stupor, lamenting the unfortunate problem of crushing on a coworker.

It *sucked.*

Denying the crush had worked for all of two-and-a-half weeks, but eventually Patrick admitted defeat. He mused on this while making bacon pasta for dinner. He was cat-sitting Miranda for Aunt Gemma; she blinked at him owlishly from the counter, judging his agony. He did not want to like Karl. He was not prepared for this stupid crush. Why should he have a crush at all? And on *Karl?* He didn't even know Karl.

Well. He knew some things. Karl was a Bay Area native, and most of his family was still here. He'd gone to school at Berkeley, studied Economics with a minor in Art History. He was bad at sports but liked long walks ("And hiking . . . but I know literally everyone likes hiking. I'm not, like, the best hiker. I just like trees. Haha."). He claimed to enjoy karaoke and museums, and once he'd brought in a tupperware full of white chocolate chip and macadamia cookies that he'd baked from scratch. Before Marquet he'd worked at another start-up, which had tanked after its series A; before *that* he'd been at Apple. It was unclear how old he was, and he didn't have LinkedIn.

Patrick also knew that Karl moved like water, like he was possessed by some internal rhythm. He crossed the room in liquid strides, and teleported from either end of the whiteboard when Patrick wasn't paying attention—which, in this situation, was almost never. Perhaps he'd been a dancer in undergrad. Also, apparently Karl didn't bleach his hair. It was that color naturally. "Some genetic mutation!" Karl said, laughingly, and Patrick had thought *what, for hotness?*

Patrick was constantly hunting for clues about whether Karl liked men. Had he ever mentioned an ex-girlfriend? Ex-boyfriend? Had he ever mentioned a type? Patrick did not know how to broach queerness without bringing it up himself, hence: never.

Anyway, nothing was going to happen. They did not hang outside of work. "I can be his friend," Patrick said aloud. He flapped a hand at Miranda, vaguely worried that her hair would get in the pasta. "He's a great work-friend, a great colleague. We probably wouldn't enjoy weekends together anyway." He set the timer one minute less than the package stated and stirred sauce in an adjacent pot. "I don't even know if he likes boys. He probably doesn't. And yes, he's really nice to me, but he's also nice to everyone. That's just how he is."

That morning Karl had randomly brought him a white chocolate mocha, with matching milky smile. "This is for turning those mocks around so quickly," he'd said.

Patrick didn't think he'd been particularly efficient. He tried not to read into it. "Thanks, dude, but now I owe you one!"

Karl said, "Okay, you can get the next one" and walked off to get his requisite granola from the pantry.

That smile though. What was it about that smile?

He missed his timer. The noodles weren't firm. Miranda meowed thoughtfully at him as he slurped dinner and resolved to get through this.

❀

"Are you coming to Pride?" Kat asked the next day, which meant: *you are coming to Pride.*

Patrick hrr-rr-rrmed. "I work Saturdays, remember? We're having a June sale. Lots of people expected that day."

"Dude, that works *perfectly.* We can hit you up and then head to Dolores Park for the rest of the afternoon!"

"I don't know . . ."

"Come on, man! Karl's going, and he's *new.*"

Why was Kat mentioning Karl? Had Patrick been obvious?

"He's not *new* anymore," Patrick said carelessly. "And I dunno about Pride. You know I'm not out."

"That doesn't matter," Kat said. "Everyone goes to Pride. It's full of straight people. You've been living here, what, two years? And you haven't been to Pride yet? You can't be native SF until you've been to Pride!" She noticed his extreme discomfort and softened her cajoling. Kat, Product Marketer Extraordinaire. "Okay. At least try to join us for an hour or two?"

"Okay. Fine. Only for you."

"Yesssss. *I love you.*" She got on tiptoe and kissed his forehead.

"Don't come to the shop," Patrick said warningly. "I'll find you at the park."

Contrary to expectations, Kat did not come to the shop with the twelve-strong contingent of Marqueters. Patrick was relieved. Kat was very spur-of-the-moment and could easily forget, or pretend to.

Myrtle had urged Patrick to partake in the festivities that morning, but he assured her that he was happy to hang around 'til the afternoon. They'd done pretty well that day: regulars coming in to pick up their herbs and tinctures and pills, and some new visitors as well, curious and buzzing from the day's festivities, browsing light spells on the shelves. The shop offered more intricate, specialized potions, but those you never saw out in the open. San Francisco laws were fairly lenient on magic, but it still wasn't something you blatantly advertised.

To nonmagical people the place would just seem like an eclectic collection of knickknacks, liquors, and herbal supplements. Their magical clientele was diverse, though it had diminished somewhat in recent years as the shapeshifters and sorcerers moved to the Pacific Northwest, or Denver, or Pittsburgh, escaping explosive rent prices and the devouring maw of the tech industry. Myrtle often sighed about losing some of her favorite customers: the Daly City diwata who was a nurse at UCSF and moved back to Manila to look after her ailing mom; a sylph that had had a falling-out with the local mist elementals and decided to try her luck being an artist in Seattle. Patrick always hoped to see a mythic creature come through, but they'd gotten so good at blending in with humans, he could almost never tell.

"It's hot," Patrick said, because it *was,* and like everyone else in this city he became sluggish and confused in anything but perfect sweater weather.

"I want an ice cream," Myrtle replied, idly petting Josiah, the shop cat. Josiah, unlike Miranda, actually allowed himself to be petted. Myrtle's gray hair was in an intricate bun-braid that morning. She was a friend of Aunt Gemma's, a long-time Berkeley resident, and utterly cool. Unlike Patrick, she seemed completely at peace with her witch identity.

"Go and get an ice cream, it's slowed down," Patrick said.

"You want an ice cream?"

"Nah."

"I'm gonna get an ice cream."

Patrick waved her off, then assumed her place next to Josiah. He was noodling on a new brew which was supposed to provide better outcomes to Tinder dates. It was powdered, meant to be something you could mix into any beverage. It wasn't a commission, exactly;

more of a suggestion from numerous regulars, bemoaning the shitty app-driven dating scene. If you liked the person, this would speed up their reciprocation. ("It's a love potion," Myrtle drawled. Patrick thought about it, then said: "Kinda, yeah.") He'd managed to make something that actually quickened attraction and improved flirting—*in theory,* as it was something he still needed to test with willing subjects—but it always took too long. It wouldn't work at all on a first date. Right now the best he'd gotten it down to was a few weeks. Which wasn't what people were looking for. He threw in another handful of dried rosemary and wondered what it was missing. Or maybe he'd put in too much of something? Vanilla? Dried tears?

After ten minutes of silence, the bell tinkled and Karl stepped inside.

He was wearing one of the garish rainbow tank tops that Kat had screen printed for everyone. Pink plastic shades from a competitor, gleaned from their last trade show, were propped on his head. His smile was bright as the rare sun over San Francisco; those gray eyes bleached all shadows from the room. "Hey, Patrick!" he said.

"Hey," Patrick answered. His heart skipped fluttering and went straight to jumping jacks. Did Myrtle go to Bi-Rite? Why'd she have to go to Bi-Rite? The line always took forever. "What . . . are you doing here?"

"Picking you up! You weren't answering your texts, so Kat sent me on a mission."

"Sorry. I was, um, preoccupied. I was meaning to go, in a bit."

"S'all good." Karl languished by the counter, where Patrick was aware that his Fail Tinder Brew was still cooling off. Patrick had only ever read the word *rakish* in books, but Karl right then was the very definition of it, despite the rainbow tank. "You seem troubled. Am I not allowed in here?"

"It's fine," Patrick said. "I just . . . I like to keep this separate from work." He waved a vague hand. Maybe Karl did magic too? Maybe that explained the hair? And the pheromones?

"I won't tell," Karl said, hand over heart. "What exactly are you selling anyway?"

Okay. Either he wasn't a witch or wizard, or he was pretending not to be. Patrick skritched Josiah behind the ears; Josiah looked at Karl with interest. "Unique brews," Pat said, because he didn't like to lie. "We get IPAs and lagers from special suppliers, mostly West Coast, but a few from Hawaii and the Midwest, too. And uh. Some kombuchas, and teas and stuff."

"Anything you'd recommend?"

Were they flirting? Patrick had no idea how flirting went. "What do you like?"

"You."

Patrick gaped. Karl slapped his shoulder, one easy motion, and snickered.

"Just kidding." Patrick tried not to feel too hurt. "I'm not picky. Hmm. Give me your favorite tea."

"*My* favorite?" He paused. "I like white teas. Gentle stuff."

"Works great." Karl reached out tentatively to Josiah, and beamed when the cat nuzzled his hand.

Patrick fought blushing with everything, which was a doomed move from the beginning. He fished under the countertop for something normal, and gratefully found a packet of White Needle. It had been taped, which meant some of it had been used, but that was fine. "Here. Free of charge. Also, it really *does* taste better when you brew it four minutes exactly."

"Thanks, dude." He was starting to sound a little like Kat. He took the packet, stuck it into his shorts, and paused expectantly. "You're really not ditching?"

"And risk Kat's wrath? No, of course I'll go. I'm just waiting for"—the bell tinkled, and Myrtle stepped in, licking a double ice cream cone and eyeing them . . . Patrick didn't want to use the word *suggestively*, but it seemed most apt—"my colleague to come back."

"I'm back," she said, waggling her eyebrows. Every woman in Patrick's life was trying to set him up. Life was grim. "And you are?"

"Karl. One of Patrick's colleagues from his . . . day job." The smile went lopsided, stupidly endearing.

"Nice. I'm Myrtle. From Patrick's side hustle. You come to finally take him to prom? It's happening out there."

"You know I don't like things that are *happening*," Patrick mumbled, while Myrtle stepped behind the counter and nudged him.

Imperiously, she said: "Go forth, you young'uns."

Patrick sighed and put on his rainbow tank above his shirt—he wanted to show solidarity. If he was going anyway, might as well be shameless like the rest of them. Myrtle gestured at the pot he'd been boiling the FTB in, asking *does this work?* Patrick shook his head. "I'll wrap it up next weekend," he said.

"Thanks for the tea," Karl called out as they left.

Pride was . . . Pride-ish. There were a lot of people milling about Dolores, fastidiously Instagramming. The cluster of Marqueters cheered as Karl appeared, Patrick in tow. Kat had stripped off her rainbow tank and was wearing an American flag bikini. Everyone was eating tortilla chips dunked in Papa Lote salsa; someone had brought a bluetooth speaker and was playing a 90s mix with generous amounts of Britney. A Coors Light found its way into Patrick's hand.

This was the first time, he realized, that he was hanging out with Karl outside of work. And it was . . . fine. Whatever. It wasn't anything special. Karl was the same: easy and smiley, spouting puns, tenderly shooing away a cluster of drunk girls who had started to twerk aggressively beside them. He was the first to offer everyone alcohol, though he didn't push if refused. He was full of small, affectionate gestures—like that shoulder-slap back in the shop—touching an elbow here, the small of someone's back there. Karl was a flirt. A massive one. No one was exempted from his winking, his casual familiarity.

One other reason why it wouldn't work. Perhaps now Patrick could convince himself.

❁

After Pride weekend, the crush went away. It was glorious. Q3 started up, and everyone started scrambling to hit their year-end goals. The v2 feature release went so smoothly that Karl got tapped to redesign their entire web platform, setting him up for a long customer discovery project with Kat. Patrick was in the middle of creating new iconography for their Marketing materials, and after that he had to update the main corp site (a priority, per the second annual board meeting), which kept him from most new product development. All this meant a good month of nearly no interaction with Karl. When they did cross paths, it was brief and collegial. Sometimes Patrick looked at Karl and thought, with relish, *He isn't even that cute!* Then Karl would catch him looking and grin, which would ruin things slightly. But not *too* much. Patrick had broken the crush's stronghold.

Besides, his thoughts were occupied with magic. The Tinder Brew was taking longer than expected, a worthy challenge that excited him about witchcraft in a way he'd missed. The problem was emotions and their volatility. You could temporarily tweak human chemistry all kinds of ways with the right proportions of salt, crushed seashells, and essence of spring, but one couldn't totally *control* it. You could just make enough suggestions that it bent to your will.

"Maybe it doesn't work because it shouldn't be made," Myrtle suggested. He'd been calculating chemical compositions for an hour, and she was bored.

"It's not forbidden, because it's temporary," he answered. It was frustrating that it wasn't even good enough to test yet. "It's a little attraction spell, old as time. The final version is supposed to only work if they're also curious, anyway."

Patrick, with his Level 0 Romance Experience, had no business making what was ostensibly a love potion. But he liked challenges. He was precise and creative, and often bored. It was Aunt Gemma who gave him the missing element he needed. She'd swooped into the city one afternoon, back from exotic travels, and dragged him out for dim sum. Patrick could not reject dim sum. And he loved Aunt Gemma; she was one of the reasons why he'd moved to San Francisco in the first place. Of course, as luck would have it, once he arrived in the city Aunt Gemma got a promotion and started consulting abroad for half the year. That was how he ended up with Miranda. She'd offered him her apartment, too, a really nice place in Pacific Heights. It was stupid to decline, but somehow it mattered that he get his own place.

"Witches must have their own sanctuaries," Aunt Gemma acknowledged. "Number forty-six. You still have the rulebook, Pat?"

"Of course."

They were having wine in her place, post Yank Sing. Aunt Gemma was always concerned with his progress in the craft, even if she knew he spent most of his time being a designer. She cheered him on, told him he had talent, introduced him to Myrtle so he wouldn't stop working at it. If not for her he would've probably quit magic long before.

She'd brought some mooncakes and shrimp-flavored Pringles from a visit to Taipei, several herbs that he couldn't identify on sight, and half a dozen new volumes for her book collection. Aunt Gemma had an impressive library; it was always a pleasure to inspect her shelves and see what had changed. *Magical Creatures of Northern California* cut an imposing figure next to *Mary Canary's Homemade Kitchen Spells*; there was a four-volume set on *Discerning the Fog (Strategies, Tactics, Symbols, and Befriending Elementals)* squished between *Romancing the Rogue* and Strunk's *Elements of Style*.

Patrick flipped through one of her new editions: a photo book of Hong Kong in the '80s, filled with neon lights and some incredibly stylish people that he assumed were actual elves and not merely cosplayers. Aunt Gemma was stroking Miranda idly (Miranda made it *very* clear she knew who her master was), sipping a glass of Prosecco. "What are you up to these days?"

"Something I call a Tinder Brew." He explained the objective and the problem he was facing: how could one shift attraction from a slow-burn, built over repeated dates, to something instant, a spark that caught fire upon ingestion?

"That's a terrible name," Aunt Gemma laughed, then: "You shouldn't be using rosemary. You have to go harder. Snake oil."

"*Aunt Gemma.*"

"Yeah, kidding. No, you could use this." She swirled her drink and lifted an eyebrow. "Right?"

Patrick blinked. "That's genius."

"Well," Aunt Gemma said modestly, and raised her glass.

The Working Tinder Brew, dubbed "Pucker-Up Powder" thanks to Myrtle's dry humor, was a hit with city spell-dabblers. Myrtle took him out for tacos. Patrick's next product was innocuous hexes to discourage pesky suitors, but he was taking that challenge easy, still basking in getting the last spell so right. By the time August rolled around and he was pulled into Karl's redesign, Patrick was confident about his newfound nonchalance against Unfortunate Office Crushes.

He walked into a meeting with a mug of meh afternoon coffee in hand. Karl was at the whiteboard, jotting down bullet points under the header *Beta Issues*. "Hey!" He turned and beamed at Patrick. "I missed you! I feel like we haven't talked in weeks. Like, not since Pride."

Patrick smiled back, utterly disarmed. "Yeah, it's been busy. But we're here now, right? Solving problems together?"

"Totally," Karl said. "And there are lots of problems. The survey results from yesterday's mocks are in . . . and they're pretty brutal. But you know I'm not the best at mocks. You're gonna have to save me."

He smiled sheepishly. Patrick had the presence of mind to think *Oh no.* God, his hair was still that color.

And it still looked good.

❀

That meeting proceeded in a perfectly normal fashion, as did the next ones. The following sprints were loaded with long evenings, but Patrick didn't mind. He and Karl made a good team. He was still attracted to Karl, but not in the *alert-alert-danger* way he'd felt when they first met. It was mellow now, and most days bordered on a fuzzy happiness. This was what some people called a happy crush, the internet told him. As long as it didn't evolve into anything else, Patrick was content with it.

Until that Tuesday when Karl asked him to dinner.

Patrick tried to play it cool. "Yeah, to talk about the upcoming sprint, right?"

"No," Karl said, his gray eyes all weirdly soft. *Sweater-weather-like.* Patrick hated that there was now apparently a bad teenage poet living in his brain whenever Karl was around. "I just want to have dinner with you." He paused, then scratched his arm, a throwaway gesture that was out of character. "But we can talk about work. Or whatever you want."

"Okay," Patrick said. He debated freaking out to Kat, or Googling "what is a date?" before deciding he needed to handle this on his own. At 6:30 Karl stopped by his desk, easy as anything, and they went off to dinner. Neither of them had preferences, so they ended up in a Thai place not far from Union Square. Patrick ordered a green curry and Karl got cashew chicken, and they split a tom yum soup. Along the way they'd discussed the current project, naturally, and also the latest episode of *Black Mirror.* Patrick relaxed, because it wasn't that different from lunch after all. They could have good conversations like this. As friends.

"So tell me more about the day job," Karl said. "The real one." He winked, which was illegal.

"The shop in the mission?"

"Yeah. With the hip lady. Why a liquor store on weekends? You . . . don't strike me as someone who drinks much." They'd been to company happy hours together before; he knew Patrick wasn't big on alcohol.

Patrick was possessed with an irrational burst of honesty. "It's actually a magic shop," he said. "We make minor potions and spells. Nothing people would really notice, nothing that's *too* influential, mostly impermanent . . . but we do come up with some pretty cool things."

"Really?" Karl's eyes were bright. "You can actually do magic?"

"Sure." He sounded like he was bluffing. He was surprised Karl kept playing along. Maybe he'd misread Karl's magical ability after all? Why was it so hard to tell this stuff?

"Woahhhh. You're a *wizard,* Harry."

"I'm a witch, actually," Patrick said, and was heartily relieved when the waiter came by with their soup.

Karl laughed, but it wasn't a mean laugh. It was a laugh of delight. "That's *awesome.*" He ladled out some soup for himself and for Patrick, and added, "Well, you can't say that and not show me something. Or is that against the rules?"

"Not really," Patrick said. He was in deep already. Might as well keep going. "Okay. Watch." He held one hand over the soup in its boiling tureen, breathed in, and concentrated. It went from bright red to deep purple, to grassy green, to milk white, before turning red again.

Karl watched, open-mouthed. "Woah!" he said. "That's amazing!"

Patrick shouldn't have felt so pleased—color-changing was *nothing,* a very basic glamour—but he didn't get to show his magic often, and the look in Karl's eyes made him really . . . proud of himself. He wondered how different things would be, if not for that conversation years ago. What if, instead of always hesitating, he'd maybe practiced magic more openly? He took his hand away and picked up his spoon, embarrassed by how pleased he felt. "I've always kinda done it, but I only found out when I was eleven. My aunt encouraged it and stuff."

"Eleven! You really *are* Harry Potter." Karl started spooning soup into his mouth. "So why be a designer at all? I mean, it's great working with you, but this is so much cooler."

This, at least, was easy to answer. "I really like designing. I like start-ups. I wouldn't enjoy magic so much if I was stressed about making money with it. I enjoy it as kind of a . . . design puzzle, actually."

"That makes sense," Karl said. The waiter swept by with their mains. Patrick didn't really want this conversation to center too much on him; he was still surprised it had turned out easy like this.

"And you? Why Product?"

"I guess I like solving problems too. And making things from the ground up. Things that are mine. Plus I love being able to work with all different kinds of people, you know? People are fascinating." He talked about getting lucky in an internship mix-up—how he'd originally gone in for a role in Operations and ended up in Product. This led to a discussion about terrible undergrad internships, which somehow evolved into general memories of undergrad.

Patrick talked about New York, the newfangled magic of living in a big city, how that and the career options had made San Francisco a no-brainer. "It's such a cliché," he said. "But I really did love it. I mean, my family's all mostly in this coast, so I knew I wanted to move back West. But I couldn't imagine going back to Fresno."

"It's cool that you moved away, though. Sometimes I wish I had done college outside of the Bay Area," Karl said. "Gone somewhere different for a while. I'm too rooted here."

"Why not go now?" Patrick asked. "You're still young."

Karl shrugged. "I can't leave this place. The hills, the weather."

"Sure."

"The job options, too."

"Good point."

"Let's just say that San Francisco and I are inextricably linked." Karl chewed the single piece of broccoli on his plate, and considered the flower-shaped carrot slice that went with it. "So you gotta indulge me: why a witch, not a wizard?"

"Well," Patrick said. "*Let's just say* that's not something you get to choose."

Karl smirked and nodded. "Magic makes its own rules, I guess."

Outside the restaurant, Karl asked him if he wanted a drink. Patrick ummed and said he had to feed his cat. Drinks felt like pushing it. He'd survived dinner—really it had been a *nice* dinner—but he needed to decompress, debrief this step by step in his head.

Karl nodded, an aw-shucks smile on his face.

Patrick inclined his head towards Market Street. "I take the bus," he said. "See you tomorrow?"

"Sure. Thanks for having dinner with me."

He'd already turned away when Patrick said, "Um, Karl."

He turned back. "What's up?"

"It's . . . it's not exactly a secret, but um. No one really knows at work. Besides Kat."

"I got you," Karl said, and waved. Patrick knew he meant it, too. Truthfully, it wasn't the hair or the dimples, or the elbow-patch jackets. It was his kindness, his way of somehow always understanding, that kept making this so hard.

He and Karl started going out for dinner regularly: pizza in North Beach, Korean food in the Richmond, ramen by Market Street. They talked about the latest updates in self-driving cars; how you got better at magic ("It's like learning an instrument or a foreign language: feeling silly, guessing, getting it wrong . . ."); Patrick's younger sister Ann who was in her sophomore year of college, taking up Biology, debating whether to become a veterinarian or a doctor; Karl's multitude of cousins scattered around the West Coast, from Seattle to Orange County; whether Marquet was growing too quickly and needed to slow down; what were some good ways of improving visual design skills; how insufferable yet lovable San Francisco was.

The dinners were only *sometimes* agony, and only because it was getting very difficult for Patrick not to wonder what they meant. It didn't help that their project meant endless meetings together, and that they were always *on the same page.*

"You can't mind-read, can you?" Karl asked once, jokingly. If only.

When Karl invited him to a non-mutual-friend's birthday one Saturday evening, Patrick hesitated only briefly. A friend's birthday seemed like a very platonic setting, and Kat would probably be there. The address was in Nob Hill; the fog curled around Patrick as he climbed up the streets, huffing, grateful for the chill so that he wouldn't start sweating. He gave Karl a call when he was by the door, and Karl came down to pick him up.

He opened the door, smiling widely. "You came!"

"Why wouldn't I?"

"I dunno. Shyness?"

"I'm not *that* shy," Patrick said, and wondered what else Karl thought of him, and how accurate it was. "Besides, my current spell involves how to avoid people at parties, so I can use this as research." *And I like spending time with you,* he didn't add. He took off his jacket as Karl led him indoors. "Where's Kat?"

"Oh, she can't come."

"Oh, really?" Patrick should've checked with her first. Now that he was here, there was no way he could bail.

"Too hungover," Patrick said. "She was out dancing 'til two."

The background music had increased during their progression down the hallway; they emerged into a giant-for-SF-standards living room that was full of stylish people holding wine glasses and paper plates filled with cheese nibbles. Karl felt strangely undone by this scene. He'd done SF house parties before, in the Marina and the Mission; he knew how to hang. But he didn't know anyone here, and they all seemed to know Karl. They even had that same strange glossy sheen to them that Karl did, a sort of high-fidelity attractiveness that made Patrick feel very . . . ordinary. And out of place. He hadn't exactly been conscious of it 'til this moment.

"Here, give me your jacket. Do you want something to drink?"

"Oh. Uh, sparkling water, if there is."

"Karl! Who's your friend?" A girl in a dark denim jumper was sitting on a loveseat, waving her rosé.

"His name's Patrick!" Karl said. Turning to Patrick, he said, "That's Sal. Let me grab your drink."

The *why-don't-you-go-say-hi* was implicit, but Patrick felt like a boneless, compliant creature by this point. He wandered over to Sal, who had extremely circular glasses and a classy bob. "Yo," she said. "Welcome!"

"Thanks. H-happy birthday?"

"Aww, thank you! So glad you could come! This is Dara, and Arnie. Come sit." Two people sitting on the floor waved up at Patrick. He sat next to them, trying to relax.

"You work with Karl?" the girl named Dara asked.

"Yeah."

"What's that like?"

"He's great," Patrick said reflexively.

"I mean, I don't know anyone who doesn't like Karl," Arnie said. "*Seriously*. I get to say that because I'm his cousin." Patrick had noticed the gray eyes, the sharp jawline. Arnie's hair was also that paler-than-pale blonde, reinforcing Karl's claim that the color was natural. She had a frail, ethereal beauty that looked like it could fit in a high-fashion ad.

Patrick wasn't sure how to direct the conversation. "I mean, he's really good at his job. And sweet. And I guess kinda mysterious?"

"He *is* sweet, isn't he?" Dara said. "About the only people who'd disagree are his exes. Remember that girl Lauren? She was the worst."

"Ah," Patrick said. He fought the instinct to touch his chest, surprised at how badly it hurt. Wasn't this what he wanted from the beginning? Some reason to stop obsessing over Karl. Some form of closure. *Of course* it wouldn't be that easy, that the first person he ever liked would reciprocate. *Of course* Karl was into girls. Maybe he even had a crush on Kat. They were always doing one-on-ones, whispering and snickering at each other.

"Are you guys gossiping about me? Don't scare off my friend." Karl appeared, La Croix in hand. Patrick sincerely regretted not asking for a glass of wine instead.

"We were about to stir up the legend of Lauren."

Karl slapped his forehead. "Please, no. Anything else. My love life is tragic, full of terrible women. Sal, didn't you just come back from Tokyo?"

"Oh my *god*," Sal said, and launched into a story about taking the wrong bullet train and ending up in Kyushu. Patrick tried to follow, but it was surprisingly difficult. *Of course* Karl being fashionable didn't mean he was queer; *of course* Karl saw him as a cool coworker. Patrick wanted to leave, but felt he couldn't. He wasn't sure if he was supposed to be having fun. He wasn't sure why Karl had invited him over. Various people would stop by and Patrick would be introduced to them, but he didn't know what for. The next hour he spent in that room felt like agony, and when it was sufficiently late enough that people felt like heading out to a bar to drink more, Patrick didn't say anything; he just left. Everyone else was too wrapped up in themselves to notice.

Beware of men's hearts, and never let them be your master. He turned this over in his mind the whole walk home. For some reason, this whole time, he'd never thought that passage would mean his *own* heart.

"Something's messed you up," Myrtle said. Since he last saw her she'd chopped her hair extra-short. She was constantly messing it up, unable to get used to it. Tonight she was hunched over, darning a protection spell into a child's sweater—a birthday gift for a friend's nephew.

"What do you mean?"

"Pat, you look *woebegone*."

Patrick looked at his blurry reflection on the countertop. He looked the same. She was trying to wrangle a confession out of him. That was such an Aunt Gemma move. He sometimes wondered if they were dating. "I'm fine," he said. "Just . . . stressful stuff at work. Lots of late nights. We're having a major product launch soon."

Myrtle murmured, unconvinced.

"Josiah," he told the cat, who was watching the street outside with lazy interest, "tell your mom to stop bullying me." Josiah flicked his tail.

"I just worry about you, kid."

Patrick grinned down at his diagrams. "You don't need to." People were always worrying about him, and it made him feel sheepish, eleven again and not standing his ground like he should have.

Myrtle, did you ever not want to be a witch? How do you deal with a broken heart, when nothing's even happened?

He dusted away the chalk on his fingertips. "What does the jar of blackberries mean?"

Myrtle hmmed. "You're supposed to mush it into jam and feed it to people you want to keep by your side. I tried it once with an ex-girlfriend. She was *not* into it."

Patrick stared. Myrtle burst out laughing. "Kidding! Hell if I know. I don't think it really means anything. It's superstition. We love superstition."

"But superstition *means* something to us."

Myrtle shrugged, shook out the sweater to see how it looked. "Rules are easy. Living despite them, that's the hard part."

There was a Starbucks cup on his desk. *Hang in there.* Karl's all-caps handwriting.

Patrick was suddenly angry. At himself, mostly, for not getting his feelings under control. But also at Karl, for messing with him like this when he—when—this had to stop. He picked up the cup and veered for Karl's desk, where Karl was bouncing on his heels, bopping along to something on Spotify. Patrick wasn't sure what to say, but it was hugely important that he deal with this *right now*. He waved a hand in front of Karl's face.

Karl pulled down his headphones. "Morning!"

"What's this for?" A measured tone, that hopefully communicated: *stop doing this to me, I'm dying.* There was the teenage poet again. Yuck.

"Umm," Karl said. "It's a stressful week? With the launch? I like you?"

"*Stop saying that,*" Patrick said, the measured tone slipping away. "You, you just—I'm sorry. I don't want you to keep doing nice things for me." He sounded like an idiot. He *was* an idiot. Myrtle was right—he was messed up—and he braced himself, waiting for Karl to say *Jeez, dude, it's just a coffee!*

Instead, Karl said, very gently: "Want to go to a conference room?"

The sting of tears. Patrick fought them with every ounce of self-preservation he still had—he always cried too easily. (He could hold it in when it mattered. He had done that, sixteen years ago, in a conversation about who he was.)

All the conference rooms were empty. They entered one where the whiteboard still held their diagrams from the day before, last-minute tweaks after their testing party brought to light two conflicting user flows. Karl eased the door shut and stood in front of it, leaning his arms on a chair, watching Patrick's face.

"What's wrong?"

Patrick gathered into himself, let out a shaky breath. This was a completely ridiculous time to be having a meltdown over a crush. If he had more experience with this stuff, he wouldn't be such a wreck. But this was first-time everything, his heart was on fire, and the boy across from him always made him smile and had no idea *how much that hurt.* There was nothing he could say that would make sense. "I'm sorry," he said dropping his gaze. "I don't know what's gotten into me."

Karl drummed his fingers on the top of the chair. "Maybe I should apologize," he said.

This was so unexpected that Patrick looked up.

"It's the flirting, isn't it?" Karl asked. He sounded sorry.

Yes would be wrong; *no* was inaccurate. Patrick pressed his lips together.

"I didn't know the right method," Karl said. "I'm a Product Manager, right? I had to do my research, but also work with assumptions. Test a hypothesis."

"What the fuck are you *talking* about?"

"I was trying to figure out if you liked me."

Patrick went red. In the glass pane behind Karl's shoulder he saw Kat reach her desk and wave at them. It was perfectly ordinary for a PM and a Designer to have a last-minute meeting the day of a massive product launch; that meeting just didn't normally involve gay feelings. "That's not funny," he said.

"What? Why are you mad?"

"Because, I—" *don't want to hope,* Patrick thought; maybe that was the start and end of it. "It's not a joke."

"I'm not joking."

"You—you like guys, or something?"

"Maybe." Karl smiled, not his usual beam of unshakeable goodwill, but something more tender and—tentative, almost. "Or the more accurate way to phrase it is . . . that kind of stuff doesn't really matter to me, given what I am."

Patrick started to laugh. "Oh my god, what's happening?" he said aloud.

"I'm saying I like you," Karl said, reaching out a hand—Patrick caught it. Wondered if this wasn't a dream—something he'd concocted for himself, a draught he inhaled so that this would happen, too good to be true. Karl squeezed his hand. "I've been telling you that for *weeks.* That's okay, isn't it?"

"It's . . . okay," Patrick said, and forgot to wonder if anyone could see when Karl raised his knuckles to his lips and kissed them reverently.

"It's going to be stand-up soon," Karl said. He let go of Patrick's hand. "We can talk about this more later." He seemed sunny, radiant, and as the clock inexorably ticked to 9:15 and others started to file into the office, he did not stop smiling. Patrick was sure he had the dopiest expression on, but right now, that didn't really matter.

It was easy, Patrick realized, in a way he didn't expect it to be. It wasn't even that different from being friends: the same dinners, the same heart-fluttering spasms, how every time he glanced at Karl he thought, *Shit, he's cute.* Except there was this separate awareness in his head—even if they'd never quite said it—they were *dating,* he was *dating a guy.* It *was* like the songs, being in love—because that's what this was, right? Now that he wasn't fighting it every minute, now that he was letting himself be okay with the feeling: sunshine on a cloudy day, hooked on a feeling. You really got me; you make my dreams come true. They didn't act differently at work, either, so no one could tell. Which was fine. Neither of them felt like being the topic of office gossip, and they collaborated so closely that it was better if no one else knew.

Kat, of course, was in on it. Patrick half-expected her to say "Fucking finally!"—but she actually laughed in surprise, and said, "Oh my god I had *no idea congratulations you two* but oh my god really?! Oh my god!" She dropped the taco she'd been holding, and they had a good laugh while mopping away salsa. "Come to think of it," she said to Karl, "you are somehow the perfect definition of bisexual."

Surprisingly, Patrick's heart still hurt sometimes. The ghost of rule number two, looming. How fragile things seemed. How he was still hiding, in a way. The happiness melted everything, made the edges fuzzy, but there were still times when Patrick was sure he was going to mess this up because of how badly he wanted it. How ashamed he was, of that wanting.

❀

The first time Karl asked if he could come over Patrick had said "Sure." Internally he'd been nervous, totally unsure of what was about to happen. They walked back from ramen at Japantown, discussing the latest trivia night at the office that had ended with Marlene from Marketing crying drunkenly about not knowing The Rock's real name. Patrick's mind was only half on the conversation.

"It's messy, sorry," Patrick warned, as he turned his key in the lock. He'd been practicing pentagrams that week, things to conjure a little spring for winter. "I don't usually have visitors."

"I don't mind," Karl said. He inspected the diagrams on Patrick's table. "Are these spells to summon a sexy boyfriend?"

"Ha-ha." Patrick cleared a stack of books off a chair and pushed his papers out of the way, while Karl migrated to his bookcase. Patrick realized his jar of blackberries was sitting in plain view, but decided not to worry about it.

"You want something to drink?"

"White tea?"

Patrick snorted and flipped his kettle on.

Miranda poked her head out from the bedroom, eyeing the interloper.

"Aw, she's such a cutie." Karl squatted down and reached out his arms to her. She turned her head aside, unimpressed, and sauntered over to Patrick to rub against his leg instead.

"She plays hard to get."

"Like you?"

"Don't know what you mean," Patrick said, but he bit his lip to keep from smiling. Karl had wandered over to the refrigerator and was now looking at the pictures Patrick had tacked up: of his family, random wedding invites, Aunt Gemma's note.

"Interesting list. What does *the shape of things can be deceptive* mean?"

"That's a secret." Patrick envied Karl his mysteriousness, a little; sometimes he wanted to do the same, be even *slightly* alluring. He handed his boyfriend a mug.

"I mean, it doesn't sound too secretive. It just sounds like good life advice." Karl took a sip, standing close. He had long eyelashes—*sooty,* Patrick thought, that was the book-word for it—and his hair had grown out from when they first met. Now he had bangs that kept falling into his eyes. He was wearing a green sweater, and there was a ball of fuzz on his right shoulder. Patrick didn't know why he was noting all of these things, except this felt like an important moment. Worth turning into a memory. Patrick brought his mug up to shield his face, acknowledged he was freaked out. Excited. But freaked out.

Karl put his mug down on the counter. "Why are you so cute?"

"Stop it. You're the worst."

"No, I'm serious." He crept closer, and because he was a gigantic flirting *idiot* he completely ignored the fact that Patrick was holding a steaming mug of hot tea and just *leaned in,* went for a—kiss—this was Patrick's first ever kiss—Karl wouldn't know that, but maybe he'd guess it—and Patrick's hand jerked, spilling tea, even as his body relaxed. The tea fell harmlessly onto the carpet. Miranda hissed like she was going *oh-please.* It was . . . really *interesting,* a kiss was, sort of mushy and Karl's mouth was soft, a kind of dissolving into nothingness, the taste of tea and dinner beneath it, and Patrick was lightheaded with this sensation, suddenly present with himself—not forwards or backwards, not thinking too hard—alive here with someone's mouth against his. Why did Karl taste like rain?

They broke apart, and he put the mug on the counter. Bit his lip, for a different reason this time. Watched Karl's eyes flicker with interest.

I can do that to someone? Holy shit.

Karl waited. This time, Patrick was the one who reached out, cradling his head—and—was it always this impossible not to close your eyes? The kiss went on forever, even through Miranda skritch-skritching somewhere in the background (*my pentagrams,* Patrick worried faintly), and then Karl slid a hand up the back of his shirt, palmed his ribs. He made some unfortunate sound into Karl's mouth, and Karl pulled away.

"Sorry," they said at the same time.

Karl kept his hand where it was, warm against his side.

"It's not that I don't like it," Patrick said. "I just, uhhh. I've never. Been intimate." He'd never even made out with someone, but the words *make out* were too embarrassing to say aloud. Even the word *intimate* made him feel ridiculous. He should have just admitted he was a virgin. For a long time Patrick had wondered if he might be ace; he'd guessed he wasn't, and recent feelings had made him *sure* he wasn't, but this was all still very new to him.

"We don't have to do anything you don't want to," Karl said. Then, since he had no shame whatsoever: "Should I take my hand away?"

Well, if it was going to be like that, he could play too. Patrick looped his arms over Karl's shoulders and looked him in his absurdly hot, thundercloud eyes. "Leave it."

He told Karl the story one October evening, rain falling steadily outside and someone in the floor above him playing Spanish guitar. How he'd come out four years ago, shortly after moving to San Francisco, back in his old apartment that he split with four other people in the Mission. He had a charm for courage tied around his wrist while he called his mom and wondered when his heart had been replaced with a jackhammer. It was cowardly, to come out over the phone. Cowardly and still more frightening than anything.

There was a long pause while she digested what he had to say.

You don't have a boyfriend, Mom said. *Do you?*

No.

You're not dating someone?

No.

So how do you know?

Patrick had pressed his head against the wall. What use was a stupid courage spell for? Why did he always feel like he had to *say what he was,* when it hurt the people he cared about?

I just—I know, I'm sure. I've known for a couple of years now.

But how *do you know?* Emphasis on *how,* like that was the part of her question he was struggling with.

Patrick had stared at Miranda, who was more at home in this city and in her skin than he'd probably ever be. Cats were not sages and they were not *guides,* she wasn't even Aunt Gemma's familiar per se, but maybe if he stared at her long enough she'd deign to give him an answer. Miranda stared back. Nothing happened. He soldiered on.

I find boys cute.

That's not the same thing. I think some girls are cute.

I would only like to date boys. By then Patrick felt remote and helpless. He thought of adding, *I would only like to kiss boys, and fuck boys, and be fucked by boys, and it has taken me forever to reach this conclusion, and for the longest time I thought saying this didn't matter, and a part of me still thinks maybe it doesn't. But a larger part of me has just gotten tired of hiding this, and not flinching away at every mention of it, and pretending that I'm not what I am. I've come here. This far. This far and I am still turned away, at this gate, this shore, I cannot cross, Mom, I've gotten this far and you still can't see me. I have carried myself here and I am at your feet.*

Is this related to the witch thing? That was Dad, suddenly—Dad who'd been listening this whole time, as Patrick had been expecting. Dad who only knew what he knew: that his son was a witch and now gay. Dad whom he loved, who loved him back, who could not know how much those words hurt. Being a witch didn't make him gay, and being gay didn't make him a witch. Patrick was just Patrick; being Patrick was hard.

No, it's not related to being a witch at all.

They were all quiet for a while.

Mom had sighed. *We love you so much,* she said. *We worry about you. We don't . . . want things to be hard for you.*

I know, Mom. Dad. He wiped his tears away, didn't inhale deeply like he was longing to, so that it wasn't obvious he'd been crying.

We want you to be happy.

Okay.

Okay.

He was tearing up again, recounting the exchange. He swallowed and said, "We've never really talked about it since, even when I go back home. I mean . . . I don't really want to talk about it either. I don't know what they think."

Karl's head was on his lap, and he'd closed his eyes during the story, making soft noises to show he was listening. Now he opened his eyes. Patrick couldn't look at him, suddenly; he gazed outside, but there wasn't much to see. Fog pressed against the windows, like a stray seeking shelter. Karl reached up and touched his cheek, gently. "Does it matter what they think?"

"It does to me."

"Sorry. What I meant was, does it matter . . . if you all love each other?"

Patrick bent down and kissed his boyfriend's forehead. Karl's skin was always cool, always tasted faintly of rain. "Yeah. But knowing that makes it matter a little less."

Halloween started off innocently enough. It was on a Friday that year, one of those unexpectedly warm fall days, the sun beaming down, bouncing off all the glass windows in SoMa. Patrick counted six Where's Waldo's on his commute. That had been his default costume (having obtained the requisite striped sweater the previous year), but Kat had been insistent about going as the Bananas in

Pajamas this year. ("Fine. As long as I get to be B2.") Karl's costume was a secret.

By lunchtime almost everyone was only pretending to work. It was too nice outside. Most people went for the food trucks then lounged in South Park for way too long. Marquet had closed a Series B in the last week and everyone was in high spirits, and the party tonight was hopefully going to reflect a *wee* bit of that cash in the bank. At 4 PM Melody started walking around with a jug full of beer, and people began queuing for the bathroom. Karl got his turn at last, and emerged wearing a T-shirt, beanie, and jeans—all bright red.

"Ooo, let me guess!" Kat clapped her hands together. "Sexy Santa? A drop of blood? Wait! A . . . *period?*"

"I'm the Golden Gate Bridge," Karl said.

Kat leaned towards Patrick. "Your boyfriend is an idiot."

"He's not the one dressed as a banana," Patrick replied.

Angeli, the newest Android Engineer, cracked ice for old-fashioneds in the kitchen. Richard the CTO appeared from behind his desk dressed as a piece of salmon sushi, and was swarmed by people wanting to take selfies. Melody dimmed the lights and put on a playlist that predictably started with Michael Jackson's *Thriller.* Random friendly relations poured in from the stairwell and the elevator, and soon the room was full of people drinking and talking and not-exactly-dancing, green lights strung up on the ceiling, the fog machine making everyone alienlike. Two girls that Patrick didn't recognize were dressed as sexy witches, black miniskirt-eyeliner-lipstick. They came up to Patrick to ask him where the bathroom was, and he wondered if either of them could actually work any magic. At some point Jeremy from Finance made a passable DJ airhorn imitation, and an image of Vodka Ice was projected on the wall. Everyone had to proceed to the cauldron in the kitchen, fish out a bottle, get on one knee and down it. Around this time Kat shoved Patrick and Karl out of the office and told them to get in the Lyft waiting outside, because it was time to hit the city.

Patrick was still lucid. He remembered most of the first club: some of Kat's friends from her first start-up were there, and half the Sales team appeared shortly after they arrived. There was a lot of standing in a circle and pumping knees. He'd discarded his banana hat-thing at the bar; now he just looked like a dude in striped pajamas. He remembered most of the second club too: a Jack Sparrow with the most endearing Australian accent bought them shots of whiskey, gratis; Kat had kissed his fake beard. Karl lost his beanie somewhere on the dance floor, maybe because some girl dressed as a cop had come by and pulled it off to rake her fingers through his hair—Patrick had witnessed this stumbling back from the bathroom. He was too far away to do anything about it. A Luke Skywalker suddenly blocked Patrick's path, laughed in a way that showed all his teeth, and tried to give Patrick a hug. He seemed to have four thousand arms. Patrick allowed himself to be hugged, laughed back, felt his stomach lurch. Luke Skywalker kissed him on the mouth. Patrick stepped backwards, into a grinding couple; he edged away from them, helter-skelter, and suddenly Karl's fingers were around his wrist like a vice, dragging him through the crowd towards the door.

"Ouch," he'd said, expecting Karl to stop. He didn't. "That hurts."

Karl tugged him through the door, didn't listen when Patrick said he needed to let Kat know they were leaving. "I'll text her," Karl said, and waved at the Uber making a U-turn for them. "Come on, get in."

"Are you angry?"

Patrick had seen Karl angry exactly twice—once when they'd pushed an update without properly QA'ing it and the support team got flooded with venomous calls and chats (he'd been in an auspiciously *loud* meeting with the Product Lead for approving the decision); and another time when someone had yelled "GET A ROOM" and a slur at them while they were crossing the street together, holding hands. His eyes weren't the gentle gray of mist anymore; they were deep storm clouds, roiling around a single point of fury. Something in them shook Patrick, fought through the haze of alcohol and the threat of nausea so that he was really *looking* at Karl. Rain broke out, slammed against the car's windshield. Karl only let go of Patrick's wrist once they were pulling away from the neon lights of the Castro, passing a troupe of angels and devils clustered on the street corner.

Patrick pressed his hands to his face, though whether that was to hold something in or blot something out, he wasn't sure. He heard Karl sigh next to him.

When the Uber finally stopped, it wasn't at his apartment like he was expecting. He didn't have time to ask any questions before Karl got out of the car, and he had to follow. Karl was at the gate, already putting his key in. He turned and looked at Patrick, still with that stormy look. Patrick went up the steps and followed him inside, suddenly uncertain. Two flights of stairs. Another key, a deadbolt, and they were inside Karl's flat, which was somehow colder than the hallway or even the night outside. It occurred to Patrick that some part of him hadn't believed Karl *lived* anywhere, that his existence didn't appear to involve anything so ordinary as an apartment, even if that was absurd. Karl flicked on a light, revealing the meticulously clean room. Patrick had taken barely two steps inside when Karl embraced him from behind, pressed his lips to Patrick's neck and kissed him beneath his striped pajama collar. Patrick tingled all over.

He turned and touched Karl's face. "You're drunk," he said. "Stop."

"I don't want to." He kissed Patrick again, almost lunging, full of want. His arms wrapped around Patrick's back, pressing him in. Patrick was surprised by the force, how it made his stomach jump, an aching tenderness in his lower belly, but—no. Not like this. Resisting the urge to kiss him back, Patrick placed his hands on Karl's temple and pulled him away, gave him what was hopefully a stern look. Did the thing he used to do to noisy kids in food courts: *stop that.* The rain outside was so loud it seemed to be in the room with them. Patrick had to strain to get his magic to work. *Stop it.*

After a moment where it seemed like nothing was happening, the storm clouds left Karl's eyes. He blinked, dazed. Then he pressed his face into Patrick's collarbone. "Oh my god, I'm sorry," he murmured. "I don't know what got into me."

"It's okay." He wanted to be reassuring, but he *was* a little worried. He patted Karl's back. "Let me get you a glass of water."

Karl was reluctant to let go. He disappeared into the bathroom; Patrick heard water splashing. He entered the kitchen, trying to ignore a spike of disappointment. On the counter he noticed the bag of White Needle he'd given Karl, way back during Pride weekend, and an infuser next to it. It would probably wake him up, get him back to normal. He rummaged in the drawers for a teaspoon, then opened the bag.

His heart dropped.

That did not smell like white tea. It smelled, instead, like rosemary and vanilla, like dried tears. A spell that didn't work, or worked too slowly. A slow-burn desire that peaked only months after ingested.

In moments of extreme panic, Patrick typically acted with supreme rationality. He took the bag. He fished his phone out of his breast pocket, thanked god he still had battery left, and called a Lyft. He said nothing to Karl, who was still in the bathroom, and left the apartment. He stood on the street outside, getting drenched in the rain, trying not to think, trying not to feel. He failed miserably.

Myrtle was surprised that he hadn't known she'd been storing the early brews in old tea canisters.

"I always save the earlier batches," she said. "You never know when they'll come in handy. Something wrong?"

"No."

"Oh boy."

"Don't ask." Patrick blinked rapidly when she put a hand on his shoulder, and was grateful she didn't press.

hey
I'm sorry about yesterday :(
God I was such a dick
I'm sorry
Can I come over?
3 Missed Calls from Karl :cloud-emoji:
I understand if you're mad
2 Missed Calls from Karl :cloud-emoji:
I love you
See you tomorrow

Had he ever said I love you to Karl?

Karl always said *I love you* to him.

He turned that over in his head. He'd always *meant* to, in his embraces, his glances, his heart emojis. But it didn't seem like he'd ever said it aloud. The words were too raw, too trusting. Maybe he'd been waiting for a way to make sure.

It was weird. And sad. That whole weekend Patrick made up dialogues in his head about how this was going to go. He forget them all when he walked into the office on Monday. Karl was waiting for him. Of course. He'd been ignoring Karl's texts and calls all weekend. The office was deserted at 8:30; he should have arranged to come in with Kat that morning, so that he could pretend everything was cool and nothing hurt. But they were in a professional environment, and they were both professionals, and he was going to see this conversation through to the bloody end.

"I'm sorry," Karl said. They were back in the room where this had all started, just a few weeks ago. "I was a little drunk, yes, but it was the sight of that Jedi dude kissing you that made me—I lost it. I totally lost it. I know I act calm all the time but I'm really not, Patrick, you make me so . . ." He exhaled. "I won't make excuses. But I really am sorry and I get why you're ignoring me but it's driving me crazy. Can we start over? Can I fix this?"

"Stop apologizing," Patrick said. He was going to have to do it after all, break his own heart by breaking Karl's, so that this would be over more quickly. After all, it was his potion. He knew how it worked. He knew it would be wearing off any day now, and Karl's sensibilities would shift and all that ache would be gone, whisked away from his being. The feelings hadn't really been there to begin with. His memories would be vague, the details filed off. Patrick was the only one who'd have to carry the broken pieces.

Which was great. He could bear it. He had lots of practice with pretending.

He looked at his first-ever crush and only-ever boyfriend and reconciled that sometimes things were too good to be true.

"This was a mistake," Patrick said, carefully. "It's . . . it wasn't real, Karl. I'm sorry. We can't," he waved a hand, then forced himself to say it. "We can't keep dating. I really like you, but I want to . . ." Say it. *Say it.* "Just go back to how we were, you know. I want you to keep being my partner, my PM, my friend." He managed a smile, tried not to register the way Karl's face was spanning an entire history of pain—*it's the potion working, it's doing its job; he's supposed to desire me. He can't help it.* Time to bring it home. "Can we do that?"

Karl squeezed his eyes shut. For a moment Patrick thought he was going to cry. But when he opened them again his eyes were clear. "I don't want to," he said. "But if it's what you want."

"It's what I want."

"Can I hug you as a friend, then?" Karl said. "It'll make me feel better."

"You really are the worst," Patrick said, but he opened up his arms anyway. Karl pressed his nose to Patrick's shoulder and breathed in deeply. Patrick nearly lost it, all the tears he'd been holding back that weekend suddenly welling up, up, up, it had been *so good* even if it had all been fake. He swallowed, gave Karl a firm squeeze, then pushed him away. At least this way they could keep working together. "It'll make sense in a few days," he said, smiling. "You'll see. It won't hurt at all."

This was easy, too, but in a different way—*acting* was easy, because that's what it felt like. They didn't need to be any different. They moved and talked and worked the same, they still had lunch together, still talked about the merits of their new design software and which emo bands they liked in high school, but that was all surface stuff. Everything beneath that was different. They could still work together, but in the silences of a meeting—brief encounters in the kitchen, packing up for home—tension stretched between them, so delicate a drawn breath could explode it.

Maybe the weirdest thing was how Karl dropped the flirtations almost entirely, just a stray gesture here and there: touching his arm when he was making a point over a mock-up, or picking stray cat hair off his shoulder. Karl always started when he did those things, as if he was surfacing from a dream. Then they would both look away.

Kat noticed, of course. Patrick didn't tell her about the potion, because the spell was wearing off now and any mention of it might have repercussions. He told her, instead, that he'd known from the beginning it wasn't going to work, and he figured it was better to call it quits early. Kat's forehead went all creased. "You were both hella wasted on Halloween," she said. "Whatever happened, I'm sure it was just . . . you know. A thing."

"No, Kat, it's not one of those things. It's really . . . it's me."

"I could've guessed that," Kat shot back, surprising Patrick with her anger. "You're always fencing yourself off, Pat. You were happy! *He* was happy. I don't get it."

"I wasn't expecting you to," Patrick said. She gave him a dark look and left. He watched her go, weary. He and Kat had fought before; he'd bribe her back with gelato the next day.

Things did, eventually, normalize. Karl went from slightly droopy to bright and sunny again, his smile radiant as ever. Patrick was surprised at how the memory of having that smile directed at him made him lonely. The loneliness was new. It was like their being together had made a space inside him that hadn't been there before, and he'd expanded to contain it, and now he was empty. What had happened felt like a dream. A temporary moment of grace: someone else's story. Something to treasure and hold close. The first crush that had come, years and years after it seemed *normal* to get one. It was a lesson, he decided. Someday he'd look back on it and the hurt would be gone, too: his broken heart an artifact to inspect.

That didn't need to be magic; time was magic in its own way.

At least they were still friends.

Patrick got a rental car and drove back to Fresno for Thanksgiving. Aunt Gemma joined him. She'd come from Asia on consecutive flights, and by all rights should have been groggy and grumpy. But she was effusive as ever, sharing all her travel adventures during the long drive. Once they arrived she bustled over the turkey Dad was painstakingly trying to roast, and cheerfully whipped up her signature blackberry tart. Ann had flown in from the East Coast and spent most of her break napping, though occasionally she wandered into Patrick's room to tell him about the latest drama at school. Ann had no magic, like Mom, but she didn't mind. She was a peaceful kid, extremely bright, and probably going to med school after all. Do actual healing, instead of the sometimes-fixers that Patrick brewed.

It was interesting, how they lived such separate lives most of the year, but could pick up where they left off the few times they were together. She lurked now in his room, like they did years ago, before they both left.

"Are you working on a new spell?"

Patrick was at his desk, fishing out notes from high school. "Yeah," he said.

"What for?"

"Mending a broken heart."

"*Really?*"

"No, not really. That's the kind of thing spells can only gloss over, not fix." He leaned back in his chair, stretched. "Or maybe I'm just not a good enough witch."

"Aunt Gemma's always going on about how great you are."

"She just dotes on me," he said. "Because we're the same."

Ann shrugged. "I'll always be grateful for when you mended Mr. Puttyface without any thread." Her purple rabbit doll, ages ago, when she'd torn off one arm in a rage. "So what are you actually working on?"

"Something to keep the cold away in winter. I had a prototype and it didn't work."

"Few prototypes work," Ann said sagely, then lay on his bed to finish her paperback. "Though I do hope that by 'winter' you don't mean San Francisco getting marginally colder in January. I could *really* use something that works in Syracuse."

"Yeah, yeah."

She turned a few pages. "So, uh. Did your heart get broken?"

"Sort of."

Ann gave him one of her owlish looks, but kept reading.

Patrick found the journal he'd been looking for. Flipping through it, he remembered what it was like *not* to feel this way—constantly thinking of someone else, wanting to be wanted. He'd wondered, on and off for several years, what was wrong with him, why he didn't get crushes like everyone else. Turned out he was just as fallible as the rest of them. He nearly missed this old version of himself: not-caring, pre-Karl. He read the journal until Mom called them down for dinner.

"How's work?" Mom asked, while they sat munching turkey and brussels sprouts.

Patrick talked about their platform redesign launch, which had been a success in that *very few clients had complained*. Kat had been publicly recognized at All-Hands for her good work with messaging, and she'd named all the team members. It had been a warm and fuzzy moment. He mentioned Karl, but only in passing: part of that project, nothing else. Aunt Gemma engaged them all with tales of getting stranded in the Singapore airport ("10/10, would recommend"). Patrick wasn't sure if she'd sensed his gloom, or simply wanted to talk.

After the meal he helped with the washing-up, then lay down on the couch and drowsed. He opened up Facebook to wish his friends a Happy Thanksgiving, and of course the first post he saw was from Karl: a picture of the Golden Gate Bridge, wreathed in mist, no filter. He'd put a heart emoji and a turkey emoji as his status update. That was it.

Patrick rolled over and wondered how long he was going to keep feeling sad. Aunt Gemma sat next to him on the couch, a decaf coffee in hand, and sipped primly.

"Pat," she said. "You got a second?"

"I've got the whole evening, ma'am."

"When I gave you that rulebook for your eleventh birthday, how did you feel?"

He sat up, straightening. He hadn't been expecting that question at all. "I felt . . . grateful?"

She looked at him.

"I felt *seen*," he said. "Like someone had given me permission to say yes to something I'd known all along."

"Did it make you a better witch?"

He scrunched his face. "I don't know that it did, it was just . . . comforting. To know that you were, that I could be, a witch."

"Do you *like* being a witch?"

"Yes." He answered quietly, because he was in his own house, still carrying shards from a conversation that should have bled out of him long ago. *Yes* was still a betrayal of *something,* though he knew by now he'd never been wrong about it. He said *yes* under his breath, but he said it with conviction, because it was true.

"That makes me happy," Aunt Gemma said. "I always worried that you did it only for me."

"For you?" Patrick laughed. "But you were never around!"

"I *know*. I mean, your mom's never forgiven me. And I always had to prod."

"No, I like magic for myself," Patrick said.

"It *is* magic, witchcraft, isn't it? I feel really lucky to have it."

"Sometimes. When it isn't blowing up in your face."

Aunt Gemma narrowed her eyes, then took a nonchalant sip, looking coy.

"Everything works out in the end," she said. "And if it doesn't, you can always blame the cats. Or the weather."

Patrick returned to work steeling himself against the onslaught of feelings he fully expected to have. Sure, they'd been "acting normal" for weeks, but every time he thought about Karl—every time they made eye contact, even every time it *rained*—his chest went tight, like some freaking romance novel heroine. Visiting home had been great, but he knew that a few days eating leftover stuffing and thumbing through old journals was still probably not enough armor against that platinum hair, those eyes that struck him like sunlight through the mist.

Except Karl wasn't at his desk that day. It was only after an hour of meetings that Patrick got to his inbox and saw Karl's all-hands email about feeling sick and working from home.

He was out for the next three days. He still replied to email, but it was hours late, which meant he was in a bad way. The front-end team had made a functional prototype of Patrick's mock-up that Karl needed to give the go-ahead on, before the back-end team could start creating new endpoints. Patrick had sent Karl a tentative ping on Slack, but besides the perpetual *out sick* status emoji he'd gotten nothing. So it was that he found himself outside Karl's apartment at 7 PM that Friday, holding a tub of chicken noodle soup and feeling simultaneously anxious, embarrassed, and irritated at himself.

Kat should have brought it. He was being a dope.

On his third try someone finally answered. "Yes?"

"It's Patrick," he said.

"Oh!" Coughing, laced with intercom crackle. "One sec."

He heard the door buzz open, and pushed his way through, up two flights of stairs, 'til he was standing at the door. There was a beat when he considered leaving the soup on the welcome mat and running away, then the door swung open and Karl peered out. He looked . . . not great. His face was flushed under pale, sick-looking skin; his hair was matted to his face with sweat. It looked washed-out, the cloudy color depressing rather than appealing.

"Hey," he croaked. "Sorry, I would invite you in, but I've caught the plague."

"It's okay," Patrick said. "I, um. I brought you soup."

"Magic soup?"

"Maybe a little." He grinned in spite of himself, and held it out. Karl took it. "Did you, um. Did you have a good Thanksgiving?"

Karl shrugged. "It was okay, until I started semi-dying, I guess."

"What caused it?"

"Heartsickness." He smiled, displaying an amazing ability to remain cheeky. Patrick sighed.

"Just promise me you'll get better. The front-end guys don't know what to do without you. Actually no one does."

"I'm sure they'll manage," Karl said. "*Some* people can." Before Patrick could open his mouth to reply, he added, "Sorry! Sorry. I'm just spaced out from being sick. Patrick, you're a hero. I will take this soup religiously until I am all better. Thank you. I really appreciate it."

"It's not a big deal," Patrick said. If Karl was comfortable flirting with him again that meant the potion had finally expired; it was totally gone from his system. They could go back to being normal. "Take it easy, okay?"

He stepped back from the door and waved. Karl waved back. For a moment it seemed like he might say something else, but the moment passed, and he shut the door. Patrick walked back down the steps, tongue pressed to the roof of his mouth, and wondered where to go from here. He felt free, and somehow trapped with it.

Karl got better and showed up the next Monday. He stopped by Patrick's desk that day. "That soup *was* magic!" He clapped a hand on Patrick's shoulder, then didn't talk to him for the rest of the week, except once to ask if he'd filed that JIRA ticket, post-standup.

One random Thursday Patrick had a sudden desire to walk through the Embarcadero on his way home. There were runners everywhere, and pigeons. He couldn't taste the water in the air so much as feel it. The wind blew dramatically so that his scarf flapped; random SoMa debris skidded every which way. There was a flock of birds wheeling overhead, V-shapes turning and turning in ever smaller circles, mesmerizing against the pink-streaked sky of San Francisco in early December.

Patrick sat on a concrete block facing the water. He watched two dudes walk past, smiling; one of them leaned in for a quick kiss. Their laughter seemed to ring as they stepped away, but maybe that was just Patrick being melodramatic.

Maybe it was okay to let himself be melodramatic sometimes. Maybe it was okay to remember the way Karl had made him feel: like sunlight, like things were going to work out. That it was all right to be himself. That no matter what was exploding at Marquet that week, no matter how angry the clients were about the latest release, they'd figure out some way to make things right, with a bit of creativity and enough coffee. Sometimes it was about Karl's smile, his stupid hair, how soft it was threaded through Patrick's fingers when he finally allowed himself to touch it, during that second kiss. How Karl, who always seemed to be dissolving and turning up everywhere, had been firm against Patrick whenever they embraced: something that would never leave.

When did the city become so infused with the memory of one boy? When did every speck of mist and every step on the gray streets become some echo of him?

A bird landed next to Patrick, shifting its his head inquiringly. He flapped a hand at it, but it didn't leave. Soon there was a whole crowd of tiny brown birds milling around him. "Can't I have a broken heart in peace?" he sighed. To his surprise, un-summoned, a gust of wind rucked up and sent the birds wheeling over the Bay Bridge.

In the nearby dog park, a French bulldog and a Corgi erupted in barks.

He stood and walked to the banister, leaning to stare at the shiny rocks and churning water below.

"I should have said it at least once," he said. "Because I really did."

He arranged his scarf again, because the wind had died down. Fog filled the road. He seemed to be alone with it, the air thick with mist. It hung around him like an embrace as he walked the length of the road, turned into Market Street, and took the bus home.

The next weekend was SantaCon. Patrick almost forgot, except he'd set a doctor's appointment by Union Square and had to walk past a distressing number of buff Santas and sexy elves. If Kat was in town she'd have obviously set up a SantaCon brunch for everyone, but she was in Chicago for her grandma's birthday. Which was great, because after all this time Patrick still had trouble saying no to her.

After his check-up Patrick bought a cup of Peet's Coffee, then walked to Union Square and squatted on one of the steps by a heart sculpture to spectate. A crowd of merry Santas passed by and waved at him.

One of them had gray eyes, over his thick fluffy beard and oversized Santa suit.

Patrick turned his head away and decided it was time for him to be getting home. Too late. By the time he'd stood and tipped back the last dregs of latte into his throat, the gray-eyed Santa had broken off from his group and was striding towards him, faster than the wind. Patrick scurried into the middle of Union Square, trying to lose the Santa in the throngs of people messing about and posing under the giant Christmas tree. By then there was no point denying it: he was running away.

"Patrick!"

Nope. He broke into a full-on run, down 4th Street, looking for some place to take a breather, some place to hide—there was nowhere to hide. He made it as far as Yerba Buena Gardens before Santa reached him and touched his shoulder gently. He would have kept running anyway, if not for the fence of fog around them, blotting out the garden, enveloping them in silence.

He turned.

"I knew it. You're still avoiding me."

Karl had unhooked the fake beard from his ears and taken off the Santa hat. He raked his hair back, pushed those floppy pale bangs out of the way, but he wasn't actually sweating. He looked, as always, immaculate. Patrick felt his chest rise and fall, cursed himself for his breathlessness. Even in a stupid Santa suit Karl was still everything he wanted.

"You freaked me out, that's all."

"I always seem to be doing that." His expression was pained.

"I know you don't mean it." Patrick was too tired to feel embarrassed; he simply felt defeated.

"Hey," Karl said, stepping close. "Can we talk about this?"

"There's nothing to talk about." He said it quietly, a last-ditch attempt at saving himself before he got too honest. He always got too honest. What did it matter anyway, that he broke his own heart further? It was smashed into pieces by now, impossible to glue back together.

"I won't let you run away from this." Somehow the mist around them congealed, 'til they were standing in a white fence, the air solid around them. *Magic,* Patrick thought. He wondered if Aunt Gemma or Myrtle was giggling somewhere, conjuring this. Or was it his own subconscious, tweaking the weather to force this conversation?

Karl reached out and touched his cheek, and Patrick didn't flinch away. He kept his eyes open, felt them sting with sudden tears. He remembered this touch. Like song lyrics, falling rain, Karl's skin always so cool whenever it made contact with his.

"Why are you running away?"

"Because it's not real."

"What about this isn't real?" He reached out his other hand, and gently cupped Patrick's face.

"What you felt—what you feel. It was a potion, the White Needle tea, it was an accident." This far into speaking, Patrick felt he could finally *look* at Karl, and not wither into nothing. "You were drinking a *love potion* that whole time and it was made to be a slow-burn and you don't really like me, you only think you do. You were under a spell."

Karl blinked. He blinked again.

"You gave me a *love potion?*" He squeezed his palms, squishing Patrick's cheeks.

Patrick yelped. It wasn't painful; just shocking. "It wasn't on purpose!"

"Oh my god." Karl took his hands away, pressed them to his face. It took a second for Patrick to realize that Karl wasn't angry; he was laughing. Laughing so hard he actually doubled over. "Oh my god, you—is that why you broke up with me after Halloween?" He made a sound that sounded suspiciously like "Arrrrgghhhh" when Patrick nodded gravely in reply. But Karl was still laughing, and Patrick was too confused to be embarrassed or angry, though he did feel a pang of dismay that he was being serious, and here was Karl, losing his shit. After a moment in which he actually wiped *tears* away, Karl said, "I'm immune to potions."

"You're what?"

"I'm an elemental." He was almost apologetic.

It was Patrick's turn to blink.

Karl grinned in frustration, which shouldn't have been so endearing. "I'm *of the fog*"—he waved a hand—"and I'm *immune* to *human spells.*"

Patrick understood all in a rush. The curtain of air fencing them in, the way the fog had crept over him like a blanket so often. Karl's beautiful *eyes.* Old magic, older than witchcraft, entire books on Aunt Gemma's shelf about them, but none he'd ever gone through with any diligence because—he didn't think he'd fall in love with one. Or that they'd be so capable at project management.

"Then—"

"Yeah," Karl said, and without pretense moved like water through the space between them, right up to Patrick so that their faces were barely apart. "Some of it *was* acting, some of it was . . . trying to do this, the way humans do. But it was true. That was all me. *God,* I thought you knew—I thought that's why you showed me your magic—I mean when we first met you immediately said *the fog.* I should've guessed you'd assume something completely different!"

Here was the blushing, arriving far too late, because Patrick *was* an idiot.

"Then . . ."

"*Yes,* what do you want me to say? I've said it before, I'll say it again: I love you." He wrapped his arms around Patrick, and all the tension left his body, so that he felt he was drifting on air, or nothingness. "My witch boy, witch love. You *did* cast a spell on me," Karl murmured, while Patrick pressed his cheek to Karl's chest, eyes filling with tears, and breathed in. The smell of rain on concrete, condensation, the air after a storm. "You just didn't know it."

Aunt Gemma was behind the counter, enjoying tea with Myrtle, when Patrick came in. They both grinned fiendishly at him; their smiles widened when Karl came in half a beat later. Patrick tried to ignore this.

Karl said "Hi." Then, "So, uh, do I have to impress you ladies? I humbly ask for your blessing to date this precious boy."

"We can't give blessings away! We're witches, not fairy godmothers. Besides, our spells don't work on you." Aunt Gemma extended Karl a cup of tea, which he took.

"Wait. Did you *know* this whole time?" Patrick's jaw dropped open.

Aunt Gemma shrugged. "Just because your boyfriend's the fog, doesn't mean he'll never break your heart."

"Patrick's already broken *mine,*" Karl said. "Multiple times."

"Smart boy," Myrtle said. Josiah meowed. It sounded like a giggle.

One weekend in February they walked down the Marina pier, taking in the salt air and circling seagulls, hand in hand. They stopped at the Wave Organ, leaning into the pipes to listen, but only one of them made any sound: a faint humming, like a moan at the end of a long tunnel. It was cold and silly to be walking here in winter, even if San Francisco could make any month seem like winter, because its chilly wind was always more apparent than its sunshine.

Karl sat down first, facing the Golden Gate Bridge. It was completely visible that day.

"Are you that happy, because we're on a date?" Patrick asked.

"Maybe. Why, am I not allowed to be?"

After taking a panoramic photo, because the view was just too good, Patrick sat down next to him, pulling his beanie lower over his head. Karl leaned his head on Patrick's shoulder. Anyone walking that way would see them from a long way off, but Patrick didn't mind.

He reached up and ran a hand through Karl's hair.

"I'm still new to all of this," he said slowly. "And sometimes I'll still freak out. Just so you know."

"I know." Karl held his hand, pressed a kiss to his knuckles. He really liked doing that. "*I* still wonder sometimes if you'll ever like me as much as I like you."

Patrick touched his lips to Karl's, briefly. It seemed the best response.

Karl sighed. "I guess I'm down for this. Whatever happens. I'm down."

Because this made Patrick too happy, and he didn't know what to do with his happiness, he stuck his free hand into the pocket of Karl's coat. "My hands are cold."

Karl laughed. "I'll allow it."

Have You Heard the One About Anamaria Marquez?

It all started when Ms. Salinas told us about her third eye. It was home ec, and we were sitting in front of the sewing machines with table runners that we were going to make our moms or yayas do for us anyway. I was pretty anxious about that project. I knew Mom was going to tell me to do it myself, because she believed in the integrity of homework. "Mica," Mom would say. "Jesus expects you to be honest, and so do I." I was wondering how to get Ya Fely to do it for me behind Mom's back when Ms. Salinas started blabbing about the ghost on the bus.

"You see, girls, most ghosts are very polite. At first I didn't even notice he was a ghost, and then I realized the woman sitting next to him couldn't see him, because she looked at me with this suplada face and said, 'Miss, are you not going to sit down?' Then the ghost shrugged, like, it's okay with me. So I had to sit on its lap, while at the same time sitting on the bus seat, and that felt so . . . weird."

Ms. Salinas was young and super skinny, which made up for her ducklike face. On the scale of teachers she was neither bad nor good. She liked to wear white pants, and a rumor had recently spread about how she liked to wear lime-green thongs and was therefore slutty. We amused ourselves during home ec trying to look through her white pants every time she turned, crouched, or bent.

"Miss S!" Estella piped up. By then we had realized that if we kept her occupied, she might forget to give us our assignment. "When did you open your third eye?"

"I was born with mine open," she said. "My dad had it, and so did my Lolo. Oh, but my Kuya had to open his. He just forced it open one day by meditating. It's really easy as long as you know where yours is." A snicker from somewhere in the back made her look at the clock. "Girls, don't stop sewing."

We obediently hopped to work. I stepped on my machine's presser foot and stitched random lines through my table runner. Someone tugged on my elbow. "Help," Hazel whispered. She gestured at her machine: the cloth was bunched up in the feed dog, the needle stabbing through it at random points. I reached over and jerked one end of the cloth until it came unstuck. It was now full of micro-holes. She made a face. I smirked.

"You trying to give your cloth a third eye?" I asked.

Anamaria Marquez was a student at St. Brebeuf's, just like us. One day she stayed after school to finish a project. At that time the gardener was a creepy manong, and when he saw her staying in the classroom all by herself he raped her. Then, because he did not want anyone to know about his crime, he killed her and hid her body in the hollow of the biggest rubber tree in the Black Garden. Nobody found out what had happened to her until after the manong died, when finally a storm knocked over the rubber tree—that was years ago, it's grown back now, *duh*—and the police found her bones.

If you look at the roots of the tree at night you might see Anamaria's face, or some parts of her naked body. If you stand in the

Black Garden and stay absolutely silent you will hear her crying and calling for help.

But you shouldn't go near, because if you do she will have her revenge and she will kill you.

It was fifth grade, a weird time when we were all changing. It seemed like every week someone was getting a bloodstain on her skirt, and sobbing in the bathroom from shame and hormones, while her barkada surrounded her vigilantly.

At the start of the semester we had a mandatory talk called "You and Your Body!" We were given little booklets with "chic" illustrations, diagrams of the female reproductive system, and free sanitary napkins. We spent a lot of our time vandalizing the chic illustrations. Lea found an ingenious way to turn a uterus into a ram by shading in the fallopian tubes, and we took turns drawing uterus-rams in each other's notebooks.

I held a slight disgust for all of this girl stuff, though I couldn't explain why. Maybe it was because I only had brothers, and some of their *that-is-GROSS* attitude rubbed off on me. My skin crawled whenever Mom or Ya Fely or the homeroom teacher made some reference like, "You are now a *young lady*. You are *developing*."

Our barkada had decided that we would tell each other "when we got ours," and that would be it, no hysterics or anything. I was more afraid that someone was going to get a boyfriend. Bea, the class rep, took every chance she could to tell people about her darling Paolo from San Beda. I was fine with Bea having a boy, and Bea was my friend too, but she wasn't part of our group. If any of us got a boy, I knew the dynamic would change so much we'd be screwed.

It was around this time, after all, that people's barkadas were getting shifted around, and that scared me more than I liked to admit. I loved my friends and wanted us to stay the same forever. There were four of us: me, Cella, Lea, and Hazel. Hazel and I were both in section C this year; Cella was in B, and Lea was in D. We had all ended up at the same assigned lunch table in first grade, and had continued eating lunch together since. We had our fights and silent periods and teary reconciliations, like everyone else, but otherwise we were one of the tightest groups around. These girls were the sisters I'd never had, and I thought we'd forgive each other anything.

So when Hazel told me she had opened her third eye, I laughed in her face and thought nothing of it.

Anamaria Marquez was a student at St. Brebeuf's, just like all of us. One day she took a piss in the third-floor bathroom and the school bully locked her in, laughing, and called Anamaria a stupid slut. No one knows why she hated Anamaria so much. When the cleaning lady did her afternoon rounds, she was surprised to find the door locked. Inside, on the second stall from the left, she found the corpse of Anamaria. Anamaria had drowned herself by sticking her head in the toilet.

That's why you should never use the third-floor bathroom. If you use the second toilet from the left, Anamaria Marquez will come out of the toilet right before you flush, and ask why you bullied her, and then kill you.

If you use a different stall, she won't kill you. She'll just float on the ceiling and look down at you and ask you, *Why?*

The annual school fair was coming up. Based on a random draw, the seventh graders were assigned the concert, and the sixth graders were going to work with the PTA for the bazaar, which would include goodies baked by the fourth graders. Our year level, the fifth grade, got the Haunted House. Bea announced this right before recess one Monday. The fair was pretty much the only time each year that boys were allowed on campus, which meant a lot of squealing. Section

A was doing a freaky dollhouse inspired by Chucky; section B was recreating the well from the *The Ring*; my section, section C, was staging a haunted traditional Filipino home; and section D was enacting ritual sacrifice. There was a cash prize for the scariest section, so Bea *insisted* we do well.

While people were yelling at each other to sign up for time slots and committees, Hazel pulled me aside and said she didn't really want to do this, now that she had opened her third eye. I laughed and continued to cram my science homework.

"What's so funny?"

I looked at her, annoyed. "Um. You just told me you opened your third eye."

"But I did." Her eyebrows were furrowed, and her eyes were taking on that buggy, frantic look they did when she was priming for an argument. I considered this. Hazel was one of my best friends, but she was also an attention-seeker—she was the only one among us who had broken the rules and cried passionately when she "got hers," describing her intense stomach pains as being "like giving birth." I mean, it must have hurt a *little,* but she was fine by the next day. Lately I had been thinking that if anyone changed anything in our gang, it would be Hazel and her weird theatrics. It was probably the lack of a real drama club in our school.

I stopped writing. "Why would you do that?"

"Because," she said. "I've always wanted to see."

I remembered our failed ghost-hunt during Stargazing Night in third grade, when we were both part of the Nature Club. We had squealed and scurried through the halls, waving our flashlights, and nothing had come out: no spirit balls, not even a little wheeze from the famed Anamaria Marquez. Then again, we didn't make it to the third floor, because as we were creeping up the stairs a security guard spotted us and told us that area was closed.

"And?" I asked, feeling the precious recess minutes drain away. "Have you seen anything?"

She shook her head. "But I've—I've started hearing things! Whispering, weird noises, sometimes singing." I couldn't tell if this delighted her, or freaked her out. I was not a ghost person. If you had *my* mom, who routinely doused the house in Holy Water, and never stepped into her parents' home without begging her dad—rest in peace, Lolo!—not to come out and spook her, you probably wouldn't be either. I preferred my dad's stance: laughing and shaking his head because Mom was a probinsyana through and through. Besides, I always had my scapular to protect me from evil. It was a gift from my ninang at baptism: a brown cloth string that linked two images of Our Lady, which I wore around my neck. Mom insisted I never take it off, just in case I died suddenly, because it guaranteed entrance to heaven.

"Sure. Any confessions from the kapres yet?"

Hazel gripped my shoulder. "You really don't believe me?"

"I'll believe 'em when I see 'em." I tried to say this comically, fakely, so that she would understand that I wasn't *trying* to be mean.

But I guess I used the wrong tone of voice, because she said, "Fine. Be that way," and stalked off.

Anamaria Marquez was a senior in high school when she committed suicide by hanging herself on the higad tree next to the parking lot. Her boyfriend had dumped her for one of the Popular Girls, and she was so distraught that she decided to teach him a lesson. She only meant to scare him and his new girl, or so her barkada said afterward. She was supposed to freak them out by *pretending* to hang herself, except it all went wrong; her foot slipped on the branch she was stepping on, or something. I'm not making this up. This really happened. It was all over the news and stuff. Of course the boyfriend freaked out, and broke up with the new girl and then had psychological issues all his life. And the tree, which was once a pretty tree, is now full of fat, hairy higads, crawling around or dangling in the breeze, and if they fall on you, you will get a really bad rash.

So that's the part everyone in Manila knows; now here's the part only the girls of St. Brebeuf know: if you walk beneath the higad tree after the school has closed down, sometimes you will see her shadow on the concrete, the shadow of a hanging girl. Don't look up. If you look up you might see her, and she might talk to you. No one knows what she says. No one who has heard her talk has survived.

Hazel got all distant after that conversation. We were still talking, but there was all this weirdness underneath the surface. I felt that she was overreacting. Everyone else said it was hormones. She would pick at her food during lunch and not say much, even when Cella would do her hilarious commercial parodies. Everyone assumed Hazel was slimming down for the boys at the fair. I thought about apologizing a few times, but then I would think, *Well, I didn't do anything wrong!* Besides, we were all so busy preparing for the fair (which happened right before the semester break) that every time the guilt crept up something would distract me. I was on the Props Committee, and spent my days badgering people to bring their lola's folding screens and old sheets and tablecloths—the grosser the better.

The Haunted House was going to be in the Old Recreation Building, which we lovingly called the ORB. It was a small square structure right next to the Black Garden, barely used after the fancy new gym was erected. Our batch could make use of the whole ground floor.

That last week was crazy. We had our usual schedule until Wednesday, and morning classes on Thursday. The fair started at five p.m. on Friday and ended with a concert on Saturday evening. We hated our school and our teachers were sadists and periodically Bea burst into tears, because our Haunted House was *obviously* going to suck. When it got too stressful people would launch spitball fights, wadding up newspaper and shooting it from the straws someone had added to our materials pile.

The school finally let us start decorating the ORB on Monday. I sat with the rest of the Props people and spraypainted crumpled balls of newspaper to look like bloody things. We draped the windows with mottled sheets and marked off our section of the floor with some plastic cafeteria tables that we covered with yellowing tablecloths. A troop of girls retrieved the random wireframe bed that lay in the corner of the home ec room. The idea was that we would have a creepy, bloody lola lying on the bed, looking for her lost grandchildren, shouting "Anak! Anak!" at passersby. We had also envisioned a grandfather clock. That was probably not going to happen. To make up for it, Bea decided that the tiniest girls in class needed to dress up in nightgowns and crawl out from underneath the plastic tables.

Hazel was still one of the smallest girls in class, although she had been the first in our group to start wearing a bra. I happened to pass by just as Reena from the Costumes committee was asking her whether she had a plain white nightgown. "I have some old shirts," she said.

"That would work! We'll just paint them. Hey Hazel," Reena said. "You look, like, kinda anorexic. What's wrong?"

"Nothing," she said.

"Growth spurt, maybe?" Reena pressed. Reena wanted to be a doctor when she grew up.

"I've been waking up in my sleep a lot. It's too noisy," Hazel said. She shrugged, and turned, probably to stop Reena's pestering. I didn't have a chance to keep walking. I smiled at her. She quirked her lips, but I couldn't tell if she was smiling back. She looked tired. There was something unfamiliar about her face, but it was probably the way the old sheets were blocking the sunlight from the windows. We had to pile them on thick so that it would *actually* be dark and scary inside our Haunted House.

To make conversation, I said, "Did you fill in your time slots?"

"Yes," she said. "Friday evening."

Then she floated away, as if something else had caught her attention. Reena shook her head and muttered, "Cramps."

Anamaria Marquez was the principal's daughter, and felt she needed to be perfect. You know that girl. There's one in every class. But no matter how perfect she was, the principal was always too busy for her. One day she didn't show up for homeroom. They found her body in the well of the Black Garden, all swollen, her mouth full of seaweed. Some people said her legs had dissolved and became seaweed, too. That is why the well in the Black Garden is full of seaweed, and the water is brown, and every frog that drinks from it dies.

Some girls might tell you to throw a coin in the well of the Black Garden and make a wish. Don't. You will be cursed. Anamaria Marquez will crawl out and eat you, and bad things will happen to your family. But if you say "Mama Mary" three times before she reaches you, she will dissolve into seaweed again.

I don't think you should try. She crawls really, really fast.

Thursday was tense and awful and most of us stayed in school until past ten, decorating the ORB and taking naps on each other's laps. Cella wandered over from 5B's display to see how our section was faring. Her face was caked with white makeup, except for the blue rings under her eyes. I burst out laughing when she approached. When B said they were doing *The Ring*, they weren't kidding.

"They made you Sadako?"

"It's the hair, the hair!" she moaned, gathering the massive amount in a fist. "Did I have any choice?"

"Why the blue eyebags?"

"They couldn't find any black face paint," she said mournfully. "I think it will work if my hair is all over the place?" She combed it over her face and waved her arms around.

"Yeah, that works," I said. Cella was the tallest of us four. Looming over me with only one eye visible and all that face paint, she actually *did* look like a dead girl who had crawled out of a well. I hoped our lolas would be able to hold their own.

"Where's Hazel?" she asked.

I found myself preoccupied with the stockings-and-old-shirts-guts I was holding. "Uhhh, not sure."

"Hey, Mica," she said, pulling her hair back. "Are you two okay? It's been kinda weird at lunch these days. Did something happen?"

I shrugged. "*I'm* fine with her. I don't know if she's fine with me. We had . . . a debate, a few weeks ago." I didn't mention the third eye. It floated into my brain, but something stopped it from leaving my mouth.

Cella patted my head. "Well, Hazel's been kinda moody since she started her period. You can tell me and Lea if you want us to, you know, intervene or whatever."

"Eh, we'll be fine," I said.

"Hey look, there's Hazel," Cella said. "Let's go talk to her."

I wanted to refuse, but Cella grabbed my arm and started tugging me. Hazel was sitting alone in a corner, with her head bent, as if she was reading something in her lap. We had only taken a few steps when someone from section B called out, "Come back, Sadako! You need to practice your groan!"

"Shoot," Cella muttered. "Okay, you go on your own. Just say you want things to go back to normal!" She ducked back through the makeshift curtain that separated her class's display from ours.

I steeled myself and decided that I could always ask her if she needed any props, in case things got weird. As I neared, I realized Hazel was talking to herself.

"I know, that one is kind of ridiculous. I think some high schoolers made that up so that they could go there to make out."

She must have heard me approaching, because her shoulders tensed. She stood and whirled around. "Hi, Mica," she said, oddly breathless. Her face was caked with dead-girl makeup, like Cella.

Our section's makeup artists were obviously better than B's, because her face actually looked convincingly withered. There was a ribbon in her hair, and someone had artfully arranged her bangs to obscure half her face. They had also inked a trail of blood from her lip to her chin, and smeared it expertly. If she weren't still wearing her uniform, I would have clapped my hands in glee. If everyone looked as freaky as Hazel, that cash prize would be ours.

"Are you practicing your script?" I asked. "It sounded kind of long."

Hazel's eyes flickered sideways. The fluorescent lights in the ORB were old, and some of them were burnt out, so certain spots were cast in shadow. The place where Hazel was standing was bright enough. I suddenly did not want to look at the shadowy space next to her.

"Um, just thinking aloud," she said. As if she could not help herself, she added in a low mutter, "Yeah, I *know,* okay? Stop it already."

"Excuse me?" I said. My palms felt clammy. I clutched my old-clothes-guts and tried to look Hazel in the eye, but she kept looking at the space next to her. It annoyed me, that she was trying so hard to freak me out by acting this way. But this had been going on for too long. It looked like I had to be the mature one.

"Hey, Hazel," I said. I sucked in a breath. "I'm sorry I laughed about your . . . third-eye thing. I was tired that day, okay? I'm sorry."

Her eyes snapped back to me. They were suddenly cool, calculating. "But you still don't believe me."

I sighed, trying not to be angry. Why was she so intent on putting the blame on *me*? Hazel could never admit to being wrong, and that side of her was coming out more and more often. I didn't like it, and it bugged me in a way that it didn't bug Cella or Lea. "Look, we can each believe what we want to believe, okay? I don't believe in ghosts. That's all."

"I told you so," she answered, but she didn't seem to be addressing me. Something icy ran down my back. Then she focused on me again, suddenly looking fatigued. She actually *swayed.* I thought she might collapse. I reached out to steady her, but she stepped away from me, like I was dirty.

"It's okay, it's okay," she said. Her eyes were wide, as if she was trying to convince me of something. "It's okay, Mica," she said, giving me a tiny grin. "Don't worry about it. We're fine."

Anamaria Marquez was a student at St. Brebeuf's, just like us. She had the usual black hair and brownish eyes and pearl earrings. Her portrait is hanging on the second-floor corridor—the one with the Music Room and the President's Office and the Dance Hall—next to the paintings of St. Brebeuf and Blessed Antonia Mesina and the Sacred Hearts of Jesus and Mary. None of the teachers or admin know why her painting is there. The truth is that they trapped her spirit in that painting, so she'll only haunt you if you walk down that corridor. You'll notice that her eyes are always following you. You'll notice her uniform, which is the same as our uniform, and you'll notice that her smile is a little sad.

Anamaria Marquez is the reason why the third and fourth floors have those extra railings. Anamaria Marquez jumped from the third floor after a dare.

Actually, I don't believe that story. I believe the one that says she was pushed. Because Anamaria Marquez was such a sweet, sweet girl, and maybe her sweetness was too much for someone.

Have you heard about the mysterious puddles of water in that corridor? It's from the painting. If you visit it at three a.m. you will see that her face is broken, and tears are streaming out of her eyes.

The next day was Friday. Fair Day. There was a lot of last-minute blood splattering to be done. I ran into Lea on my way to the bathroom to wash my hands for the hundredth time, and she breathlessly handed me a sandwich. "Here. Extra. She told me you were gonna forget lunch," she said.

"Who?"

"Hazel," she panted. "Gotta run!" Lea was vice president of her class and looked extremely harassed.

So Hazel and I really were okay. Great. I hadn't slept so well the night before. At one point in my dream, Cella, in her Sadako attire, had crawled out of a papier-mâché well and begged me to open my eyes. I had woken up in the middle of the night with a bad taste in my mouth, and nearly jumped when Mom blearily stuck her head in my room and asked me what was wrong. "You have Holy Water on your bedside table, Mica, remember," she said. Then she reminded me not to forget my prayers, and I had to convince her I hadn't. I was already so sleep-deprived that week I could barely think. So it was a relief that Hazel wasn't still mad at me.

The gates opened to outsiders at 3:30 p.m., though they couldn't enter any attractions until 5:00. There was a massive scrambling behind the scenes when it hit 4:00, but somehow, by 4:55, we were all in place and ready to go.

As usual, the Haunted House was one of the biggest attractions. Girls from other year levels and their boylets started streaming through, as did the occasional cluster of teachers. With all the props in place, and the overhead lights turned off completely, we actually seemed to be doing pretty well. Our first Lola, played by Bea, got especially loud screeches from the groups shuffling through. "Anak! Anak!" she howled, rolling her eyes as far back as they would go. "Nasaan ang aking mga anak?!"

"Lola! Lola!" went the two "Little Girls" on duty. Abbie and Erica were roughly the same height, and someone had outfitted them in matching white smocks. They crawled out from under the table and lolled their heads, reaching out with grasping fingers. "Lolaaaa!"

I was responsible for guiding people out of our display and into Section D's. I was wearing an old dress—someone from Costumes had cut out the waist part and sewn fake intestines onto it. I bobbed my head and went "Salamat, salamat" before directing visitors around the folding screens, which blocked Section D's altar from view. They had a pretty good chance of winning because of the holy statues they had amassed. I don't know how they did it. If I so much as asked for one of the baby Jesus figurines from our home altar, Mom would throw a fit.

There was a short break at 7:00 so that we could rest and switchover for the next shift. The fair closed at 9:30. I checked the list and saw that the next Little Girls were Hazel and Yanni. Bea was looking over my shoulder. The next Lola, Sammy, was yawning behind her. "Have you seen Hazel?" Bea asked. "We only have twenty minutes. Shouldn't she be with Costumes by now?"

"I'll go find her," I said. I wanted to thank her for the sandwich, anyway. I entered the ORB Bathroom, which Costumes had invaded. It was a mess, with piles of clothes and girls in different stages of undress. I waded through, asking people if they had seen Hazel. One or two girls thought they had seen her wandering around outside the building. It looked like she was looking for someone, they said. "If she comes in here, tell her she needs to get into position," I said.

I darted out of the ORB to find the fair in full swing. It was already dark. The deep purple sky was starless. Bugs swarmed over the big stadium lights they had erected around campus. The scent of kettle corn hung in the air. A gaggle of seventh-graders laughed exaggeratedly as a group of boys with overly gelled hair passed them. To my left was a row of parlor-game booths, courtesy of the high school students. To my right was the Black Garden, barricaded by the old metal gate. I gave it a cursory glance, already set on grabbing some kettle corn, but that thought vanished as I spotted Hazel: already in costume, standing beneath the biggest rubber tree.

Anamaria Marquez was a student at St. Brebeuf's, just like you and me. When she was in fifth grade, she died from a mysterious illness. She really loved to study, poor Anamaria; she dreamed of becoming a great scholar one day, perhaps becoming the principal of our school.

It never happened, but her love for the classroom was so strong that she never left. Sometimes you will see a bright light winking against the classroom window, and if you stick your head out the window, you will see a girl huddled beneath it. Her skin will be rotting. She will look up at you and ask if you've done your homework. If you're a good student, she will spare you.

If you're a *bad* student, she will ask you *why, why,* and she will latch on to your shoulders and you must carry her until you die. No one will see her except for you, and the only way to get rid of her is to visit the Monastery of the Poor Clares and offer them a dozen eggs every day for twelve days. And don't even think about lying. If you lie she will leap into your mouth and possess you, and make you claw off your own face.

I pushed through the gate and walked in. I found that my hand had flown to the scapular around my neck. I realized how ridiculous I was acting, and jerked my hand away, but I stopped walking forward. I called out to Hazel from where I stood.

"Hazel? Your shift's about to start! Are you done with your makeup?"

Hazel turned, slowly, to face me. I saw that she was standing right in front of the rubber tree's hollow. I couldn't tell if she already had makeup, or not. She was pale, but not in the cakey way, and the rings under her eyes seemed real. Her mouth moved. I could not hear what she was saying.

"Hazel, come on," I said. I heard a loud roaring in my ears, and realized it was my heart. My voice came out pleading. "Hazel?"

"Mica," she wheezed, with great effort. "Mica, I'm sorry."

"What? Hazel?" I couldn't help it; I moved forward, staggering toward her, my fake guts swinging as I tried to avoid the roots of the rubber trees. "Hazel, what's wrong?"

"I'm sorry," she whispered, starting to cry.

"What?" My skin was prickling. "Let's get out of here, Hazel." I didn't look at the tree and its drooping branches; I didn't look at the roots. I didn't look at the well to the left of the tree; everyone knew it was drained, anyway. "Let's go. Come on." I paused right before a tangle of roots that snaked between us and reached out my hand to her.

She shook her head. "Not until you say you believe," she whispered. Then I saw—the impression of fingers on her neck, as if someone was gripping her throat. "I opened it because I was curious," Hazel wept, struggling to get the words out. "And I still can't see. But then she found me, and she keeps *talking to me*. She wants you to say," her breath hitched. The finger-shaped dents on her neck deepened. "*Say*," she choked.

Something dark bubbled up from the pit of my belly. Something dark stirred the trees. The rustling sounded like the chatter of young girls, our friends, our own voices. We were alone in an abandoned school, and it was pitch black—midnight? Three a.m.? I could not turn my head to look back at the gate or the lights of the fair.

"I believe," I whispered, gripping my scapular, gazing at Hazel, whose eyes were bulging. "I believe," I said, louder and louder, "I believe! I believe! I was wrong!"

Hazel's eyes rolled back. Her feet slowly lifted off the ground.

"It's my fault!" I screamed. "Now give Hazel back to me!"

Hazel wheezed and gasped, as if she could finally breathe again, and she dropped down, stumbled forward—I let go of my scapular and reached out my hand to her, shaking uncontrollably.

Cold fingers grasped the wrist of my free hand, and cold lips brushed my cheek, and a cold voice whispered sadly in my ear, "I know."

Anamaria Marquez was a student at St. Brebeuf's, just like you and me.

She is standing in the middle of our circle right now. You can't see her, but I can. She is happy we are talking about her, even if some of our stories are stupid; even if some of them have got it all wrong. At least we know her name. At least sometimes we think of her.

Syringe

"I wanted to be a doctor," Merlie says. She watches her nurse, Ada, scroll through her patient information on the bedside projector. Ada puts on her best empathetic smile. It's perfect programming, and Ada is so pretty, with her clear skin and immaculate eye makeup.

"Is that so?" Ada asks. She picks up an injection from a tray at the other end of the room, and tears off the protective plastic.

"Yes," Merlie says. "Even before I found out that Rufino was sick." She used to be so careful about this topic. They even decided on *zucchini* as a code word for the pain. After treatment, she would sit next to Rufino on his hospital bed, and knead his shoulders until he gave her a weak smile. *Zucchini?* she would ask, and he would say, *Yep, zucchini.*

Ada seems to be considering what to say next. Or maybe that's being too generous; maybe Ada already has five different responses pulled up, and is pausing simply for effect, because that's what a human nurse would do. Ada says, "I'm so sorry for your loss, Mrs. Romualdez."

"Oh, don't be sorry," Merlie says. She doesn't add, *You're really not, anyway.* "It happened a long time ago."

Ada walks over, the kindness in her eyes not betraying the rapid swish of data behind them: now she is pulling up Merlie's file, checking through her personal information, zooming in on the line that reads: *Spouse—deceased, Rufino Romualdez.* The quick calculation: twelve years, three months, nineteen days. The fact of his death means nothing to her. She holds the needle poised, and Merlie holds her breath as the injection slides in, even if she should be used to this by now. Even if she knows that tensing up will make it worse.

"All done," Ada says, tossing the used syringe in the trash. She sticks a patch of gauze on Merlie's arm and applies pressure to it. Merlie suddenly feels the urge to grab Ada's head and shift it so that her barcode can be seen. She's curious about which healthcare provider made this model. She wants to know how old this model is, or how new. Do the Nurses™ need to pee? Do they ever need to recharge? Ada looks up and catches her staring. She opens her mouth and pauses; Merlie can almost hear the whirr-click of a recorded message, except that's only in her brain, they've smoothed all that audio stuff by now. "How are you feeling?" Ada asks.

"Not great," Merlie answers. She leans back into her pillow. She wants orange juice, and cinnamon rolls; she wants Patsy to come by with Danica so that they can color together. She wants to read the papers but she's afraid of turning to the obituaries. She wants to watch TV but hates herself when she does. She is very tired but she does not want to sleep. She wants all these things and none of them.

"What can I do for you?" Ada asks.

"Nothing, my dear," Merlie says. She's old, and dying, and *nothing* is the truth. It's not worth it to lie to something that won't know the difference.

Sometimes they let Rufino come home, between treatments. When he did, he usually wanted to drink, and since there were no Caregivers™ to police them, she said okay. She wanted to drink too.

Rufino was thin and bald and his skin was gray and patchy in places. His veins were so *blue*, running under his skin; they made her stomach flop. Yet she couldn't help thinking those veins were such a beautiful color.

She had been teaching full time at the University of Manila, toying with the idea of returning to school for medicine, but his sickness had put that out of the question. Besides, the six years of study that she would have to undergo—*at least*—could be accomplished by one of the new Doctor™ wireframes in an hour. That's what happened to cousin Mercy, losing all her patients to a computer. Thankfully, they hadn't brought those into the universities yet; hospitals had first dibs. And if one of them could save Rufino, that made it all worth it. She poured him another glass and crawled on the couch, next to him. They toasted to science.

"Someone will find a cure," she mumbled, cradling his warm head with her elbow. He made a sound of contentment that twisted her guts. "Or if not, we will find a cure."

"For what?" he asked, blinking drowsily at her.

She swallowed, suddenly too sad to speak. The grief rolled over her in a slow, sadistic wave. This man, this warm head, should not die, she thought. Why should he die, when I love him so much, when he loves me? Why should it matter so little, what I want, what I'd fight the universe for?

Rufino suddenly started laughing, his back shuddering against her lap. "There's no cure for lovesickness," he wheezed, pulling her down for a kiss.

"She told me she wanted to be a doctor," Ada tells Ada. Ada nods. They are in the break room, drinking coffee that another Ada brewed that morning. They are both tired, or as tired as Nurses™ are allowed to be. One of the Jessas comes in, pours herself a cup of coffee, and sits across from them. Her eyes are open, but she might be asleep. Ada wonders what makes their sleep different from Mrs. Romualdez's sleep—all that snoring and shifting, and muttering that sounds like conversations with her deceased spouse. Once, Mrs. Romualdez rolled over and said, "Don't come near me!"

Ada's processing unit told her that her patient was dreaming, but the observant part of Ada second-guessed this and recorded, *Maybe she is doing this on purpose. Maybe she does not like you watching her all night.*

Well, I must, Ada's decision-making unit declared. *She is in very poor condition.*

"Your Patient Merlie Romualdez talks very much," Ada tells Ada. Ada nods. "I think it is quite nice," Ada admits.

"She is a very sad woman," Ada says.

"Ah," Ada says. They are programmed to have empathy, but there is a limit to how deep it can go. This is what makes Nurses™ better than humans—not only can they handle the physical toll better, they are also psychologically immune to despair. The Nurses™ have saved many nurses from depression. From tiring physical labor, as well, but that is not their concern.

Across the table, Jessa opens her eyes wider and drinks some coffee. The clock on the wall tells Ada that she must go and check on Mrs. Romualdez soon. Her patient will probably be crocheting, or video-conferencing with her daughter Patsy. She will probably point at Ada and ask Ada to wave, and tell Ada to sing something in a foreign language, or to recite some sections of her favorite book, which is *The Count of Monte Cristo*. This will delight Patsy's daughter Danica. Ada's processing unit will indicate that her cheer-up objectives are successful.

"How are you feeling?" Ada asks Mrs. Romualdez, applying pressure to her arm. The motion allows her to quickly calibrate all of Mrs. Romualdez's vitals. Mrs. Romualdez smiles at her. She is always more gentle after a cranky spell. Ada is grateful for this patient.

"Better," Mrs. Romualdez says.

Ada considers her possible responses. "Good."

"Ada," Mrs. Romualdez says, "are you ever tired?"

Ada considers what to say. Her pause might be a tad too long, because Mrs. Romualdez continues, "Well, I guess not. But won't you come rest here for a bit?" Mrs. Romualdez pats the coverlet of her bed. Ada's decision-making unit runs its predictive tests. All outcomes will be fine, so Ada moves forward and, as gently as she can, sits on the edge of the bed. It dips beneath her weight, but Mrs. Romualdez doesn't seem to care. She leans her head against Ada's shoulder. Ada pats Mrs. Romualdez's arm. "Thank you," Mrs. Romualdez whispers.

Her head is bent, but Ada can tell she is crying.

Ada will not judge. There are no algorithms for sadness, anyway. She strokes Mrs. Romualdez's hair. She calculates whether she should say, "You would have been a great doctor." Something tells her to stay quiet.

Asphalt, River, Mother, Child

The girl does not come to Mebuyen, so Mebuyen goes to the girl.

She is standing ankle-deep in the river, looking down, her mouth open. Mebuyen notices, as she draws closer, that the child's calves are skinny, her cheeks chubby, and her SpongeBob SquarePants sando has a bullet-sized hole above her ribs. Mebuyen frowns as she steps into the river, waiting for the girl to speak.

"Why is this river so clean?" the girl asks. "I can see my feet!" She lifts one foot, then the other; her voice is high and filled with wonder.

"It isn't clean, really," Mebuyen says. The dirt they are standing on is packed with fears and pains, the current made of tears, the silt of sadness. There are no fish, not even algae. Though it is sweet to drink, the water cannot be used on anything in a garden—Mebuyen has tried, and grumbled at the results. "It's just clear, at the moment."

The girl turns her gaze to Mebuyen and blinks. "You're bomba! Why?"

"I don't like clothes," Mebuyen says impatiently. "What's your name, anak?"

"Adriana po." Mebuyen reaches out her hand, and after a brief hesitation, the girl takes it. Her skin against Mebuyen's is warm, still full of life, and she curls her fingers into Mebuyen's fleshy palm as if suddenly afraid. "Where are we going?"

"To my house. You can rest there a bit."

Adriana considers this. With her free hand she fingers the hole in her shirt. Then, with a slight tremor: "Am I dead?"

Mebuyen sighs. She was hoping the girl would not ask.

The girl shares her story as if she is recounting something peculiar that happened at school: thoughtful, but not with extreme anger or sadness. She sits at Mebuyen's table, elbows splayed, drinking the sweet milk Mebuyen poured for her. "This tastes like Yakult," she says. Mebuyen wonders whether to take that as a compliment. She has not felt concern in a long time, and the emotion sits heavy in her chest, like a stone.

There was a man, Adriana starts, then scrunches up her face. I was playing jackstones on the second floor. There were three of them actually, who came in. They . . . I think they were police. They were all wearing blue shirts and um, um, blue pants. I did not see them come in but I heard them come in so I ran to the staircase to see. They shouted "Bonifacio! Bonifacio Magsaysay! We know you're here!" Lolo Basyo was outside helping Mama make tinola. Lola came out from her room and saw them and screamed, so I ran down the stairs to—to be near her. My lolo came in through the screen door, they said "That's him!" and then I heard a bang, and then . . . everything stopped. That's why I think I'm dead po. They shot me yata.

You were shot by the police?

Mebuyen brewed herself a glass of pandan tea, but she has not been able to drink, intent as she is on listening. Mebuyen is never cold, but she warms her hands against the glass anyway.

Adriana shrugs. Her face grows sulky, like she doesn't want to talk about it. Mebuyen softens, in her heart if not in her gnarled face, and asks Adriana if she wants another glass of milk. The girl nods eagerly. "Do you have TV po? I want to watch *Naruto.*" Mebuyen realizes this visit may last longer than she expects.

Juan Miguel Pulag, known to friends and family as JM, has not slept in two days. His mother doesn't know, though she tells him, jokingly, that he looks like he has seen death. He does not have the heart to say: that's not funny. It's not that he doesn't have *time* to sleep, the way it was back in high school when some nights he'd only have twenty-minute naps between textbook chapters. This is different. These days, he lies in bed and stares at the creaky ceiling fan forever, and when he closes his eyes it's as if he's still awake, and there is no darkness; only the ceiling fan, lazily spinning. Sometimes there are shadows behind it that slowly shift into shapes like hands and faces. Then he opens his eyes again, drenched in sweat, cold to the bone.

Sometimes he hears, far-off but steadily growing louder, like someone slowly turning up the volume on a TV, the cry of an old woman—startled at first, high and sharp, followed by a wail of despair that stretches, endlessly, until the sound cannot possibly be human anymore.

Adriana-a-a-a-aaaa. The old woman grabbed the girl, clutching her hair, her shoulders, patting her face gently, then with more and more force.

JM doesn't remember who pulled the trigger, but when Sir Marco barked at them to chase Bonifacio Magsaysay, he followed his orders. He ran out the back door, gun held out, and the mother outside screamed, of course she did. As he chased Bonifacio Magsaysay down the street, neighbors rushing out of the way, he continued to hear the woman's cry, stretching that *a-a-a* to eternity. He lost Bonifacio Magsaysay in a crowded market, him and Digo both. Without a criminal in hand he dreaded it more: returning to that house, to see blood on the floor, the little girl covered in it.

JM is sure he did not pull the trigger. JM is *pretty* sure he did not. He is a good shot. His hands never tremble when he holds a gun. When they returned, him and Digo panting, the mother was at the door, staring blankly. Her tinola soup was boiling over; he switched the stove off. Sir Marco could be heard from the street: "Why did she run down the stairs? Look what happened, because of that!"

JM's mother isn't wrong. He has seen a lot of death before. He is not some candidate fresh from the academy, jumping at every little thing. It was unfortunate, what happened, but he always knew the price to end the war on drugs would be high. He'd known from when their new president stepped into power. They were told things would be difficult, but in the end the world would be safer-better-more-productive, free of crime and the scum of the earth, those who succumbed to the sweet siren call of shabu. And JM, like all his fellow policemen, wanted the Philippines to be free. *Your mothers, sisters, daughters will walk safely through the night!* the precinct chief told them, a few weeks after they started, when some were growing faint of heart. *Their shrunken minds are useless to our society. Don't you see?*

JM saw. JM did not question what they did, because he knew what good it would bring.

On the third day, Nanay makes him lugaw, his favorite from when he was a child. While stirring in toyo, he sees the line of soy sauce turn red, the rice blending from gray to ghastly pink. He chokes. Nanay turns to him, concerned, but the lugaw looks normal again. "Nasamid lang po ako," he says.

"Drink water," she advises fondly.

He falls asleep for the first time since the little girl died. In his dream the old woman passes him a cup of her granddaughter's blood. She tells him to drink it, and calls him a sinner.

"Manang Em, Manang Em!" Adriana has taken to calling her this. Mebuyen does not mind. The last few days, in response to Adriana's wistful droning about being bored because there's no TV and now she won't know what happens next on *One Piece,* she has set Adriana to work on her garden, where she grows okra and kamote and corn. She has a finicky banana tree that turns out sweet little latundans from time to time. And a precious lemon tree that she does not shake, for fear of how many might fall. There is no way to mark the seasons, here in the underworld, Mebuyen's town with its endless river and little stone house. The sky turns from a pale gray day to a soft blue night, and there are no stars. She recognizes all this only because of Adriana's endless questions. Mebuyen answers, and tries not to grow fond. She's too old for that sort of thing.

Adriana muses aloud: "Why did they come for my lolo? He voted for the president, you know. He wasn't a pusher. Lola said he went to the police station to make sure he was safe. We thought he was safe."

Then: "I wonder why they shot me?"

This, Mebuyen cannot answer.

She is preparing her milk when Adriana calls her, so she does not rise immediately. "Manang *Em,*" Adriana repeats forcefully; Mebuyen lumbers off her stool to see what the matter is.

There is a new visitor, kneeling by the river. A beautiful girl, looking dazed, dreamy. She looks twenty, twenty-one—still a child to Mebuyen, but not quite as young as Adriana. She is wearing a Barong Tagalog, which Mebuyen finds odd, until she looks more closely and thinks: *Ah.* Adriana is capering near her, full of adrenaline. Closer now, Mebuyen can see that the girl is wearing makeup, expertly applied, but tears have smudged the mascara, and the color on her cheeks is chalky.

The girl notices this scrutiny, and with dignity, says, "It's not waterproof makeup, *okay*? That's too expensive."

Mebuyen smiles in spite of herself. "What's your name?"

"Babygirl Santos," she answers, defiant, like a pageant contestant. At this she finds her strength and stands, regally. Mebuyen notices that despite the barong, Babygirl is wearing heels—beautiful, shimmery, four-inch heels that make her tower like a gorgeous pillar. "My name is Babygirl Santos, twenty-four years old, from Tondo. My talent is singing like Whitney Houston and Ariana Grande. I am also very good at dancing the cha-cha and K-pop covers. I am *not* a drug dealer!"

Hay naku, Mebuyen thinks. She may have to visit her brother in the world of men, little as she likes to.

For dinner that night they have mashed bananas and cassava cake. Mebuyen is not sure if they can taste anything—she has never bothered to ask—but she knows the physical sensation of food, of chewing and swallowing, is comforting to those who visit her. Many of them cry when eating their first meal. But Adriana did not, and neither does Babygirl, who has broken through her bewilderment to become effusive and bubbly, much like the beauty queen she was in life.

She tells her story like something out of a telenovela. They knocked on my door. They said my real name—Eduardo Reyes—so macho, no? I hate it—and I immediately knew what it was about. But they were wrong! I haven't taken drugs in like three years. And the last time I sold one was eight months ago and it was to some rich boy in Makati, which of course as you know, he won't get caught, because he has a driver and a huge condo. So they called my name and the knocking became banging and my sister, Janelle, the sweetheart, she looked me dead in the eye and said *Do not open the door.* And I said, Jel, Jel, where can I hide? They're going to kill me! She told me to go upstairs and they kicked the door open as I was going upstairs and, yun nga, there was nowhere to hide. I crawled into the closet. Janelle screamed at them as they came up the stairs, and they found me, of course.

Our house isn't very big kasi.

I shouldn't have been home. I'm so sorry Ma had to see it all. She was standing by the Santo Niño as they dragged me out, then she fell to her knees bigla, pleading. Don't take my child away! He's my only son! She was crying and crying. Outside the street was empty and the sky was medyo reddish. Janelle tried to grab the arm of one man and he shoved her away and pointed his gun at her. Do you want to die? he asked. I was calm then, I knew there was no way to escape, and the funny thing was, he didn't sound angry or threatening—he actually sounded scared. Like he was begging her not to follow.

Jel, I called out to her. Jel, tama na, it's okay. Stop na. It's okay. Tell Mama I love her. Tell Papa I love him, I'm sorry I could never be his son. The one dragging me hit my mouth. A bloody mouth tastes like salt pala. Shut up! he said. Nag-English pa siya.

I think they took me to a side street. It smelled like pee. There was garbage on the floor. I prayed to the Lord that I trusted He would not put me in hell even if I am transgender. I don't pray very often but I was scared. I kept thinking don't let it be painful, I don't want to die suffering. They asked me two questions and I answered, then the one that shouted at Jel came forward, and the one that dragged me told him to shoot. And he shot.

Babygirl sighs. "I'm glad I'm not in hell," she says. "At least—I don't think this is hell?"

"It's not," Mebuyen says.

"But what *is* this place? Does this mean I don't have peace?"

Mebuyen hands her a glass of milk. "This is Gimokudan—my domain. You're safe here. But as for your second question, I would like to know the answer too."

Babygirl drinks the milk, then looks at Mebuyen's boobs. "You have so many," Babygirl says wistfully. "Can't I have just one set? Not even here?"

JM is not surprised when the sister of Eduardo Reyes appears on TV. Beneath her name, Janella Reyes, is the subtitle: *sister of the deceased.*

Her eyes are bright, huge and accusing, as she says to the reporter, "What they are doing is wrong. What they are doing is murder. They killed my innocent sister as if she were a pig. Are we pigs, that you can treat us like this?" She looks at the camera; it's as if she's looking right at him. "Shame on you." Her tone is low and even, each syllable clearly enunciated. "Putangina niyo, you murderers. We will not let you get away with this."

The words make his body twinge all over, but he doesn't change the channel. He recalls how she tried to grab his arm, how he pushed her aside and asked her: Do you want to die?

Later that night, back at the station, his captain had clapped him on the shoulder for a job well done. He kept looking at the image of the Virgin Mary behind the shoulder of his superior. Her eyes were downcast, and her mouth was a small, sad curve. He wondered what she was looking at.

He felt proud; he felt like vomiting.

You're wrong, he thinks at the TV. *Your brother was not innocent. He was a drug user and a drug dealer, and he deserved to die.*

The news report goes on to tally the number of reported extra-judicial killings that month. Nanay, watching with JM while stringing some beads on to rosaries to sell at church on Sunday, moves her glasses higher up her nose. "That wasn't far from here."

"No," he agrees.

"I will pray," Nanay says, "For your safety. They fight back, don't they? It's so scary."

He does not tell her that her prayers might be petitioning for the wrong soul; that the Virgin's gaze in his mind is now locked forever on a body just beyond his vision, lying at his feet.

Babygirl and Adriana become fast friends. They spend the underworld-equivalent-of-day playing in the garden, tending to plants, having dance-offs, singing duets. Babygirl has a beautiful voice and often sings about love, in English. *Some people want it all,* she croons, holding an imaginary mic. One time Babygirl braids Adriana's hair all over, securing it with a pack of clear elastics they found in Mebuyen's kitchen. They often walk by the river, sometimes wading in it, sometimes keeping to the bank and drawing in the soft soil with twigs.

"Where does the river flow to?" they ask.

"The next place," Mebuyen answers. They look at each other and shrug.

Mebuyen mashes rice in a bowl and pours milk over it, but this tells her nothing. She boils bananas in a pot and empties the grayish water onto a plot of soil in her garden, but there isn't anything to read in the soaked compost. Finally, after a lot of grumbling, she decides to visit the world of men. She sends her emissary, a little maya bird, to let her brother know she will be ascending. She makes sure to add that because it is so *rare* for her to do so, and her knees are particularly creaky these days, he *may* perhaps wish to meet her halfway.

He greets her at Carriedo Station in Manila, wearing a nice button-down polo and maong jeans. Lumabat looks older, but his skin is much nicer than hers, which makes her a little jealous. Mebuyen has not come up in what men might describe as a decade, so she feels proud of her sleeveless shirt and khaki shorts, which make her look like any other manang. She notices everyone holding a small, rectangular skinny box, and glaring at it, their thumbs pounding away.

"Those? Those are cellphones," Lumabat says. "Oh, they call them smartphones these days."

"Phones? But they aren't talking at all?"

"They're texting. Or surfing the web. You know, Facebook?"

Mebuyen is mystified, but does not try to understand. The world gets stranger each time she visits.

Over lunch at Ma Mon Luk, she explains her quandary. "They're different. You know how I haven't had a visitor in a while, that men these days aren't beholden to our magic? But suddenly, there they are, by my river . . . they're *older*, they're not infants, but somehow they are still innocent." She pours soy sauce into her mami, brooding. "The river cannot wash their stains away. It runs clear, not dark. They aren't moving on to the next place. What have you observed?"

Lumabat chews through a giant siomai. Although neither of them will admit it, the strange textures of mortal food are rather delightful. "Their dreams are very brutal," he says. "All red and black, very vivid. Very *loud*. They float up to me, as violent almost as the journey I took to the heavens—it's mesmerizing." He takes a sip of 7-Up. "And the sky is full of smoke, though whether that's from the traffic or gunshots, it's hard to say."

She frowns at him. He sighs. "All right, all right. Let's wait until the sun goes down, and I'll show you. But I warn you, it's not very pleasant."

They pass the afternoon walking through the tiangge at 168 Mall, and Mebuyen palms a pair of pearl necklaces that she thinks Babygirl and Adriana might like. She has nothing to pay with, so she merely takes their essence and memory, humming to herself. Lumabat buys a metal keychain in the shape of a kampilan.

As dark approaches, Lumabat takes her hand, and they walk past Divisoria, drifting up to the corrugated rooftops of Barangay 19. They land on the steel and rust, and wait. Mebuyen feels a change in the air. The city is growing electric, and when she opens her mouth to breathe in, she tastes fear.

Scene A: A masked person on a motorbike rides into a subdivision. Outside his house, a man sits on a plastic chair, smoking a cigarette and rubbing circles around his exposed belly. The masked person stops in front of the man, and the man stands in alarm. The masked person trains a handgun on this man and shoots once, twice. The man falls, hand still on his belly now covered in blood. The masked person tosses a sign by the body: *Drug pusher ako.* Two children playing one street over scurry for their houses, not even screaming, just running, running as fast as they can.

Scene B: A woman is yelling at her man, who laughs at her while taking down the laundry, in the narrow crevasse between their house and the neighbors'. Two men storm in, wearing masks, yelling a name.

The man raises his hands. Says, "Don't shoot!" They tell him he's on their list, they ask him to deny it. He turns, counter-clockwise, towards his woman. He takes a step, they scream at him not to run, he doesn't run, a gun goes off. The woman drops to her knees, as if she has been struck, but no—it's only his blood, as she pulls him onto her lap, as she wails like something being slaughtered.

Scene C: A boy is holding a wooden carton with cigarettes and mints and packets of Piattos and Chippy. He is no longer selling. He is on his way home. He walks with his head down, his slippers slapping the asphalt. When he sees the policemen waiting for him he freezes to the spot. The police approach him. They handcuff him; one seizes his arms, the other grabs the scruff of his shirt. They proceed down four streets, to an alleyway that smells of garbage and shit. The boy cries the whole time. The boy says *please*. The boy asks why. The first policeman, more heavyset, puts a gun in the boy's hand and tells him to run. He does not run. Instead, he falls to his knees. The first man gestures to the second man, who shakes his head, slightly. The first man raises his gun and fires, and the boy collapses. They leave something next to his broken body before they depart—a small bag with white powder.

"Why are their lives so cheap?" Mebuyen is trembling; the words are spoken into her fists, balled at her mouth.

Lumabat is quiet.

"I think I've seen enough," Mebuyen says. Lumabat nods. He holds her elbow, gently, as they find their way back to Carriedo Station, the streets now mostly empty.

Mebuyen inhales. She smells the salt off the backs of men who have worked for decades only to die like small animals, and children who go to sleep at night barely expecting tomorrow. She smells the desperation in a grandmother's twined fingers, praying for her grandchildren to return, to survive. The tang of a woman afraid of what she might find when she goes home, an acidity that spikes in her armpits and the nape of her neck.

There are too many of them, like grains of rice. It's more than her breasts can nurse and her heart can hold.

"It's good to see you, manong," she says, patting Lumabat's cheek, a small sign of affection that is unusual for them.

He returns the gesture, says, "Would that I could intercede. But alas—it is no longer my time."

He returns to his sky, and she sinks down to her world. She does not go to her house immediately. Instead, she stands in the river for a long time, wondering when she stopped knowing how to cry.

The boy turns up the next day. He starts his story almost as soon as she sees him—after he stops gawking at her. He tells it in a breathless rush as she takes him to her hut. She doesn't have the heart to tell him she already knows.

He finishes with, "I wanted to be a policeman, ma'am. I wanted it so *badly*. Since I knew I couldn't become a ninja like Naruto, it was my one and only goal. I was going to protect everyone. I was going to be astig, and fight the bad guys, and wear a cool uniform. I studied so hard for it. Honor student po ako." He gulps, swipes at his eyes. "I still want it, even if I know I can't ever be. Even if that happened. That's crazy, isn't it? I'm crazy. My head's broken."

"No, it's not," Mebuyen says gruffly. She palms the top of his skull, whole beneath her hand, and kisses his salty forehead.

JM cannot face his mother. She might see the welt under his eye where he was struck by Sir Marco. She might ask him why his boss would do such a thing, and he would have no answer. *My hands shook. I didn't say no, but I didn't fire my gun, either. It felt wrong. It was wrong. I think it was wrong.* She calls to him from where she is ironing his shirts, asks him how his day went. He says he's tired, that he's going to take a bath.

Seated on his narrow bed, he tries to look at nothing. Instead he finds his eye drawn, again and again, to the diploma hanging on his wall. *The Philippine National Police Academy hereby confers upon Juan Miguel G. Pulag the degree of Bachelor of Science in Public Safety, with Secondary Honors.*

The gothic font, sharp letters spelling out his name, always made him proud. It told a grand story, of a boy from a barrio and his mother, her hands raw from washing clothes, yes, you're familiar with that story, it moves your heart on Sundays or in the right Globe Telecom ad, it's a story of *inspiration*. Because he made it. Against all odds, against the estranged and womanizing father, the so-so grades in elementary, the looming garbage mountain that formed the backdrop of JM's childhood—he finished high school, he finished his training, he became a policeman, like he always wanted to. How Nanay *wept* on graduation day, her lips quivering as she fastened the medallion to his shirt. And, a few weeks later, with his first professional fee, how he had treated her to a meal at Aristocrat, even going so far as to order overpriced Coke from the menu.

As he looks at the certificate, a stain appears at the corner and creeps across, slow and inexorable, like the trickles of blood beneath his victims. Not *his* victims—*the* victims. He is not victimizing anyone. He's upholding justice. He's carrying out the orders of his president. They're supposed to eliminate every last one of them; he understands this, so he is mystified by the pain in his gut, the way he blinks repeatedly because there is no stain, that's impossible. He stands and walks over to the certificate. The parchment is clean, dull cream protected by the cheap frame from National Bookstore.

He turns to the mirror on the opposite side of the room and touches the puffed skin beneath his eye.

"Sir," he says aloud. "Sir, there are other ways to do this."

He doesn't sound convinced, even to himself.

Over dinner, Nanay comments on his eye—of course she notices it beneath the band-aid. He tells her some overly rushed commuter struck him with his elbow in the LRT. She nods, because she cannot fathom him lying to her.

The boy's name is Romuel. He's a bit makulit, but painfully earnest. Mebuyen overhears him and Babygirl telling each other dirty jokes, and rolls her eyes. They chase each other around the river, holding Adriana's hands as they splash in the water. They swing her between them on counts of one-two-three-wheeeee!

Romuel is invested in the mystery of his death—in what it could *mean*. He wonders whether it can change things, and it shifts the peace of their days. Aren't people talking about it on Facebook? Twitter? Insta? Won't someone have to pay? Babygirl is empathetic. Adriana is fascinated. "Because it can't just keep happening," Romuel pronounces. He's drawing a gun in the soil with a stick, three dead bodies next to it: a girl, a boy, a woman. Self-portrait of a slaughter. He is not afraid to think about it. "It has to stop somehow. I think. If I was strong and old I would stop it."

"How?"

"I don't know. I would definitely do something. Especially if I was a policeman." He shades in the pools of blood.

"But the police killed us," Adriana mutters. She pokes more holes into her sketch-body with a finger.

"I know that! Stupid girl!" Romuel springs to his feet, throws his stick down, scuffs his own drawing with his foot. Adriana bursts into tears. Romuel walks away.

Babygirl wraps her arms around Adriana and rocks her. "Let's not fight. None of us are wrong. We're not wrong."

Romuel walks ten paces, turns around, walks back, scratching the side of his face. He apologizes to Adriana. Offers to draw her SpongeBob.

Mebuyen watches all this from a short distance away, sucking on her cheeks. She pats one of her breasts absentmindedly, and thinks about human pain. Does anything make it worth it? Do they gain something, from feeling the world, feeling everything as if it were fresh and raw?

The little maya bird roots around in her hair before delivering Lumabat's message: *Is there a boy named Romuel with you now? He's all over the news. They're asking for justice. They're speaking his name, on the streets, on the web. They're chanting his name.*

Mebuyen closes her eyes. She mouths their names; tries not to think of the countless others she has let go of, will let go.

It's Romuel who asks, over dinner one night, "Why can't we move on?"

Mebuyen figured this time would come. She doesn't admit that some part of her was hoping she might never be asked. The other two put down their utensils, and look expectant. Mebuyen stands and beckons, warns them not to let go of each other. They link hands, and with the steely determination of an old woman who has felt fury and sorrow in endless cycles for eternity, Mebuyen walks from her world into that of dreamers. She rips right into the darkness so that it bleeds rainbow ribbons around them. She knows who she is searching for. When she finds him, he is curled up into himself, already shivering.

Juan Miguel Pulag wakes up in a dirty alleyway. An old, flabby woman in a duster, with monstrously frizzy hair, is staring him down. There's a greenish tint to her skin, and he cannot help but notice that her breasts are enormous. He knows this is inappropriate, but that's just a tangential thought; he's mostly preoccupied with the three figures behind her. A little girl in a SpongeBob SquarePants sando; a beautiful drag queen in what could be a prom dress; and a boy with an impish smile, though the mischief doesn't reach his eyes. There's regret, instead. And a growing ember of what might be rage.

JM's eyes move slowly from one to the other. His chest spasms.

He scrambles to his feet, tries to run. The little girl scurries and blocks his path. *Her blood all over her grandmother's shirt.* He remembers her name, and vomits into the shit-smelling concrete.

"I don't think this is only your fault," the old woman says, "but you have to apologize, just the same. Then the river will start flowing again."

"Oh, is he the one who did it? Sayang. He's cute pa naman." The drag queen walks up to him, inspecting his face, and he backs against the wall, sweating. *Are we pigs, that you can treat us like this?*

"The entirety of this is bigger than him, and carried by many, of course. But he's one of the few I can get through to." The old woman comes closer, and he screams, unable to help himself.

"Stay back!" he shouts. "I'm police! I'm trained! I don't want to hurt you!"

"Then don't," she says curtly. "I don't wish you harm, either."

"We're trying to do the right thing," he stammers. He can feel every drop of sweat sliding down his back. He is trying to recite a Hail Mary and not lose his mind at the same time. "We're trying to clean up the Philippines. They're wrong, they're hurting our society, I want—I want my future children to be safe."

He pulls his gun out. She gazes at it warily. "Put that down."

He raises it.

"Manang Em!" The boy steps in front of the old woman, his arms spread out. He glares at JM. "You will not hurt her." His eyes are a mirror: that's definitely rage, burning in them, but grounded in the unshakeable knowledge that what he's doing is right. He looks so much like a boy JM recognizes that his finger trembles where it's hooked against the trigger.

"I'll be all right, Romuel," the old woman says. "He can't hurt me." The boy moves aside, but stays close to her. Protecting her. As a man should.

Romuel. Romuel de Vera. Romuel de Vera, seventeen years old, an honor student. He wanted to be a policeman. His parents loved him very much. How do you sleep at night knowing you killed an innocent? Hashtag Stop the Killings. Hashtag Justice for Romuel.

JM retches into his closed mouth. He swallows.

"I don't see how the mountains of bodies is cleanup," the old woman says. "I don't see how nightmares is your reward for something *good*. Where is your mercy? Where is your sense of doing what's right—what one human would *do*? I am not human, and even I know."

In her eyes he can see beyond himself, to some space where there is a small boy who wants to be a policeman, wants his mom to stop scrubbing her hands raw, wants his dad to see what a fucking fool he was for leaving them, wants to do the right thing, always. *There are other ways to do this.* But how can it be wrong, when everyone else is doing it? How did he become this? The boy next to her is the boy from his memories, and the boy next to her is dead.

The boy is dead. JM killed that boy.

"Stop," he says, weakly. She reaches out her hand to him.

"It's okay, anak. You have a voice. You have hands. You have your life. You don't have to fight anymore. You just have to open your eyes, and see."

He rests his finger on the trigger.

Her eyes narrow. "Don't," she says. "You'll regret it."

He fires. Quick and fluid, she wraps her hand around the barrel. The gun explodes; the bullet blasts into his shoulder, and pieces of it strike his face. He howls with pain.

"Anak?"

"No!" He screams, but it's no longer the old lady, it's just his own Nanay, poking her head into his room with concern. He's wet, he realizes—he has pissed in his sleep, the first time since he was a toddler. He gasps; he can't get enough air. His vision swims. His insides are on fire. Nanay comes over, carefully, and sits on his bed. She gazes at him with love and worry. He cracks. He cries into his hands. "No, no no no," he repeats.

She rests her hand on his shoulder, rubbing up and down. He leans into her and cries like he will never stop.

But he does. The next day, he takes a temporary leave from the precinct, and wonders what to do with his free hands, with the blood still lingering on them. How to rebuild? How to revive that boy, give him the justice he deserves? There are no answers, there is nothing easy; but JM is tired, at last, of running away. Tired as well of standing still and nodding along. He has to live. He can at least do that with his eyes open.

There is a dark bruise on his shoulder that aches even at the gentlest touch.

There is no sun in the underworld, but the sky is bright. Mebuyen feeds them a last meal, as delicious as she can make it. Looking out at the river, she sees a flock of birds circling it, a deep brown cluster—and she hears the rush of water, at last. Her heart is relieved, but she is wise enough to recognize the tinge of loneliness beneath it. Well. There will always be new ones. And these three, they may lose their names and the exact bodies they moved through in the land of men, but they will not lose their essence in the next place. This is the hope Mebuyen clings to, for everyone who passes through her town.

So: the ritual. She takes them to the river, and they stand in the shallow waters.

"You'll need to stoop a little," she tells Babygirl, then Romuel. The only one not too tall for her is Adriana.

She scoops water in her hands, and pours it over them, one at a time. First their joints, then their heads. As the water runs down their bodies, the darkness of their pain trickles out, seeping into the river as a smoky stain, blending into the gray current. "Don't cry," she snorts. Babygirl flicks water at her.

"I don't want to go," Babygirl says.

Mebuyen has spent eternity not being soft—not since the first babies came to her, with their wide eyes and their sweet puckered mouths, shortly after her quarrel with Lumabat. She tsks. She says not to worry; she doesn't know exactly how men experience it, but she suspects there's a lot of family on the other side, maybe even sisig and bibingka or whatever it is Babygirl likes to eat. Definitely there is endless rice. "And you can be who you are there," she says. "The way you are here."

This seems to cheer Babygirl up. Sometimes it's the oldest ones that are most like children.

"All right," Mebuyen says. "Let's get going."

"Wait," Romuel says. She glances at him, wondering if she missed a spot, and promptly gets caught in a tight hug. "Salamat, manang," he whispers. He squeezes her tightly; she is surprised by his strength, then not. Her arms quiver as she wraps them around him.

"Me too!" Adriana chirps, then they're all pressed in tightly together. Mebuyen is never cold, but right here, she feels warm. They hold each other for a long time.

"I'll miss you," Adriana says.

Mebuyen breaks the circle. "Yes, yes. Now let's go."

They wade through the river in silence, until Babygirl starts singing: a song about not being afraid, not being left alone. The melody is cheerful, and makes Mebuyen's chest ache.

They reach the part where the river is met with a canopy of dark trees. Mebuyen kisses them all on the cheek, and lets them go. They continue down the river, holding hands, waiting for the light to change. Not once do they look back.

Hurricane Heels (We Go Down Dancing)

In hindsight, we should have expected things would go to shit. Like always. But it was Friday and Selena was getting married, and we wanted to drink and dance and not blow up monsters for one night. That's how I reasoned, anyway, as I slipped through orange slime on my way to Aiko's motionless body, wondering why the fuck we'd been so careless, how quickly could we stop the blob monster from pummeling downtown.

The evening had started at Ria's house, where she'd baked penis-shaped cookies and gotten everyone fuzzy little tiaras. It was already hilarious, how bad we were going to be at this. We *tried*. We even dressed in the appropriate colors—I came in a dark green shift, holding my gift exchange: a voucher for the hip new coffee roaster in Bushwick and a picture book of hot guys holding puppies. At least one of those was bound to make the recipient happy. Ria opened the door, laughed at my makeup—despite efforts, *glam* was not in my vocabulary—and waved me in. Natalie was sipping light beer, ignoring the pink champagne that had been poured into delicately frosted glasses. Aiko was running her thumb over the books on Ria's shelf, picking out titles at random. Selena got up from where she was patting Ria's French bulldog and gave me a tight hug. She was wearing a sash that read *Soon-to-be-Bride, Motherf*ckers!*

"I'm *still* the last one?" I'd tried to get there early, but my timing jinx was in full force, even as I'd braved the subway (and one too many catcalls) in this unashamed party getup.

Selena faked a frown. "We expect nothing less from you, Alex," she said.

"You're just a bunch of early birds."

"Whatever—leeeet's get *started!*" Ria had been appointed grand dame of the bachelorette party. An obvious choice: besides Selena, she was the least awkward. She knew her way around a nightclub, got swanky discounts from her event planner friends, and was queen bee at social life. She made us gather in a circle around her low, tasteful dining table. I ate a frosted penis cookie. We toasted Selena's impending marriage to the impeccable Robert Myers, and Natalie added that should he ever break her heart, we would break his bones. Selena smiled sweetly and told us that she'd break them herself. We did the gift exchange, in which Ria shrieked upon receiving my offering, and I got an extremely practical Amazon gift card from Natalie. Next we played five rounds of a drinking game that made absolutely no sense. I remember tossing down cards and screaming whenever hearts came up. Then I think we played a round of spoons, using utensils with boobs on the handles. By the end of it we were buzzed and ready for dinner.

Dinner was at an exceptional steak and seafood place on Madison Avenue. Someone got Dungeness crabs as an appetizer. As I cracked a juicy leg open I thought *Oh god, who is going to pay for this?* I turned towards Ria, who winked. "Splitsies, dahh-ling," she said. Well, that was fair. I eagerly returned to my crab. The waiter—who I'll admit looked rather dapper in his suit—was overly flirty with everyone, but especially with Aiko, who eventually said, "Dude, I'm taken." Aiko was the most pokerfaced liar. We had a good snicker about that.

All in all, a normal dinner. For us. I had to give this some thought. I'd been *almost* successfully ignoring the fact of Selena's impending marriage to the impeccable Robert Myers, and what this would mean for us; for the unbeatable equilibrium we'd had for years, or at least since we were wide-eyed ingénues in our training bras, attending summer camp in the same forest where goddesses roamed the earth and had too much time on their hands.

No one had asked. Or if anyone had, I didn't know about it. Was Selena quitting? Was quitting an option? Would she be bequeathing her magic watch—it looked rather like a Baby-G and I'd always been a bit envious of it—to a new, trusted girl? Or would we then be reduced to four, lacking her pink bleeding into our rainbow, lacking her grace and her Bountiful Hammer Smash, which indeed could break bones?

Was Selena going to be happy? Or was all this speculation irrelevant because even after marriage she'd still be with us, same as always? Had she ever called on the goddess, demanded release? Was marriage an accessory to freedom?

I couldn't ask. I desperately wished someone else would ask.

"Dessert?" The waiter reappeared, slightly crushed but gallantly trying. We got lava cake and crème brûlée and strawberry cheesecake. I ate until I was bursting, then ordered a dessert coffee, because we were going to stay up past my bedtime, and I could be a royal baby with enough sleep deprivation.

"Next: put these on," Ria said, passing out headbands with penises stuck to them in lieu of alien antenna. Natalie burst out laughing. Aiko looked ready to die of embarrassment, but she wore it anyway, after Selena gleefully jammed a pair onto her head. We left in a parade of bouncing penises, and emerged into the cool Manhattan evening, where the city's bright lights and faint pizza smells bore no warning of the terrifying monster that would soon emerge from dark dimensions.

"Where to?" I asked, hopped up on party drinks and Irish coffee churning together in my belly.

"Abs," Ria answered.

Aiko said "Oh dear god, no," but the rest of us just decided that the hilarity must continue. We trooped forth, expertly sidestepping potholes in our heels, a candy-colored group of five. It was stupid yet inevitable that we had all ended up in New York. Like the laziest of superhero clichés. But fighting was easier in a group, and besides, I didn't really think of myself as a superhero, even if my fist—in the right glove—could punch its way through an oversized worm or a particularly aggressive stalker. We were best friends and magical girls—now ladies, now women? how bizarre—and that was it.

I don't think any of us believed it, when we got chosen and were still wondering what to do with our hands, our lack of fear. Then our first monster appeared, all dolled up for us to slay it, and we realized—this wasn't a joke. That's what I felt, anyway, vomiting after a tentacle slapped my stomach, whitehot pain searing across my insides while everything inside me screamed *I don't want to die, not yet,* and *why, whywhywhy;* then my eyes focused on the bracelet the crazy forest lady had slipped onto my wrist, and my mouth was suddenly whispering that song she'd been humming—

my mouth was suddenly apart from me—

and a bright light lifted me up, a strange song of pain, warping into a blouse around me, a skirt, wrapping over my hands and feet and neck, long strands of it billowing behind me in a dazzling array of rainbow colors that hurt my eyes, like I was standing in a disco on the cheapest acid, not that I'd ever tasted acid then, not that I'd ever imagined anything *like this.* But there was a strength filling my arms and legs and a song of power lurching against my breast that I wouldn't have believed, for a second, could be mine. I was shit at sports and did better with mental computation—Kumon Math, baby—and blowing up starcrafts on my computer, but suddenly I was jumping to my feet, suddenly I was doing a freaking *backflip.* I could still taste the vomit that had leaked out of my mouth but the white light slapped itself around me—into *clothes*—and began filling my fingers and fists, and the bracelet had extended into a chain whip that dangled from my hand.

The galactic octopus made a curious squealing sound when my whip lashed into it. Although my body remained on autopilot, fragments of my consciousness started returning, and I thought of the other girls—Aiko I knew from down the street, but there was the peppy blonde one and the boisterous new girl that screamed *leader* and the gorgeous gymnast with the lazy grin—and were they alive? I whipped back a tentacle that had lifted itself out of the water to wave at me, and heard a chainsaw-rev, saw a set of silver teeth smashing down so that grayish liquid sprayed everything. I wobbled backwards on the heels of the boots I was suddenly wearing, and picked up a corner of my skirt, dazedly wondering where my favorite cargo shorts had gone.

"Alex?" another girl asked, closer. One hand tugged my shoulder back—I seized it, staring at her, not sure what the hell my face was doing. She said, "It's Selena," before ducking and hacking at something behind her with what appeared to be a battleaxe made of light.

When the octopus finally collapsed in the mud and our clothes morphed back to the raggedy casual ones we were wearing before everything went to shit—when the aches filtered into our bodies, pounded into our heads, reappeared as hastily healed scars and scratches along our limbs—I found myself at a loss for words, the whip now a bracelet on my wrist. I sank down into the muck and exhaled, and the one thought in my head was: *I'm glad I'm not alone.*

Aiko crawled up to me, half her face caked with blood. I lifted my hand to touch her, caring more for her than I ever did in all our years as neighbors, but she shook her head *no.*

"It healed," she said.

"What did you get?" I asked. She looped one finger into her necklace, and her shoulders trembled with fatigue. "I thought she was a hobo," I finally managed. "A really pretty one."

Aiko cracked a horrific, broken grin.

I don't want this, I thought of telling her, but what good would it have done? Instead I cried, a warbling cry that quickly dissolved into sobbing. We gathered in a circle, heads bent, bodies broken. We cried more that day than we ever cried in another battle, or at least that's what I remember. Tears are a byproduct now—a moot point, a waste. Tears won't carry us through to victory. The fear of losing each other might.

Who's been the closest to dying? Hard to say. Natalie once spent a week in intensive care, and I remember this cold-iron feeling in my stomach every time I stopped by the hospital. She'd looked—fine, mostly, which was the scary part, except she wasn't waking up. Ria kept Natalie's earrings, which seemed to have grown dimmer, lacking that unearthly light that turned us all into weapons, warriors. Natalie finally woke on Selena's watch, and when I got the text I cried like anything.

The next day I held her face in my hands while she smirked and said, "You're so weird, you know that? Stop worrying."

I'd gotten both legs crushed in a golem's grip, once. I didn't feel pain so much as shock, the numbness spreading up my thighs. But they'd yanked me to safety, and after a few days with the goddess grace doing its thing I could walk again, despite the doctor's better judgment. They took turns playing card games and Jenga with me, until I was better.

It was tough not to get casual about injury. After realizing how much everything *hurt*—it became a constant refrain, easy enough to swallow. Maybe the healing wouldn't last forever. But even now, after all these years, we could still leap and spin and slice with the best of them. There was a lot to be said for experience, even if the fighting looked sloppy. Aiko was a twice-over taekwondo black belt, and Ria knew some arnis, but neither of those things directly translated to curb-stomping a monster in the eye, or using a scalloped blade to wedge through a screaming banshee. It was magic, and it gave us strength. If we woke up one day with a million cuts and our vital organs fucked—well, we'd just have to deal with it, like we've had to deal with every fucking day since.

The poster outside the strip club—ahem, male revue theater—said *A Wild Night of Fun!* punctuated by Faceless Abs. Glittery clubgoers stood waiting: giggly, drunk, uncertain about how obscene this was going to be, or *could* be. Did they want it to be obscene? Did they want Faceless Abs lapdancing them for just one night when they could be Wild Grrrls? Was I being mean because I overate and felt bloated, and one of my best friends was getting married, and I was a big enough bitch that I couldn't be *happy* for her, couldn't even admit that I felt betrayed?

Natalie squeezed my elbow. I turned to look at her and burped. She laughed.

"You okay?"

"I'm fine," I said. "Are we really going in there?"

"Ria will kill you if you back out now," she said. "You didn't help plan, so you gotta go with it. And if you quit we'll each have to pay $20 for your reservation."

"Okay, okay," I said, because Natalie did not need to go Accountant on me right now. I took her hand from my elbow and held it. When she looked at me wonderingly I remembered myself and flopped her wrist back and forth, like this was some kind of joke. She let me, which was nice of her. "You think Aiko's going to make it?" I asked, inclining my head at our friend. Aiko noticed me staring and pursed her lips. I shrugged. For some reason I was still holding Natalie's hand. I put it down hastily.

The bouncer pulled back the black cord that was keeping us out. Everyone cheered. "Kill me," Aiko mumbled as we shuffled onto the dark steps.

"Haha," I answered, while wondering why the hell anyone thought dark staircases for drunk clubbers was a good idea. We made it, somehow, and were ushered to plush couches right by the stage. A table full of cocktails sat ominously next to us. Presently a bartender in a tight tank came to take our orders—light beers for everyone, and a round of tequila shots. When he returned with our drinks he extended the garter of his pants, ever so slightly. Ria smoothly tucked a dollar bill inside it.

"The night is young," Ria said, raising her shotglass. Leaving her lips, the words sounded like a warning.

Magical girls. Ria was the anime fan, both the least and most freaked out; the one who called a meeting in her tent the evening after we'd emerged from the forest and cleaned ourselves up. She asked each of us what the hell we knew, and what we could do. Asked us what the goddess told us, how the goddess had appeared to us. What did we want, why were we broken? What were our character types? Besides Selena = perky it was hard to tell, and even Selena could be dangerously unpredictable. After we started shouting over unfair casting, hating each other, Ria stopped trying to make a manga narrative and started leading us instead.

Ria was the only one who never, ever denied it. She knew everyone around us—parents, schoolmates, siblings—would go on living their lives, unseeing. She knew the destruction would somehow take care of itself, that undoing it would be the work of the goddess's other minions, that the media would make up its own stories. We would *not* be seen or identified. She admitted that it was crazy, that monsters from the dark beyond did not exist in our neat suburban life. "That doesn't mean it's not real," she said through a burst lip.

In truth, Ria probably never wanted to be leader, but someone *had* to be. She was the only one who knew, even in those first few months, that if we didn't fight, someone would get hurt. That people could die, and no amount of magic clean up could reverse that.

She was the one who held a knife to her wrist when we couldn't stop the part of that playground from smashing down on a little boy and girl. They didn't even have time to scream. They just *went,* and there was dark red seeping from under the metal and *Oh god they were dead.* We weren't fast enough or strong enough and they were dead.

I wrenched the knife from Ria's grasp and backhanded her. I felt terrible, but while she collapsed in sobs I still found it in me to shout: "Ria you idiot, you crazy idiot, we *need* you, don't do that, don't you ever freaking do that again."

Days later, post-saving-kids-screaming-in-a-bus, she apologized.

"Thanks, Alex," she said. "I didn't—I don't actually want to die. I just couldn't believe it, when those kids—"

"I know," I said. I gripped her hand. I couldn't say *Thank you for being strong enough for all of us,* but maybe if I held on tight enough she'd know it anyway.

I tried to quit, my freshman year of college. I deleted my online accounts, changed my email address, moved to California and begged Mom and Dad not to tell the girls where I had gone. I was deluded enough to think that—maybe if I drowned myself in enough schoolwork and partying—the goddess would decide that I was useless, unworthy of being her warrior. She'd retract her blessing. I'd lose my powers, sure, but I could stop fighting.

I was still awkward. I still sort of hated socializing. But I did college *with a vengeance,* hoping that would create normalcy. I kissed boys and girls, joined five different on-campus groups, tried to forget the feeling of slick guts through my fingers, the shrill scream of someone being stabbed through the armpit, the acrid burn of venom spilled on my back. It seemed to work. My bracelet didn't ping once, didn't drag me to the scene of trouble, that whole first semester.

But I couldn't avoid Thanksgiving. Mom wheedled. Dad promised turkey. Plus I felt like shit. Like a coward, and *lonely*. I cried through the weekends when I wasn't partying or hungover. I used incognito browser windows to check on the girls, make sure they weren't dead yet. We'd all chosen someplace other than Jersey for school. I couldn't help but say yes to Thanksgiving, especially when Mom mentioned fried rice, which she always used in lieu of stuffing.

Back home, I left my bracelet—now cheap and childish-looking, a girl's plaything—on my dresser. I wouldn't bring it with me the following semester. No beams of white light here, no glowing crowns for the crimefighting princesses. *It's done,* I thought. *That whacko goddess has gone and recruited others for her army.* The pure of heart could wage war on darkness—but that wasn't me, anymore. College-aged was too old. I was free.

Then a herd of wraiths descended on our town. We regrouped. I felt emphatically out of shape, but the white light splintered into the same old uniform around me—smooth blouse, smooth pleated skirt, and how did I ever find my beautiful powerful whip ugly or weak or cheap? It was priceless. Shoving the wraiths back through the portal into their world still felt more natural than shoving random clubbers' tongues down my throat. This was home, in more ways than one, whether I liked it or not.

Even now, I wondered if that brief period of freedom had been the goddess's way of showing me that I had no choice.

We stood in the field after the battle. Ragged, mudslick, autumn leaves latched onto our aching bodies. Because the monster had been orange, Selena made a joke about pumpkin pie. It was Natalie, surprisingly, who said, "Why are you such a *white girl*?" We laughed ourselves sick until it was time for dinner.

"Oh my god, that dude just slapped his junk on her head."

"His"—giggle—"*what?*"

"Junk. I don't want to say the word *dick* here. It's just—ew, he did it again."

"Dudes are gross."

"That one's pretty cute."

"Does Rob have better abs than that guy, Selena?"

"*What?* Oh my god, I can't believe you asked that. Haha. I need to pee."

"Answer my question, guuuurl."

"Ria, are you already wasted? You can't be wasted. It's only eleven."

"I don't think Rob even *has* abs."

The man on the stage gyrated around a lady sitting on a chair, sidling across her lap while she smiled in discomfort. Aiko had discarded her penis headband and retreated outside for a smoke. Selena, who had already disappeared twice for special service, came back from the restroom and sat down beside me, wrapping one arm around my shoulder.

"Alex," she shouted into my ear. "I feel like we haven't talked all night."

"I know," I shouted into her ear.

"Are you okay?"

"Yeah! I'm fucking stoked!" I fist-pumped. "Are you excited to get your turn on the stage?" We had paid extra for that; I hoped it was worth it.

She shook her head a vehement no. I laughed. I held one of her curls in my fingers.

"Selena," I said, and found I did not have the willpower to shout. "Selena, are you going to be happy?"

"What?" She leaned in closer. The music got louder, because the man on the stage was now swinging back and forth in his leopard-print thong, a feverish Tarzan.

"I hope you'll be happy," I said, a bit louder.

She pointed to her ear and shook her head. I shouted, "I hope you get a fireman routine!"

She laughed. She mouthed, *Thank you.*

Then the club exploded.

❁

These days I mostly loved no one, although I had tried a handful of times. I mean, I loved my family, and I loved our group in a special, barnacle-like way, but that was a given. Once upon a time I had loved Natalie differently, and in some scattered moments I could admit that those times were not entirely over, but the few months we were girlfriends had been difficult. We mutually called it quits after a year of breathless kisses and exhausted cuddling, with everyone sort-of-knowingly-but-hesitantly-teasing. Our friendship—and the group—survived the breakup. Sometimes I got this searing, painful certainty that we still loved each other, but holding onto a relationship took a special strength that I didn't have just then.

After Natalie and I said friendship was what we both wanted, I decided to throw myself into work. Software development was the only career I'd ever considered having, and in between monster-crushing I wrote code for a mid-sized tech firm on the Lower East Side. I gave off enough Vibes that most people in the office didn't try to learn much about me. Even if I could manage a conversation now, I still preferred a night in with Street Fighter or LOTR. I figured I was just burned out on human interactions, after a spectacularly social college life left me drained and hollow. At least I learned that I did not like the Sex Thing much. (Fun fact: not all magical girls are virgins.)

But maybe loneliness was something we all struggled with. I first realized this when Aiko and I were stuck in a coffee shop by ourselves. She took moody sips of black coffee; I poked at the latte art the barista had drawn in my foam. In the last two weeks there had been three fights. We were tired, and five people was so few. There were probably others, but we were as blind to them as they were to us.

Aiko was a nice person to be upset with. She never judged you for being tired or bitchy, and she never BS'ed her feelings. Over the rim of her cup, she said, "I think what sucks most is how *no one else* sees, you know? It gets pretty fucking lonely. I don't even care about the pain or exhaustion anymore, but there are days when I want to walk into walls until I black out."

"We're not alone," I said. She just stared at me. There were starburst scars across her knuckles that made my mouth dry.

I didn't know how Selena and Rob managed to last this long. I'd never asked, and they'd been going strong for the last four years. I liked Rob well enough. Like everyone else close to us, the goddess magic cast a spell on him. He looked at Selena and saw the Marketing consultant, not the girl holding a giant axe, splattered with guts and grime. He thought of us as her "wild childhood friends."

A year ago, pre-engagement, Selena sat each of us down, separately, and told us she really loved him, that she was not giving this up. We all said *okay*. I wasn't sure if I *really* agreed, but I cared about Selena and her happiness, so.

Slime splattered everywhere. Debris rained from above. People stampeded. I was thrown back by an invisible force, crashing into the table full of cocktails. Screams, roars, crescendoing with animal keening. Chiseled torsos and flashing sequins, and the ceiling crumbling to reveal Manhattan sky, jeweled lights, and an enormous, slavering blob monster.

There have to be others, I thought, muzzily, standing in the midst of all the broken glasses. Blood and what smelled like Bailey's dripped from my elbow. *How can there be no other girls in this room who can fight? Younger girls, better girls, girls who aren't yet sick of this.* And then—*Selena, Selena, oh god I just wanted her to have a good night, we didn't even get to go fucking dancing yet and now this.* I stood and yanked off my heels, anger rising past everything. *Selena deserved a good night,* "she deserved a break, you big fucking monster, why the *fuck* did you have to go and ruin it?" I screamed, even as someone seized my arm.

"We gotta go!" Ria's voice, unutterably calm, though when I looked at her there was dread in her eyes, through the hair tumbled around her face, the dirt on her cheek. She tugged again and we ran while Jello Blob squalled and ejected a hissing stream of acid all over the plush couches. Someone screamed. Server? Tarzan? Twenty-first-birthday-celebrant? All of the above? Flecks of acid got on my shoulder, sizzling through my dress straps, the pain like sharp darts. Holy shit. We lurched out, breathless. Fucking Irish coffee. I retched on our last step, turning my head so that I missed Ria. Where the hell was everyone else?

I grasped my wrist, and my insides turned to ice. "My bracelet," I said. "Shit. I left it—"

"I know," Ria said. "Me too," *fuck,* sometime during the third drinking game?

"Ria! Alex!"

Aiko, already transformed. Beautiful, dependable, *angry* Aiko, the necklace now a cannon melded into her arm.

"Natalie's getting your charms, so get clear! I'll hold it off!" Aiko shouted, turning to blast a hole in its wobbling orange guts.

Whenever I watched a battle, everything slowed: all detail, all precision. Aiko leapt, landed on top of a subway entrance, and fired shots that streaked through the sky, bright-blue. Screaming everywhere. The crowd running the hell away—great, good. The blob shooting at Aiko so that half her skirt got burned in its wake, and Aiko falling to the ground in a loud string of expletives. She flipped in midair, skirt swishing; cannon fire, then her body getting slapped away by a blobhand. She landed with a crunch, coughing up blood. Ria yelled at me to get to an alley, goddamit, before her voice splintered away as a nearby deli's glass shattered. I raced towards Aiko, mind numbing, certain she was dead, certain she would be okay. The monster saw me scurrying into its field of vision and pigsquealed, and I wished, not for the first time, that desperation by itself could work magic. That the goddess would come fight her own battles. I held my arms up in a stance, in front of Aiko, and said, "You just try, you big fucking bully!"

A globby hand, heading straight for me, orange and vile and about to crush my windpipe—

Selena in a blaze of pink, hacking it apart. She had a sickening gash on one leg, probably from the exploded stage.

"That's my bridesmaid, fucker!" She grabbed me and hauled me back. "Alex, *what the fuck?*"

"Here," Natalie, this time, suddenly right behind me. "I got her." When Natalie had her earrings in magic mode, she could teleport. I'd always thought that was unfairly cool.

One gloved hand held my wrist, the other forced my bracelet up to my elbow. White light spiraled around us, melding to fit my body in the dress I was wearing for Selena's sake. Beside us, our bride-to-be stood, battle-axe lengthening in her hands. Rage lined her face, seethed through her, while tears smudged makeup down her cheeks. She leaped and spun, backlit by the moon, and dove down so that her axe cleaved a chunk of monster. Acid gushed up in globs, and she flicked it off her arms in a furious gesture, slicing, vindictive, even as she spat out red. Classic Selena, radiant and violent as fuck when she wanted to be. Natalie was next to Aiko, helping her up, holding a hand against Aiko's probably broken ribs.

"Over here, you little bitch!" Ria yelled, beneath a billboard for *Chicago,* chainsaw roaring.

The white on the peripheries of my vision sparked away to rainbows, to nothing. I pulled my whip taut between my hands. I raised my arm and let it whistle harshly through the night.

"We are never going to be free of this," Selena said in the aftermath, wearing the tattered remnants of her dress. Tears ran down her face.

She looked more mad than sad, just a girl who'd had an awful night. Somehow her sash had survived the fight. The club, unfortunately, had not.

We picked through the remnants of the monster, as Natalie and Ria hurried Aiko to the nearest hospital. Selena found its glass heart: our offering to the goddess, the leftover manifestation of malice. She clutched it to her chest and wept as it dissolved, a swell of white filling her hands then fading. When her palms were empty, she sank to her knees. "I'm tired, Alex. I'm tired. So tired."

I held her, and rocked her back and forth, whispering, "Things might still change," and "Shhh, shhh, I'm here." I stroked her hair, wiped her cheeks. Her tears were warm and heartbreaking. I thought *But if this ends, if we do finally become free, will we still be together?* I felt selfish and awful and bonetired, and also—for one brief, treacherous moment—glad it wasn't over.

"It could have been worse."

"I know."

"You took it like a trooper, though," Natalie said, plucking a can of beer from the cooler. We were all set for a chill afternoon. A hard drive of several Netflix series, a DVD copy of Ria's debut—we were eighteen and had put on the most embarrassing dance number as part of her entourage—and Selena's oft-played box of Taboo. Aiko was sitting up in bed and clicking through her laptop, deciding what to watch. Injured's privilege.

Outside the hospital window the sky was dense with clouds. The street was quiet. At least for today, it seemed like the goddess and the forces of evil did not give any shits about us.

"I mean, it could have happened on your wedding day."

"I *know*," Selena said with a shove, so that Ria toppled on the couch we'd dragged next to the bed. "God, it could still happen."

"It won't," I said, knocking on Aiko's headboard. "No way."

Selena smiled at me, eyes crinkling. Her arm was in a sling that by now was probably more for show. She'd be out of it in time for the wedding next week. I smiled back. If a monster came then, I would personally crush it to bits, with apologies to the bridesmaid's gown.

Only Unclench Your Hand

They're killing chickens again in the backyard. Last time, a headless chicken ran in and danced blood puddles around my feet. I can't relax, because of a massive thrumming headache, so I grab my textbook to get a few pages in by the river. As I make my way down the rocky path I hear Tito Benjo laugh and Aling Dinday scream for the chickens to stay still. I should be used to noise, from Manila, but here in the province, every sound is amplified. In a village this small, you can hear everything for miles.

It would be good for my review, Mom and Dad said. Why not spend a few weeks there? When you get home, you'll be all set to pass the entrance exams. So, shortly after New Year's, they drove me here to stay with Tito Benjo in the old farmhouse. Tito put me up in Mom's room, with the creepy secretary desk and the miniature Santo Niño on the bookshelf. The house is in worse shape than I remember: floorboards croak if you step on them wrong, and Aling Dinday warned me not to lean against the stair banister. Without my parents and cousins, it's too quiet and empty, so I spend most of my time outdoors.

My parents were right about the lack of distractions. I can barely get a cellphone signal, let alone a few bars of Wi-Fi; even then I have to work from the village carinderia. I finished my study plan in three weeks, with time to review. Only downside is I've been overthinking whether I really want this degree—but I'm heading home at the end of this week, and there'll be plenty of time to doubt my life choices there.

I reach the stone bench by the river and lift my arm to block out the sun. There's a mosquito latched onto my elbow, sucking furiously. I swat it, and blood smears across my palm. "Damn bug."

"Damn bug," someone echoes behind me, the English exaggerated. I turn, grinning, and seize Edna by the armpits. She shrieks as I lift her into the air. "No, Ate Macky! Bloody hands!"

Laughing, I put her down and wipe my hand on my shorts. Edna is the daughter of Aling Dinday and Manong Edgar, the caretakers of Tito Benjo's farm. I think she's nine, though she's tiny enough to be six. The last time I was here she was so young; she barely spoke, and ran away whenever she saw me. Over the last month, though, she's become the little sister I never had: leading me on walks through town, and laughing as I help around the farm, 'til Mang Edgar and Aling Dinday shoo me away, horrified by my attempts at labor. Edna's one of the few people in the village who humor me, who don't mind the English I mix with fumbling Tagalog, or the short hair and comfy clothes that get me mistaken for a boy. If not for her company, it would have been a lonely visit. I might never even have set foot outside Tito Benjo's property.

"Whatcha doing? Studying?"

"I want to. But my head hurts."

Edna grips her chin with one hand and her elbow with the other, striking a "brainiac pose," which she mostly uses to mock me. "If you have a headache, you should see Mang Okat."

"Who?"

"Mang Okat," she repeats, tugging on my arm. "Our healer."

"It's fine," I say. "I get these headaches pretty often." I don't mention that they've gotten worse, or they only started last year, when I decided to try for law school. I don't mention that I think faith healings are whack, fit only for *Rated K* and other sensational news.

"He can fix it!" she says, still tugging. Because I like Edna, and my brain hurts, and I don't think I can concentrate anyway, I let her drag me off.

Edna bounds up the steps to Mang Okat's house, which to my city-girl sensibilities looks kinda like a hut. "Manong! I brought someone new for you!"

"New?" He peers out. His weathered, wrinkled face eases into a grin. "Ahhh-ahhh! Sir Benjo's niece, the Manileña!"

"Hello po," I say, ducking my head as I enter. He gestures for me to sit on a plastic chair by the window. I can't refuse. Edna perches on a bench across from us.

"What's the problem?"

"She has a headache," Edna says.

"Yes po," I answer, helplessly. Mom got my head checked when I first complained, but the brain scans showed nothing. Their only advice was to take painkillers, but I've already had my quota for the day. I decide to go along with the inspection; my headache can't possibly get worse. Mang Okat slaps his hand on my forehead. It's greasy and smells of herbs.

"Hmm-hmm." He turns to his table, which is covered in vegetables and herbs and jars of—potions, I guess, or liquids that are supposedly potions. He turns back, holding a glass filled with water in one hand, and a small bamboo tube in the other. There's a black stone in the glass. "Stay still," he instructs, holding the glass against my head. I glance at Edna, who smiles back encouragingly. Mang Okat dips the tube into the glass and starts blowing into it, so that the water bubbles. He hovers the glass back and forth around my head. I feel profoundly weird. To distract myself, I watch the movement of a bug across the floor: it looks like a giant fly, but it has no wings. Some kind of beetle. It skitters from one wooden plank to another, then races up the window ledge and disappears over the edge.

At once, the pain in my head evaporates. The sudden, sweet relief extends from my forehead to my shoulders—I didn't realize how severe the ache had been, pressing against my skull. "Better?" Mang Okat asks.

I nod. My breath comes languid, easy. I'm filled with a desire to sleep, even if I generally hate naps.

He holds out the glass. The water has turned murky green, with solid particles floating in it. "This was inside you," he says, before dumping it out in a plastic bucket.

"Thank you," I say, rather awed.

Edna beams. "Told you so!"

I pull a crumpled fifty-peso bill from my pocket. "Here, Manong." I hold it out.

He waves it off, brow wrinkling.

"Sige na po," I say.

"Oh, just take it, Tay," someone says from the door.

"Ate Senya! I thought you were still in Manila!" Edna launches off the bench and wraps around the legs of the woman entering. She looks a little older than me. Her mouth is curved in a tired smile, and she has severe eyebags. She's wearing a yellow tank top stained with sweat so that I can see her bra through it, and a sky blue skirt. She wipes her face with the back of her hand while setting down a woven bag of groceries.

"I came back two days ago," Senya laughs. "Sorry I didn't go see you. Lots to do." She pats Edna's head because Edna is still wrapped around her like a leech. Edna's face shines with stark adoration, and a jolt of jealousy runs through me.

"Welcome back, anak," Mang Okat says.

"Tay, you should stop healing for free. Besides, I think the Manileña has some cash to spare, no?" She grins—probably to show she's only ribbing me—but it stings, even if I'm used to it. After a brief pause, Mang Okat takes the bill from my fingers. He passes Senya, gives her a quick kiss on the cheek, then holds out his hand. She slips him a pack of cigarettes, and he stumps out of the house.

Senya eyes the bucket against the wall, lips quirked.

"Your dad is pretty amazing," I say, feeling a perverse need to defend him. Quack powers or not, I definitely feel a million times better.

"I know," she answers, softly. "I'm glad he was able to help. Don't you have any paracetamol, though? I bet it's more effective."

I decide not to argue, and shrug.

"Ate Senya, be nice. I like Ate Macky," Edna says.

"I'm always nice." She crouches down to whisper in Edna's ear, and they giggle. Feeling left out, I gaze out the window. There's a cockroach creeping on the ledge. It scuttles down the wall, across the floor, towards Senya. She doesn't pay attention, even when it crawls between her feet, disappearing under her skirt. It emerges on the other side and drops between the planks of wood.

Edna has to go shopping with Aling Dinday the next day, so I take my backpack and decide to try my luck with the carinderia Wi-Fi. My head feels so light, I practically skip down the road. Mang Edgar waves at me from where he's knee-deep in a bunch of Tito Benjo's goats. I wave back. No matter how old I get, whenever I visit, Mang Edgar and Aling Dinday don't seem to change—they're familiar and caring as ever. I know they appreciate me hanging out with Edna; I've not been able to convince them Edna's the one looking out for me.

The lady at the carinderia knows me by now. She fills a paper boat with greasy chicken skin, squirts banana ketchup on top, and hands it to me with a bottle of Coke. I settle in at my favorite table, waving away the flies that cluster in bunches, hoping for scraps off people's plates. I'm holding up my MiFi, searching for a signal, when I hear glass shatter.

"Fuck you!" a man shouts. Someone shouts back, "Let go of me!"

The Carinderia Lady frowns at the street, but stays where she is, waving her flyswatter back and forth. I dash outside. Mang Okat's daughter—Senya—is trying to wrench her arm away from some shirtless dude in low-hanging shorts. Broken glass litters the ground. My eyes fix on the knife he is holding. Senya is gripping the jagged edge of a beer bottle, but the knife will be faster, more precise.

"Hey!" I default to English in my anger. "Let her go!" The man turns; even from a distance I see veins crowding his eyes, nearly popping with rage. There's a thorny heart tattooed on his left bicep, menacingly flexed. I'm scrawny and empty-handed and not that near—but my family has owned land here for generations, and I'm the niece of Tito Benjo, former governor. You don't fuck with politicians. "I'm warning you," I add.

He releases Senya's arm and stalks off, still clutching his knife. The look of searing rage he throws at her, then me, makes me want to run after him and beat his head with a stick—but I don't. Senya rubs her arm, not meeting my eyes.

Once he disappears from sight, she says, "You didn't need to do that. I can take care of myself, Miss Macky."

Her formality surprises me—that she thinks of me that way, too. "I know, I just—what an asshole."

Senya manages a huff of laughter. She comes over, still rubbing her arm, and chucks the broken bottle into the trash. We walk to my table.

"You're . . . funny, you know that?"

I smile. "You want some chicken skin?"

She shakes her head but takes a seat. I sense the Carinderia Lady watching us, but Senya glances at her and she starts loudly talking into her cellphone. My cheeks grow hot. If she's assuming things, it's not that different from what I deal with in Manila—the casually tossed-out *tomboy*, the more piercing *lesbo*. I've got my friends, my humor, and enough self-preservation not to let it get to me most of the time. It's not supposed to fucking matter, how I dress and who or what I like. But I can't escape the blabbering mouths, not even here.

I drum my fingers on my laptop. My MiFi has zero signal. "Why was he threatening you?" I ask, finally.

"Does there need to be a reason?"

"Um. I guess . . . not really."

She shrugs. "Well there is one, in this case. I told him I didn't want to see him." She rubs one finger down my bottle of Coke, still cold from the icebox. A ring of water from the condensation stains the plastic tablecloth. Her wrist, where he squeezed it, is starting to bruise. "We didn't even date that long, but lately he's been so aggressive. I don't worry for myself, but it bothers me that Tay's here. The problem is, I always forget about him when I'm back in the city."

"What do you do in Manila?"

"I study nursing. I'm old," she adds quickly. "It took Tay and me a while to save enough. He wants me to go work in a hospital abroad, after. That'll make it worth it. But if I do end up going . . . well, Tay does okay for himself, but . . ." Sadness crosses her face. I remember Mang Okat kissing her cheek, her exasperation at his work. The dusty wood of their hut, smaller than Tito Benjo's living room. She seems to catch herself, and fixates on the textbooks piled next to my computer. She picks one up. "Law?"

"Hopefully."

She sighs. "Corporate, right? Or something like that?"

"I haven't decided yet." I haven't even gotten in. But she's right; from my older cousins in Ateneo and UP, litigation doesn't seem like the right track for me. I've never liked confrontation. And I can put my Econ degree to better use helping companies solve their problems. It's what my parents do.

Senya dips her finger in the ring of condensation and drags it around the tablecloth. "Doesn't matter, I guess. Miss Macky, you and Sir Benjo and your family, whether you're in Manila or visiting here, you'll probably be okay. People like him"—she jerks her head at the road—"they won't bother you. They won't try. If anything happens, someone would at least attempt to solve it."

"That's not true," I answer, though I wonder: *What the hell am I even defending?* "Even in Manila—stars and athletes and people from—people with power—they get attacked sometimes. Sometimes their cases don't get solved, too. Look at uh—Nida Blanca."

Her finger draws figure-eights on the tablecloth. "Is that the same thing?"

I can feel my face growing hot. Of course it's not. But what would she have me say?

"Don't be mad," she says, lightly. "I'm not accusing you or anything. It's just that here, we learn justice isn't usually for us. If you wait too long, you lose too much. And if what you're saying is true, even for the rich . . . then why would you want to study something so useless?" She looks up from her water-tracing, eyes calm and piercing.

My mouth feels dry. I take a sip from my Coke. "Even in small ways, I want to help." But the words sound feeble, apologetic. She's right. I'm not going into criminal law. I'm not cut out to be a burning Defender of Justice. It's too easy to get disillusioned, and the rewards are few, or that's what my relatives tell me—and some of them have been practicing for decades. "Same reason you're doing nursing, right?"

Senya nods, slowly, but with more deliberation than I could ever muster.

Senya doesn't linger. She smirks at my offer to see her home, and I spend too much time feeling embarrassed about it.

I stay at the carinderia until evening, when the flickering fluorescent just won't cut it for reading. The sky still has a faint streak of pink way in the distance, but I use the camera flash of my phone to light my path as I walk back to Tito Benjo's, since there are few streetlights and too many potholes.

Halfway there, I hear violent retching somewhere ahead of me on the dark path. The local alcohol is cheap and goes straight to one's liver. Tito Benjo asks me to drink some with him every now and then; I hate the taste, but I've never been great at saying no to my elders. Besides, Mom told me to be extra-nice to Tito since he lost the last election. Every time we chat he says he's having fun taking a break, minding his kalamansi and the new fish farm. *Have another glass, Maria,* he insists; then he changes the subject.

I scoot to the other end of the road and hold my phone up so I don't step in anything nasty. A man is doubled over; the wet chunks of his dinner splatter the ground while he heaves. My light catches the mess he's making, and I see tiny black balls of . . . what looks like hair, stained red with blood. He vomits again. More dark balls splat on the ground, with shiny pink things that look like slugs or tongues. He glances up, panting. "You," he manages, one hand gripping his bare stomach. "What the fuck did you do?"

"Uh," I say, 'cause I've never seen this man in my life—then I notice the knife poking out of his shorts, the heart tattooed on his upper arm. He retches again. Even if he's a fucker, if he's barfing out his intestines, I have to do something. "Do you need—"

He flings me a look of stinging hate, spits, and staggers away. I cringe, relieved and grossed out. Already a trail of large black ants is approaching the vomit. Feeling sick, I run the rest of the way back.

Tito Benjo laughs.

"Puking out hairballs? Like a cat?"

"Tito, I'm serious."

"He probably ate something spoiled for dinner." Tito Benjo shrugs. "And, you know, some people can't hold their drink. Not like you and me, eh, Maria?" He winks.

Don't call me that, I don't say. Instead I mumble, "He was threatening someone outside the carinderia today. And he carries a knife around."

"Lots of people do, here. You can't stop them. Unless they've actually done something, you can't report them or anything. But hey, you tell your tito here if anyone threatens *you,* okay? You just say my name." He laughs. "So anyway. How are your studies going?"

"Okay, I guess." *You and Sir Benjo and your family,* Senya had said. Our name.

"I'll be in trouble with your mom if you don't pass your exam. Haha!"

"I'll pass, don't worry." I offer him a smile. Tito Benjo laughs too much, but he's mostly a good guy. The village respects him, he's not had any crazy scandals, and he treats Mang Edgar and Aling Dinday well. He's even offered to send Edna to college. It's just that the opposition candidate last time had a pop-star daughter.

I peck him on the cheek, excusing myself for the evening. In Mom's old room I lie in bed and think about this house with its concrete walls, the gate around the perimeter, bars on the windows and double locks on the doors. The path is long and the farm surrounds us and no one would dare. I think of Mang Okat and Senya in their hut; Edna and her parents in their own hut, just on the edge of our land. That drunk raving through the night, a knife in hand, the smell of blood and vomit hanging off him.

Edna appears the next day, while I'm heating up leftover tinola soup in the kitchen. "Nanay says you're going back at the end of this week?"

"Yep."

"You didn't tell me!"

Edna doesn't play much with other kids in the village; I realize that I'm a rare friend of hers, too. "Sorry! I thought you knew." I pass her a bowl of soup. "I'll come back in the summer"—but I won't have an exam to pass then, so there's no reason for me to leave Manila. And I'll probably be taking an internship, or summer classes. "I'll *try* to come back in the summer," I amend.

"Try, okay?"

"Uh-huh. Na, you've changed so much. You used to run away from me!"

"You were scary then!" She giggles at the memory. "And I didn't know it was okay to talk to you." With the rest of my family around, she meant. Maybe her parents told her not to bother us.

"I'm not scary anymore?"

She shakes her head. "Only when the goat bumped you. Your scream was scary."

"The *goats* are scary."

We sip our soup in peaceful silence until Edna pipes up: "Ate Senya said we could visit her later. She's making mais con hielo."

"Oh," I say. For a second I don't know what I'm reacting to. I'm glad Senya's all right—crazy ex-boyfriends are the stuff of too many fucked-up homicide cases. But it's weird she's inviting me. She was so condescending yesterday, or maybe I was just too sensitive? There's something about her patient look that makes me guilty.

"So let's go?"

"Umm." I wonder whether I can use studying as an excuse, but Edna blinks hugely at me. We have such little time left together.

"It's *mais con hielo,*" she pleads.

"Okay, okay." Honestly, it's not just elders I can't say no to.

On our way to Mang Okat's, I inspect the ground, both hoping and not hoping to find proof of last night's encounter. There's vomit at some point, but in daylight, the color is more watermelon pink, nothing like blood at all. There are no hairballs. Edna skips over the trail of ants creeping across the mess, engrossed in her tale about the dog they temporarily adopted that died from kidney stones. I make affirming noises as I fall into step next to her. If she notices nothing weird, then neither do I.

❀

Senya beams at us when we arrive. She seems happy about something, but all she does is hand us knives so we can all help crush ice in plastic cups. It's a burning day; the ice is already half-melted by the time we pour condensed milk and corn kernels into it. We don't talk much, sitting on the steps of her house, eating our frozen treats. For a moment I act ridiculous, closing my eyes. I don't hear cars or smell pollution or feel like someone's about to snatch my phone out of my pocket. The province feels peaceful, otherworldly, and I'm glad it's not Manila. I'm glad the freeways don't extend to here; I'm glad I have no urge to take a selfie with my dessert and give it the appropriate hashtag.

Edna sings a song in Ilocano. Aling Dinday used to sing that song for me and my cousins, when we were small and didn't want to take our siesta or get in the bath. Senya joins in during the chorus, winding her hair into a braid over her shoulder. I hum along but awkwardly get some notes wrong.

"Your Nanay used to sing this for me," I tell Edna. "Though I never knew what it was about."

She shrugs. "Some kinda love song."

"The worst kind," Senya says. "The singer wants to die because they're so lovesick."

"Oh, I thought it was about the moon!"

"Well, they're singing *to* the moon."

Mang Okat emerges from the trees blocking our view of the path. We're standing to greet him when he shouts for help. He's dragging something—someone.

I get to him first and let him drape the arm of the person he's carrying over my shoulders. I don't ask, just move. Senya and Edna watch as we climb the short steps and deposit the body on Mang Okat's narrow wooden bed. The man stirs, moans. There are open sores on his cheeks and neck, down both arms and over his chest:

cuts and scrapes that gleam raw, wet and weeping. His wounds are all colors, a grisly sunburst spectrum of red-yellow-orange-purple-black, already graying at the edges.

Mang Okat grabs a bottle off his workbench, full of wood chips and herbs suspended in oil. There are three tiny crosses attached to the bottle's base. He twists it open, and the potent smell of rum leaks out. He pours the liquid over the man's chest, smearing it into the wounds. The patient makes a gargling noise, voice thick with pain.

"Tay, do you need help?" Senya asks.

Mang Okat shakes his head. His eyes linger on Senya's, then flit to mine, but I can't decipher the look in them. "I think you girls should go."

It takes an effort to walk away. I can't tear my eyes from the sight of the man. The smell of his skin, warm and slick with fluid from his wounds, hangs heavy in my nose. There are weeping sores even on the soles of his feet. Before turning completely, I see a black bug crawl—out of his wound, or next to it?

"Ate Macky," Edna calls. I sprint down the steps.

We reach the river. I lean over the bank, knees against my chest, breathing deeply. I can feel sticky patches on my arm where I made contact with his lesions; my shirt is stained in parts. I stare at the water, watch my reflection stare back.

"Who was it?" Edna asks.

"I couldn't tell," Senya says. I turn to look at her. She sits cross-legged, fingers twiddling the grass. "His face was messed up. Tay's gonna use up a lot of strength, trying to fix that curse."

"Curse?" I stand. "That was a curse? It looks like he got—*I don't know*—sliced by tons of invisible knives! What even *were* those wounds?"

Edna and Senya look at each other, then at me, almost pityingly.

"A mambabarang did it," Senya says. "I guess you wouldn't encounter one in Manila."

"A what? What the fuck is that?"

"They curse people," Edna answers. I shouldn't swear around kids, but she doesn't seem to care. She's ripping up blades of grass, shredding them into pieces with her hands. "They're like . . . the opposite of Mang Okat. You can bring them money, or things they want, and they'll curse your enemies. Or sometimes they'll curse people to get back at them for something." She won't look at me as she says this.

"You're not scared?"

Edna shrugs. Her face shows an emotion I haven't seen from her 'til now: pity tinged with judgement. Her "smart" Ate Macky knows nothing. "If you don't do anything wrong, they won't get you."

"What the hell? There's someone like that in the village and you just—haven't they tried catching the person? Shouldn't they?"

"The mambabarang won't get caught," Senya says. Her gentle voice makes me feel like I'm acting hysterical. "It's not like there's only one. If they were found out, the village would murder them, or send them away. So they're careful. They won't let others talk."

I remember how the man yesterday glared. It wasn't only rage, but a kind of fear, in his expression. *What the fuck did you do?* he asked. He was asking *me*.

It's true I warned him. That I'd wanted him restrained somehow. But I only meant my family name. I don't *know* how to place a curse on someone; I wouldn't ever want to.

"It's not me," I say, without thinking.

Silence. Then Senya bursts out laughing, doubled over, shrill and gasping. It's the loudest sound I've ever heard her make. Her laughter makes me feel ridiculous, but I'm relieved in a way: if she thinks it's impossible, it must be. I had nothing to do with it.

"Of course not, Miss Macky," she says. "You'll use the law instead, right?"

I stare at her, mouth open. My hand trembles—do I want to hit her? Or cover my face? Edna gazes at the river, neutrally.

"You wouldn't do a cruel thing like that," Senya continues, back to her soft voice, like something escaping a dream. The words seem kind, but her eyes tell a different story: *you wouldn't dare, and anyway, why would you ever need to?*

I take a bath as soon as I get home. Since it's not my usual time Aling Dinday hasn't been able to heat up any water; she makes a fuss, saying it won't take long, but I assure her I don't mind. The cold water wakes me up, makes me angry. *It's a feeling,* I think. *At least.*

I stare at the tiles, unseeing, running soap over my body. I keep wondering if I've ever wanted anything, if I've ever had to fight for anything. I don't notice the bug until it skitters up my calf, the brush of its legs against my skin nightmarish.

It's huge. I shriek. I fling my leg out, slap it away with my hand, slippery with soap. Half-crushed, it tries to crawl away; I waste a whole tabo of water drowning it, heart pounding as it swirls into the drain. I don't know whether I've killed it or helped it escape.

"Macky?" Aling Dinday calls from beyond the door, summoned by my abortive scream. "What was that?"

"Nothing," I reply, a trembling hand against my chest. "Just a bug."

Tito Benjo and I eat in the carinderia that evening. We do this once or twice a week, so Aling Dinday can have a break from cooking our dinner. I nudge stewed goat around on my plate, while Tito Benjo debates basketball with three manongs in a nearby table. I can't eat or I'll be sick. I'm about to ask if I can go home when Edna crashes into our table, tears streaked across her face. "Ate Macky! Governor! Itay—Itay is—"

We run, with Tito Benjo puffing behind us. Edna stops on the edge of our farm. The moon is so bright, I don't need another light to know that there's blood everywhere. I smell it rising from the grass; when I kneel down beside Aling Dinday, sobbing as she cradles Mang Edgar in her lap, I feel it, slick against my knees.

"Who—" I ask.

"We don't know. He went out to buy some beer. When he didn't come home—" Edna can't continue.

"I'll get the car," Tito Benjo says, voice pinched. He charges off.

"Manang," I say, crouching next to Aling Dinday. "Breathe. It's okay. He'll be okay." It's irresponsible to say that, when we don't know what kind of injury he has, which weapon was used. I grip one of her shoulders; with my other hand, I touch Mang Edgar's wrist. There's a faint pulse running through it. He makes a breathy, croaking sound—hope flares treacherously in my chest.

"Who did it?" Aling Dinday sobs. "Why? *Why?*"

Someone drunk. With a hot temper. Looking for trouble. Someone who felt like a free beer. A stranger from out of town. A stranger in one's own town, with a grudge. What if they were trying to get back for something?

"Edna! Manang!" Senya comes running down the road, with Mang Okat behind her. When they reach us, Mang Okat kneels across from me, and Senya pulls Edna into her arms. "We got your text. What *happened?*"

"Manong, manong, please," Aling Dinday breathes, clutching Mang Okat's hand. Her voice wobbles.

Mang Okat rubs Mang Edgar's forehead, his lips, his shoulders. "He needs a hospital," Mang Okat says, sounding defeated. "This isn't something my healing will work on."

Aling Dinday draws a heavy breath, as Tito Benjo's car comes up the road. He brings it as close as he can, then jumps out. Carefully, he and Mang Okat lift Mang Edgar into the car. Aling Dinday wipes her eyes and climbs in after them.

"You stay and watch Edna," Tito Benjo says. "It could be robbers. Lock up the house."

I nod, knees and fingers wet with blood, shaking, shaken.

❖

Senya calls the police. They come—the barangay captain and one barangay tanod, both of them in pambahay. They take notes and ask questions, inspect the ground cursorily, flashlights shining on the wrecked grass. They assure us they'll drive around town for suspicious individuals—tonight, and again tomorrow. *Medyo mahirap lang kung walang witness. Pasensiya na po, ma'am.* That last toward me. I give them my number, ask them to please call if they find anything. Edna is silent, unlike herself. Senya smoothes Edna's hair, murmuring, but even she has to leave eventually.

"Please keep me updated," Senya says. Edna and I lock up the gate behind her. We stop by Edna's house so she can grab her toothbrush and a saggy little doll named Kokoy. When we get to the main house, I set all the locks on the doors, and check the windows too.

I call Tito Benjo. The first two times he doesn't pick up. The third time it's choppy because of bad signal, but I manage to make out that they're at the ER. "I'll call you with updates," he says tersely.

I turn on the TV, but neither of us care to watch. I tell Edna it'll be all right, that the hospital isn't too far, Mang Edgar's super strong—but that last just gets her crying again. Eventually I give up and say we should go sleep. It'll make time go faster. Edna doesn't protest. She curls up beside me on my bed, Kokoy ensconced in her arms, tears streaming out of her eyes. I wrap my arms around her narrow shoulders.

"Ate Macky," Edna murmurs. I tense, not wanting to say the wrong thing. "We have to find out who did it."

"Yes. Shhh, shh. It's going to be okay." I remember the leisurely way the policeman crouched, curious but not urgent.

"We have to make them sorry," she adds. The words should be menacing but there's no heat to them. She's merely saying what she wants, like a kid. *Because she is a kid.*

"Yes." But if the police don't find anything, what recourse do we have?

"You'll help, Ate Macky?"

"Of course." When Tito Benjo returns, he'll certainly complain to other officials.

"Promise?"

"Promise." I still don't understand what happened. It's not that Mang Edgar wouldn't hurt a fly—I think that, but I don't *know* that. I don't know anyone in this village, really. I'm removed from how they live, sheltered in this house; nothing touches me. I get to have no fear. I will *always* get to have no fear. "Go to sleep," I say, 'cause I'm good at that: looking away, letting someone else solve things. "We'll hear from them in the morning."

Edna goes quiet. I don't know if she's asleep or not. Images keep flashing in my mind: Mang Edgar tending goats, his missing front tooth, how troubled he was by my attempts to help Edna weed the garden. How I thought being here meant he was safe—we were all safe, with Tito Benjo in town and my family's name like a talisman.

It wasn't a curse. Mang Okat had said so. So who would want to hurt him? Why?

Does there need to be a reason?

If you wait too long you lose too much.

How easily you can hold death in your hands. How there can be no consequences. Words on a page or judgement handed from on high seem so pathetic. I pull my blanket up to my chin; helplessness, at least, can't follow me into sleep.

"Ate Macky."

I startle awake. Edna is crouched by the bed, her fingers on my arm. It's still dark. Outside our window the moon hovers, bloated, dull silver.

"What is it?"

"Come on." Edna stands. "We've got to hurry." She starts out the door.

I trip out of bed, pull on my slippers. Edna seems to vibrate with energy as I undo and redo all the locks on the main door. She walks briskly down the path, waits as I open the gate, but doesn't continue to the street like I expect. Instead, she crosses the goat fields, past rows of tito's kalamansi and sticky corn, right into a thicket of trees—the forest beyond our farm.

I'm afraid I'll lose her in the darkness. There's no path, but Edna walks on surely, steadily. I have to hold my hands out to keep from tripping on roots or getting scratched by branches. I don't know how long we continue like that; I still half feel like I'm dreaming.

Eventually I see a dim fire—the glow of several candles, beneath a balete tree, its gnarled roots stringing to the ground, splayed against the soil. I blink to focus. Someone is kneeling before the candles, wearing a sky blue skirt, hair wild over both shoulders.

She sees us and grins. Her eyes are half-lidded, glazed with a strange ecstasy. Edna sits cross-legged on the ground. She looks up at me, eyes prompting. I'm shaking slightly, but I sit next to her.

Senya holds out her hand. There are fat beetles on it, the same kind I'd seen in her house. The revulsion in me is so strong that I gag. She skims their shells with one finger, makes a clucking sound in the back of her throat. Then she drops them onto her lap. They rove around in lazy circles. She withdraws something from her shirt pocket: a needle, with white thread running through it, ghostly in the moonlight.

She picks up a bug and pierces it with the thread. My hands curl into fists; my fingers dig painfully into my palms. Senya pierces the bug, again and again. The woods are silent, but with each movement of Senya's stabbing hand screaming erupts in my skull. Screaming, laughter, crying, screeching. Worse than the worst headache. My breath comes in sharp fragments; I touch the skin beneath one ear, expecting to find blood.

She does this to two other bugs, then sets them down on the floor. Instead of curling up or twitching to death, the bugs appear unharmed. They begin moving in a line, pale thread strung between their black bodies, and that's when I notice the cloth doll lying next to the candles. It looks like Kokoy, only smaller.

The bugs burrow their way into it. Senya watches, hands folded in her lap. The doll flops back and forth as the bugs tear their way through it. Then, from the same holes they bore in, the bugs burrow their way out. Senya whispers to them—or to us, or to the candle flames?—and their black shapes scuttle into the darkness, thread trailing behind. The sounds in my head slowly die away.

Senya sighs. She looks drained, the bags under her eyes alarming, but her mouth curves into a peaceful smile. Edna stretches her hand toward Senya, and Senya takes it. After a moment, Edna reaches her other hand to me, and I reach for Senya's, closing the circle. Their fingers are slim and cool in my grasp.

I witness the fierce concentration in Edna's face, the dreamy anticipation in Senya's, so different from how she is during the day. For a few seconds Senya's eyes meet mine and she nods at the maimed doll. *What do you think, Miss Macky? Our way.*

Like a secret offered up. Locked beneath my tongue. A power I can't understand, that I give myself to because it's the least I can do. I promised—which means, until the end, I'm not sure the choice is my own.

We stay like that, waiting in the dark, while the candles burn and darkness twists and seethes around us. The peaceful town with its unremarkable terrors, asleep. It feels like a long time before the screaming starts, but it could have been mere minutes. In a village this small, every sound is amplified.

Tears are running down Edna's face. She squeezes my hand tighter, the fury in her eyes matched only by the serenity of Senya's smile.

I look down at my feet. I imagine the skin along my veins cracking apart, gushing with blood; dark beetles crawling out, making their way up my ankles, my knees, eating into my belly. Pouring out of me, trailing my guts with them, slick with blood. I think of the man holding his knife towards Senya. Mang Edgar in the goat field, singing to himself: a song for the moon, about love and death; a song Aling Dinday probably sings to him, teasingly, swaying her hips, like she did to me, as a kid. Like she probably still does for Edna.

I curl my toes and hold their hands, and we wait until the screams stop. We wait until we are satisfied.

My shirt is crusty when I wake up, from Edna's tears and snot. She's rolled away from me, and is facing the wall. I can't remember when we came back. I'm not sure we ever left.

I fumble for my phone. No messages. I hold it outside the window, trying to get a signal. After a few moments, there's a ping: *Tell Edna Mang Edgar will make it. Tks.*

Tito Benjo comes home that morning, and charges off to barangay hall after a quick breakfast. Aling Dinday and Mang Edgar are back a day later, after the village has found and buried the bastard that did it. He's a stranger, not from this barangay, or the next one. Tito Benjo seethes that this wouldn't have happened if he were still governor. We'll never learn the motive, if there was one at all.

Mang Edgar's head is heavily bandaged, but his laughter when he sees Edna is warm and bright as ever.

I stop by Mang Okat's house my last day in town. Edna's sulking, but I've promised to make it up to her by bringing a souvenir from Manila next time. Christmas seems more likely than summer, especially if Tito Benjo decides to host. With luck, I'll be in law school by then. I wonder if it will mean more to me.

I find Mang Okat and Senya on the steps, shelling boiled peanuts.

"I'm heading back to Manila tonight. Manong, thank you again for your help the other day."

"No more headaches?"

"None. No patients today?"

Mang Okat shakes his head, then stands. "That's right—I have something for you!" He enters his house and rummages around his bottles.

Senya holds out a handful of shelled peanuts.

"No, thank you," I say.

"Ready for your test?"

"Sort of. I'll feel better when I take it. At least it'll be over."

She laughs as Mang Okat emerges and hands me a tiny bottle, filled with oil. "Just rub a bit of this on your head when it hurts," he says.

"Thank you, manong." As I fumble my pocket he waves his hand: *don't bother.*

"Just take it," Senya says—to me this time. She sets aside her bowl of peanuts, stands, and gives me a quick, awkward hug. "Good luck."

"Thanks."

I'm halfway down the road when I turn back to them, bottle clutched in my hand.

Senya gives me a small smile and a wave. I wave back. Something crawls up the side of my neck, perching behind my ear. I pinch it between my fingers, hold it away, let it drop to the ground. I see, briefly, the black thread trailing from its body, before it scuttles off to safety.

"I want to know the fires your hands bring—"
— *Having Been Cast, Eve Implores,* by Barbara Jane Reyes

Tonight, as in every night, she smiles when the door opens. Her arms loop over your neck; she leans in and rests her head against your cheek. She looks down at the basket between you. "Is this for me?"

She already knows the answer, but: "Yes, my jewel."

It's four golden mangoes this time, and a bunch of lakatan bananas, stubby and sweet. She lifts a mango to a patch of moonlight, turning it pale silver. "From who?"

"Aba Ignayon."

"Which one is he?"

"The one with a very square chin. His head is like a box."

She laughs; her laughter soothes the knot tightening in your chest. As her sixteenth birthday nears, the number of suitors grows by the day. They come from farther lands, ever distant shores. The gifts they bring grow more numerous, more elaborate. They are given audience for an afternoon, discussing with her parents. Sometimes they are blindfolded and taken to a dark room, where they kneel, waiting in agony, 'til at last they are permitted a glimpse. You sit with Anyag on the other side of the wall, watching her hold her laughter while she carefully pushes her smallest finger through a hole cut into the wood. There is usually a sharp intake of breath on the other side. Then you both wait, quavering, until at last a door clicks shut, and you fall over each other, erupting in giggles.

Part of your pain comes from not knowing what will happen when she marries. Will she stay here and become a lady of the village? Or will she leave with him, for some faraway place where you can no longer be part of her life? These thoughts haunt you more than you care to admit. To distract yourself, you inspect her weaving progress for the week, the colorful tapestry only begun: the impression of a woman, bare-shouldered.

"A sirena?"

"Mm-hmm." She takes a banana and peels it. "I dreamt of one," she says. "She sang the song of Buyi-Lahin, so sweetly. While the men rowed close in their boats . . ."

"Dreaming of men now?"

She shrugs, talks while chewing. "And why not? They're only people. You *know* the only man I've ever seen is my father, so I have to imagine. Anyway they're no different than women, besides what is between their legs." She snickers. To her, men's bodies are funny. She has never had reason to fear them, of course, which is a relief. But that could all change, one day not too far from now. You decide her curiosity is a good thing. It might make the wedding night easier. She continues: "It was strange; in my dream, Buyi-Lahin was no man, but a woman without hair, who rode a steed of dark copper . . ."

While she recounts her dream, you gather the materials for bathing: clean clothes, a smooth stone to polish her feet and elbows, coconut milk for her hair, salt crystals, and a midnight cloth to shield her from view, even if no one dares come by the river, lest they be put to death for straying eyes. You would hold the knife yourself, slit their throat, pluck their eyeballs, partly because it is your duty: she is your handiwork as much as her family's. And partly because you love her, despite all your efforts not to.

She doesn't make it easy, but you're good at difficult things.

"Shall we bathe, then?"

She nods and drapes a veil over her head. You follow her down the steps of her tower, into the quiet night outside.

When your mother was a girl, there were still two moons. Like Bathala's eyes, she would say, working a long blade over her fire. You always imagine Mother the same way: sweat shining on her brow, curls plastered against her neck and cheeks, sparks dancing at her elbows. At her throat glints the amulet you now wear. On her sturdy neck, it was more like a choker, the bright pendant reflecting forge fire. *What a delight it was, to look up and see them both there, an assurance that everything was safe; that we had not been forgotten by the gods.*

And? What happened?

And one night, when the two moons were glowing bright and beautiful, it came for them: the Moon-Eater, rising out of the ocean, groaning as it ascended over the land. The trees shook and snapped in the force from its beating wings. It had rows and rows of silver teeth, each one as big as the boulders lining the caves of Aman Puli. Its ribbon-like tail was serrated at the edge—here, mother holds up the knife she is sharpening, ridges flashing in incandescent light—*and it lifted in a tremulous zigzag, out of the water. When it flickered, a shower of saltwater fell on our rice paddies, our homes. For days after everything smelled of salted fish. Our skin, our hair. Our hands.*

You shudder at the idea of a mouth so large it could swallow ten of you in one go.

It rose, and rose. It was every color. We stood transfixed—unable to move, unable to stop it. It sank its jaws into one of our moons, which disappeared down its throat. We saw the shape of our moon roll down the length of the monster's endless body, shining through those giant scales, while the monster laughed—its laugh like a roar—for it had taken something precious from the children of the earth, and it was delicious: our moon, our suffering. Its great orange eyes trained on the next moon . . .

"Our moon," you breathe, and look outside the window, even if it is daytime.

Yes, the moon that remains with us. For just as soon as it had eaten the other moon, the beast could already feel it melting away, like the six it had swallowed in your ancestors' times . . . Its hunger was insatiable, and our moons were never meant to last outside the sky. It sank its teeth into our last, final moon, and our hearts lurched in our chests, for we would soon be cast into darkness every sundown . . .

And then, three things happened at once. The village priestesses, your great-aunts among them, took up a chant. Their voices, straining through panic, rose like cutting knives, and the pitch made the bakunawa blanch, the great moon bobbing out of its jaws. The village warriors began to pitch their spears at the beast. Driven by the chanting, some spears found their mark and pierced the bakunawa's side. But what little effect it had! The bakunawa merely roared at us, a sound that still rings inside me today (here, her eyes water, though whether it is from the rising smoke or the memory of that cursed night, you know not. She blinks the tears away because her hands are grimy, and continues). *What made it stop was not the spears or the magic, but the high, clear voice of Hugan-an, who emerged from her house, to everyone's shock.*

Hugan-an, our precious jewel. Hugan-an of fabled beauty. It was the first time any of us had seen her—those not of her family. For she was a binukot, protected from birth, shielded from view, in order to be as pure and unstained a gift for one suitor most worthy . . .

She sang a song we did not recognize, with words that she was making up, words that were not handed from our ancestors: leave the moon be, leave my people be, and I will be your bride, Moon-Eater, if it pleases thee. She walked on the sand toward the shoreline, and the priestesses stopped banging on the gongs and kulintang, and held their breath. Her father ran from his house and screamed for her to return. But she was so sure, she was unyielding.

The moon emerged from the serpent's mouth, fixed itself in the sky, shining brightly, while he dove and took Hugan-an in his jaws . . .

Like the moons, she sparkled as she disappeared down its throat. The beast fled back into the sea. We had finally learned the secret of keeping our moons alive, after he had already taken six. And he may never take another, so long as she is his bride . . .

But how her father sobbed! Despite everything the village gave him, nothing could ever make up for that sacrifice, and he died of heartbreak not long after.

She stops working the blade, and sets the polished steel down. "I pray it does not happen in your lifetime," Mother says. She is speaking about the return of the Moon-Eater, and the loss of a binukot. Having completed her work for the afternoon, she reaches out to you. Neither of you know that in just a few months, she will be dead from a blood illness. Your living relatives will barter you for coin, and you will become a servant at the house of one such jewel. You nod and press your head against her chest, breathing in her smell: smoke, comfort, a sorrow that has never left.

You help Anyag shed her clothes by the river: undoing the pearled clasps of her top, first, then the hooks of her skirt, the soft woven undergarments. You set them aside on the grass while she removes her earrings, the clips in her hair, the necklace with two thin braids of gold. Jewelry from her family—she is not allowed to wear gifts from her suitors, not yet. Her mother keeps such offerings in trays, stacked in a dining-hall cupboard. Pearls the size of lanzones, green gems that mimic the eternal depths of the ocean, ivory cut into intricate starscapes. And letters, love poems, the most delightful or daring of which you read to her in the evenings. It's a curious game: you choose the words you think will make her fall in love with the suitors you like best (how can you not judge, even knowing it isn't your place?). You read them to her as sweetly as you can, but lightly, too. Your guilt and shame coalesce with envy, but you never let it leak through your voice.

"I liked that one," she says sometimes. Sometimes, she says nothing.

Sometimes, she smiles at you in wonder, and something skitters under your skin, a fey creature with too many legs.

What if you were to write her a letter of your own, just to tell her how you feel? No one would know. But you cannot bring yourself to do it. What use would it be, even if she turned to you after and said, *I liked that one*?

You can't fall in love with your jewel. You have always known it, but never dreamed it would be a problem. Every time you think you've managed to escape your feelings, they flood back. A smile, a look, a sharp word: needles to the heart, as sharp and biting as if you'd been actually stung. You would tell her to stop doing that to you, but she doesn't mean it, isn't even aware of it. You know her as no one else does, and this makes you ashamed; this knowledge should not make you love her.

Anyag wades into the river. "Gah!" she says. "It's cold."

"You always say that." You unfurl the cloth and step into the river, up to your ankles, and wait.

After a moment, she says, "Sing for me?"

"Anyag . . ."

"I'm bored."

"Only if it's a duet, then." You're toying with your own feelings, pushing the boundaries of what you can bear. You recklessly start the song about three stupid monkeys splashing in the river, and the turtle that outsmarts them all. Anyag joins in, playing the high-pitched parts of the baby monkey and the grumbling murmurs of the turtle. After the last verse, you laugh, expecting her to join in. There's a pause that makes your heart skip—then she finally does.

"That song never gets old, does it? We've been singing it for years." She pokes you through the cloth. "I'm done."

You wrap the cloth around her. "Some things never change."

"Yes. Some things stay the same for a long, long time." She sighs. There it is: from the moment she said *I'm bored,* you were expecting this. What a longing she must have, to see more of the world, instead of being locked away. No sun, no other humans, no freedom to wander her own village, except at night, with you keeping watch.

Her cage a tower, and you its guard—or is it dragon, fending off any who come to lure her out?

It's your duty, but sometimes you wonder how much damage you're actually inflicting. You understand why she'd want more than this, so you say: "Things will change, soon enough. Your presentation is only a few weeks away. I am certain your future husband will show you more of the world."

"True," she says. There are countless things unsaid in that *true.* You string them together in your mind: excitement, eagerness, resignation. A thread of wistfulness—no, that's only your own hope manifesting. Without warning, she asks: "Will my marriage make you happy?"

"Your happiness is my happiness."

"That's not an answer, Amira." She sounds a bit scolding, and you laugh and tell her it's true, ignoring how your heart aches. Why does it feel as if both of you are speaking in code tonight?

She dresses herself while you wash her garments. For reasons you cannot fathom there's a nervous taint to the air between you as there has never been before. Then a thought strikes you: *she knows.* She knows how you feel, your desires like poison, and she does not know what to do with this knowledge. How to break your heart carefully. How to tell you that what you want is wrong: not only because you are both women, and you are a servant, but most importantly because she does not feel the same. *It doesn't matter,* you think desperately, while you twist the cloth to let out water. *It changes nothing! Just ignore me.* You wish she would understand that you know your own foolishness and want nothing more. Your heart pounds loud enough to drive moon-eaters away.

When she speaks next, however, it's with her usual nonchalance. "Will you teach me something new tonight?"

You feel your body unspooling from lost tension. "You mean the last verse of the *Twenty-two Laments of Matang-ayon?*"

"No! You know what I mean."

She should really be practicing her dancing and singing—she always forgets that last verse, no matter what you do. But ever since you made the mistake of teaching her the sword arts years ago, she has been preoccupied with learning nothing else. As with everything, you cannot say no. That first time, she plucked the dagger from your scabbard, and held it aloft in her fingers, like it was just another offering of fruit. Her eyes grew bright with the possibility of acquiring something that opposed tenderness. Something that let her be powerful rather than delicate. Respected, rather than revered.

You're skilled at this, aren't you? You had never shown her, not 'til then. But you are the blacksmith's daughter, and even after your mother's passing, you continued to train with the village warriors. Someday, when you are no longer in the service of Anyag, you plan to join them. And there perhaps find another girl with bright eyes, who can sing silly songs with you, who can actually be yours, if only in secret.

This, at least, is familiar territory. "Of course," you say. But not out here, where someone might see. She keeps her blade in her fruit bowl, under the mangoes and bananas, the one sweetness you alone can offer: self-protection, even with the hope that she never has to use it.

Anyag has a talent for the blade. It might be her quick steps from years of dancing, or the creativity born of being a captive. Tonight she gets in close enough that you strike her on the hip without thinking. She claps her hand to her mouth instantly, muffling a cry. You grip your weapon and crouch next to her, cursing yourself and the tight confines in which you spar. Her skin is hot to the touch. She makes a sound like "Tsst!" through her teeth, then immediately says, "Don't. Apologize."

"But it will bruise . . ."

"No one will see." She touches your cheek, unaware how you melt. "I'm glad you're taking me seriously."

"I always do," you answer, mock offended. She meets your gaze. *Look away,* you plead silently, but she does not. In the end, you're the one that drops your head; she removes her fingers from your face.

The next day you blunt the blades you use to spar. A bruise you can cover; a gash would be too much.

There is only one other binukot in your village, and she was married two summers ago—three days after her presentation—thus rescinding her status. Since then the village has hummed with anticipation for Anyag's own coming-out. It is strange that the person you know best in the world is spoken of with such wonder.

I've heard that her hair is darker than black, for it has never seen the sun . . .

Her skin pale as the sand on the shores of Aman Puli . . .

When she dances it must be like a diwata gracing our earth . . .

They look to you, hungry for a tale, some inclination that they are right. You could spin so many threads for them from memory; you wouldn't even need embellishments. But part of your duty is silence, keeping her a desirable mystery. "She is learning her epics well," you say. You don't add: her smile is like cool water after a burning day; her touch a suffering the skin yearns for anyway. You will love her from the moment you lay eyes on her, but even then, not half as much as I do.

You have never spoken to the apid of the other girl. Freed, now, from her bonds, she tends to her family's farm of root crops. You have sometimes thought of things you would like to ask her: Did it hurt, when you said goodbye? Do you ever see her, now that she lives in the home of Seryong Baniig? Do you miss those days of servitude, teaching her poems and brushing her hair, or are you glad they are over? Does your existence now bring you peace?

You fear that her answers will hurt. Not knowing, you are sure, hurts less.

A week before Anyag's presentation, a nobleman sails into town, his ornate boat calmly docking on the beach. He proceeds to your master's house, standing by the gate with a cool-eyed confidence that hushes the world around him. He has no attendants, which is odd despite your village's current peacekeeping policies. His robe is a deep blue threaded with silver, large sequins all down the sleeves and back, glinting fiercely in the sunlight. His chin is sharp as cut glass, and his thin lips curl in a resting smirk. There is no doubt what he has come for.

His name is Lisoryo, and he has traveled from far away to make his intentions known.

It's a hot day when he arrives, and everyone melts in his presence. The other servants preen while they bring him chilled calamansi juice and boiled corn, shaved into a bowl and topped with grated coconut. Before dining, he rolls back his sleeves; your eyes trace the delicate pattern of his tattoos, finely drawn scales from his elbows to his wrists. He looks up and catches your gaze, and your throat tightens. The lady of the house smiles with her mouth slightly open, so that he can see the gold in her teeth. The master of the house refuses to speak directly with him, as he does every other suitor, but studies the dowry the man has brought in a large wooden chest: six globes the color of no gem you have ever seen, a pearlescent white with shades of gray, beautiful enough to make the heart ache.

"What are they?" Anyag's mother asks.

"Crystals," he answers. His voice matches his face: quiet, smooth, with a resonance that gets into your bones. "They were bespelled by a witch in the southern sea, whom I traveled a great distance to barter with. I assure you that it would be impossible to find others like them. During the day they are merely beautiful, but at night they give off enough light to brighten the whole village. Of course, I would need your daughter's hand to prove this." He shuts the chest, with a meaningful snap.

You are called to introduce yourself, and to receive his letter for Anyag. There is not a trace of sweat on him despite the blistering sunlight filtering everywhere. You kneel, your head bent, until he asks you to show your face. A bead of sweat crawls from your hairline to your chin, and his eyes follow it languidly.

"What is your name?"

"Amira, sir."

"Amira. But you are only a child yourself. Can you polish a jewel and make her sparkle, being so young?" His eyes are the midnight black of the ocean when there is no starlight. Anyag would find them very poetic.

"I descended from a family of smiths and priestesses. We were poor, but I learned to sing the epics before I could speak, and I have sought to enrich my jewel by being her dearest friend."

"Her *dearest* friend." He seems to savor the sound of his own tongue. "How well does your jewel recite her epics, Amira?"

You should lie. *Terribly. Her voice breaks above a certain note, and she always forgets her last verse.*

"Very well, sir."

"I look forward to hearing her, then." He holds out a letter, which you take. His nails are very long, filed nearly to a knifepoint. It must be a foreign custom. This close, you can sense strong magic on him, but not like that of your village, the soil and storms you carry in your blood. His magic is deeper, scavenged from the depths of places you've never trespassed, with edges of salt. You tuck the letter into your belt, assure him that Anyag shall read it tonight, and withdraw to a corner of the room, where you wait for the visit to end. It lasts forever, while he describes his realm, his great conquests there, how Anyag will live like a princess beside him, and have her every dream fulfilled. He will stay until her presentation, and he will not back down.

When he finally stands to leave, his eyes find yours again. He smiles, briefly, holding your gaze. For a moment, it feels like you are drowning, as you choke on air, on the knowledge that you've lost.

❁

Not that she is a prize to be won. The trouble is, you can't help thinking of her as *yours*—and yourself as hers. If only you could erase all your memories together. She calls you her best friend, months after you start looking after her. Her last maid, a soft and simple older woman, was let go after she was found with child. Someone your age might be a better companion, so long as you can keep her out of trouble. You are nine and she is seven. Your hands are rough and calloused, and hers are soft as a newborn's. Your hair is short and curly like your mother's, while hers comes down to her waist in one shimmering sheet, which she constantly twists into knots.

You are an orphan and have no home, but you come from good blood—despite the disease, of course, but at least it is not transmittable. Your last living great-aunt has you stand before the lord and lady and recite the *Twenty-two Laments of Matang-ayon,* and then display the first six movements of Soaring Eagle, Claws Outstretched. Afterward they speak to her in quiet tones and hand her a cloth bag that tinkles. They take you in, for your knowledge of blades and epics both; you are promised freedom after Anyag's presentation, with enough gold to reopen your mother's forge if you wish. She is a binukot and has no other friends; until her partner is chosen she is to remain in her tower, never to see the sun. She may as well be an orphan: even her parents do not visit her unless necessary. You are lonely and she is lonely, mirrors to each other, as you walk the same black pool of wondering why you exist.

You do not like her then, but you understand duty. Looking after Anyag is a distraction you can direct all your efforts to, numbing enough that you don't have to think about loss.

"Amira? Why do you call me your jewel?" In the candlelight her eyes are luminous. She is missing one of her front teeth. You are writing out an epic poem together, and she is already bored.

"Because that's what you are." Stories are easy, and they give life order, a piece of driftwood to cling to in the storm of grief. But even stories must be accurate. "Because that's what you must be, for you are a binukot."

"So what are you?"

You blink in surprise. No one has shown this much interest in you, not since Mother.

"Me? I'm your . . . hmm. I teach you what I know. I stay with you, and protect you from bad things."

She pokes her tongue through the gap in her teeth. "Hmm. Sword," she says.

"What?"

"You're my sword, then. I am your jewel, and you are my sword." It is so simple and easy; it must be true. "Amira, my sword," she repeats, sing-song, while reaching for your hand. Twining her fingers in yours, you have a feeling of finding purchase on land at last. Belonging, if not to this fine house, than at least to this room, this girl.

In the years that follow those words become your guide. The promise you will keep until you can keep it no longer. The ache you carry every time you are near her and not.

"What's wrong?" she asks, seconds after opening the door. You curse how easily she can read you.

"It was very hot today. I couldn't train like I wanted." To distract her, you take the letter from your basket and hold it up. "A new suitor came, from far away. This is for you."

"Did you not like him?"

What you think doesn't matter. You did not miss the long look your lord and lady exchanged, after he left; how your master touched his wife's arm, while she bent and murmured how this suitor lived so far away. He embraced her, and said perhaps that was for the best. "He brought a beautiful dowry—magic crystals the like of which I'd never seen. And he had fine robes, and the most intricate tattoos, like fish scales on his forearms." You start laying out dinner: rice porridge with two teaspoons of salted fish, a lighter meal for this final week that the lady insists on, so that Anyag may appear irresistibly slim at the time of her presentation. Anyag used to complain, but does no longer. She understands inevitability.

You try not to watch her reading the letter, as you pour out mint tea, then slice a mango lengthwise and crosswise.

She folds it, frowning. The moon tonight is faint; in the faded candlelight you can't tell if she is blushing or not.

Silence gnaws holes into the air until you ask: "What did you think?"

She glances at you, and you are chilled by her look—piercingly remote, as haughty as she must be on her presentation day. Already not yours. But she was never yours.

"What does it matter to you, what I think?"

You could say nothing, but she has asked you a question, and in delivering that look it's as if Anyag has reminded you of your place, which she has not done except in the rarest of moments. Suddenly you are seized with a desire to end everything, tonight. If you break your own heart, at least no one else has that option: not the gorgeous Lisoryo, or the lord and lady, or Anyag herself. You tip your head in apology. "I shouldn't have asked. It does not concern me."

"Right." Anyag exhales, then puts the letter away and takes her seat for dinner, not looking at you. You eat together in stony silence. This is safer. If she is angry, the next week will be easier—saying goodbye, parting ways. You are thinking so hard about what you'll do once the presentation is over that you almost don't hear her saying: "I'm your shackle. I keep you bound here, and it makes you suffer. You think I haven't noticed, how you drag your feet around me, how your eyes are always blank and faraway? How you don't *talk* to me anymore?" She scrapes her spoon around her bowl, voice thin. "I know you can't wait for this to be over. But I wish you could still pretend to care about me, at least until then."

Your lips part, through your shock. "I *do* care—"

"Because you're my sword." Her eyes are ablaze. She isn't sad; she's *angry*. "Because it's your *duty*. Well, it won't be for much longer." She smiles then, a different smile than every other night. You realize that for all her lighthearted banter and dreaminess and passion for practicing with a dagger, Anyag is *brittle*; she's been crumbling away in the furnace of what's about to happen, and you were too wrapped up in misery, too busy protecting yourself, to notice. Anyag drops her spoon into the bowl. She has not touched her food. "Amira. I am going to be wed to a stranger. I am moving from this cage to another, more elaborate prison. You will be freed, at last, but not me. Not me."

Her eyes brim with tears. She turns her head, because your jewel—your best friend, princess, home—has always been proud. At once your choices, safety—your wreck of a heart don't matter. You skirt the table and fall to your knees beside her. You wrap your arms around her. She pushes you away.

"Don't *act*," she says.

"I'm not acting."

She keeps shoving you back, her hand on your collarbone. "Then answer: What does it matter to you?"

It matters because I love you. Because I can't bear to let anything hurt you. Because I have no choice, because it won't make a difference, and I am weak. I could only ever teach you weakness.

Words escape you. In the end, the answer is in your swiftly pounding heart, your fingers threading through her hair 'til they rest at the top of her skull to turn her face towards you, ignoring how she pushes her elbows against your chest. You look into her burning eyes, lean in close. You press your lips to hers, still distantly hoping she'll hate you afterward, so that you can take the years of falling for her and coil them into a ball in your chest and say goodbye to them forever. At the same time you are hoping she *understands* what you're trying to tell her: you never wanted this; she is the most precious thing to you and you are a coward; your only hope is that somehow you can still make things right.

Anyag freezes. She stops pushing, and the lack of force makes you fall against her. Your hands splay on either side of her, clutching the table for balance; your heart thuds against hers. You pull away, ready to slice yourself open with your dagger if she asks—maybe even if she doesn't.

"Amira," she says, quietly. "Do you mean that?"

You nod. Tears crowd your eyes, but you don't let them fall; you've shown enough weakness, tonight.

Anyag sighs. She places her thumb on your mouth, feels your lips tremble beneath her touch. When she smiles, it's different than before—weary and gentle, like she knows how easily she can break you.

"Then let's fight for our freedom," she whispers. "Yours and mine."

Did you ever hope for it before?

No—it's not like you. You stick to what you know. The stories you shared, the songs your great aunts burned into your memory, the poems you and Anyag made up together. Not once did you speak of freedom. The word carries with it so much weight, even as it edges tantalizingly close to betrayal—and misery, even, for if things go wrong you could lose everything.

Why had you never dreamt of it? Why did you never think you could possess it, too?

Of course Anyag has dreamed of freedom; has been thinking of this since forever.

She has never seen the blue sky or the sun, yet her visions for the horizon extend much farther than you could ever fathom. She sees a world that has no limits, a world even you could own.

It will only work, Anyag says, once they believe she has left with her new husband. The best time to escape is following the marriage feast, just before they set sail; to save face, he will not dare to let anyone know that his bride has left him, and her parents will not have to bear the burden of shame. By then the other suitors will have departed and the town will be muzzy from three days of drinking.

"And how do you know who you'll leave with?"

She smiles. "Isn't it obvious? He must be the one my parents admired best, for his dowry and conquests and confidence. You must choose."

When Lisoryo returns, you have a letter for him. *Dear Night Sky, dear Veil, hear me. A lullaby aches in my rib cage. Today, I am a dovecote, and there are songbirds cooing inside, twittering, goldened, precious. How they all at once alight as I open my body to your waning autumn moon. I am waiting for you to fill me.*

You watched Anyag write it out, grinning at her own audacity. "You think he'll believe it?" she asked.

"Powerful men never doubt themselves," you answered. "Take care not to let the ink bleed through."

He receives the letter with a knowing smile, but does not open it in front of you. He thanks you, then asks if you might sing for him.

You have no idea what to do with his request, except comply. "Will a verse from *The Twenty-two Laments of Matang-ayon* suffice, sir?"

"More than."

Feeling caught and foolish, you sing verse eight, about Matang-ayon's sojourn to the Eastern Valley of the Sky, to seek the hand of the bride of darkness. His ankle is caught between two grinding bits of cloud, and his flesh tears, but he does not cry, for he is a hero.

As you sing you feel Lisoryo's magic reach for yours, sly and searching; you divert it gently, as if you do not know what you are doing. Anyag always wanted to meet other sorcerers to exchange stories with. He is dangerous, not only because of his face and his wealth. You finish the song, and he breathes in, satisfied.

"You could come with us," he says evenly. "There's always a need for more beauty in my garden. You could make yourself useful with the palace's defense—and you would have all the training you desire, for your sword arm and your magic, both." He licks his lips. "Besides, I'm sure the jewel would love to have the one who first polished her quite near."

You don't bare your teeth, but you can't return his smile, not even as a lie. "Thank you, sir. But I know where my place is."

"The offer stands." He clasps your shoulder, briefly. The tips of his nails dig lightly into your skin; you fail not to shudder.

The rest of the afternoon, while he is eclipsing the other suitors who are making their case for Anyag's hand, you play the part of a good steward, standing silent in the corner. While he is waxing poetic about his domain by the sea and the vast riches of his people, you imagine how just days from now, you will make a break for freedom. You will leave in the dark, with no witness but the moon—customary for you two, but next time, it will be different. The day after, when the sun rises, Anyag will not have to hide, and you can watch together, hand in hand.

After practice that evening, out of breath from dancing and sparring, Anyag asks, "For how long?"

You wipe your sweat, not really attending. "Hmm?"

She's not looking at you, so you don't see her expression. "For how long have you loved me?"

Your face, already warm, turns hot. There's no simple answer. You've spent half your life looking after her, memorizing every note in her laugh, the way her eyes grow glassy when she's ill, how she has grown more distant from her parents with the passing years ("They don't see me, Amira, not the way you do"). You've adjusted the cant of her hips in the middle of a song, the way she holds a knife, the words she breezily recites: *Abya Malana, Matang-ayon's temporary lover, cannot look him in the eye, for she is afraid the looking will render her speechless. And without her words he will see her truly, and find her incomplete . . .*

That first year together, when you were weary and grieving, you once awoke from a nightmare to find your face against her chest. She was stroking your hair, as your mother had done before she fell ill. "It's all right," she said, the once momentous gap of your stations rendered to nothing. "You can cry. It doesn't matter here." You couldn't even apologize, broken as you were, and you sobbed instead, on this girl who was much smaller than you, saving embarrassment for the morning after. She only laughed and said it was nothing.

You *loved* her then, but as your only friend, your reason to keep going. It's different than now. You don't know how it turned into this. One day you looked at her and she was brighter and more beautiful than anyone had a right to be, and something in you begged to keep her just a while longer. That was when you knew to be afraid.

This girl knows too well how to play with your feelings, but you've known her for just as long. You want to make *her* heart beat faster too—it's not lost on you, that she didn't kiss you back, that she doesn't trust your loyalty—to her? Or to her parents, your masters?

You are trying not to hope that *freedom* necessarily means *together*, but how will you know for sure? You reach out and grasp her arm.

"Will you believe me if I said always?"

She shakes her head, grinning. "You once threatened to spank me if I made a joke instead of concentrating! Abya Malana, Matangayon's temporary lover," she repeats, sing-song, even as you pull her towards you and hold her. "Cannot look him in the eye, for she is afraid the looking will render her speechless . . ."

"Is that what you're doing right now?" Her head is against your shoulder; you smooth her hair, as you've done countless times before (but not like this. Not *like this*). "Not looking at me?"

"Maybe."

"I've loved you for a long time, my salt and stone, my ivory bone. And I will keep on doing so, and hurting for it, won't I?"

She kisses your shoulder, a drawn-out motion that makes everything in you tingle. She kisses your neck, your cheek. Your nerves are strung so tight, you are certain one inhalation will break you apart. She touches her lips to your ear. "Maybe," she murmurs, and you are too breathless to reply, too ablaze with want to be angry.

The presentation is a story. Like a story, it has a beginning and an end.

The drums start when the sun goes down, the kulintang blending in after a few beats. Anyag's parents have spared no expense, and the entire village comes to witness the spectacle. In the first few years after Hugan-an's sacrifice, the village feared for their binukot, for the coming of the bakunawa. But that was countless seasons ago, and the moon remains, and the monster has become one terror your people do not fear. The young maiden's death, still recent enough to be in the memory of some, has become the stuff of legends. With it has come the elevation of every other binukot: their purity, talent, and beauty are such that even celestial beings—*monsters,* no one says—are content with them forever. If you take a binukot as a bride, then surely you are blessed by the gods.

There are seven suitors in total, arrayed in a half-circle, waiting for Anyag to make her entrance—but everyone's gaze is on Lisoryo, who has come wearing a silver band that sits like a crown upon his brow, black paint lined sharply around his eyes. His robes graze the sand even when he stands. The lord and lady sit on rattan chairs with golden embellishments, decked in their best finery, faces impassive as they survey the gathered crowd. The sun melts into the sea, and the sky turns from red gold to pink, to blue.

The other servants light lamps. The drums slow, and soften.

Now the cast is in place, save the main character. At the door to Anyag's tower, you hold a lit torch. With your other hand you touch Mother's amulet, begging her spirit to be with you, even if what you are doing may be wrong.

Behind you, Anyag breathes out to steady herself.

"Are you ready?"

"I'm ready," she says. Quiet and firm. "Stay with me, no matter what happens, Amira."

You reach back and twine your fingers together. You listen to the drums. For a minute you are afraid, then you remember to trust her, your worry dissipating.

"Yes, my jewel."

You rehearsed this moment so many times in moonlight, walking in a secluded area of the beach. You practiced the movements in her room, with all the furniture pushed to the sides. *Watch your feet,* you'd tell her, and she'd laugh and shove at you and do it worse, just to hear you mutter in frustration. She does none of that now, regal and delicate as she emerges from behind you and stands, blinking, in the light of your torch. Theatrically, she removes her veil. The crowd murmurs, gasps running from mouth to mouth so that it sounds like the wind whistling.

Anyag descends the steps of her tower while you keep pace behind her, so that your firelight barely brushes her skin. She carries the tapestry she completed last season—one with a great eagle soaring over the sea, the moon hanging above everything. As she walks to the half-circle where she will perform, you step away, standing just beyond the ring of lanterns; despite everything, your heart is bursting for her to *do this well,* this moment you've spent years over, the moment to take their breath away. It is the one gift you can give this village, before you betray it. The crowd hushes. The only sound besides the steady thump of the drums is her anklets, stacked so that they ring like bells with every step. She spreads her tapestry on the sand, so that all can see it and marvel: the delicate weave of color, the intricate story that her hands have brought to life. She straightens, and stares every suitor in the eye, briefly. She takes her longest with Lisoryo, their respective gazes magnetic, and the moment stretches tight: a breath held long enough to suffocate.

Then she smiles, the proud smile of an enchantress who knows the power she commands, and she raises one arm to cover her face. She stretches out one leg. The gong sounds, and she begins to dance.

She's not perfect—no one is, or can be.

But she's *breathtaking*. Close enough to a diwata that no spell, no song, would get her closer. There's a moment when the lady, her mother, looks at you and nods. Pride swells through you. Anyag lifts her arms, and your heart is dragged with them; she rolls her shoulders, and you are out to sea; she smiles, and you are not here.

With a start you remember that it's not her you should be watching. You glance at Lisoryo. He is resting his chin on one hand, long fingers obscuring his mouth, but his eyes never leave her. In the glare from the lanterns they are no longer fathomless black pits; instead they reflect the gold at her wrists and ankles, the haze of gentle fire. You recognize desire, kindling. It's the suggestiveness of the song, calling a warrior to sweet rest: *Buyi-Lahin closed his eyes, leaning on the fair maiden Ka Bigtuang's lap, and slept for a thousand days . . .*

The music stops. The crowd cries, expressing their admiration, their awe. Anyag stands before her parents and kneels, her forehead nearly touching the sand, until her mother says: "Rise, my jewel." She goes to them and kisses their brows. The firelight illuminates the sweat on her skin. The suitors, shaken from their stupor, stand and wait for her approach. Over her father's shoulder, she catches your eye—and winks. She's excited and fearless, exhilarated from her victorious performance, and you can almost hear her think: *We've got them. With this, it begins.*

They give her away that same evening. There is no argument —there never is—but her choice freely coincides with theirs, which is all anyone can hope for. The other suitors understand how this goes; they are gracious in their defeat, and will travel to other islands to find their wives. As they are leaving, Lisoryo and Anyag exchange their first pleasantries, where the lord can see them. You are summoned by the lady and instructed to pack up her meager belongings, for the newlyweds will sail tomorrow, just after noon.

"Tomorrow?" You had expected the festivities to continue for a day or two longer, for the wedding feast to come in the traditional three days, after which you would immediately depart, leaving her husband behind.

"Master Lisoryo has been away from his domain for more than a week now; we agreed it best to have them sail immediately, given the potential for storms, and so that Anyag will start her new life—with joy and excitement." The lady falters. You consider possible liabilities: she has no love for this village, and though she cares for her family, the only thing Anyag can truly be concerned for is—you. You swallow and nod, hoping your lady thinks it only extends to this—the tearful goodbye between sisters, dear friends.

"Then the wedding ceremony will be . . ."

"In the morning. At first light."

"Understood, my lady." If the wedding ceremony is tomorrow, then she will sleep at the foot of her parents' bed tonight, as is custom. So you will have to approach in darkness, and hope that Anyag has realized as much as you. Hope that she hasn't forgotten your plans in the glare of admiration and longing that Lisoryo casts her way—for when you look at them again she is staring at him with an expression close to heartbreak.

You've packed everything you need. Both her dagger and yours are in your belt. It is past midnight, and there is no time left to second-guess things. You leave the servants' quarters for the main house, and creep to the room of your lady and master, praying to find her outside the door. She isn't. You wait; perhaps she has simply gone to sleep—or maybe she has decided, at the last, not to run away. After the seconds become unbearable you push the door open, gently. On the bed lie your lady and master. There is no sign of Anyag on the cot next to theirs.

You will yourself not to panic, but know immediately where you must go. You race for the shore, running faster when you see Lisoryo, and Anyag beside him, walking with her head bent. They are almost at his boat.

"Stop!"

Lisoryo's expression is somewhere between disgust and gloating. Anyag's eyes grow wide, then harden. "Stay away!" she yells, but you don't listen, you run right up to them even as you wonder what you will do—separate the couple? Threaten his life? Then the village would have you beaten with bamboo rods, and branded for your insolence. But you are fueled by instinct now, and your hand flies to the knife at your side.

"What are you doing?"

"I'm leaving with my husband. It is no concern of yours."

"What did he tell you?" She wouldn't do this, not for no reason, your Anyag wouldn't—

"I owe you no answers. Don't talk as if you own me," she says, coldly. *"Leave us."* A slap to your face would have been kinder. You look at her eyes, searching for any enchantment, and find none—only steely determination. Your heart crumbles like soil squished in a fist.

"I'm tired of waiting, my bride," Lisoryo drawls. He inspects his long fingernails.

"We're going," she says shortly, and turns away.

"Anyag—" You grab her arm. Lisoryo sighs, steps forward, and backhands you so that you sprawl on the sand. You are surprised by his strength. When you blink up at him, head starry with pain, you are further surprised by his narrow eyes and the way his teeth are sharp within his smile—sharp as his fingernails; sharp as a dragon's fangs. The amulet at your throat begins to burn with a memory, of standing on the shore to see one moon gulped down, then another . . .

"You're . . ."

"Oh, have I been found out? There are too many clever girls in this village."

In a flash you are on your feet. You will die for striking a man unarmed, but you are certain that he is no man. You try to slash him across the side, but he merely sidesteps and kicks you hard in the stomach. You drop to your knees.

"Master Lisoryo." Anyag's voice wavers. "Come now, you said you would harm no one."

You cough out spit and blood. "Anyag! He's not human!"

He laughs. "Human? No, but after taking the sacrifice of a human maiden I learned the shape and sounds of one, the simple artifice, the cues I need to make you believe. How I *loved* Hugan-an—her skin, her hair, the exquisite sweetness of her marrow . . . but the last of her radiance is gone, and I hunger once again." He seizes your face. "Your precious jewel *knows,* slave. The only thing that has given me patience is how delicious I know she will be. You've heard the story. You know her song." His fingers dig into your cheek and you are unable to move, your breath coming short. You do know this song; you know how it must end.

"Don't hurt her," Anyag says.

"Oh, don't barter, beloved. You have nothing to threaten me with."

Your blade is tight in your fist as you lunge up to take another swipe, at his neck this time—he jerks his head away, but you get him across the cheek, a fine tear that drips a single trickle of black blood. He sighs.

"I pity you, how you forget to be afraid. But I suppose hope is one of the best seasonings, for humans."

You don't see him move, but suddenly there's a searing pain in your stomach—you cry out, your nerves buzzing as he kicks the side of your head and stomps on your knee. You touch your stomach, and your hand comes away wet with blood; you cough out spit that tastes of copper. He didn't strike anything vital, though there are sparks in the corners of your vision that you try to blink away, as you scramble to your knees—but Anyag is standing before you, face tilted up to the man who is also a moon-eater.

"Enough," Anyag says. "It's me you want, isn't it? If you're starving so badly, why don't you take me now?"

"Well, if you were in a hurry, dearest, you should have said so! There is no need of this filthy skin, then." The glamour begins to slip from him, his skin turning to scales, melting into the midnight blue of his robe, as he grows and grows—

"Anyag!"

"Don't." She looks back at you, her eyes hot with tears. "You shouldn't have followed, so you wouldn't have to know. I must do this, Amira. See to your wound. Do not die."

"No!" You watch in horror as he bends into a monster behind her, lashing out his enormous tail, eclipsing the moon. She turns to face him and mouths the song that will be her requiem: "Leave the moon be, leave my people be—"

She does not even finish before he snaps his jaws around her. You scream and scream as he takes to the sky.

There's a moment, watching him spiral upwards, through the haze of your disbelief, that you realize what a story this will make: how Anyag saved your village, how like Hugan-an she made the most perfect sacrifice so that you all may have light, so that you may keep your moon. And there would be no pain this time, for no one but you would know. Everyone else would think that they had simply stolen away in the night: newlyweds so in love, unable to wait. If he spoke true words, his next visit would not be in your lifetime.

Then you remember the brightness of possibility, when Anyag asked if you would fight for freedom. You did not raise a jewel just to watch her die; even if this is how the legend goes, you cannot let it end like this.

His long tail has just left the ground; you leap up, run forward, and stab your dagger into it as hard as you can, chanting for power through the blood in your mouth, as your feet leave the earth. The bakunawa flicks its tail but you've wrapped one arm around it now, the other still pressing down as hard as you can with your dagger, drawing blood in thick black gouts. For nothing will you let go, not the world. You are calm in the depths of your sorrow, and if Anyag is dead, then at least you don't have to live without her—at least you tried.

The bakunawa screeches, all human speech gone, as you sail over the ocean—it coils around you, wind rushing. When you turn your head you see the dark depths of its throat, the bright jagged line of its teeth, closing around you. You wrench your knife from its flesh. There's a snap as air and wind and noise disappear. You fall into nothing.

You reach out blindly with your dagger, and catch on to something—a distended piece of flesh, somewhere in its long throat. The creature bucks, seizes, and your head rattles, but you drag yourself onto the ridge of bone, rolling away from the edge. You gasp, savoring the air—it reeks of the ocean and decay, but you can breathe in here. The flesh is soft beneath you, slimy but not acidic like you'd imagined, and you roll onto your knees, shaking. The inside of the beast is massive, but the place you've landed seems to be solid, at least, living flesh pulsing beneath you. You blink, trying to let your eyes adjust to the darkness, but there's no light save the dim steel of your blade.

How did he consume Hugan-an? Did he take his last bride below the sea, and spit her out, and eat her bit by bit, to make her suffer? Or did she live out her life in this dark cavern, alone and starving, eventually fading away to nothing?

How will you find Anyag here? You remove your top and wrap it around your waist, to staunch the bleeding. Your desperation, and the last vestiges of your magic, can only go so far.

"Anyag!" you shout. It echoes back at you, dismal, desperate. "Anyag! I'm here!"

Nothing. Your heart quavers. At least you still have your weapon. Perhaps you can still find the beast's heart, and slay it, before dying. At least you won't have to wait long, if she's truly gone.

Then, from somewhere behind you, a faint echo: "Amira?"

"Anyag!" Cautiously you stand, wary of falling back into the pit of the monster's insides; you turn and reach out, but there's only emptiness. You walk deeper in, one hand pressed over your nose to avoid the dizzying stench, the other stretched out before you, searching. "I'm coming!"

You walk blindly into the dark, grasping the air, until your hand collides with something—another hand, a set of fingers. They twine with yours, shivering, the movement uncannily familiar. A sharp intake of breath, a stuttered cry—and then your arms wrap around each other, even in this place that might be your grave. You grip her tightly, like she might turn into nothing the minute you loosen your hold on her. Her fingers dig into your bare back, trembling. Blood slicks your arms, gashes from where his teeth grazed her (but didn't snap her apart—he wanted to savor it—he said as much). She's *alive*. She's *whole*.

"You fool," she sobs into your chest. "What are you doing here? I told you to stay behind. Your wound—"

"It'll heal," you say, hoping it will be true. "I promised to stay with you, remember?"

She barks out a laugh, and pulls back slightly. "Then we'll both die here?"

"I won't let you die." You wish you had a light to see her by, but all you have is this familiar sensation: her cheeks beneath your fingers, wet with tears. You rest your thumbs on the corners of her mouth, feel her lips part, searching for words. Anyag has always known what to say, but caught here without hope, even she might hesitate.

Her arms slide slowly down your back, and loop around your waist. She exhales. "Then I won't let you die, either."

You remain standing like that, holding each other, for a moment. Then you step back and fumble at your belt, unlatch her dagger and press it into her hand. "We have these," you say. She holds her dagger tightly, considering. You skim her arm, feeling for cuts, and she stops you by clutching your hand—*No need. I'm fine.* She makes a thoughtless humming sound, as if you are merely in the dark of her room and not in the belly of a monster.

A sudden thought crosses your mind—a flicker of possibility. You hum with her, letting the idea take shape. You have nothing better, and neither of you dare wait—already you could be sinking into the sea, miles away from where anyone can save you. You have to try.

"We can change her song," you say. "We can make a new one. Just as Hugan-an did, that time."

"But my magic isn't—"

"We have to try." You're both more comfortable with swords than with spellwork, but against the bakunawa, brute force will get you nowhere. Anyag nods, keeping quiet. You sense her thinking, determining how to lay down the words, what to sing so that you might live, or if not, take this monster with you in your perishing.

"Bathala," she starts, her voice thin and shaky. "I, your humble daughter, have nothing to offer—"

But I raise my eyes to you, beseeching, my arms uplifted, reaching—

I call on you to fill me with your light

That I might take this blade and shatter darkest night . . .

You take the thread of her chant, her magic, and weave it into yours—just as you first guided her hands to mimic a dove's wings, taught her to swing a sword—but this is her power, her right for the sacrifice of becoming binukot. She is destined for this.

And you have been singing together for years.

You repeat the words, join your free hands, feel power thrum through both of you. The sensation of warmth flares around your neck—your mother's amulet, her anting-anting, alighting, the last gasp of protection from your blood relatives responding to this plea as you shut your eyes and beg, beg, beg—for you deserve to live, too, you deserve a chance at joy. Not everything has to be a sacrifice. On your third round of the song, something changes. You open your eyes and there is light in the darkness, a bright fire, dancing over both of you, crackling, growing—

Your song begins to echo. You don't dare stop singing it, but another voice joins it, then another, and another, each note different, some a throaty hum, others at a pitch higher than humanly possible—a melody of moons, and the spirit of a girl who gave her everything to save a village and would give no more, not this time.

Has he heard you? Bathala listens and does not in turn, and anyone invoking him knows that. One must accept what fate rolls out in due course, inexorable as the ocean and the slow growth of trees, the tide drawn in and out, the shape of a song that has been carried in a heart for years and years at last finding itself . . .

The light collecting above you spirals down into your blade. You keep singing as you hold the blade out, no longer a simple kalis but a beautiful kampilan, curved and deadly, sparking fierily, then growing longer and larger until it is a giant shaft of light.

You see Anyag's face at last. Her eyes are scrunched, set with her will to fight: one answered prayer among so many abandoned, one dim ember sparked to flare all of your guttering hopes. Her hand in yours tightens; in the other is her blade, and you see that it is now a burning pillar of light as well.

Then Anyag's eyes snap open and she nods, bidding you to strike. You face opposite directions, determined to slay the beast together. You arch your arm, and thrust with all your might into the darkness, throwing the light, pushing your magic out as far as you can—the amulet at your neck explodes, and the wound in your gut opens wider—but you do not let go, Anyag's hand clutched tightly in yours, her voice high and clear above all the others.

The world wrenches apart; the floor beneath you gives way. You free-fall in the midst of the wildest screeching, a scream so inhuman and endless that your head feels like it's tearing. But light is spilling through—and air—and the sound of the ocean, and drums beating. You are not beneath the sea at all—you are still in the sky. Just as you two were fighting a battle inside of the beast, the village was doing its best outside of it. Your sphere of light keeps growing, extending from both ends of the hilt now, splitting the beast apart around you, until its scream is cut off and you close your eyes against the glare of light, brace yourself for an endless fall. Only then do you stop singing.

You aren't expecting Anyag's hand to find yours, as you drop through the air, still trapped in the gutted neck of the bakunawa. But it does, and you are only a little surprised as you curl your fingers together.

The first thing you see is Anyag's face, fractured through your bloody vision. Her hands rest on your stomach, sealing the wound with the last of her newly strengthened magic. Everything hurts, but you're alive.

"My jewel." Your voice is cracked, having spent it all in spell and song. You lift one hand and she grips it, weakly.

Behind her floats the moon. You are lying in the carcass of the moon-eater. You are floating in the ocean to the beat of drums.

You don't dare hope that you are free.

"Amira," she answers, and her smile is bittersweet: she has grown up, so impeccably, and it has nothing and everything to do with you, with who you are together. "Don't call me that. When we leave this place, I can be your jewel no longer. And you cannot be my sword. It won't work."

Your heart splinters, a loss as distinct as your mother's amulet, now an empty piece of string around your neck.

"I refuse to be something you must take care of and defend at every turn. I want to stand with you on even footing, and face you freely. Rather than your jewel, *let me be your shield,* for I can protect you. I cannot honor that unless you do."

You ease yourself up so that you are sitting. You do not touch her face, but you press your forehead to hers, look her in the eye. "Have I ever said no to you?"

She grins. "Yes. Lots of times."

Fair enough. You don't know what it will mean, to be together after this. You've never known a life where you don't feel beholden to her, simultaneously paving her way and blending into her shadow; where your hopes aren't tethered to hers by default. "It won't be easy for me."

"I know. But you're good at difficult things."

You nod, and her smile goes from tentative to delighted. There will be time enough in the future to determine how things must be: where you will live, how. What to say to her parents. What songs you will sing. Bathala is not known to bestow favors twice, and you already know your future cannot be in this village. But for now. *For now.* None of that matters.

Anyag turns her face slightly, so that half of it is cast in moonlight.

"I want to see the sunrise," she says. "It'll be my first."

"Okay."

She leans into you, and you do the same, balancing each other out in your exhaustion. Right now, you have all the time in the world. Time enough to watch the moon melt into the horizon, and wait for the sun to appear, as blindingly bright as its promise of tomorrow.

All the Best of Dark and Bright

Melanie broke up with him during the start of summer break. There was something particularly painful about this, as if she had decided on the start of summer because then she might be able to meet someone new over the next two months—at the beach, maybe, or her tita's house in Tagaytay, or wherever she was going to go without him, without *thinking* of him—but she was still calculating enough that they had spent the first three months of the year together. They met up for milk tea. He paid eighty-five pesos for her peppermint with pearls. She took a long sip and said, quietly, "I don't think this is working out."

If it was still the school year he could have said, *What, the group project,* or *Sorry, I have to go because my mom needs the car,* or *You've had a rough day, can we talk about this some other time?* But it was summer. There were no excuses. He frowned when he looked at her, and he knew it was an ugly frown, accusing and pitiful. Like, *I paid eighty-five pesos for your drink, dammit, and this is how you repay me?* He didn't mean for his face to do that, but it did.

"I'm sorry." She laced her fingers around her cup. Didn't meet his eyes. "You're still one of my favorite people, Macho. I'm just being honest."

What could he have said to that?

His real name was Matthias Antonio, but when he was a toddler he had somehow been conned by the yayas and his older sister Cely to strike muscleman poses on cue, so they started calling him Macho. This was adapted by the neighborhood kids and eventually his classmates. By the time he was in fourth grade and it was a completely unfortunate matter, nobody could be persuaded to call him anything else. This was made worse by the fact that he *wasn't* macho—just average. Average wasn't a terrible thing to be, at least to his mind, but it was still a bad nickname. Only his parents called him Matt, and Mama Santi, when she was still alive, called him Matthias. People who got exhausted by nicknames with multiple syllables sometimes called him Mach.

Melanie liked his name. She found it funny. She called him Mach-oh, usually, with an emphasis on the *oh*. It sounded extra-embarrassing that way, but by the time they met he had stopped investing unnecessary emotional stress into this issue. When he entered college some people called him Matt, because that was what he wrote on all his first-day nametags, and most teachers called him Mr. Lorenzo. It was only the people who knew him from high school that couldn't shake Macho. Melanie was one of those people, but she was also one of the people he cared enough about not to mind.

That weekend, when he was still in a haze of post-school-year-exhaustion and post-breakup-depression, they went to Lolo's Zoo to attend a family reunion. These reunions happened fairly often. Mom got nervous around Dad's family, so usually it was only Macho and

Cely that went. In exchange for good food and a chance to receive random pocket money, all they had to do was greet relatives. It wasn't a bad tradeoff, especially when Macho started handshaking instead of cheek-kissing. There weren't a lot of kids his and Cely's age, so they had developed the habit of sneaking out after dessert, to stare at the animals in the zoo and make jokes about their personalities. The dodo bird was a creepy stalker, the monkeys were hyperactive punks, and the arapaima was a forty-year-old family man.

Sometimes after their usual tour of the animals they would spy on the Duende Forest, which was really only a tiny enclosure of overgrown plants that could be accessed through some mossy steps beside the hidden restroom. There was a thick cluster of bamboo in the middle of the Forest. The zoo caretaker said that duendes lived in it. He loved showing them the marble-sized boil on his left leg, as proof of their curses.

Today, Cely was absorbed with her handheld and didn't feel like walking around, so Macho went on his own. He taunted the dodo bird and the monkeys, and stared at the arapaima until he felt grossed out by its size, then he walked over to the Duende Forest and observed the naked girl standing in the cluster of bamboo. She didn't seem to notice him. He decided there was something wrong about this, so he said, "If you don't come out, the duendes will curse you."

She jerked at the sound of his voice. Then she squinted at him, as if trying to decide whether he was suspicious or just perverted. After a moment, her face relaxed. "I don't think I should leave," she answered. "This isn't really the right place. Maybe if I stay like this, I'll go back."

Macho tried to decide, by her physical features and voice, whether she was younger or older than him. He couldn't tell. She looked fifteen for a few seconds, then around twenty-one, then suddenly a lot older. Her voice was sweet and friendly but also low. She talked deliberately, clearly. "Okay," he said, because that was easier than him dealing with what was clearly A Situation.

She stood amidst the bamboo. He watched her. Because she seemed so unembarrassed, he felt pretty nonchalant. A few minutes passed. Nothing happened.

"I think you'd better come out," he said.

"Okay," she conceded.

The thing was, Macho and Cely were used to seeing naked women, because their mother was Danila Perea(-Lorenzo), who was famous for her nude paintings and sketches. She taught a nude-drawing class, where people paid her to look at their sketches, and she paid models to stand naked in the middle of their sala, which doubled as her classroom. Her nudes hung in hospitals, malls, and art galleries. The president had one in his private collection. Critics talked about Perea's *lovely breasts, lovely backside,* and *sultry, albeit remote, stare.* It took a few years for Macho to realize they were talking about her rendering.

The naked girl who stepped out of the bamboo cluster, and walked through the rest of the Duende Forest before ducking under the little wooden barrier to join him, was exactly the kind of girl his mother would love to paint. She had dark, wavy hair and flawless, almond-colored skin. Her face was perfect. He took off his jacket and put it around her shoulders. She might have been a little crazy, a little heat-stroked, sun-dazzled. It was a scorching day. (Macho liked wearing jackets no matter what the temperature was.) She smiled at him, gratefully. Maybe *he* was the heat-stroked, sun-dazzled one.

"What's your name?" *Who are you* was the better question, but this sounded gentler.

"Uh." She looked blank for a moment. "I guess you can call me . . . Maganda?"

He didn't say *Wow, that's humble* or even *Wow, that's vain* because he was not a jackass. Gelo, his best friend, might have made that kind of comment, because Gelo sometimes confused being cool with being a jackass. Or maybe Gelo was just less self-righteous and funnier than Macho. He didn't usually compare notes. Gelo was a lot more invested in what girls thought about him, but Macho had been the one with a girlfriend, after all.

Melanie had been his soph-night date. That meant they'd been together four years, three of them official. Four years was a long time. It was all of high school, and all of college. Fifteen and nineteen were completely different ages. Melanie had braces during prom, but for the two years afterwards, she didn't. Macho had stupid hair during Senior Ball, but his hair improved a lot in college. Four years made the person you wanted to text every five minutes into the person you argued with about movie themes and stupid things like being late, not really being sorry. But some people got married after four years, too. What happened after four years was completely unpredictable.

Not quite as unpredictable as Maganda, but still.

He needed to get her some clothes. Cely had some left in one of the guesthouses here from a while back. They would be too small, but at least they could cover Maganda up. They walked through the Zoo back towards the dining place. Macho deliberately picked the areas no one was hanging around—the dodo bird fence, the empty raccoon and squirrel cages, the section with screeching parrots. No one else had a nude artist mother. Maganda seemed fascinated by their surroundings, even if she was the most fascinating thing in them.

"Where are you from?"

"From the Bamboo." She saw his expression, laughed, and added, "Don't get me wrong. I've walked around the outside world for many years. Several times. It was just, you know, the moment to step back in, to become new again." She bit her lip, like she had decided against saying something. "Anyway, we went, like always, into the Bamboo. Only this time it split and I was somewhere else."

"We?"

She tried not to hesitate, but he still caught her pause. "My partner. I'd rather not mention him right now." She shrugged. "When I stepped out, he wasn't there, and neither was the bird."

So she had a boyfriend. Macho could guess what they did in the Bamboo. He decided to let himself be sidetracked by extraneous detail. "What's the bird?"

"The one who pecks the Bamboo apart."

If he was Gelo, this was the point where he would have said that her innuendoes were *crazy*, like, was she a *porn star* or something, and he and Melanie would chorus, *Gelo, shut up!* In another part of his brain, he was thinking, *I've heard this one before,* but he didn't want to explore that idea further. Yet. They reached the dining place. Macho directed her to a row of flower bushes. "Wait here," he said, like he didn't trust her not to run inside and make everyone scream. "If anyone comes by, crouch."

"Wait. What about you, where are *you* from? What is *your* name?" Everything she said in that low, sweet voice sounded like a story.

"My name is Matt and I'm from Quezon City. And," he continued, because those eyes demanded the whole story, "most people call me Macho."

"You mean, strong?"

He nodded. *Okay,* he was still not completely over it. Maganda went "*Hmm*" and *looked* at him again, as if she was seriously considering something. He felt exposed by her huge, brown, lasering eyes. This was unacceptable. He wasn't the naked one. "I'm going to get my sister," Macho said, and did.

Cely was only a year older than Macho, so he usually called her *Cel* instead of *Ate Cely,* and didn't feel guilty about it. The most outstanding fact about Cely was that she was a hardcore gamer. It was difficult to have a sister who was a better gamer than you, even if she was older. She had finished three *Metal Gear Solid* games in the first week of summer break, and was only not playing the fourth because she had gotten distracted by *Pokemon Black* on the DS. Macho's guy friends were in awe of her. Also, Cely was kind of pretty, because their mother was pretty, and she got better grades than Macho. He didn't know how, because she was in a five-year Engineering course, and spent a lot of her time in various virtual worlds. He suspected that she had replaced her need for sleep with a need for coffee and Mountain Dew.

Because Cely played videogames, including shooters and horror titles, she was not easily freaked out. So when Macho told her that he had discovered a naked girl in the Duende Forest and needed to get her some clothes, Cely nodded, saved her file, turned off her DS, and excused herself from the table. Maganda was crouched behind the bushes. She stood when they came out.

"Hmm," Cely went. "Well, my clothes won't fit, but they'll have to do." To Macho, she added, "She's *way* too mature for you."

"Hello," Maganda said. "You must be Macho's sister. I'm Maganda."

"And confident!" Cely pronounced. "I like that. Let's go to the guest house, shall we?"

Luckily most of Cely's childhood clothes were oversized. They fit quite nicely on Maganda, although none of Cely's old bras did. She offered Maganda an old bikini top instead. It worked passably. Macho said it was probably okay for them to go home now, so they told Maganda to wait beside the bushes again, and said goodbye to their relatives. Cely kissed ten cheeks, Macho shook ten hands, and Lolo thanked them for coming and gave them 500 pesos each. Then they filed into Macho's Pajero. Cely graciously let Maganda ride shotgun.

The whole drive home, Maganda stared out the window, and sometimes asked them what this or that was. She seemed genuinely amazed by everything. She laughed at the statue of Jollibee when they passed one, and crinkled her eyebrows when a kid knocked against the car window, brandishing a handful of colorful cloths. Halfway through, in a patch of bad traffic, Macho decided he needed some guidance.

"Hey. What are you going to do now?"

She scrunched her mouth up. "Hmm . . . I don't think I have any choice but to go back. I don't exactly belong here."

"Yeah, but how?"

Cely was listening to this conversation with great interest, Macho knew, even if she was in the middle of a *Pokemon* tournament.

"I guess I have to get to the right Bamboo. I have to find him." She sighed and crossed her arms. "He's probably looking for me, too."

"Where is the right Bamboo?"

"I don't know." She yawned, like she was bored with this question. "Maybe the bird will come and tell me. Do you know anywhere it could be?"

"No idea."

"It's fine," she sighed. "It always ends up the same, one way or another. Even if things in the middle are different. Even if I *try* to make things otherwise. I'll keep looking, but it's not worth worrying about. Can I stay with you in the meantime?"

Cely leaned over her seat, making eye contact with Macho in the rearview mirror. "Sure you can, it's summer break," she answered for them both.

Maganda got Tito Danny's room, because he would be at his Baguio loft for the next three months. Tito Danny spent half the year in Baguio, making landscape paintings, and half the year here, making nudes. He was very competitive. Macho knew it was hard to have the same profession as your sibling, especially if she was your older sister and therefore had the right to bully you when it suited her. Even worse, his mother was really quiet and sneaky when she was being mean. Macho had witnessed her offhand comments about misshapen nipples, Tito Danny yelping *I'm not trying to be realistic!* and his mom snickering. She loved teasing. It would probably help Tito Danny if he learned how not to react.

They introduced Maganda to their mother as Maggie, a third cousin from Dad's family. That was quite enough. Mom didn't like to know much about her husband's clan, but she was nice when she *had* to know them. Dad felt much the same. Macho and Cely knew their parents' relationship was complicated, even if they loved each other, at least as much as either of them could. It was probably better that Dad went abroad almost every other month. This time he was in Singapore. He had packed his bigger maleta. They suspected he didn't know his third cousins, anyway.

Mom's eyes got mega-wide when she shook Maganda's hand. "Do you, by any chance, model part time?"

So Mom hired Maganda. They were going to start the next day, but Danila Perea could only paint four hours a day at most, so Maganda would have a lot of free time. She came to Macho's room the next morning. Cely was camped out in the family den because she had pulled an all-nighter to finish *Pokemon Black,* and was now back to *Metal Gear.* Macho was researching potential Bamboo locations. He kept finding dead Geocities links.

"If you tell me more about your partner, maybe we can figure it out."

Except he already knew. On the car ride home he'd let his mind start considering, because Maganda's appearance had dissipated some of the post-breakup-depression and filled him with curiosity instead. When he was five he'd spent three nights at Children's Medical from a massive asthma attack. Before he started puking in the lobby he'd been staring at the giant mural of the first Filipino man and woman, their painted smiles faint, fake. Malakas had blocky shoulders and abs, and Maganda's hair had been artfully arranged over her boobs. The real thing was much, much prettier.

"I'm not in a hurry," she answered, which meant, *I still don't want to talk about it.* Maybe things between her and Malakas were complicated, the way it was with Macho's parents.

"Is it a cycle, then? Like you go into the Bamboo every hundred years, and come out, and the Philippines is totally different?" He swiveled around in his chair. He didn't want to be annoying; it was just so *interesting*. Besides, she didn't seem to mind. "Were you there during Rizal's time? Do you know who Rizal is?"

"He was short," she replied, "But a really good artist. And he wrote nice poems. Of course I know who Rizal is. Don't you think I know my history?"

"So the Bamboo usually splits open somewhere in Manila?"

"I've been all over."

"What other legends are true?"

"Do you know the legends, then?" She sat cross-legged on the floor next to his bed, while he drummed away on his laptop. "Did you read them when you were younger?"

"I know *your* legend." He could feel himself turning red, like he'd made some kind of stupid confession, so he barreled on, "I didn't know it continued."

"All stories continue, Macho," she declared, as if this was obvious.

Mama Santi was the one who told them stories. She read out to them from her furry brown rocking chair every Sunday. She had a lot of slim, hardbound, beautifully illustrated Philippine folklore storybooks. Because of her, Macho and Cely knew the legends of the ampalaya, banana, lanzones, corn, pineapple, makahiya, termite, scaly fish, salty sea, and seven thousand islands. Most of the legends involved crying girls who got turned into something, either as punishment or as a reward. Mama Santi had a happy storytelling voice, and she made everything sound pleasant, even if it was about a girl turning into a peanut. After the reading sessions they would walk around the village, enter the park, and she would tap things with the end of her umbrella, like termite hills and tree trunks.

"The village sprites like me," she used to say. "I'm their friend. Look, they're waving. Because you're my grandchildren, they won't hurt you, so you can play around here without worries. But beware of the snakes. They like to leap out of trees when you aren't paying attention."

Macho had never seen a snake in the village, but if leaves were rustling loudly he always heard a sort of hissing in his head.

Mama Santi died three years ago. It was a peaceful death, one in her sleep. She was even smiling a little, like she knew something funny; like there was some great, witty secret about death. They entertained guests for three days at the wake. It seemed like lots of famous people knew Mama Santi. She had worked in all sorts of places and touched all sorts of lives.

Cely sobbed like crazy when they put Mama Santi into her tomb at the Perea mausoleum. Macho had never seen Cely cry, not even when her memory card got corrupted and all of her PSX files got deleted. She emitted hacking sobs and whistling whimpers, and then got really quiet. She didn't talk for a whole week afterwards. Mom was crying too, and Dad had his arm around her, which was weird because they rarely showed physical affection. Macho knew his own eyes were quietly gathering tears, but at that point he didn't even feel like he was in his body. He was somewhere in the casket, with Mama Santi, asking her to tell him another story, and another.

All stories continue, Maganda had said. Mama Santi would have been so delighted with her.

He did not believe he was the reincarnation of Malakas. That made no sense. There was no way Maganda could think so. They couldn't be partners. He still couldn't even figure out if she was too old or too young. Being a legend probably made you a step out of time, unfixed in age, distorted by the imaginations of various people. Besides, he was Matthias Antonio, and he had always lived this life. He had no recollection of anything else.

When Maganda was done modeling for his mother, he took her out to inspect potential real Bamboo spots. The village park was first. She stood in several different clusters of Bamboo, and shook her head each time. The little kids in the jungle gym stared at them. He gave up and got them both cones of dirty ice cream.

"Do you have a girlfriend?" She seemed to decide it was her turn to interrogate.

"Had one." Last week seemed like ages ago.

"Tell me about her."

Macho was grateful that she didn't clarify whether they broke up or not. He wasn't sure if they really had. He couldn't remember what he did at the milk tea place, after she dumped him. "Okay, but only if you tell me what happened with Malakas."

It was the first time he had actually said the name. She pursed her lips, like, *Not a bad move, kiddo.* "Fine."

This is what he told her: Melanie was Gelo's friend first, only Gelo wasn't interested in her romantically, because she was flat-chested or something like that. After sophomore night, which was a set-up, they met again for Dairy Queen, and again for coffee, and again for McDo. She liked horror novels and soccer and she got fantastic grades, so it was not surprising that she became an Engineering major, like Cely. Her hair always smelled clean. She had dimples. It was going to suck when the school year started and he would have to randomly see her. Guys would be all over Melanie.

He left out the part about wanting to call her, just to see how she was doing. And the fact that they'd kissed only three or four times, but that didn't matter because they liked watching movies and talking about all kinds of Stuff. And about how she had squeezed his hand during Mama Santi's funeral, how she turned her head and cried into his shoulder, even if she barely knew his grandmother. The only reason he pulled his floating being out of Mama Santi's casket, or tried to, was so that he could wipe the tears off that beautiful girl's face.

This is what she told him: she didn't want to go back, not yet, because the lights were fading along the beach and she liked the taste of the breeze and the Bamboo was stuffy. Besides, she wasn't sleepy. The bird was squawking at them to get a move on. *Why can't I do what I like sometimes,* she said. Malakas tried being sweet to her. She got annoyed with him. She wanted to walk away. He grabbed her wrist, and it hurt a ton, and this pissed her off. He didn't mean to, she knew that, he just didn't know his own strength. After all those years, he still didn't. He was sorry. He followed her across the sand on his knees. He was kind of an idiot, because his muscles were all spread out and not concentrated in his head. The bird kept squawking so she gave in and walked to the Bamboo with him. But she was still mad so she didn't let him hug her, and she kept him at a distance with her feet, kicking at him, while the Bamboo closed its two halves. Maybe that screwed things up.

Macho couldn't be sure, but he bet she had left some parts out, too.

"I was being unfair that day, to be honest. I just didn't feel like going through it again, and he didn't have to be so smug and pushy about the fact that we *had* to." She crunched the tip of her ice cream cone. It was the first time he'd seen her angry. Her eyebrows seemed to go way down in her face.

"If you get into fights, how could you have a million children with him?"

She looked surprised for a moment, then she laughed. The question seemed to ease her out of anger, back into gracefulness.

She smiled at Macho, coyly. "Do I look like I've had a million children?"

No, but that was how the legend went. And besides, Macho and everyone else he knew was descended from one of those million children. He wondered if his ancestors were the ones who ran outside or hid in the walls or sat in the stove. He wondered if Maganda and Malakas had really grown tired of them, and beaten them with wooden spoons. If they didn't want to have that many kids, they should have stopped having kids. Okay, he knew it was easier said than done. He looked at Maganda again, who was a vision in faded skinny jeans and a white blouse. Maybe she never actually had kids. Maybe legends didn't reproduce; that was how their own stories stayed relevant.

There was a silence in which they both watched a little girl make it all the way across the monkey bars. She raised her arms over her head when she reached the other side, beaming with pride.

"Do you love him?" Or was she only forced to love him, because that was how the story went?

Maganda sort-of-snickered-sort-of-giggled. It was a weird sound, coming from someone so beautiful. "Mach-*oh*, the love doctor," she said, and smooched his cheek. She was really flirty for a legend. Was Maria Makiling like this too? "I'm still mad at him, so I won't answer your question. Let's go home."

Strike one: two and a half years ago, he told Melanie that they were moving to California. Melanie was upset about it. She didn't want to talk to him after that. Why is it so out of the blue? she wanted to know. Well, Dad had said so, what was he supposed to think? The green cards that his aunt had applied for decades ago finally got approved. They were all going to go, and then suddenly they weren't. His mom and Cely were happy, and even Dad seemed kind of relieved. Maybe next year, Dad said. They were all still sad about

Mama Santi during that time, and did everyday things like they were in a sludgy time warp. You never know what's *really* going on, Melanie said. But she was still glad he wasn't leaving.

Strike two: he wasn't really ambitious. He didn't know what he wanted to do after college. He couldn't become an artist like Danila Perea, even if he could sketch pretty well, because it seemed too risky and he didn't have that much faith in his art. His grades were in the C+ to B range. He was taking Economics, but he wasn't sure why. Sometimes he thought he was interested in supply and demand, but he might have been making those times up. Melanie wanted to go to graduate school abroad. Whichever good school would take her. Okay, he said, good for you. You're brilliant, Mel, I'm sure you'll get in. Won't you even try to stop me. Do you want me to? I think you'd still go. You deserve to go. Yeah, but I don't think long distance would work. We could try maybe. Why don't you ever say or do what you really want to? (He didn't say this, but the answer was, *Because I don't know what I really want.*)

Strike three: since last year, there were actually times when they ran out of Stuff to talk about. He found it hard to say he really, truly cared about her, he wanted to make things work again, he just wasn't sure how. Maybe he had assumed it was a phase. Maybe more-than-three-years meant this was it, this was going to work. Once, when she was being moody, he said, "Well, what do you expect me to do? What do you *want?*" And she shook her head like *No, I don't have to answer that.* Only she did answer that, the following Thursday, over milk tea. It wasn't exactly what he wanted to hear.

They tried the area in school where people went when they needed to do secret things, and two other parks, and the atrium in the mall (quickly, while the guard wasn't looking), and the empty field near the airport, and the one near his high school, and the one in Cely's high school (she snuck them in). None of them worked. It was a good thing Macho liked driving. They went home every day exhausted but cheerful, feeling productive. Maganda made good conversation. She was open about her opinions, and Macho felt like he knew her. He suspected this was Mama Santi's doing, because she liked embellishing her legends, and probably made some up in which Maganda *did* argue with Malakas, and the bird was this kind of sleazy, obnoxious troublemaker.

Mom made many beautiful paintings, some in which Maganda was wearing a baro't saya, or a sarong, in addition to the naked ones. The painting class adored Maganda. Cely introduced her to *Tekken*, where her Zafina became a force to be reckoned with. She also liked using Nina Williams.

"Thank you for letting me stay with you," she told him randomly (or well, after kicking his Jin's ass with Zafina). "I'm really enjoying myself. I love your family."

"Well, they love you more. But thank god it's summer vacation. Otherwise it would be hard to find the time to do all these things." He decided not to ask for a rematch, and watched Zafina writhe around onscreen.

"There's always time," she answered. But time didn't *pass* for her, so that wasn't a fair statement. He felt unhinged when Maganda was profound, which was often, but this wasn't surprising. All the women in his life were profound and talented. He was okay being who he was, but maybe that was part of the problem. Maybe he wasn't supposed to be. Because Dad wasn't around half the time, he didn't know what the correct manly response was, or if it even existed.

"Does time even matter to you? You said things always end the same way." When he talked to Maganda, he kind of sounded profound. But that wasn't why he talked to her.

She kept her eyes on the screen. "The fact that the things in the middle change, that still matters. I like experiencing different things."

Even if she existed before time, even if she was pretty much perfect? He didn't know her as well as he thought. He couldn't pinpoint how he felt about her. Sometimes she was like an older sister, then a wise friend, then someone he longed to replace Melanie with, then a complete enigma, a legend that was breathing across from him and smiling like there were still things she had to learn. Like the myths they spoke of considered this world, his world, a different kind of mythology, legendary in its own way.

Gelo came over with some beer, because he had heard about The Dumping from one of Melanie's friends, and needed to comfort his bro. He was rapidly sidetracked by Maganda, and after their introductions, dragged Macho away by the arm. "Your cousin is *hot!*" He made a gesture that could have meant *shapely female body* or *I want a piece of that.* Macho had already forgotten about the third-cousin thing. She seemed like a permanent fixture in their lives, and it had only been eleven days. "Can you hook us up, please, pare?"

"Dude, no. She's too good for you."

"What! The hell, I set you up with Melanie!" Gelo knew right away that he had said the wrong thing. Macho hoped his expression wasn't too bad, but it probably was. "Shit, sorry, dude. That's not what I came here for. Here, here. Beer." Gelo was awesome when he put some effort into it, which was why they were best friends. He was still obviously delighted when Maganda went over and helped herself to the beer, but Macho didn't mind. Today she was like a cool friend-that-was-a-girl, and he was looking forward to tomorrow.

Tomorrow was the day he saw her crying. Maybe she was missing the Bamboo and her idiot boyfriend with the washboard abs. Maybe she was missing her one million children, wishing she could take it all back, that she had never scared them away, some as far away as California. Maybe she just had those random summer blues, when you felt alone and betrayed for no reason, but you couldn't focus on anything else because there was nothing else. Maybe she woke up from a nightmare about losing someone she loved.

It was 1:00 a.m. and she was in the kitchen crying over a glass of milk. He came down to get his laptop cord, which he stupidly forgot, and never was able to remember, because she raised her head and she was looking seventeen, exquisite and dewy, lost and confused. He walked over to her and put his arms around her, without thinking, and she put her head on his shoulder. "Why are you crying? Don't cry," he whispered. "It'll be fine. It always ends up the same, remember?"

She cried some more. Maybe that was the wrong thing to say. If legends cried, he thought, that meant they also felt sad, scared, tired. Maybe they also lived and died, except they did it over and over. He kept his arms around her, and rocked her back and forth. His next discovery was that legends also kissed, just like real people; they also shut their eyes, and their mouths were warm, their lips were soft. He held her close. The room was utterly dark. He felt her tears against his face. Legends held secrets too, and maybe some of these were hazy secrets full of touching, sensations, the click of doors in the early morning. Macho never figured out, afterwards, if any of that had been a dream or a memory; a story he had written by himself, or with someone else.

The text message came a few days later. By then they were only looking for the right Bamboo half-heartedly. They never talked about the crying incident, which Macho could still only half-remember. They played *Tekken,* and sometimes he joined the nude-drawing class, and sometimes he thought about the future without immediately thinking of Melanie.

Tell Maganda i've been lookin all over for her. Sooo exhaustin. Meet us by the art exhibit at d Fort, Boni High Street, 5 PM. -Bird.

He showed it to Maganda over breakfast. She sighed, but whether it was with exasperation or relief, he couldn't tell. "Well, I'll be ready by 3:30," she said, because she had a good grasp of travel time by now. Then she went away to get ready for her last nude-painting session. Macho went over to the family den and told Cely. She cut Solid Snake off in the middle of his sentence, and stared at him. "Don't screw this up, kid brother," she said.

"What do you mean?"

"Like what you did with Mel." Cely, like their mother, was quiet and sneaky when she was mean. He hated that about her. But his anger melted a little when they were getting ready to leave, and Cely embraced Maganda for a long time. It was weird to see Cely *really care*. "I hope things go the way you want them to," she told Maganda, and Macho realized that the two of them had had a lot of conversations he didn't know about.

They drove toward the Fort, mostly lost in their own thoughts, until Maganda told him she knew the girl who had become a banana, and really she was quite happy being a banana. She made a lot of people happy being a banana, because bananas were a popular fruit.

"Didn't she want to be a girl? I'd rather be a girl than a banana."

"She became a banana to prove her love."

He parked the car. "What does that even mean, *prove your love*? How do you know what to do?"

Maganda was quiet. Then she said, "Why don't you ask Melanie?"

"I'm not asking about me," he answered, because that stung. "Are you not mad at him anymore? Are you going back to him?" This whole time he'd been nice, delicate. Suddenly he was tired of the secrets and the magic. He felt like demanding an honest answer. Even a heartbreaking one.

"I thought you knew my legend," she said, and he remembered holding her while she cried. But she wasn't crying this time. She looked tired, also, twenty and broken.

"Sorry," he replied. "I do know it." He imagined Mama Santi jabbing him with her umbrella. Cely telling him, *fail.* "Why don't we go?"

They got out of the car and walked to the art exhibit, which was spread out over the central field. Macho immediately spotted the bamboo fixture in the center, which looked like it was made of glittery green-and-blue plastic. It was segmented, huge, with sharp edges and red plastic leaves that sprang from it in artful curlicues.

Standing beside it was Malakas. Like Maganda, he was a lot more amazing in person. His abs didn't look blocky the way they did in the Children's Medical painting. He could be posing in every billboard along EDSA. He seemed cool and funny, as if he deserved to be surrounded by hot girls. But the only girl next to him looked like a high school student. She was wearing glasses, had a sharp chin and tiny eyes. Standing next to her was a lady clad in leather pants and a weird, feathery shirt. There was something wrong with her face—the flat part over her mouth was huge and pointed.

"Thank god!" Bird squawked. "You really made a mess this time! Come here, come here."

Maganda and Macho came over. He hadn't expected Bird to be a girl. Malakas broke into a huge smile when they came closer. Maganda returned his gaze, and Macho deliberately tried not to see the expression on her face—love, or indifference. Either would be tough to swallow. The high school student rolled her eyes. "Did she give you a hard time too? Because Malakas was a pain in the neck." Macho hadn't expected her voice, clear and self-certain. Up close, he noticed that her face was very proportional.

"No, not at all." He tried to smile at Maganda, but she wasn't looking at him. This made his gut twist, so he turned his attention back to the high school student. "I'm Matt, by the way."

"Alina," she replied. "Are they going to do this or not?"

"Of course they are," Bird snapped. She seemed to finally notice Macho, and fluttered her eyes. "*Thank you,* by the way." She clapped her hands together. "Okay, you two, take your clothes off and step inside."

A crowd was starting to gather around them. People were talking and bringing out their camera phones. Macho didn't blame them, but he suddenly wished he wasn't a part of this.

"I didn't know there was performance art scheduled!" someone exclaimed.

There *was* something theatrical about the way the two legends slowly, carefully, removed all their clothes. Bare skin clearly suited them better. Little children started shouting. Women, hypnotized by Malakas, grumbled as they led their children or husbands away.

"Come, my love," Malakas said. It was the first thing Macho had heard him say. He didn't sound like an idiot at all. He sounded like he meant it, like he was so relieved and happy. Maganda probably *had* been unfair. Macho knew what she was like when she was angry, or sad. Malakas climbed into the plastic Bamboo sculpture. It was unpoetic that it wasn't a real tree. Macho was disappointed. He had wasted a lot of time, looking for the right Bamboo. And Maganda *could* have elaborated more on this whole ritual thing.

"Well, I have to go now," he found himself saying. He turned and started pushing through the crowd.

"Macho, wait," he heard Maganda say. But he didn't turn around. He didn't hear whatever it was she wanted to say.

He drove home. Cely had already eaten dinner. Mom wanted him to look at her newest painting. He agreed, to prove he was stronger than they all thought. It was beautiful, one of her best yet. Maganda came alive in it, stunning in her cluster of bamboo. He told Mom what he thought. She beamed at him. "Do you want it for your room?"

"No, but thank you. It would look kind of suspicious, I think. Maybe you should send it to Tito Danny?"

She liked his suggestion, and kissed him goodnight. His phone buzzed as he was climbing the stairs. It was a message from Melanie.

He read it, and couldn't tell if he wanted to smile, or start crying. Instead, he took a bath, then went to his room and fell asleep.

When he woke up, he was no longer on his bed. He was still lying down, but vertically, as if his bed had been propped up. The wood against his back was smooth and cool. He couldn't see anything, but he knew it was bamboo. He also knew he was naked, but he didn't feel cold at all. The air wasn't as stuffy as he imagined. He moved, to see if there was anything else in this darkness. He stepped on something that jerked back. It was a set of toes.

"Watch it," the girl across from him laughed. He couldn't see her face in the dark. Couldn't tell if it was Melanie or Alina, Maganda or someone else. He couldn't tell from her voice, either, but he knew it was someone he had met. He knew it was someone he cared about. He reached out to touch her shoulder.

"Who are you?" he asked. He felt her hands cupping his face. She was trying to figure out who he was, too. Then her hands curled behind his neck, and she leaned against him. There wasn't a lot of space, here in the Bamboo. He decided this was all right. This was something he wanted.

"Macho," she murmured. He realized that she was really sad, but he didn't know why. For some reason, this made him feel like crying, but he didn't. "Matt. Matthias. Malakas. Tell me something. A story you know. Something honest that will make me happy."

He thought for a moment.

"I care about you," he said. He felt her smile against him—just a little grin, but it mattered, because it seemed like he had finally said the right thing. He couldn't keep all the pieces together, but this was a start. Maybe they could help each other out. He smiled back. He held her, and waited for something to peck the darkness apart.

The cool air and long winding roads remind her of Baguio; but even Baguio never got *this* cold, cold enough for boots and a thick sweater. Baguio didn't have air that tasted like saltwater, and when they went to Baguio, it was always with Mom and a whole host of cousins and titos and titas. Baguio never had this stillness, the kind that makes the movement of birds across the road startling; she watches them flap away through the mist and wonders what they are called, where they are going. She elected to stay in the car while they got the room keys from the concierge, and when Rhea runs back to tell her they got a *suite,* it's gonna have *two floors,* isn't that *awesome,* she looks back blankly. With no one else around, Rhea is incredibly *loud.*

"Stop sulking, Ramona," Dad says as he climbs into the car, his good humor threatening to waver. She is the only one who can bring out the chinks in it, get him to raise his voice, slam doors, glare. She isn't afraid of her father, but that doesn't mean he isn't scary sometimes. His forehead bunches up in the rearview mirror, and beneath it his eyes are watching her.

The weekend has only started. She unfolds her arms and says, "I'm just hungry."

She doesn't say *I don't want to be here.* She doesn't ask about the mist or the birds. She just puts her hand on her stomach, like she's *starving.*

The forehead in the rearview mirror smoothes, as Rhea chimes in with her impeccable timing: "Oh, me too, can we please go somewhere with fries? I really want to eat fries!"

"Of course, anak." Dad laughs as he turns the key in the ignition. "You want fries too, Ram?"

"Sure," she answers, then distracts herself by gazing at the clusters of pink flowers that line the road as they drive up the hill.

She feels like she is being watched the minute she sets foot in the room, but it's no different from the past few days, the weariness after the funeral. It's fatigue, she tells herself. Besides, the walkway outside is well-lit and wooden; if someone walks across, she will be able to hear the footsteps, loud and clear. If someone knocks on her door, she can look through the peephole and decide whether or not that someone can be let in. There is a balcony that no one can climb. There is hotel security.

She turns on all the lights and sinks onto the couch, turns on the television, opens a book.

She starts telling the new story over lunchtime, partly to shut Rhea up, and partly because Dad stood up to answer his phone and never came back. Rhea listens intently, slurping her milkshake, while Ramona relates how Susan goes to the resort to take a break, because she is sad, because her husband just died. The resort is exactly like the one they're going to. It's all misty, and there are pink flowers on the road.

"I don't like the name Susan," Rhea says.

"Look, who's telling the story?"

Rhea sucks on a french fry to make it soggy, then mashes it in her mouth. "Fine."

"So Susan was lying down on her couch, reading her book, and she was getting a little sleepy, and then she heard this sound outside—like someone whistling. You know, like a guy having a good day. So she gets kind of scared, she stands up and looks through the hole in the door, but no one's there. She goes back to the couch and reads. She thinks she hears the sound again, but she ignores it."

Rhea presses her lips together and goes, "Phoo-weeet! Like that?"

"No, more like . . ." Ramona wets her lips and tries to whistle, but it doesn't work. She knows exactly how it's supposed to sound, but the sound won't come out. "It's a *tune*," she insists, when Dad comes inside and slides into his seat. "Well, that's all I've got for now."

"No way!"

"What's going on, girls?"

"Ate Ram was telling me a story," Rhea says. "You interrupted!"

"Oh, please, go on ahead." He fishes among the fries, slathers them with ketchup. Smiles widely at his daughters, as if to say, *Let me in on your secret.*

Ramona smiles back, as if to say, *It's just between us girls, Dad.*

"Hey Dad," Rhea suddenly hops up in her seat, talking with her mouth full. "Can you whistle?"

He smacks his lips and whistles: low, melodic. Like someone having a good day.

"Is that what you meant?" Rhea asks. Ramona nods, trying not to feel chilled.

She falls asleep twice reading the same page before she decides it's time for bed. The room is too big for herself, alone—but it was all they could offer on such short notice. Maybe she can ask them to switch her out tomorrow; maybe they can give her a smaller place, for a cheaper rate.

The stairs are long even if the steps are short. She is dizzy, oddly breathless, when she reaches the top. In the shower she feels her skin prickle, but it's probably only the contrast of hot water and cold air.

Besides, she left all the lights on downstairs.

Besides, she has been listening, carefully.

If someone were here, she would know. She *thinks* she would know.

Outside the window, the breeze in the trees makes a curious whistling sound, like a man having a good day, walking down the street.

Rhea dashes inside the room and stomps on the carpet without removing her shoes, loudly claiming that she's gonna have *the sofa bed, the sofa bed, la la la LA!* Ramona enters much more sedately, lugging in two duffel bags and her laptop case.

"You're not getting the sofa bed, you're sharing with Dad. You're *smaller* than me. You'll fit better." Having her own space is one of the few perks she can claim as an older sister; besides, she's more affected by Dad's snoring than Rhea is.

"No, the sofa bed is mine!"

"Listen to your sister, Rhea," Dad says calmly, wheeling in his overnight luggage.

"That is so *unfair,*" Rhea wines, letting the last syllable roll out as she speeds up the stairs. She could get hurt, running up so quickly like that in her socks; but Ramona's not their *mom,* so she doesn't say anything. There is a brief, blessed pause as Rhea's feet thump on the landing. "Oh my GOD! There's a *Jacuzzi!*" More prancing. It sounds like a thunderstorm brewing above their heads.

Ramona sinks down on the couch, exhausted. The drive was only three hours to Baguio's six, but she's jetlagged, lonely, and dislikes the cold. The only thing she wants to do is connect to the free internet and talk to someone, anyone, who isn't Dad—trying too hard to please them—or Rhea, who can't shut up for five minutes.

"You like the place?" Dad asks, hands in his jacket pockets. "Fresh air is a nice change, huh?"

"Yeah," Ramona says. "Real fresh." She squints at the wood chips by the fireplace in the corner—*a real fireplace,* she notes—then lets her eyes wander to the balcony outside. There's a seagull perched on the balcony railing. It stands still as stone, looking out somewhere.

"Ramona," Dad says, "I'm really glad you're here." He claps a hand on her shoulder, then turns and climbs the stairs.

She slips into bed after saying all her prayers, and feels the tears coming on—the nightly tears, the usual sad drowning, because he's dead and he won't be coming back, he left her all alone. (She didn't cry at his funeral, not once, not even when her mother-in-law wept madly against her shoulder, not even when her sister shook her head and said, "I'm so *sorry*, Susan! If only you had kids!") She pulls the blankets up to her eyes and lets the tears soak them. Thinking, *He could be right next to me. He would have put his arm around me, right around here.* She would be listening to him breathe, treasuring every breath.

That's when she realizes—she *does* hear breathing.

The last time they went to Baguio was four years ago. Ramona cried on the way there, but she doesn't remember why; maybe she had a fight with Rhea, who wasn't so noisy then, but was really into pulling hair. Maybe she was sad about missing someone's party. It couldn't have been so bad, after all, because she cheered up when they got to Camp John Hay and they ate in Le Souffle and she had wet rice—risotto—and then she and her cousins tried to make the glasses sing by running their fingers over the rims. They ate weird stiff fruity cake for dessert, which wasn't that good, but then Tita Darlene let them buy some chocolate bars from the gift shop, and those were *really* good.

The next day they went strawberry picking in the morning and they were all super-excited because none of them had ever eaten strawberries (but that was before Dad got kind of weird and moved to the States, before she ever heard Mom say she hated him; and that was before S&R started stocking strawberries for a thousand pesos a box). But the strawberries were teeny and *sour*, so they had to mash them up with milk and sugar before they tasted good. In the afternoon they went horseback riding, which was fun until about halfway through, when Josh got a massive allergic reaction, hives sprouting from his ankles to his neck. They galloped back to the hotel (or maybe just trotted, whatever) and spent the rest of the day watching *The Simpsons* on TV, while the adults had coffee and Talked About Life.

Baguio was fun and Baguio wasn't lonely and when they were in Baguio her parents still talked to each other, still said they loved each other, and didn't pass them back and forth like volleyballs. Dad didn't go drinking, make weird phone calls, or not come home sometimes; Mom didn't smash plates and point her finger at him, when they thought Ramona and Rhea were sleeping. Two years after their last trip to Baguio, Ramona and Dad were alone, and she yelled at him that she hated him for making Mom cry. He hit her on the arm and called her a little bitch, his eyes so wide they reminded her of cartoon characters with their eyeballs bugging out.

The bruise lingered for more than a week, and whenever Rhea asked her what happened, she said, "I fell." And whenever Mom asked her what happened she said, "I fell."

Six months after the bruise faded, Dad left for America. She sobbed when they said goodbye, but a part of her felt that she wouldn't mind not seeing him much anymore; a secret part of her felt that it would be fine, if he never touched her again.

She gets up. She left on the kitchen light downstairs, the staircase lights, the bathroom lights; but after her prayers she turned off the bedside lamp because she never slept well with too much brightness. She flicks the lamp on, looks around the room, but no one's there. Looks outside the window, but the second floor doesn't have a balcony, only the first floor does. But she's sure she *heard* it—an even, steady, *breathe-in-breathe-out,* somewhere in the room; there was a hint of a whistle to it, a low melody that scraped against the lips.

One night. Ramona decides she can manage. She tunes out for most of the afternoon with the homework she brought from school, at least half successful with her plan to use the rest of Christmas break—here, with Dad, in America—to catch up on all the readings her teachers insistently piled on. Rhea watches TV upstairs, which is distracting because the sound floats down, and she keeps channel surfing so that every other sentence gets cut off. Ramona clips on the headphones that Tita Darlene sent her for Christmas—by express courier delivery, because they stopped having family reunions when Mom and Dad stopped living together—but she didn't have time to fix her iPod before they left, and she hates all her current playlists.

At around five Dad loudly calls out that they'll be leaving in thirty minutes for fish and chips on the wharf, but be sure to wear a jacket *and* a coat because it's probably going to be freezing, so close to the water. "Okay," Ramona shouts back. She watches the sun sink outside: so quickly, so early, like it can't wait to be gone.

Her hand is shaking as she hits the little icon on the phone. It rings for a long, long time.

"Hello, Concierge." Blearily. But it's a relief to hear another person's voice, after the whole day's quiet.

"Hello? Hi. I'm calling from Room 501. There's—I think there's someone in my room."

There's a pause on the other end. "Room 501. Ms. Susan Peters?"

"Yes." She tries to keep her voice from shaking.

"Ma'am, are you saying that there is another person in your room?"

"*Yes.*" This time it doesn't work; the single syllable cracks. "Please, can you—I don't know, send someone over? Have security check out the rooms along here?"

"Did you lock your door, ma'am?"

"Yes, of course."

"And your windows?"

"I'm telling you, there's someone here—I *heard* someone breathing, here, in my room!"

The pause this time is long enough for her to realize: she's a widow; her voice also trembled when she called to make her reservation. She must sound *old* to them; old and fearful.

"I'll let security know, ma'am. They'll look out for suspicious persons in your area. They may knock on your door and ask you some questions."

"Please," she says. "Please, I don't feel safe."

"So Susan is American?"

"Yeah. I guess so. Why?"

"Nothing." Rhea licks caramel from her fingers. "Make her Filipino."

"Stop licking your fingers, that's disgusting," Ramona says. She fishes around in her own bag of chocolates and saltwater taffy, looking for something that won't be as messy to eat. They're at the Boardwalk, wasting the pocket money Dad gave them, and she's telling the story again while Dad is buying souvenirs for his coworkers, or that's what he says he's doing anyway. "And she isn't Filipino. She's real, you know. She was really here. She really stayed in our room."

"Yeah, right!"

"No, I'm serious." She looks at Rhea while unwrapping a candy bar. "You can call up the hotel registrar and ask."

"Shut up," Rhea says, but her mouth twists with discomfort. "Your story is stupid."

Ramona shrugs and pops the chocolate into her mouth, waiting.

"So who was it?" Rhea asks, a minute later. "I mean . . . it's stupid, but I still want to know what happened. Who was breathing, in the room?"

Ramona sighs laboriously. Curiosity always wins, in the end.

Susan decides to turn on all the lights. She can't sit still, waiting for security to come check on her. She walks around the room, slowly, carefully, like she might step on something broken; but it makes her feel better, being able to *see* everything. Maybe she *was* hearing things. Or maybe it was a presence, trying to be felt? Maybe it had been a friendly gesture, from someone she loved? The idea makes her feel a little more like herself, like she *isn't* frightened—she moves towards the stairs, decides that she can turn on all the lights and see everything for herself, then call the concierge again and tell them *never mind*, to prove she isn't crazy. And everything will be fine. She'll have to sleep with the lights on, but that's okay; she isn't going to pay for the electricity anyway.

She has gone down two steps when someone places a hand between her shoulder blades and pushes.

The real reason why she doesn't want to sleep next to Dad is because she has this dream, sometimes—where she is lying on her bed and Dad is choking her. He's looking at her and his eyes are wide, wider than is probably humanly possible. Wide like a bug-eyed cartoon character; like a crazy person on a TV sitcom. She wakes up and he's choking her and she makes these terrible gasping sounds, and then her vision narrows to the brilliant red veins leaping out of his eyes, before she blacks out. She wakes up from these dreams feeling sick, confused, wondering why she's still alive—then she remembers they're only dreams, and most of the time Dad isn't around because he doesn't live with them anymore. If he *were* around, it would be weird, like he'd tried to kill her but really hadn't.

Now that he *is* around, it's a little weird, and she's scared about going to sleep that night.

Maybe if she tells her story properly she'll be thinking about it until late at night and she won't sleep; she can sleep tomorrow instead, when it's sunny. *If* it's sunny. If the mist doesn't eat up the sunshine.

It was just a bruise on her arm, just one moment when she wasn't careful with what she said, and he wasn't thinking. Dad still loved her, right, even if he called her a little bitch that one time? Dad didn't love Mom for a while but he never *hit* her; and a lot of the time, he really tried his best. Rhea never seemed to think it was weird, how he frowned then smiled so quickly, how he had wanted them to visit *so badly*. Ramona will sleep on her own tonight and Rhea will be upstairs with Dad, and maybe they will both be thinking about Susan, but what is going to happen to Susan won't happen to them.

This is what happens to Susan: she falls down the stairs, the rest of the twenty-two steps, and hits the cupboard door, but she scrambles to her knees, thankful that the steps were short, wondering if her wrist is broken. She looks up at the man standing at the top of the stairs. His eyes are wide, wide and bloodshot, but there is something happy about them—like it makes him happy to see her. See her roll down the stairs, and hit the cupboard door. See her stare at him with her mouth slightly open, her eyebrows at a sharp, terrified angle.

Beneath his wide eyes, the man has no nose but a small, puckered mouth, and when he breathes in she hears a tinny whistle, the air vibrating on the bevel of his lip. When he breathes out the sound is stronger, sweeter, and he starts heading down the stairs, whistling while breathing, breathing while whistling, and she screams.

"So he's like Voldemort."

"No, you idiot. Voldemort has a nose, except it's like a snake-nose, with slits. This guy doesn't have a nose at all."

"Okay, fine. Whatever. Why does he want to kill Susan?"

"I don't know. I never said he wanted to kill her."

"Well, isn't he going to kill her?"

"He's just hurting her," Ramona says, scrunching her jacket in her fingers, hoping that Rhea's nightmare will be worse than hers. Nothing ever seems to bother Rhea. Sometimes she wishes she could have Rhea's brain; *be* Rhea. Then she remembers what a pain Rhea is. Maybe that isn't such a good idea—but it *would* be nice to be that empty, happy, or selfish, once in a while. "He just wants to hurt her," she repeats, and isn't really surprised to feel the phone buzzing in her pocket; to read the message from Dad, telling them it's time to go back.

She runs into the room, hears his footsteps quicken on the stairs, looks for something to grab, rattles off a prayer in her head. There is a bin with wood chips for the fireplace; a poker is sticking out from the middle of it, a blessed answer, and she makes a dive for it and spins around, holding it before herself like she imagines a sword must be held. He whistles a laugh then says something she doesn't hear, something like, "I'm really glad you're here," and she makes a quick decision between the balcony and the door, decides that the door is safer, but how will she get past him? He moves towards her, he's suddenly very close, she screams again and tries to hit him and he grabs her arm. He grips it hard, hard enough to bruise. His eyes are wide as he snarls, "You little bitch!" but his mouth is small and his lips are pursed, so it comes out musical, like a whistle, like someone having a good day.

The Skype connection finally gets through. Ramona moves to the balcony with her laptop, even if it's cold outside. She doesn't turn the video on, in case it uses too much bandwidth. Mom's voice on the other end is a little fuzzy, but sounds happy. "How's it going?"

"Fine," Ramona says. "We had fish and chips and then we bought saltwater taffy. I think some of it is still stuck in my teeth."

Mom laughs. "Brush your teeth carefully." The Mom-like things she says can be annoying, but halfway across the world, they're comforting instead. Sometimes Ramona wishes she told Mom the truth about the bruise. Sometimes she wishes she told Mom about the dreams, so that she wouldn't have to visit Dad every time he asked them to, simply because it's fair. There's shuffling on the other end, of papers and maybe feet, like Mom is in the office.

Ramona wants to say, *I can't wait to fly back home in three days.*

Or, *Dad is being really nice but did you know, his eyes can go really wide?*

Or, *Susan is running away from a man without a nose, Mom, she was right in this room.*

"I miss you," she says.

"I miss you too, honey," Mom answers, automatically. There's the click of a pen on the other side; maybe Mom is writing out the Christmas Gift Expenditures, like she does every year. "Is Rhea okay?"

"Yeah. She's so *noisy.*"

Mom laughs again. Ramona shivers, although the wind isn't really all that strong; the mist isn't as dense now as it was in the morning. In the moonlight, the pink flowers look nearly white.

"Is, um, is your dad okay?"

Ramona hates this question. She doesn't even know why Mom asks it. She doesn't know if Mom cares or not, but she knows the only meaningful answer is *Yes, yes, he's fine*. One of these days she might crack, she might say something stupid; if she hears this question again she might ask *Why did you leave him? Or did he leave us?* or she might yell *I hate you both*.

Which isn't true. Except when it is.

"Yes, yes, he's fine."

"Good," Mom says. "Honey, my lunch break is almost over. Call me again tomorrow, okay? Tell Rhea I love her. Tell her to brush her teeth."

Ramona logs out of Skype, smacks down her laptop lid, and looks at the flowers again for a few minutes. Then she steps back inside the room, announces to no one that she's going to take a shower, and enters the bathroom. There's a big light above the toilet that is unusually bright and warm; she can feel the heat radiating down on her while she squats and takes a piss. She takes a hot shower, hot enough so that the mirror above the sink gets misted. She draws in a pair of eyes, and a little pursed mouth, mindful that Rhea takes hot showers, too.

She grins to herself, twenty minutes later, when she hears the shower head stop gushing. When, after a brief moment, Rhea emits a small, strangled yelp.

She kicks him where she thinks it might hurt, and misses; her foot connects with his knee instead, so that one leg bucks. She tries to wrestle his hand away from her arm, which is hard to do because she's still holding the poker, and then she remembers that she's *holding* it so without thinking much she jabs it towards him and it buries itself in his thigh and he howls with pain. The sound is like a train coming in, the wind gushing out of that tiny mouth so loud and metallic, she jumps away from him, leaves the poker embedded in his thigh, fumbles for some wood chips in the bin before dashing for the entrance, but he leaps after her and catches her ankle, so that she hits the bathroom door. They fall on the tiles together.

"*Ate!*" Rhea shouts, running out of the bathroom. "I can't believe you *wrote* that!"

"What?" Ramona asks, innocently looking up from a game of Quinn.

"I hate you!" Rhea wails. "Dad!" She charges up the stairs.

Ramona snickers and enters the bathroom again, to brush her teeth for the second time. It's only when she's rinsing out her mouth that she catches the words written in the mist, under the eyes, right where she had drawn a little puckered mouth that is now nowhere in sight: *I can see you.*

His hands close around her neck. He squeezes.

Ramona spits the toothpaste water out of her mouth and backs out of the room, as Dad and Rhea come down the stairs.

"What's wrong?" Dad asks.

"I didn't write that," Ramona says.

"Yes you did! You did!" Rhea insists. She's crying, Ramona realizes—hot, angry tears.

"Dad," Ramona says, because Rhea is a little girl and she doesn't know what she's saying, "Dad, I swear I didn't write that. I think someone else was in here. Someone might be outside."

"No!" Rhea screams, a little hysterical. "She's making it up to scare me! She's telling a story about Susan and her dead husband and the whistling guy!"

"Dad, please, check outside," Ramona says. The whole conversation, Dad's eyes have been widening, so that now they're nearly leaping out of his head; she sees them dart to the words still clear on the mirror. The eyes that she drew in have started to condense from the shift in temperature, coming in from the living room; the lower eyelids have started to drip down, giving them the appearance of tears.

"Okay," he says. "Rhea, stop crying. I'll be right back."

He walks out the door, forgetting to bring his jacket with him.

She can hardly breathe—she *can't* breathe—but she grips the wood piece in her hand and swings it with the last of her ailing strength, so that it smashes into the side of his head. Something warm and wet hits her hand; his grip loosens from her neck, and she gasps for breath, looks up to see his wide eyes and their horror, the horror that mirrors her own, the nightmare that won't leave, the veins popping from the corners of the whites in his eyes, turning gray.

She shoves him off and runs for the phone and screams at them to come, and while she's doing that someone rings the doorbell and it's security and she says, *Look right here, in the bathroom,* gesturing at where he lies sprawled with blood gushing from his head—

Only he isn't there anymore. Instead, there's a box on the floor, with a little pink flower on the lid. There's a folded paper tucked under the pink flower. On it is written: *I can see you.*

Ramona locks the door. Rhea glares at her, tears still running down her face.

"What are you doing?"

"Don't let him back in."

"What? Who? Dad?"

"That's not *Dad,*" Ramona says. "Whoever he was, he was the one who wrote that on the mirror. He wants to hurt us." Her heart is racing, pounding so loudly she thinks she might go deaf with it. "Here," she says. "I'll prove it to you." She steps back inside the bathroom, stands in the space where the man with wide eyes and no nose fell, looks hard at the tiles. She can hear someone's footsteps, distantly, outside—coming from the other end of the suites. Walking back towards them. She looks around desperately, and then sees it wedged beneath the wooden plank under the sink, nearly hidden behind extra rolls of toilet paper: she reaches her hand in and pulls out a small box, with a little pink flower on the lid.

"What's that?"

The footsteps get closer and stop outside their door. "Hey, who locked—Ramona! Rhea! Open the door!"

Rhea turns her head towards the voice.

"Don't open it!" Ramona shouts.

"Why? Ate, stop it!" Rhea's face crumples; she looks terrible. "You're really scaring me! Stop!"

"Open up! Ramona! Rhea!"

She ignores the noise. "What do you think is inside?" She asks her sister, gesturing at the box. "The nose he never had?"

"STOP!" Rhea shouts.

Her hands tremble on the lid, but she keeps on talking. "The puckered mouth that whistles?"

"What the hell is going on in there?" The person outside is starting to get really angry. She can almost see his eyes popping, the whites in them crowding with red. "Open the door, goddamnit! It's freezing out here!"

"DON'T OPEN IT!" Rhea sobs.

Ramona nearly laughs.

"The staring eyes?"

Curiosity always wins, in the end. The person outside is banging his fist, then his shoulder, against the door. Soon he will come inside, and then they can't run away. But Ramona will be fine. Ramona knows what is just a nightmare, what is just a story. Even if Rhea and Mom and Dad and Susan don't.

"Let's find out," she says, and lifts the lid of the little box, and looks inside.

A Canticle for Lost Girls

Have you ever noticed yourself on your knees and thought *Oh, I don't like this?*

I'm braiding Andy's hair, struggling through a complicated style I found on Pinterest, when she catches my eye in the mirror and says, "Mommy, how did you and Ninang CJ and Ninang Tisha become friends?"

Andy's eyes are humongous. There's a deep dimple on one of her cheeks. She's incredibly cute, and I don't think that just 'cause she's mine. The only thing I don't like about her is she has this slight manipulative streak, like when she calls me *Mommy* or Ray *Daddy*. Lilting, sweet. Ray always falls for it. I try not to. Is it cruel to think of your own child this way, to be suspicious of her? But I'm suspicious of everyone. Ray can't decide if he finds it unseemly or attractive about me, saying, *You're so praning all the time, I feel like I gotta protect you,* while he kisses me and cups one of my breasts through my pambahay. I love him too much to tell him I don't think I need his protection.

"Our moms were all lunch mothers, so we hung out during lunch in grade one. Then in grade two and three we did summer swimming classes, and were in the same section, and joined the Cooking Club together." I finish braiding the left side of her hair and secure it with a Goody elastic. She cries "Ouch!" but doesn't really mean it. Already she's squirming out of my grip to check how it looks in the mirror.

"I still have to do the other side," I say.

"Okay. Mommy, you're so slow," she giggles.

"I don't want to hurt you, so I'm trying to be careful." Her thoughtless jab stings, even as I think *what am I doing, making my lovely daughter even lovelier?* I know what a terrible idea that is. I know so well I can't even tell her the truth about CJ and Tisha—how we spent most of our time at St. Agnes not being friends, hurting each other in that special way young girls do. How we love each other now only because we called the dark as one voice. How that happened our junior year of high school, at our spiritual retreat, when we summoned a cruel thing to destroy our CL teacher. How I don't regret it, and I wonder what that makes me, even as I deny the answer: a thing with secret claws. A face in the mirror that swivels, unhinging secret jaws.

Our feet were dirty when we entered the retreat house, our heels and soles covered in dried mud and dust.

They'd arranged the chairs in a circle around the room, and asked us to spread out. Before descending the bus for volunteer work at a village halfway between the city and the retreat house, they'd passed out slippers for us to wear instead of rubber shoes. It was so obvious they were up to something, message-wise.

For two hours I sat inside a sari-sari store with Janelle Montalban, helping Aling Babes, our assigned manang, sell turon and Maxx candies and cigarettes. We chitchatted about *Eat Bulaga,* which was playing on the TV. Janelle and I took turns cradling the chubby infant that Aling Babes had been carrying when we arrived. Several times a manong or child came by to ogle at us through the bars, sometimes smirking and calling out "Uy, sexy." There was a man napping in the back room that kept coughing; each time he did, Janelle flinched. Back on the bus, she told me that at some point when I wasn't paying attention Aling Babes had mentioned that the man—her son—potentially had TB.

When we'd all found our seats, Ms. Caledo, our homeroom teacher, asked us to stand, then led us in a prayer of thanksgiving for our safe journey. We implored the Lord for a holy, enriching retreat. At "Amen," she continued, "Now, girls, take your seats. Myself and your other teachers will be washing your feet."

Silence, flickering from amused to unnerved. Sir Tonio and Mrs. Lagdameo appeared, smiling solemnly, bearing plastic basins and pitchers. "As Jesus washed his disciples' feet, so too will we wash your feet, as a reminder of our need to always remain humble and willing to serve others," Ms. Caledo intoned. One of the retreat house aides entered and handed her a basin. Picking points in the circle at random, the teachers started their work.

We made eye contact with each other, grossed out and nearly laughing, until I saw CJ's expression across the room. Sir Tonio and Ms. Caledo were closing in on either side of her. As they neared, her face grew more alert. She was trying not to look at Sir Tonio, bent over Kat's feet, oblivious to the way Kat made an exaggerated gagging face. CJ's body shifted away; her unease radiated to where I watched, useless, inert. She swallowed, and my own throat tightened, my mind closed on the word *please*. When her eyes met mine I wanted to look away but couldn't, all my guilt simmering, pinning me in place. *If she's so scared of him, maybe it was her picture, after all.*

The spell broke. Ms. Caledo reached her first. CJ's body uncoiled, nothing too obvious, just her shoulders slumping so that she looked again like the slob everyone accused her of being. Two bodies away, Sir Tonio had reached Tisha; from this angle I could only see the back of his head, but he looked up at her for longer than he did other students. Tisha glanced down at him, smiling her smile of perfection, but she didn't let it last—she lifted her head as he dropped his, and scanned the room for someone to charm. I stopped observing before she could catch me. Luckily, Mrs. Lagdameo knelt before me then, and in her motherly voice said, "Hello, Raquel."

"Hi ma'am," I answered, smiling with effort. Mrs. Lagdameo gestured. I held up my right foot, allowing her to pour water over it. My toes curled from the cold. The teachers weren't using soap, so it wasn't like we were *really* getting clean. The water in her basin was the color of weak coffee, and made me feel sick.

We were inseparable in second grade. Mama always told me that, but of course I remembered, too. "I don't know why you and CJ and Tisha aren't friends anymore," she would sigh. "What happened to you girls?"

It bothered me how easily she could bring it up. I missed their friendship too, but I was tired of feeling sorry for myself. Besides, how could I explain all that had happened in the six years since? How in fourth grade we all went to different sections, and things started to change, so quickly it was hard to tell what was going on. We missed eating together for a week, because of various things. Then Tisha started having lunch with some other girls in her section, and CJ got so moody I suddenly didn't want to hang out with her. How that was the start and end of it.

How could I tell Mama that Letitia Tan had become one of our batch heartthrobs, growing taller and slimmer in the span of one summer? How in seventh grade she started dating a high schooler from La Salle, which cemented her reputation as one of the most formidable girls in our batch. She wasn't part of the *main* popular girl barkada, but had her own posse. Her fierce bluntness was sometimes cruel, but it was difficult to hate her. Not only because she was pretty; it was widely known that she was smart, that she regularly got honors. We did not have a friendship confrontation when things started crumbling in fourth grade. After that year, we simply didn't speak. It was like our whole history as childhood friends didn't matter. And it didn't, not really, the loss barred from my mind except in those rare moments when we would pass each other in the hall and I'd think *You traitor, we once roleplayed* Pokemon *together for a whole summer, how could you forget that?* I was Squirtle. CJ was Bulbasaur. Tisha was Charmander.

The only interactions we ever had were as part of the high school paper. It surprised me when Tisha joined, in second year. I was on the News team and she was part of the Literary team, but occasionally we had club-wide workshops, where anyone could share creative work and get critiqued. Both times Tisha submitted long, rambling, hard-to-understand poems that used the word *blood* a lot. She was amazed that everyone read them as meditations on violence. "They're love poems!" she protested. But there was something satisfied in her expression when people interpreted her poems the wrong way.

Nor could I tell Mom about how Carmina Jane Crisologo had gone the opposite direction, slipping from the safe middle of the class to one of our pity cases, a girl on the fringe. I couldn't explain why to Mom, or even to myself. It's true that CJ got her period in the middle of PE and stained her gray gym pants, but that had been true of many other girls. Maybe it was that she turned goth in fourth grade; it wasn't a good look, the leather jacket and emo artwork that she doodled in class. How she seemed *angry* all the time, and that was exhausting to be around. So I decided not to be around it. It hurt less than I thought it would. Maybe Tisha had shown me there was no remorse in discarding something that no longer fit right.

It's also true that CJ's boobs grew enormous, that throughout fifth grade she'd worn ill-fitting bras and people started calling her the Nipple Queen. Then there was that incident in grade six when she burst into tears during music class because there weren't enough kulintang available and she didn't get a chance to play. It didn't seem to me that stupid, to be honest—the kulintang were only on loan at our school for two weeks, and CJ had always loved music. We'd done sleepovers before where we took turns being Britney and Christina Aguilera. But it wasn't a good idea to speak up about it.

I felt sorry for CJ when all that started, but I didn't know what to do. I didn't want to get sucked in. I felt it happening, an electric current under my skin. I still remember the first time I deliberately avoided CJ at lunch. I asked Faye Pajero, my seatmate, if I could eat with her to review for our Sibika exam together. Faye said yes. I made it sound very temporary. From that point on I was always hanging with different barkadas—a benevolent satellite. Safe because I never landed. This meant that CJ lost her one reliable friend—but the thought of being ostracized like CJ terrified me, made me get literal stomachaches. I couldn't let that happen. If at times CJ tried to come over and I shooed her away and her eyes showed utter betrayal—if sometimes my stomach hurt anyway, watching someone whisper as they scuttled past her, like she was some kind of disease—well, it sucked, but could I blame myself? What was I supposed to do, go down with her?

No. Not if I'd managed to dodge that bullet. It wasn't easy to have no fixed barkada. There were weeks when I felt shunned, too. But like, *I got it.* I didn't have any particular draw as a person. I wasn't ugly, except my nose was a bit squashed. In academics I was a flat B across the board. I wasn't a varsity girl. In grade five I won the batch spelling bee so people associated me with being a bookworm—a role I latched on to so I could have *something*, though it didn't feel entirely honest. If, for a couple days, girls felt like not talking to me because I was kind of a loner, I could stand it. I said very little, so there wasn't much to bully me about, nothing that could be used against me. By sixth grade I had been quiet and gentle enough that I could have lunch with different groups, who deemed me harmless. No one adopted me fully, but people were fine with me being there, chiming in occasionally. By the time high school rolled around we'd pretty much cemented our roles. Though I said hi to Tisha whenever I saw her, I didn't do more than that. CJ I didn't even speak to.

We were never all in the same section again until junior year—which is when the boob pic happened, which is when the retreat house happened.

But those intervening years—what happened, Mom? We grew up. The natural selection of private girls' schools took its toll, its flesh sacrifices. Some of us ascended and some of us sank. I was with the majority, too close to the bottom, paddling furiously for fear of drowning.

Our first retreat lecture was about the flight from Egypt and the seven plagues. I *think* the point was that Pharaoh was overly stubborn. As a closing activity, we were told to write our personal plagues on cuartilla paper. I had written *fear of cockroaches* when there was an eruption of snickers to my left. Someone had written *CJ* on their paper. "Hey," I whispered. They quieted, but probably because they thought I was troubled by the noise, not what they'd written.

"Shut up," Tisha, who was nearby, said. "The sooner we finish this exercise the sooner we'll be let out for break." That silenced everyone. It was one of Tisha's powers, the ability to strike with a well-placed sentence. It seemed unlikely that she was defending CJ, who sat alone in a far corner; but I'd learned by then not to question Tisha's motives or actions.

We were led in prayer by the visiting priest, imploring the Lord to make us more like Moses, willing to follow His command. After, we were finally allowed to get to our rooms and organize our things. My roommate was Danica de Dios, a nondescript girl who'd spent elementary school in the States and came to St. Agnes in first year. By then the organism of our class was fixed; new entrants were rapidly assessed and appropriately relegated. The novelty of Danica's accent wore off.

When it was clear that she wouldn't be a ringleader of any sort, she was allowed to freely perch with whichever girls would accept her.

She spent most of her time with Cassie Yuchengco and Maica Silang, who'd also lived abroad for some portion of their childhoods. As a barkada, their biggest claim to fame was that they led Props for our batch production of *The Wiz* in first year. Unfortunately, Cassie and Maica were both in section B, which left Danica as a sometimes-loner in our class . . . like myself. At our field trip to Casa Manila a month ago Danica and I ended up as partners—I'd managed to avoid CJ—and from then on it was an unspoken agreement that though we were hardly what one would call *friends,* we'd fill that gap in each other's required pairings as needed.

The retreat house rooms were simple. I was going to say *dismal,* but that would've been me exaggerating to make it funny. It only looked dingy because we were spoiled Agnesians. The beds were narrow, the pillows deflated. The room's single window looked out onto brown grass; dust motes swirled in the yellow light shining through it. An image of the Sacred Heart of Jesus, blue-and-red rays strobing from his chest, occupied a side table, which also held a dusty plastic bottle of holy water. "This bed doesn't look that clean," Danica said, warily. She put her bag down and sat on it anyway. We ignored how that launched more dust motes into the air.

"It's okay," I said. "Neither are we." It wasn't a joke, but we grinned at each other like it was.

I enrolled Andy in St. Agnes. It didn't make sense to send her elsewhere. I wasn't going to put her in some other private school that I knew even less about, and Ray and I couldn't afford an international school, not without drastic lifestyle changes. For all that I didn't have the best time there, I believed in the basic pedagogy and quality of the education. Besides, it made my mom happy that we could now claim three generations of Agnesians.

Ray left the decision to me, "since you're the mom." Sometimes I wish he'd have more of an opinion on Andy's childcare, if only to challenge my reasoning.

Luckily, Andy loves school. She's eager to see her friends most days. Her grades are better than mine ever were. Of course, she's only nine. From experience I know this is where—if it isn't already—things get hard. You start to care more, about everything. Your body betrays you. Your face secretes *oils*. You get conscious about your chest. You need to use pads. Next year, as a fourth-grader, she'll be bestowed with that ungodly label, *pre-teen*. Her batch will migrate to the building opposite the high school. Underclassmen will look like babies. Upperclassmen will seem looming and lovely; she will share a building with girls who pluck their eyebrows and wear deodorant, and no longer allow their yayas to put their hair in pigtails.

Andy amazes me. Sometimes I feel like I've given birth to a tiny alien. The fact that I can't predict what she does, or that her world is so different from mine, makes me anxious. The truth is I never stopped being anxious, but I've gotten better at normalizing everything, *pretending* I've got it figured out. Ray thinks I'm super religious because I never want to do it, but the fact that I've even had sex is proof of me overcoming fear. Andy is the product of all that, a little warrior, a little genius. It's weird how she makes me a gushing mom, so I try to contain it. I didn't like it when my mom gushed, either. I just love her so much. I'm relieved that I do. I'd feel terrible if I didn't.

Our late afternoon retreat session involved singing some mass songs, then Sir Tonio led reflections on the Passover: "Your lamb must be a year-old male and without blemish. You may take it from either the sheep or the goats. You will keep it until the fourteenth day of this month, and then, with the whole community of Israel assembled, it will be slaughtered during the evening twilight."

Sir Tonio always read like he was performing, pausing between sentences to glance at his audience and check if the words were *sinking in.* The year before, I had interviewed him for the *Agnes Gazette* for our special feature on teachers who'd been at school longer than three years. When I asked what his favorite part of being a teacher was, he laughed—fakely. Like he thought laughing was the thing to do in that moment, so he did it. He said, "The students, of course. My students are the best thing about this job."

I'd bent over my notebook, scribbling to capture this bit of teacherly magnanimity. Something inside me squirmed. Something between a shudder and a prickle raced down my spine. But we were sitting in a corridor in plain view of everyone, and anyway, he wasn't my teacher. Not then.

This year it became fashionable to hate on the male teachers. We agreed that they were all either married, gay, or extremely unattractive, so there was no risk of us falling in love with them. During lunch, in the backs of our notebooks, we made Venn diagrams and sorted our teachers into categories. Sir Tonio was married, so *presumably* he wasn't gay (though the same rule didn't apply to the stylish chem teacher, Sir Leo).

The class was divided on whether Sir Tonio was cute or not. I could kind of see it. The glasses gave him that air of a nerdy Ateneo boy all grown up, and he was younger than a lot of other faculty. What we couldn't figure out was why he taught *Christian Living.* The frontrunner backstory was that he'd been a choir boy and never got over it. Sir Tonio's main issue was that he sometimes said weird shit during class, like that time he told Abby Tuason, "You have beautiful eyes," or when he rhapsodized about relics then leaned over Tisha's chair and said, "What about you, Ms. Tan? Which of your body parts do you think the Church might keep to venerate?"

The class went still. I was surprised he'd dared to challenge Tisha like that. It amazed me that the teachers didn't realize her power. Char Laguatan started hiccuping, which was an opening for Sir Tonio to retreat, but Tisha remained cool as a cucumber and said, twirling her hair around one finger, "Probably my lips, sir." She didn't even justify it. She didn't need to. Char hiccuped furiously; Sir Tonio grinned and moved away. The class, as one body, giggled tentatively.

In the fading light of the retreat house rec room, Sir Tonio droned: "Do not eat any of it raw or even boiled in water, but roasted, with its head and shanks and inner organs. You must not keep any of it beyond the morning; whatever is left over in the morning must be burned up."

For much of the semester the verdict regarding Sir Tonio was that he was slightly creepy but harmless. Last month, though, because of the boob pic, a rumor started that he and CJ were having sex. No one really believed it, but everyone found it funny, or pretended to.

It was getting dark. I wondered why the fluorescents didn't come on, until the teachers brought out candles and sorted us into small groups. Our task was to share stories of our own "flights out of Egypt." We were supposed to talk about personal struggles, like bad grades, or fathers with affairs, or grandparents with cancer. Instead we talked about prom, which was five weeks away. Queenie Paterno and Lucy Esguerra were doing the Skyflakes diet; Lucy claimed she hadn't seen results, and instead got LBM. Jana Chuatico grumbled about the Xavier boy her mom was setting her up with, because he was only interested in pure Chinese girls, and she was only 50% Chinese. We complained about how ugly the invitations were, despite *Moulin Rouge* being a decent theme. When it was my turn to offer up a prom woe, I talked about how my modista kept changing the design of my dress. That satisfied everyone.

Presently the teachers and retreat house aides brought dishes to each group: a flattish piece of bread, a bowl of clear soup, a single lump of chicken breast, skin unappetizingly pale. Sir Tonio walked to the center of the room and said into his mic, "We have just now brought you unleavened bread, and bitter herbs in the form of soup. Sorry walang lamb, so we provided chicken instead. Mas cheap eh."

Someone laughed so that he could get on with it. "You will share this meal with each other. It is the only dinner you will have, like the Israelites before they fled. Try not to have leftovers."

We started on the communal meal. It seemed odd that this was all they would feed us, but something about the exercise was tender, gently amusing. We tore humble strips of bread. We twisted the soup bowl slightly each time we sipped, so as not to indirectly kiss each other. None of us wanted the chicken, but for the sake of the kitchen staff, we each took a forkful, chewing 'til we could swallow. We remained somewhat hungry, which was good for the dieters; the hunger made us feel pious. In the dramatic candlelight, everyone's face was an interesting shade of orange. We chattered genially, until the meal was over and we were dismissed.

The lights in the first-floor dining room were open. The quickest girls to the staircase noticed and immediately raced down, laughing. Spaghetti, garlic bread, and barbecue were waiting for us as we swarmed the room, suddenly ravenous.

"I knew it!" Abby exclaimed. Of course they wouldn't let us starve. The night was young and so were we, and we deserved every delicious thing.

One afternoon Andy asks me if she needs a training bra. My eyes snap to Andy's chest like a creeper. It's flat. There's a high chance Andy will simply inherit my A-cups. I'm upset by her question, though I know it's better than her starting to visibly . . . poke through shirts. CJ in fifth grade comes to mind. I wonder which of Andy's friends planted this idea in her mind, made her start to worry. In a barkada worrying can be infectious.

"Come here, baby," I say. She comes. Recently she's started to care more about her appearance while going out, but at home she's the same as ever. She's wearing her ratty Elsa-and-Anna shirt, that CJ gave her two birthdays ago, and some boxer shorts from SM

Department Store. I hold her shoulders and swivel her from side to side, inspecting whether there's a critical mass of boobage that needs to be hidden.

Andy sighs. "Mom, stop being weird."

Better to be safe than sorry. It'll happen sooner or later. Maybe I can get her a T-shirt bra. At the moment she's still mostly nipples, but I don't want her to feel left behind.

"We can look next time we're at the mall," I oblige.

"So I *do* need one?"

"Um, not really, I think. We can ask the saleslady for her opinion."

"Oh," she says. I can't tell if she's disappointed or relieved. I should be better at reading her. She shrugs. "Okay."

I accuse Ray of being the doting parent, but it's both of us, really. I hate the thought that Andy will be like other only children, supremely spoiled, self-centered. *You turned out okay, though, didn't you?* Ray, who has four siblings, murmurs. I shut him up with a kiss and don't tell him he's wrong.

About the infamous boob pic. No one knows where it originated. One day one girl had it, the next ten did; three days later our whole batch had either glimpsed it or specifically declined to see it.

I saw it. I didn't want to. It appeared in my inbox, a forwarded message with the subject line "LOL." I assumed it would be one of those harmless chain emails with lists of stupid Pinoy names or *if-you-don't-pass-this-on* curses. Instead my screen displayed a girl's chest, her shirt rucked up, a camera flash obstructing most of one breast: a reflection in a dirty mirror. The image was cropped at her neck. I deleted the email, emptied my trash bin, looked over my shoulder in case one of my parents was lurking.

My heart rate had picked up. Seeing the picture felt dirty—and scary. The boob-owner was anonymous, and the email had no details, but it was definitely being passed around with *some* name attached. None of us were safe.

A day or two later, while standing in line for fries at recess, Lei Pecson turned to me and said, "Have you seen it? CJ's boob?"

"Oh . . . was that CJ's?" I answered stupidly.

She shrugged. "I heard it was CJ's."

"It could be anyone's."

Marisela Binuya, who had just placed an order for jumbo-sized sour-cream fries, said, "I heard she sent it to Sir Tonio. But it wasn't actually Sir Tonio, it was a senior pretending to be Sir Tonio."

"What? Gross!" Lei gagged. "Why would she? He's not even that cute."

"Oh, you didn't know?" Marisela passed over two crisp twenty-peso bills, grinning at the fries lady who put a ten-peso coin back in her hand. She dropped her voice in a show of discretion. "I heard they . . . *did it* . . . in the faculty bathroom on the third floor. You know, the one with the shower."

I can't speak for others, but at sixteen, the idea of sex—even just the *word*—filled me with dread and disgust. I knew how it worked, of course. I'd been on the internet, and in second grade I read this picture book called *Mommy Laid An Egg* that my Math tutor had in her bag, presumably for some other student. I'd paged through it while she took a phone call. Its stick-figure depictions of "doing it" were faintly horrifying. I'd wanted to talk about it with Tisha and CJ, infect them with my newfound knowledge, but I didn't know how.

Thankfully that duty wasn't mine. Starting fourth grade they'd given us free napkins once a year, and talks delivered by various alumni encouraging us to shut our legs, not dress like sluts (or, as they phrased it, "temptingly"), and remember that boys were animals. There were also cautionary tales that got passed around—the sophomore who dropped out because she got pregnant; the girl who'd been threatened with expulsion because she was caught giving someone a blowjob at the Xavier fair. She got a temporary suspension instead. I was twelve when I heard that rumor. She'd been one batch above us, in seventh grade. "What's a blowjob?" I asked, flushing when everyone broke into laughter.

(Sometime in college, "sex" became just a word. It didn't suck everything up with gravity, like a black hole. This happened not because I'd become a slut, like all those alumni feared. In fact, the only person I've ever slept with is Ray, and even then it was a few months after we got engaged. I still wonder why I didn't wait until marriage, since we were so close already; but I loved him and thought it would make him happy, and I didn't mind. Tisha once told me sex is supposed to be fun. At my stricken look she smirked and said, "Yeah, even for someone like me," which made me feel terrible.)

"Barbecue, large," Lei said to the french-fry lady. Turning back to Marisela she said, "I feel sorry for Sir Tonio's wife. Like he already sucks for cheating on her, but for a girl like CJ? So sad."

"CJ's not that white," I said, wondering *Why the hell am I even saying so?* There was no point in being her defender. It *could* have been her boob. If I pressed the issue, there was a non-zero chance the boob would be attributed to me. Lei and Marisela looked at me, then at each other. The french-fry lady coughed. "Small plain," I told her, grateful for the distraction, then mumbled, "I mean, she's not as white as the girl in the photo."

"How would *you* know?" Marisela said. "Have *you* ever seen CJ's boob?"

During swimming lessons the summer before third grade, we'd once clambered out of the pool because some kid barfed in the deep end. We'd been disgusted, even if the vomit had been far away. We imagined the vomit was everywhere, hardly diluted by the chlorine. In the changing rooms there was only one shower stall open. We stripped out of our swimsuits—CJ, Tisha, and I—and rushed into it, laughing. We were eight. CJ didn't have boobs then.

I shook my head, claimed my french fries, and fled.

❁

CJ is a doctor. She's a heart surgeon at St. Luke's. Apparently she did amazing in med school, and when she got into her residency program she was ranked in the top five something-something nationally. When she was in med school it was hard to meet with her, but she always tried. She'd catch the tail end of our dinners in Megamall or High Street, wearing her white coat, haggard but happy to see us. It's gotten better post-residency—she still keeps crazy hours, but the more senior she gets, the more control she seems to have over her schedule. It's strange to think of CJ cutting people open and saving lives, when once upon a time she couldn't walk through the cafeteria without someone snickering.

After the retreat house, CJ never confronted me about my cowardice. How complicit I was, all those years, in ostracizing her. It was enough that we were friends again, or so I liked to tell myself. Honestly, she'd be entirely justified in hating me. If I were in her shoes, some small part of me always would.

All it took, really, for her to become "normal," was us giving her a chance. When we started hanging out again, I realized her preteen awkwardness—the moods, the incessant arguments, the belting of My Chemical Romance songs to annoy people—had mostly faded. It was just that no one gave her the opportunity to be chill. It was easier to think what they always thought: that CJ was a loser.

For years I didn't dare reach out to CJ because I didn't want her to cling to me. But even after we became friends again she never got overly dependent on us, never emphasized her worries or shared what those years were like for her. She and I had both been burned before. The difference was that CJ got stronger, while I had turned hunted, needing frequent validation.

In St. Agnes reunions—at debuts, and later on, people's weddings—our batchmates often tell CJ, "Oh my god, you bloomed!" It's like they have amnesia about the way they'd treated her in elementary and high school. CJ lets them. It doesn't matter to her if they're fake. "It's not *intentional*," she explains. "I'm sure they now believe that they were nice to me all along." She doesn't care, she assures me. She stopped caring long ago. She has more important things to worry about, like her patients, or rejecting the persistent suitors that have plagued her through her med career.

Andy and CJ have an interesting bond. Sometimes Andy will say something incredibly smart, some science factoid or historical trivia. When I ask her how she learned it she'll say "Ninang CJ taught me!" CJ always gives her books as gifts. Andy is a real bookworm, not like I was, faking it because it gave me something to be. Whenever CJ tells her, "I want you to love reading like your mom did," a part of me wonders if CJ *understands*, too, what a fraud I was. How I still don't know if I'll ever grow out of it.

In the middle of the night, I woke up desperate to pee. I tried ignoring it, but it didn't go away. I decided to get it over with. I'd once wet the bed when I was already in fourth grade and was eternally traumatized about relapsing. I gathered my hoodie tight around me as I pulled on my slippers, careful not to wake Danica. The hallway outside was lit by a weak lamp on an altar halfway through it. It held a small metal crucifix and a bottle of holy water in the shape of the Virgin Mary. Above it was an image of Jesus, solemn, unruffled by whatever shenanigans a building full of high school girls might get up to. In a slightly smaller frame was St. Agnes, gazing chastely into the distance as she clutched an unblemished lamb and a palm leaf.

We'd learned her story back in kindergarten, through a picture book. Her death was conveniently unillustrated. Somewhere along the way we'd imbibed the utter *irony* of having a virgin as our patron saint—because of the reputation Agnesians had. Whether we were actually worse than other schools was besides the point. Our exclusivity—the way our English sounded, how we were always chaperoned by yayas—simply added to the gleefulness with which other schools declared us sluts. We couldn't dispel the rumor. Some of us believed it, even.

Every girl knew what her own score was. Every girl was deciding how she'd like to define innocence, purity. There *was* a line, the school told us—for them it was drawn all the way back at wearing halter tops and using the word "bitch," but even when one had committed an error, you could safely backtrack with enough good behavior . . . unless you let someone *take that thing*. That was the point of no return. So shut your legs, girls, please. That, which made you most precious, was reserved for God and your future husband. Allowing trespassers meant sin.

Of course, there were ways to scrub out sin. The Catholics in our class—almost everyone—had "highly recommended" confession the next day of retreat. Even then, however, a sin left stains, if only in one's conscience.

The bathroom was at the other end of the hall. I flicked on the light as I entered, trying not to look at the mirrors. I never believed in Bloody Mary, but it wasn't worth the risk. I ignored the chill of the toilet seat against my thighs and pissed. I couldn't avoid the mirror while washing my hands, so I focused on the clock in the reflection—1:32 a.m. I glanced at the dusty towel hanging on a ring by the sinks, and decided to air-dry my hands instead.

When I looked back at the mirror, someone was behind me.

"Oh, shit!" I sprang into the air, heart juddering.

"Ay, sorry," the person replied. "Is that you, Raquel?"

Nervous tears prickled my eyes. I'd left my glasses in my room. It wasn't like my eyesight was terrible, but between my terror and the crappy lighting it took me a moment to recognize Sir Tonio.

"Oh my god, sir, don't do that," I couldn't help saying, rubbing tears from my eyes.

"What are you doing? It's late."

"Yes. Sorry. I just, uh, I had to use the toilet." Had he heard me peeing? Gross.

"Sorry for scaring you. I didn't mean to." He came closer. I wanted to step back, but the sink was behind me. He noticed I hadn't moved, and stopped. "I thought someone left the light on by accident."

"I'm all done," I said. He was still wearing his clothes from the day. That was strange, but I didn't want to see him in his pajamas, either. I hesitated. "What about you, sir? Why are you awake?"

"I'm patrolling. In the first-year retreat last month two students decided to sneak out at night, so we want to make sure everyone's still in their rooms."

"Oh, okay." It wasn't exactly cold, but I felt clammy. I clutched my forearms, waiting for Sir Tonio to move, or leave. He made a sound like "Heh," which was mortifying, then he stepped into the hall. I followed, uneasiness singing through me. "My room's that way." I pointed.

"I know," he said. The way he said it made all my hairs stand on end. I swallowed against an urge to—run? cry for help? do *something*—because this was my teacher, and if anyone saw us together in the hallway I'd be the subject of the next rumor about Sir Tonio's sex life. "All teachers have a copy of the floor plan," he added, which wasn't very comforting.

"Goodnight, sir," I said, grasping for respect, the one feeling that could rise above my ambient discomfort.

"Goodnight, Raquel."

I turned away so I couldn't see his eyes. I didn't want to know if they were trained on me as I walked down that endless corridor. I never heard his footsteps. Back in my bed, swaddled in the dark, I kept listening for something, but I didn't know what. It took me ages to fall back asleep.

❈

Usually screaming roosters served as our retreat wake-up call. They were the worst, blasting through the windows at top volume as the sun rose. This time, though, we were awakened by the scream of a classmate. It was impossible to tell who. Fear shot through my sleepy body. Danica and I exchanged glances; I got to the door first and poked my head out, shielding the rest of me.

Lianne Gutierrez was kneeling in the hallway, hands pressed against her mouth. The door next to her was covered in blood, top to bottom, in a nasty crisscross pattern. It took a moment for me to realize that the blood outlined, roughly, a star in a circle. The air felt thick, greasy. Our swirling murmurs intensified, cresting when Ms. Caledo and Mrs. Lagdameo rushed over, still in their pantulog. Something about seeing Ms. Caledo's skinny calves made me panic; it was too human. Mrs. Lagdameo helped Lianne up, and Ms. Caledo touched the door handle and swung it open.

There was a short groan from within. Ms. Caledo said "CJ!"

CJ emerged, shuffling to the doorway, rubbing her eyes. "What's going on?"

She noticed everyone in the hall gazing at her first, then Lianne sobbing in Mrs. Lagdameo's arms; finally she noticed the door.

"Holy sh—!" Even in the insanity of the moment, I admired her effort not to curse in front of teachers. She backed away from the door, coming to stand next to Mrs. Lagdameo and Lianne. "What—who—"

"Someone has played a very terrible prank," Ms. Caledo said. Now the shock was wearing off, she was stabilizing, returning to her role as our unflappable professor. We all liked Ms. Caledo. Except for that one time she overshared about her love life during our field trip to Casa Manila, she was a good homeroom teacher. "CJ, Lianne, I'm so sorry. Are you girls okay?"

Lianne sniffled and nodded. CJ continued to gape.

Ms. Caledo gazed at us, passively observing from our doorways. "This isn't funny, girls. I don't know who did this or how, but you cannot bully your classmates this way. If whoever did this wants to come forward, you can find me or Mrs. Lagdameo. We don't wish to take disciplinary action on the whole section."

There wasn't even a moan of distress; everyone was too shocked. Tisha had the room next to CJ's. Her face was white as a sheet, staring at the blood-splattered door. Tisha had never been great with blood. (We discovered this when I cut my foot open on a broken tile once during swimming class. She got woozy at the sight of all that red drifting in the water. It didn't hurt much, but her panic made me panic. CJ called the teacher, who told me to stop swimming for the day.)

Mrs. Lagdameo had also recovered. "This is a cruel prank," she echoed.

"Mrs. Lagdameo, that's *so much blood,*" Tetet Rodrigo piped up. The word *blood* seemed to sharpen the stench, the B-movie goriness of it all. Tetet was our section president. She soldiered on, displaying the goody two-shoes resilience that convinced us all to elect her, despite knowing she would sometimes be annoying. "Do you . . . do you really think someone would do this as a prank? What if . . . what if we're in danger?"

"Tetet, there's an evil *star* on the door," Ms. Caledo answered, exasperated. "Every year a student sticks a sign with the word *DEVIL* on someone's door. This is the same thing, except someone here has been incredibly cruel to some chickens."

This sounded reasonable. We had all, in four years of attending overnight retreats, been in a section with at least one DEVIL-sign controversy. Of course someone had splattered chicken blood all over the door. We all knew the coop two minutes away from the kitchen, from which the retreat-house staff procured our morning eggs. We'd all seen that tactic deployed in an episode of *Megane-man Case Files* in fifth grade. Next to our sensible teachers, our morbid imaginations were tempered. It made sense: CJ was in that room, and on some level, everyone was out to get CJ.

CJ seemed to accept this. At any rate she was handling it better than Lianne, who became her roommate only because Lianne's actual retreat partner—Ylena—got a fever two days ago and wasn't allowed to come. CJ glanced up and down the hall, scrutinizing us, as if she were turning over rocks to check for bugs beneath. Asking: *Can't I blame any of you?*

The spell was broken by two retreat-house aides hustling over with a bucket, a mop, and a pile of rags. They sloshed the door with water and started wiping away.

"Go back to your rooms, girls," Mrs. Lagdameo said, sounding tired. The roosters chose that moment to break into their demonic morning chorus. "Breakfast is in an hour."

My eyes followed the way the blood ran, pinkish, down the door. Lifting them, I caught CJ's gaze. She was looking directly at me. After a beat, her lips quirked. It took me a moment to realize she was smiling: a sad smile, a kind one. It held a secret, and burned like poison through me.

If CJ is Andy's brainy, medical ninang, Tisha is the ambisyosa one that's already trying to figure out Andy's career path. For birthday and Christmas gifts, and sometimes for no reason at all, she gives Andy baking sets, jewelry-crafting kits, and last year, a one-year subscription to an online coding course for kids.

Tisha got into Ateneo on a partial merit scholarship, and became head of the Marketing Association senior year. She spent a year in Unilever's leadership training program in Singapore, then another two in Manila, rising through the ranks until she became assistant brand manager for oral care. Throughout most of that time she'd had a tumultuous relationship with one of her similarly accomplished coworkers. She was miserable, but there was glee to her misery, to the way she would cuss out her boyfriend then tell me, "You really lucked out with Ray, Raquel, he's such a sweetheart."

Ray *is* a sweetheart, but I let Tisha say that because I know there's no way she'll go after him. After all these years she still has that *thing* that makes people do a double-take when she walks into a room: effortless charm, or straight-up sex appeal? In high school it was a covert weapon, sealed beneath our checkered blue uniforms. In college, and ever after, she honed its dangerous edge to perfection, using it to her every advantage.

The year Ray and I got engaged, Tisha dumped her boyfriend and moved to the US to earn an MBA at Wharton. She flew home to Manila for our wedding the next summer with a new plus-one: a classmate from the Netherlands. Marit was gorgeous, blonde and lean. She looked straight out of a Lululemon ad. It boggled my mind to see them together, to think of Letitia Tan, perpetual heartthrob, as *not entirely straight*. I wondered if this was why none of her previous relationships had worked: not that first La Salle high school boy, or her Marketing org co-president in Ateneo, or her rival-turned-lover from Unilever. At some point, when the photo-ops stopped and I was finally able to eat a slice of my wedding cake, I saw Tisha lean over to whisper in Marit's ear, before pulling back to beam at her. CJ, also at their table, pointed at one of my nephews, aggressively getting down on the dance floor. The three of them laughed.

"I'm not gay," Tisha said, when she came home post-MBA, newly single. She seemed confident and at peace, ready to take on the world, or at least as much of the world as being VP of Marketing at her hot new e-commerce start-up allowed. I choked on the boba tea we were drinking. Tisha smiled at my awkwardness. "I'm not straight, either. I don't know, I don't care about those things. I think my parents still want me to be married, like you, and have some guy's kid, like you. I do think I still want that for myself too. Eventually. Maybe. Or maybe I'll stay single forever, like CJ. It's really fun, being single."

"Right," I said. My eyes watered slightly. I always felt too much around my friends. I wanted so badly for Tisha to find a beautiful love, but maybe that wasn't feminist of me. How could I be a better friend to her? Did she even need me to?

I must have looked worried, because Tisha sighed and rolled her eyes. "You're overthinking things again. I'm not like this because of what happened! You're the only one that's still haunted by that whole thing—you know that, right?"

Haunted is a funny word for what happened.

By breakfast we'd regained a sense of normalcy, though the Bloody Door Incident was all anyone could talk about. Someone had already declared that there weren't any chickens in the trash that morning, but that much blood certainly required several chickens. Someone else said the chickens were probably buried in the fields farther away. Who hated CJ so much that they'd go through all that trouble? What if it was a psycho who'd come in off the street—was our security guard slacking? And poor Lianne, getting dragged into all this. It was too bad Ylena got sick.

No one came forward, which made the teachers angry, but they decided to proceed with the retreat as usual. They had the rest of the semester to pursue disciplinary action. Of course, there was always the possibility—this with flip giggling—that it was, indeed, the devil.

Breakfast was the best part of retreat. Whatever the kitchen did to make their tapa the perfect mix of sweet and salty, we had no idea. Tisha was at the other end of my breakfast table, pushing scrambled eggs around her plate. She was still unfairly pretty, but she looked *bad*—her eyebags were enormous, her lush lips nearly white. She was wearing a cardigan even if the aircon was off. The conversation drifted around her; if there was something we were good at as high school girls, not forcing an issue was it.

"Tisha, are you not going to eat your eggs?" Meggie Palabyab, one of Tisha's kabarkadas, asked.

"I don't know how any of you have an appetite."

"I mean, wasting food is bad." Meggie reached over and snatched up a forkful of Tisha's eggs.

"Be in the rec room in fifteen minutes!" Sir Tonio chirped. He'd emerged from the teacher's special dining room. We groaned, although there was no tapa left; after the Bloody Door, it seemed strange to discuss spirituality, or make short comics about the Gospel.

"Sir, where were you this morning?" Lei called out. "You didn't get to see the door!"

"I had a headache," Sir Tonio answered, then added, with a solemnity that seemed by this point unnecessary, "I'm glad none of you were injured. Don't worry, girls, we're going to find out who did it."

After yesterday's foot-washing incident, I had an impulse, whenever Sir Tonio was in the room, to glance at CJ for her reaction. But she was calmly sipping her orange juice, a conspicuous gap between her and the other girls at her table. Tisha, on the other hand, seemed to get more fidgety; her shoulders twitched as Sir Tonio spoke. Maybe he'd caught her peeing in the middle of the night, too; maybe it was that he'd held her feet yesterday, and looked at her longer than he needed to. I didn't blame her look of distaste, but I wanted to ask her about it, check if she was okay.

It wasn't something I'd felt towards Tisha in a long time.

These muddy feelings got lost in the overwhelming blah of our morning session: Bible readings, fifteen minutes of silent reflection in which I fell asleep; learning a song that went "Pharaoh Pharaoh, ooo baby, let my people go!" complete with cheesy dance moves. After lunch, Mrs. Lagdameo lectured us on the parable of the Prodigal Son. The rest of the afternoon was free for us to write palancas, except for those who were attending confession.

I didn't like retreat-house confession. There was no confessional. Instead, you sat across from the priest and tried not to look at him while blabbing your sins, but you also looked *a little,* because not looking felt extremely rude. Confession itself I didn't mind so much. Every now and then I left them feeling like I'd actually been cleansed, teary-eyed and awed with it. But I always wondered what it meant that my sins never changed: I'd taken the Lord's name in vain, I'd been lazy, I'd been rude to my parents, I'd eaten too much. My sin catalogue was vanilla, derived from an illustrated guide to confession that we received before our first holy communion. A good thing, maybe—but why did I keep making the same sins?

It occurred to me that I had a new sin this time, though any way I phrased it would not convey its awfulness. The priest had a mild face, like a potato. He said nothing as I entered and greeted him, though he nodded to encourage me. As I rattled off my sins I felt my chest tightening, until at last I spoke my new confession: "I've allowed people to be bullied. I've stood by and let people say mean things about other people, even when I know it's wrong. I've been doing this for years."

The priest bobbed his head, affably, like I'd told him that it was a hot day. I decided I didn't want to end on the sin that felt most suffocating, so I added, "And I wasn't there to comfort people who needed comfort," thinking about the bloody door and Lianne sobbing. How sure I had been that I couldn't make a difference. There were so many other people who could help; teachers for whom it was their *job* to help. The excuse was sensible, and still an excuse. "For all these sins and more, including, um, the ones I've forgotten. Please forgive me." I stared at the faded maroon tiles of the study they used as the confessional, waiting.

"When you don't help someone, whether it's when they're being bullied, or when they are, as you said, in need of comfort, oftentimes it's out of fear," the priest began. "Recall from Psalms: *The Lord is my light and my salvation. Whom shall I fear? The Lord is the stronghold of my life.*

Of whom shall I be afraid? You have nothing to fear because the Lord is beside you. You can be assured that doing the right thing will please Him. Allow that to give you strength."

"Yes, Father," I said. It was a better message than I expected. I was already certain I couldn't act on it. As penance he gave me three Hail Marys, and suggested that if possible, I apologize to those whom I'd hurt by not intervening.

Since there was no actual chapel in the retreat house, they'd lined up chairs outside the confession room and placed cushions on the floor so we could kneel without hurting our knees. On the opposite side of the door were all the girls still waiting for their turn, fiddling with their hands and resisting the urge to chat, to retain the air of solemnity. Tetet had gone in after me; CJ was next in line. Her eyes were closed. I wondered if she was praying. Looking at her, I felt moved and troubled by her calm. Her *smile* from this morning, all the mysteries it contained. How tranquil she looked now.

I had no business feeling bad that I couldn't defend her. I was only trying to make myself feel better. *I wouldn't have done it any differently. I don't know if I would, now. I've worked so hard to be okay like this. If God can really see my soul, doesn't He know it's impossible not to be afraid? Why give me this fear?*

CJ opened her eyes. I closed mine and clasped my fingers together, looking more pious than I wanted to. My knees hurt despite the pillow. Was there such a thing as kneeling too hard?

My pregnancy with Andy was easy all the way up to the delivery. I don't remember most of it—the hours bled together as I drifted in and out of half-sleep and intense, stabbing pain. By the time she emerged I'd sobbed myself dry.

I've never had baby mania, never had intense feelings about other people's kids, no matter how doe-eyed or chubby-cheeked. Holding Andy in my arms felt like a miracle. I got overwhelmed pressing my cheek against her skin, which had somehow formed within my skin. The fear was also new: having made this life, it was now something I couldn't bear to lose.

For a long time I wondered if I could actually have a child. Even while pregnant, some part of me was convinced it would all go wrong, that I couldn't deliver a healthy baby—because of what I'd done. What I once dared do. My high energy, the fact that I wasn't sick or suffering throughout, made me even more worried.

I don't trust things that are easy. I always feel like there's a trick somewhere. This was true when I met and fell in love with Ray. It's true for raising Andy, because she's pretty much an angel—tantrums are rare, and her teachers all agree she's great. Sometimes I'll be grasping at the right way to mother her, then she'll wrap her arms around me and say *I love you Mommy* and my anxiety crawls away for another day. It's true for friendships: how CJ and Tisha and I have remained friends for over a decade now; how in college and at work I made other friends just fine. I don't know why it was so *hard* in St. Agnes. That these things got better, that my life is normal, feels like the extended setup to a nasty plot twist. Sometimes I wonder what I've lost, bracing for it.

I suspect it'll come from Andy, one day. I don't want to be disappointed in her, nor do I want to control her. I need to embrace that she'll grow into her own person. I always want her to need me, but I also want her to be strong and independent. I want her to be beautiful, but I don't want anyone to hurt her because of that beauty. I want to protect her from everything, but getting hurt is part of growing up. How can she learn the world without it getting its claws into her? Can I break those claws into bluntness? Is it wrong for me to want that?

Palancas were always the highlight of retreat. A month before, teachers would send letters to parents asking them to write to us, to share their hopes for our spiritual growth and bright futures. We could also write letters to each other, and solicit letters from friends in other sections. On the second night of retreat, everyone sat on the floor of the rec room, opened their envelopes, and unleashed their emotions. A fat stack of palancas assured at least two hours of sobbing by candlelight, against soft piano music.

Because I didn't have best friends, most of my crying came from my parents' letters. I always finished within an hour. My dad sent goofy cards. My mom would handwrite three pages back-to-back, telling me how proud she was of me and encouraging me to pray for guidance through all the challenges I faced at school. That sentiment always made something in me twinge, as I wondered: how much of my loneliness did she know? Which hurt more—my mother's ignorance, or helplessness? My favorite ninang sometimes sent a letter too, though that one usually made me laugh.

Tonight, though, there was an extra activity before palanca reading. Entering the conference room after dinner, we observed that the chairs were lined up in two columns. "This is called the pillars of truth," Sir Tonio said. "Please sit in alphabetical order." We complied, warily. "You should now all be facing one of your classmates. When the bell rings, everyone on the left column will have twenty seconds to speak to the person on the right column. Girls in the right column, you can only listen. You can't say anything. When the bell rings again, everyone will move one seat to the left, and those at the top of the left column will shift into the right. We hope you take this opportunity to share with each other what is truly in your heart—all the things you wish to tell each other, anything you regret, anything you never got the chance to say." He paused for effect. "Be kind, and make use of this opportunity."

I was on the left column: the speakers. I looked at Romina Tanjanco, who blinked at me, clearly wondering what I could say, given that we'd barely interacted in our twelve years as batchmates. Some girls were already giggling at each other, plotting to say a green joke or resurface incidents from elementary school best left buried. Truth was a rare commodity among us; it so often meant visceral humiliation. And it was hard to be truthful when we barely knew ourselves in the first place. Truth required scraping away the hard shell of combat weariness we'd gained over years of surviving our girlhood and each other, to get at the strange softness of *who we actually are* underneath. We hadn't even been buttered up by the palancas yet.

Sir Tonio rang a bell, the note clear as a warning in the room's muted energy. I leaned towards Romina, who leaned forward. Maybe this was an opportunity—I could be kind first, which would make them want to tell me kind things, too. "You're nice, Romina, and I never forgot how you helped me during that seventh grade field trip when I fell and scraped my knee." Romina nodded and gave me a tiny smile. I strained for more things to say. "And I know you've been working hard on the prom committee, so thank you."

The bell rang again, and we shifted seats. Tisha squinted at me, her lovely face sickly in the candlelight.. Her exhaustion made me weary, as I grasped for words. *I wanted to keep being your friend,* my brain suggested, but no—that would just make us both feel bad. If Tisha could find better friends, be more popular, why shouldn't she? I gave up on being diplomatic and said, "I've always found you very pretty, Tisha . . . and I feel like you have good leadership skills even if you're not a class officer. When you speak, people listen." In a burst of honesty, I added, "Sometimes you look really tired, though, and it worries me." When I pulled back Tisha had opened her mouth, but she was on the silent row, and the bell was ringing again.

Relief. If I could survive Tisha, everyone else was easier. Next was Felice Sysip. I told her I laughed a lot when she played the possessed boy in our second year CL play. If I thought even a little, the memories came easily, years of togetherness sharpening into clear moments. There was something nice or at least funny to say to everyone. I told Tetet she was smart and did a good job as our class president; I told Lianne her voice was beautiful, especially when she sang the responsorial psalm for St. Agnes's feast day.

I let my guard down. When the bell rang again, CJ was before me.

Her face was dispassionate, like she'd weathered whatever it was people had said to her. When she noticed it was me, her eyebrows drew together in worry. Her expression surprised me. The guilt I'd been carrying for weeks bubbled up. I remembered my confession penance. It was my moment to do something, and nothing would make it less awful, so I leaned close and whispered, "I'm sorry that I don't speak up for you when I should. I'm too afraid. I know it's not right, I just can't stop worrying that I'll be even more of a loner. Except I—I knew it wasn't your picture. I should've said so." I hated that I was mostly apologizing to make myself feel better.

I wanted CJ's wrath. Or her disgust, or disappointment. But when the bell rang, all her face held was a wrecked understanding: *I get it, don't be sorry*. It crushed me. I barely registered what I said to anyone else, 'til at last I was on the silent aisle, and it was my turn to receive feedback. I looked at Lilliam Arceo and my breath caught in a spike of anxiety: What if all anyone said was, *I'm sorry for ignoring you?* Lilliam caught my shoulder and said, "You're, um, nice, Raquel. You're so quiet sometimes that it's hard to get to know you. But I think you're a nice girl." I started to say a relieved *thank you* then remembered I wasn't allowed to speak. Since we had time left, she added, "I never forgot how in Cooking Club in grade three you gave me some of the palitaw you made with CJ and Tisha."

I recalled that palitaw, my delight as the white circles floated to the top of the boiling water. We'd fished them out with forks, sprinkled them with sugar and grated coconut. Third grade was the last time we'd been an official barkada; it stung, that even others remembered. The bell chimed, and Sandra Yu told me she was still impressed by my Spelling Bee win. I started to relax. My guilt towards CJ was tempered with relief at my classmates' comments. Maybe I'd done something right by holding myself apart after all. It confirmed my theory that while I didn't stand out, my classmates at least didn't harbor ill will towards me; if they tried, they could even say kind things, resurface a positive interaction or two that had slipped my mind.

When I faced Tisha again she was clearly upset, unlike the previous round. I swallowed. Her voice was cold in my ear. "You don't need to worry about me, Raquel," she said. "You don't even know what you're talking about. I can take care of myself. I remember that about you, always trying to be *caring*—God, it's annoying. What for? Go find another outlet that's not me." I looked at her, but she was gazing past my shoulder, eyes bright like she wanted to burn holes through the wall.

I wanted to take her wrist, clasp fingers, let her know she wasn't alone—the disgusting audacity of that. Her pride would never let her. My fear wouldn't let me, and what if I was reading it wrong? What was I missing? What was Tisha so defensive about? *Something is happening here that I don't understand. It's better for me not to.* It didn't help that Sir Tonio kept urging us to spew our emotions all over each other. By this point some girls were crying, sniffling as they dredged up sweetnesses or sorrows long buried under the endless days of class together. By the time I was facing CJ again, I felt lightheaded, dizzy from overthinking and the oppressive outpouring of feelings in the room.

CJ slid forward so that our cheeks were nearly touching. I couldn't see her face. Her voice shook as she said, "I know why, Raquel. I'm so sorry." The words caught me completely off-guard. CJ, apologizing after what *I* had done? It was so wrong I opened my mouth to speak, but CJ continued, "We haven't really gotten along the past few years, and there were times I hated you for it, but there's no way I think you deserve that. Don't worry. I won't let him. I know what to do. We're going to be all right."

The next bell made me jerk. CJ gave a brittle smile as she moved seats. I couldn't stop the creep of realization, even as I resisted—*No, I don't want to know this. No, no, no.* As things clicked into place. My head filled with buzzing, punctuated by the ringing bell; I couldn't fathom the hand that held that bell, the arm that shook it gently. The voice telling us the next person would be the last. I had understood wrong. *Sir Tonio in the bathroom last night.* My imagination was acting up. *CJ's face as Sir Tonio approached during the washing of the feet.* We were safe. *Every teacher has a floor plan.*

We were safe.

You have it wrong, CJ, it's not me, I'm not the one—

But if it wasn't me, it was someone else. The thought sickened me all through my blood, down to my toes. The bell chimed, twice. Girls were gasping, from all the tender utterances we'd had to endure.

"Please help us stack the chairs in the corners of the room," Miss Caledo said. I felt calmer with her near. *Mother-mother-mother,* I pleaded. *Don't let him be alone with us.* The ugliness of what I was still trying *not* to understand reared its head. I ignored it by hanging on to her words: "Come and pick up your palanca envelopes and a candle. When you're finished, please return quietly to your rooms."

I wanted to talk to CJ. I didn't. I needed to ask her what she knew. I couldn't. *He can't do this to us,* she'd said. So it was her, and—oh. Oh. Tisha's venom, the quiet warning in it. *Oh.*

I hoped that I was wrong. CJ wouldn't meet my frantic gaze as she paced to a far corner of the room, a slim envelope in her hands. *What do we do with this knowledge?* Tisha plopped herself by a column on the far side of the room. *What if she wants it?* The teachers started playing a cassette tape, piano versions of the Bukas Palad mass collection.

"Miss Mendoza," Sir Tonio said, too close, too close. I sucked in a breath. "Your envelope. Are you all right?"

"Yes, sir. Thank you sir." I took the envelope, swallowed, found a place to sit. I couldn't focus on my letters. My heart couldn't read the words. I wished that I didn't know, didn't care. I was already justifying running away, whether I could live with myself if I did; how I'd feel if the answer was *yes*.

When you have a kid you don't want them to know about any of your bad traits, but you're still *yourself*, with all those same flaws, now magnified in your child's trusting eyes. Did I ask to be so loved, giving birth to her? Did I want to be a superhero, invincible? It wasn't a consideration, not when we first decided to have children; not even when I first held her in my arms, a squishy bundle covered in my slick. I wanted the world for her then but I didn't care about my place in it. I had no inflated thoughts about what I needed to be. In many ways I was still my own person.

This changed when she started asking questions. They were easy at first, straightforward enough. *What's that? What's this?* Then the whys, the hows. Sometimes my first answer wasn't strictly correct; there started to be more times when I didn't know. It shocked me. How could I not know? How could my child ask a question I had no answer to? What did that mean? Still, it seemed impossible to tell her *I don't know*. Instead I'd make something up, as reasonably as I could, and reassure myself it was the best answer she could get.

I never considered myself a perfectionist. Survival, simple joy, was enough. Until Andy. Why couldn't I be a cooler mom for her? Been a renowned doctora, or gotten an MBA at an Ivy League school. I know these feelings are useless, that beating myself up for things I can't change is standard operating procedure for me. I can't even tell her about the one time I was wholly, undoubtedly, proud of myself.

She saw it once, anyway.

Mom, why do you have this on your throat? My daughter pressed her chubby fingers to the faint lines there, so that my whole body tensed.

Oh, baby, you can see it? No one else can. Except for Tisha, and CJ.

Hmm?

When I was a girl I helped save someone, and got this out of it.

You're a hero, then?

Oh, not really. I only helped.

Oh. She wavers, trying to decide between disappointment and acceptance. *You still helped though!*

I did, I say, not adding that I almost didn't. I'd called on that bravery just once in my life, and maybe never again. Not unless Andy needs it. I hope she'll never need it.

Andy doesn't see me as human yet, I don't think. She'll get there over time. Needing a bra, getting her period, texting some boy in mysterious teen lingo. I remember how it happened for me: when I realized my mom couldn't do anything for my situation at school; how I held my breath every recess, wanting to be allowed to exist. I resented her ignorance even if I did nothing to improve it. She loved me but didn't know my life, couldn't make anyone else do anything *for* me—that would be so against the rules.

What rules?

Those silent rules that plague us. The softness of our bodies, the spaces between our legs. The world's propensity to take. Our instinct to be cruel and kind to each other—how we'll laugh at a clumsy bitch who falls, then feel benevolent when we help her up. We're so good at that sort of thing, this worldly secret: what we'll do to survive, which is anything, because nothing matters more.

What I'd give so Andy never learns this. So survival can be a given.

There was no chance to speak to CJ after palanca reading. I usually left earlier than the other girls because I had fewer letters, but almost the whole point of palancas was to leave you weary and cried out so that you went to sleep lightheaded and muzzy. People never felt like talking, after. Their hearts were too full. I tried to remember which room was CJ's. It wasn't like I could knock and randomly enter rooms until I found her. What would I even say? *What did he do to you? What do you think he's doing to me? Because I think it's not me, I think it's—*

The not wanting to confirm. The hope that I was wrong.

We should tell someone. We should get help.

The terror of saying it; the longing to have absolutely no part in it.

I brushed my teeth, half-hoping to run into CJ in the bathroom, but no one came except a red-eyed Char. Back in my room, I had already changed into my pajamas when Danica arrived. I crawled into bed and said "Goodnight." She murmured a reply while stepping out with her toiletry bag. I curled onto my left side and kept my eyes trained on the bars of light that striped our ceiling, coming in through the thin curtains. *I'll talk to her when we're back at school. I'll find a way to help.* The idea reassured me slightly.

I slowed my breathing and shut my eyes. I was trying so hard to fall asleep that it seemed, for an agonizing stretch of time, impossible. When it finally happened it came quick as a sudden blow to the head: one moment the anxious discomfort of wondering; then darkness, like a hammer stilling the body.

I awoke with a jolt, soaked in sweat, shirt clinging to my skin. I sat up. I'd had a dream but couldn't remember it. I didn't want to. I rubbed my face, checked my watch: 2:46 a.m. Nearly Bloody Mary's hour. Danica breathed softly across from me. I fell back on my pillow, closed my eyes, beyond frustrated at sleeping so poorly despite being so tired. I hadn't packed a spare shirt since we were only staying two nights. I felt gross and sticky, and couldn't stop shivering, hot and cold at once. Maybe I was coming down with something.

I dug around in my backpack for a panyo, wiped my face, considered washing up. I did not like the idea of going to the bathroom. I couldn't handle finding Sir Tonio roving or—worse. I rolled over. Sleep said *fuck you.* Pulling on my slippers, I shuffled out of my room, nerves taut.

Someone was standing in the middle of the corridor, hands clasped in front of the altar. In her pantulog she looked tiny, suspended in the warped lighting of the hallway, but the shadow behind her was enormous. My body spasmed with fear. I'd left my glasses again, but I knew it was CJ.

Her eyes snapped to mine. They were wide, like she was trying very hard to *see* something.

"Raquel," she said. There was another voice threaded through hers.

I tugged on the back of my shirt with a shaky hand, peeling it from my body. This was an opportunity, right? I had wanted to talk to her.

"CJ, what are you doing?" I whispered because I didn't want to wake anyone. My heart seemed too loud, climbing my chest, squeezing through my throat, pounding louder and louder in my skull.

CJ tipped her head to one side. The motion threw her off-balance; she staggered and caught herself on the wall. Giggling, she lifted her hands then held them out to me.

"I'm asking for intercession," she said dreamily, and moved forward. I wanted to back away, but I froze, watching her hands, her easy smile, get closer and closer. "Don't be afraid, Raquel. She will protect us."

"I don't know what you—"

"*Shhh.*" She touched an ice-cold finger to my lips so that my entire body flinched. In the silence that followed I heard, so distinctly it seemed less real and more imagination, a creak and thump somewhere above us. "We should hurry," she added, her eyes taking on a sudden intensity: a hyper focus that saw nothing. When she dropped her hand to twine fingers with mine I let her, tugged by her urgency and my wild thrashing heart. *She's in danger.*

"Okay," I said, not sure what I was agreeing to. CJ's palm was cold and dry against my sweaty one. We made our way down the hall to the staircase. My knees shook as we climbed, but CJ's hand, tight over mine, was filled with an alarming strength, dragging me up step over step.

I can walk on my own, I wanted to tell her, but my mouth was arid, like I'd eaten a pack of polvoron. I couldn't even taste my saliva, still sour from sleep, as we ignored the dining hall and kept ascending.

If we're going where we're going why do you need me?

How did you get this strong?

Who are you asking intercession from?

This last one I managed to say aloud, as we reached the second floor and moved towards the makeshift confessional.

"From someone stronger than us," CJ answered, and that second voice was there again, this time tinged with laughter. For a moment, the words of our daily prayer to St. Agnes—which we would recite, as one student body, right after the Angelus every lunchtime—came to mind. *Remember now the dangers that surround me in this vale of tears.* CJ squeezed my hand and stepped in front of the door. I squeezed back, eyes narrowed, chest all tremors. CJ turned the knob and swung the door open.

Tisha was on the couch. Sir Tonio was on the floor between her legs. Her jogging pants were around her ankles, her panties just past her knees. Her hands were on his shoulders, elbows bent like she was straining against him. The air smelled like sweat and girl-hood: the anxiety we were introduced to when we started having to wear pantyliners and worrying about our period; the shame we felt, encountering a makeout scene or reading the sexy parts in a Nicholas Sparks novel, as our bodies responded in that traitorous, forbidden way—except this was shame electric with fear, a tremor so sharp in the air my mouth fell open.

Sir Tonio's arm moved. Tisha gasped—the kind of shudder-gasp I've only ever done when I can't breathe properly—and croaked, "No, no, no." The light from the hall fell onto Sir Tonio's shoulder and Tisha's face, cutting a pale strip from her chin to her hairline. She glanced at us, and her eyes—Letitia Tan's proud, indestructible eyes—held the same living fear that filled the room from its dusty tiles to the ceiling.

Sir Tonio went, "That's it, babe, relax," then finally noticed the light over Tisha's face. He turned, still with the presence of mind to keep his voice down as he said, "Who the hell—"

Hell—now that was a funny word for Sir Tonio to end on.

Years later, I will try to understand what exactly it was that I saw. I will blame my inaccurate memory on my lack of glasses, how that blurred all the details. I will tell myself: there was no way for me to make out the subtleties in Letitia's expression, what exactly Sir Tonio's face did as a shadow spilled between me and CJ and moved into the room. I will hope that the shadow came from us both, but I know it was CJ who called it, with her blood and spirit, made a sacrifice at the altar downstairs or the foot of her bed; *she* was the one who boldly took pain and shame and numbed them to something we could use without hysteria, forged them into something sharp and deadly. The courage of a girl who wouldn't flinch in the face of a whorehouse or torture or the edge of a blade against her neck, the bleating of lambs transformed into a fever chorus of ghosts, manifested in a *thing* that crawled to Sir Tonio, who tried to stand and instead was rammed bodily into the floor.

CJ's knees buckled. She let go of my hand and went "Ahhh, ahhh," and foam poured from her mouth. Any other time I would have panicked, screamed, fled for the teachers; but I could see Tisha's pale thighs across the room, Sir Tonio bucking on the floor as the thing held him down, though he was fighting it—pushing against it, with that inhuman strength men sometimes get, desperate to prove themselves right by winning. *I won't let you,* I thought, with a calm that was not my own, and with inexplicable clarity I drew a fingernail across my neck. The skin parted as easily as if I were using a knife. Blood dripped down to the collar of my shirt as I knelt next to CJ and threaded my hand with hers again, my brain snagging on the phrase *give us strength, give us strength, give us strength.*

In our hour of need and against the evils of the world—the shadow sucked every drop of strength I could give it. It reared back, lifting Sir Tonio, and slammed his head against the floor again. I could feel my energy going dry, spit stringing down from my mouth as I fought to keep my mind on that one thought: *give us strength.* CJ choked out, "Help," and I didn't know who she was talking to, but suddenly Tisha moved from the couch to the floor, clawed at her own neck with one hand. Her shadow flowed into ours as the pressure in the room shifted from broken fear to the glacial inferno of rage.

The shadow bent over Sir Tonio, stretched over him, and he *screamed.*

I hadn't known that a scream could be so satisfying. That fear could taste like this.

The being had no wings and nearly no face. The being was a darkness made of blood and force and the belief of three girls who were not afraid of fire, and before our tenuous hold on it could snap Tisha said "Fuck" and cut her power off. The shadow keened, reared back, its mouth trained on us as I wrenched my self away from it, ripping any shreds left tying it to my soul; next to me, CJ, on her elbows in pools of her own spit, did the same, a sloppy break like someone cutting through cloth with blunt scissors. The shadow dissolved, back into each of us or whatever dimension it came from. Sir Tonio lay still on the floor.

I ignored him and crept over to Tisha, my body spasming. I didn't know what I was doing until I reached out, touched her cheeks, felt her shudder. One of my hands carded through her hair, trembling.

"Tisha," I whispered.

She kept shaking, but her eyes were hers again. "I'm fine," she answered. She lifted onto her knees and pulled up her underwear and her pants, the motion exacting, devoid of shame. CJ padded over to us. There was blood all over her neck and collarbones but no visible wound, no stains on her shirt.

From where we were, piled against the couch, we could see the mess of Sir Tonio. Blood had poured out of every hole in his face;

his head was haloed in red, vivid against the faded tiles. His eyes were open and white as eggshells. His fingers twitched. I wished I hadn't seen.

"We s-should go," CJ said, slurring slightly. We struggled to stand. We made it out by leaning on each other, Tisha strung between us as we staggered into the hall. It surprised me that almost no time had passed. It felt like the night had been split open: gutted and poured down our throats, all the bitterness and satisfaction of *knowing.* A prayer surfaced in my head again. *So young yet made so strong and wise by the power of God. Vessel of honor. Flower of unfading fragrance.*

In the hallway downstairs, limping to the bathroom, we crossed her portrait. Her gaze remained heavenward, but her expression looked different. Before, she had sometimes seemed blank to me, unfocused. I'd missed it all along: how she was giving witness to something, unable to speak.

Having finished Andy's hair, I insist on taking some photos before we head to the mall. She says *"Mommy!"*—exasperated—then gets into it, flashing different poses while I use portrait mode. We're heading to the mall for our respective hangouts: Andy with her barkada, to celebrate someone's birthday at Chili's then Q Power Station; myself with Tisha and CJ, at a new Asian-fusion place that's partly-owned by one of Tisha's investor friends.

I check myself in the foyer mirror one more time. Over the years I've gotten better at dressing up; Tisha had a lot to do with it, taking it upon herself to style me when possible. In high school that would have mortified me. As an adult, I don't mind admitting that it's nice to look good, or at least *okay*, next to her. I put in effort the way anyone going to Rockwell would, but admittedly I step up my game when meeting my best friends, because we're Agnesians with a reputation to keep—or new reputations to uphold, anyway. (I started going by Elle when I went to college. Tisha and CJ always tease me about it. I think my college friends and coworkers would be surprised to know about my loner past.)

"Do you have your gift for Mela?" I ask as we head out the door.

"*Ye-e-es,*" Andy singsongs, gesturing at the bag in her hand, which contains a 12-piece jelly-pen set and a pretty notebook we picked out together. I tell manang we'll be back home for dinner, and we take the elevator down to the condo lobby. Andy and I are preoccupied with our cellphones while waiting for the car to arrive. Midway through someone's long post about a miracle diet, I reach for Andy, petting her arm. She squirms, eyes fixed on her phone screen, where a dog is harvesting tomatoes. "Mommy, you keep touching me today. What's wrong?"

"Nothing, baby."

"Mm-hmm. You only call me baby when something's wrong, too." Andy slips me a sideways glance, then takes pity and wriggles closer. "Look, Mama. I learned a new dance in the game." She swipes with her finger. The dog throws a tomato into a basket and starts break dancing. I giggle as our car rolls into the driveway. Are moms allowed to giggle? If they can't understand the thing—maybe?

Tisha took a shower. The running water sounded thunderous. She hissed when the lukewarm spray hit her. CJ and I washed our faces and mouths off in the sink. I felt weak, insubstantial, probably from blood loss, though there was no cut on my neck, no blood on my clothes. There was only the faintest trace of a scar; CJ had one too. She touched hers tentatively, and I found myself doing the same.

"My room's closest," CJ said, voice cracking. "I'll get a towel and panty for Tisha."

"Wait—don't leave—" Tisha cracked the stall door open. Her face poked out at us, warning. I marveled that she could look angry right now. I couldn't muster any expression.

"I'm here," I said, as CJ nodded at me and went. "Don't worry, I'm not going."

Tisha narrowed her eyes, but went back to showering, leaving the stall door slightly open.

CJ came back a few minutes later. We waited together. It took us a moment to notice Tisha speaking; the water pressure wasn't strong, but it still obscured her words, as did the wooziness we felt. "I thought it was exciting at first," she murmured. "I thought it was kind of fun. It was—we only ever kissed. Until we got here. I didn't want—I *told* him I didn't want to." It sounded like she was telling herself. The water switched off. Into the silence she said, "Maybe I was asking for it."

I shivered. She opened the door wider. CJ passed her the towel and underwear. Tisha took them both and dried herself off. I remembered the summer we'd crammed into the same shower stall, laughing as we struggled out of our swimsuits. Our bodies had been so different—our lives. Back then there were things that made us cry, but there was so much less to make us afraid, or angry, or betrayed.

"Tisha, did he . . ." CJ trailed off. "Yesterday, I mean. I put a ward on the wrong room."

Tisha shook her head, pulling on her pajamas. There were bruises on her arm that I'd missed earlier that day, because of the cardigan. "No. Not that far."

My body convulsed. What we watered down, to make it not so bad. How Tisha had always been so strong. How I'd started breaking right before palanca reading, at just *the idea.* How that seemed the most natural thing in the world to do. How CJ said no. How Tisha said no. How, because I didn't think too much, I let myself say *no.*

"CJ," Tisha started. "I didn't—I thought it was wrong for him to go for you too. I was *jealous.* I'm so fucking stupid. I just—I couldn't let people find out about us. It was easier to both let it be you and hate you for it."

"You're right. That was a real bitch move."

Tisha's shoulders hitched. But CJ didn't look angry. Just tired.

"It doesn't make what he did to you okay. It doesn't make what he *tried* to do to me okay."

"I'd rather you hate me than pity me."

"I wish, for once, you would drop the tough-girl act."

"It's not an act!" Tisha blurted, then clapped her hands to her mouth. Angry tears stood in her eyes. She glared at us, shaking her head; she didn't trust herself to speak.

"Hating you won't make me feel better," CJ said, firm and quiet. "I used to think it would. But it won't."

She glanced at me, and I swallowed. "You too, Raquel," CJ said. "This whole thing was stupid."

"CJ—I'm sorry—" And I really was, *finally*. Sorry for all of it, and not because I was ashamed, but because CJ *hadn't deserved it.* Not for being goth and not for wearing a shitty bra; not even for being socially awkward. I could have made a difference. I would, now. It was like finding the will to cut myself open for that shadow: I could do what was right, if only I stopped being afraid.

"You don't have to be nice to me, either," CJ said. "I did this because I wanted to."

Tisha seemed to have calmed. She rubbed her eyes and brought her hands down, clenching them into fists. "Still," she muttered. "I ought to give you something. Even if it's selfish of me to ask that."

"Fine," CJ said. Tisha and I waited. She frowned at us. "Answer honestly. Was it your boob, in the picture?"

"My b—no!" Tisha laughed. It sounded completely ridiculous, given the moment, and was therefore perfect. "No, *that was not my boob.* Clearly not!" She slapped her own boob, so thoughtlessly that CJ gave a huff of laughter, and I started cracking up too. In a second the three of us were gasping for breath, laughing, as if we'd been telling green jokes in the bathroom this whole time. Tisha was wiping her eyes again, but for an entirely different reason. "It was some dumb internet photo, I bet. Okay, okay. I'll tell everyone it was not your fucking boob. It was no one's."

"That would help," CJ said.

"I'll back it up," I answered, dutifully. It was too little too late, and I didn't have Tisha's cache—but another voice could help. Maybe I'd even find the will to go beyond that. CJ stared at us, and Tisha and I looked at each other. Something was different.

"So, what now?" CJ said.

I spoke before I'd had time to think about it. "Do you—do you want to sleep together?"

Tisha sighed. "If anyone sees us they'll call us lesbians."

I nodded, face heating, shifting weight from one foot to another. Of course. In three hours when the roosters crowed maybe I'd startle awake and find this was all a dream; Sir Tonio would call out reminders at breakfast; CJ and Tisha and I still wouldn't talk to each other. If it meant Tisha never got touched I'd rather that be the truth—instead of the nightmare she'd braved, and the nightmare we'd summoned. If we pretended none of it happened, then maybe none of it did happen. If Sir Tonio wasn't dead. If Tisha was really all right.

"But," Tisha continued. "I don't think I really give a shit."

CJ looked contemplative, then nodded, grinning. "We can go to our own rooms before everyone else wakes up."

I don't know why that made me so happy. We held hands as we went into the hall, like we were six instead of sixteen. We crashed in Tisha's room because she insisted Meggie slept like a log. Meggie was facing the wall, thin blanket pulled up to her nose. The bed couldn't exactly fit us, but we squished into it anyway, tucking up to make ourselves smaller. It felt like we were one thing: CJ against the wall, Tisha between us, me on the edge, leaning in to keep from falling.

I couldn't sleep, but my body was so exhausted that I dozed. In half-sleep it took me a while to realize Tisha was crying again. She was trying so hard to keep it in. A bright, engulfing hate filled me. I touched her hair. She sniffled. I wished we'd torn him apart. CJ's hand found mine over Tisha's hip, and we curled in tight, trying to make space for ourselves, an existence free from anything the world could throw at us and expect us to simply suffer and suffer.

Screams. The human kind. I sat up in my bed—I barely remembered slipping away to it, CJ and I patting Tisha's face, telling her to keep sleeping. They'd found Sir Tonio's body.

Danica mumbled, "Again? What now?"

"I think they're yelling . . . *something,*" I answered, slowly relaxing. It was Juana, the angry woman from the condo next door, who insisted on screaming at us every retreat, presumably because we were too noisy. But it had been *palanca reading* last night; we'd been positively quiet.

"MGA HUDAS!" She screeched. "MGA HUDAS KAYO!"

"Oh, it's Juana," Danica said. She looked over, sleep-rumpled, and startled. "Uh, Raquel. Are you okay?"

"What?"

"Your face looks—um—you look really tired."

"MGA MALALANDI!" Juana yelled.

"Oh," I touched my cheek. "Yeah. I kept waking up last night."

"Sorry, was I snoring?"

"No, I just. I kept having weird dreams." It struck me that I was having a perfectly normal conversation with Danica. Or did we always talk this way? It wasn't scary or nerve-wracking at all.

"NAG-RETREAT PA KAYO!"

Juana yelled at us throughout breakfast, which was probably why we didn't hear any other shriek. It was only when we were polishing off the scrambled eggs that Miss Caledo solemnly told us something had happened to Sir Tonio, and he had been taken to the hospital. Our morning chatter erupted into a flurry. CJ, Tisha, and I found each other's gazes.

"What happened to Sir Tonio, ma'am?" Tetet asked.

"We don't know," Miss Caledo said. "It—it might have been a stroke." She looked regretful saying it, because that simply increased the chatter. I wondered if the blood from the confession room had evaporated after all. Whatever we'd done, it left no obvious traces.

"I hope he gets well soon!" Romina said. Miss Caledo seized this opportunity to lead us in a prayer for Sir Tonio's swift recovery. I mouthed along, the words detached from everything I felt. After breakfast we had thirty minutes to brush our teeth, pack our things, and head to the bus. On our way out Juana stood by the road, jeering, her face livid as she accused us of being sluts and traitors. No one knew why Juana hated us so much. Legend had it that three years ago a batch had taken great pains to taunt her from the rooftop. She'd already thought us incorrigible bitches before, but now she was set on telling us so with great gusto. The school had repeatedly tried to calm her down, to no avail. She'd become a retreat fixture, in her own way.

As we filed into the bus, I noticed that CJ was already in the back row, claiming the same spot that she took on our way over. Normally people loved the back row as it was the farthest from the teachers, but it was a dead zone if uncool people were there. Danica settled in close to the front, for easy access to snacks. Traditionally you were seatmates with your roommate, but I had a sudden burst of bravado. "I'm going to sit at the back," I told her. "There's more space."

"Uh, okay," she said, unable to help stealing a look at CJ, who was leaning her head against the window.

I walked up to CJ and took one seat away from her. "Hi," I said, offering a smile. Again, this was easy. I felt like I belonged in my own skin. It was a weird thing to think.

"Hey," CJ said, eyes widening. She slumped into her seat. "This isn't—thank you, or sorry, or anything. I told you, you don't need to."

"It's not that," I said. "Can I sit here?"

She shrugged. "Yeah. Okay. If you're sure."

We lapsed into silence, 'til I said, "Have you ever thought of recording Juana for your alarm?"

That got her to smirk. She asked about my parents, and we caught up as the bus continued to fill. Our talk was interrupted by

Tisha coming to stand before us, somewhat imperiously. That was her default Tisha-ness. I forgave it.

"So," she said, her proud expression both challenging and faltering. CJ and I glanced at each other, mystified. It was one thing to be all right in private. *Publicly* acknowledging us seemed like overkill, for Letitia Tan. But apparently, as she'd said, she didn't give a shit. "Is this seat free?" She nudged the one between us with her knee.

"Um. Yeah," I said.

Tisha dropped into it. We didn't stop talking the whole drive home, except for the last thirty minutes, barely moving in EDSA traffic, when all three of us fell asleep, heads lolling on each others' shoulders.

Everyone was weirded out. They didn't know how to deal with Tisha talking to me *or* CJ. For a week or two they speculated that we were blackmailing her, but there was no evidence and the three of us simply didn't care. We started eating lunch together. Tisha and CJ came over one weekend to watch some DVDs, and Mom got overly emotional serving us Tang and grilled cheese sandwiches, like when we were little.

We went stag to prom, satisfied with each other as dates.

We got a substitute CL teacher. Sir Tonio apparently had a brain aneurysm. He was alive, but it was hard to say when he would be well enough to teach again.

The retreat house got partially destroyed in a freak fire over the summer. In our senior year of high school, retreat was held on-campus instead. We read our palancas in the auditorium, crying as we hoped for the future.

Andy comes with me to the restaurant to say hi to her ninangs. Mela and Mela's yaya will pick her up shortly. I've made Andy promise to check her cellphone every 30 minutes, and ensure it's not on silent mode.

Tisha is at the restaurant, having shaken off the shackles of Filipino time while in America. Two waiters, probably a decade younger than us, are failing to discreetly stare at her while she scowls at the menu. The resto's decor is pretty, warm wood with metal accents. There are open tables, but it's busier than I would expect for a new place. Tisha looks up as we enter, dazzling us with her smile: upper teeth resting on bottom lip (she taught me that technique, shocked I didn't know it, in senior year). Andy rushes to her, arms out. Tisha stoops to embrace her and Andy smooches her cheek.

"Why are you so *big*?" Tisha says, fake-aghast.

"Ninang, you said that last time."

"But I swear you've gotten even bigger!"

CJ arrives ten minutes later, looking annoyed.

"Sorry I'm late!" she huffs. "Traffic along EDSA."

"We just got here," I say. Andy comes around the table and gives her a hug. We take our seats, and I listen to my best friends catch up with my daughter, asking her about school and her barkada and what she's been reading, while I browse the menu and feel my heart swell and swell. My girls, all together. How they saved me when we saved each other. The waiters come by to refill our glasses and ask if we know our drink orders; we apologize and say we need more time.

"Your hair is so pretty," CJ admires.

"Mommy did it," Andy says.

I wink at them, feeling more proud than I probably should.

"Andy!" someone calls from outside the restaurant. Mela is at the entrance, waving. Andy and I get up; Tisha says, "Wait wait wait, let's selfie muna."

The four of us crowd awkwardly before one of the eager waiters offers to take it for us. Tisha checks his work. Leaning over her shoulder, I murmur with satisfaction. Outside the restaurant, Mela kisses me on the cheek and calls me tita. I'm used to it by now, but it still makes me feel old. I chat with her yaya to make sure she has my number, double-check that Andy has enough allowance ("Yes! Stop worrying!"), and give her one last hug before they go off.

"See you in a few hours," I say. "Stick with your friends. Be safe, okay?"

"I'm nine, Mom," she mutters, long-suffering. In front of her friends, I become *mom* and not *mommy* or *mama.*

Nine is so young, but I don't tell her that. I keep clutching her, so she relents and says, "Okay. Don't worry. I'll be fine."

Since I'm soft, since Andy is everything to me, tears spring to my eyes. I watch as she and Mela walk away, exchanging tips on tomato harvesting.

Tisha and CJ are ordering by the time I get back to the table. I don't mind. They know my taste, and I'm the least-picky eater anyway.

"Why are you teary?" CJ asks, a knowing grin on her face.

"I can't help worrying. She's getting to be that age, you know."

"You can't stop her from growing up." Tisha sips her Thai iced tea.

"I know, I know. It's not like I want to stop her!"

"She's got us," CJ points out.

It's not enough, because nothing ever is. But it makes a difference. There are ways of fighting back, especially if you're not alone—which Andy isn't. She's already learning it, I'm sure. I can trust in *that,* at least, much more than anything else in the world. I flag a waiter to order my own iced tea, ask Tisha to send me the photo, and let my daughter go where I can't see her.

I've wanted to be a writer since kindergarten. I've worked at it all this time, but I recognize that I'm still here mostly because I'm the luckiest when it comes to people.

I'd like to thank my editors and publishers, Gavin J. Grant and Kelly Link, for giving this collection a home at Small Beer Press. Thank you for bringing these stories together. I am so grateful for your collaboration and support.

Thank you to Alexa Sharpe for the beautiful, striking cover art.

Most of the stories in this collection were first improved by editors taking a chance on a newer author, a kindness I'll always remember. Special shout-out to Dean and Nikki Alfar, John Joseph Adams, and Carl Engle-Laird for their early encouragement.

For help with a story rewrite, thank you to Apo Española and Patricia Hernandez. For granting the use of her beautiful words for Anyag's letter, thank you to Barbara Jane Reyes. For the *Impunity Series,* which was crucial to writing "Asphalt," thank you to Rappler and Patricia Evangelista.

Many friends have made my life brighter, allowing me to ask silly questions and share barely-coherent ideas. Your companionship makes it possible for me to create and enjoy myself.

Thank you to my high school barkada, the mellishes: Ina, Wowie, Nikki, Meggie, Chesca, Mia, Kat, Iris; Isha, for being a rock; Sara, for coffee and words; Mara, my inadvertent story-doctor; Maddi, you're a derp. I love y'all and hope we can be sabaw together until we're grandmas.

Thank you to my lady knights, Nica Bengzon and Stef Tran. So many of the stories in here wouldn't have made it over that hill of self-doubt, fatigue, and straight-up embarrassment without your cheering and flailing. You make me braver.

Thank you to friends from P5, AJSS, Heights, and Guidebook. Thank you to my English and Lit teachers through the years. Thank you to Ninang Meg, for sending me books as I was growing up, and introducing me to the work of Diana Wynne-Jones. Thank you to those who gave me space to share my stories, and second homes in lonely cities: Katie Williams, Iain Whiteside, and Ainsley Kelly in San Francisco; Sara Saab, Emma Cosh, and Chris Kammerud in London; Jess Barber, Ian Muneshwar, and Cadwell Turnbull in Boston.

At Harvard Business School: my Section F Fuegos, Que Fiesta, Joy Luck Club, HOTS, Barkada, Titas of Manila, Duo-friends, my professors, my Harvard fiction and poetry workshops, and so many who were generous with their time, care, and intellect—thank you for broadening my world.

When I was a new writer, struggling with community and my place in it, several folks took it upon themselves to welcome me. I can't thank everyone, but among them are Aliette de Bodard, Zen Cho, Kate Elliott, Cindy Pon, Rochita Loenen-Ruiz, Sam J. Miller, Mia Sereno, Usman Malik, Vida Cruz, Neon Yang, Priya Sharma, Charlie Jane Anders, Shelley Streeby, Fran Wilde, Julia Rios, Victor Ocampo, Helen Marshall, and Sofia Samatar—at various points, though you may not have known it, you helped me take my own writing more seriously. I hope to do that for other writers.

Tamsyn Muir, thank you for feeding me ice cream and asking what I'm writing next; you know what it has meant to me. I'm glad we once upon a time wept over the same OTP.

Many fanfic writers inspire me, and shape how I string words together. On LiveJournal, FF.net, and AO3, I learned what it meant for a story to make one's heart sing. To these authors: I hope you're still writing, and taking care no matter what.

Thank you to the Clarion class of 2013, my beloved Rocketship Spatulas, for teaching me that it was okay to pursue my weird, and inspiring me with your words: Brandon Haller, Kodiak Julian, Will Kaufman, Marie Vibbert, Jessica Cluess, Christian Coleman, Eliza Tiernan, Gabriela Santiago, Zach Grafton, Angus McIntyre, Sophia Echavarria, Thom Dunn, Matt Schnarr, and Pieter Lars van Tatenhove.

Special thanks to Patrick Ropp, for taking care of me during my Pittsburgh summer; Brandie Coonis, for mirroring my heart, and understanding so deeply what it means to love sad; and Alyssa Wong, for being with me in the trash heaps, for making me laugh, and for always believing in my stories. I wouldn't have lasted if you weren't with me on this path, and I hope to keep writing alongside you.

To my Clarion 2013 teachers: Andy Duncan, Nalo Hopkinson, Cory Doctorow, Bob Crais, Karen Joy Fowler, and Kelly Link—thanks for teaching me to stick with it.

To all readers, however and whenever you've encountered my work: thank you for giving my words the gift of your time. It means the world to me.

Finally, I'd like to thank my family. To the Yaps and Santiagos, titos, titas, cousins, and all—you have always kept me grounded, and bundled in your kindness. To my parents, Ato and Jojie, and my siblings, Fonz and Denise: mek mek in the blek blek. I love you guys. Thank you for giving me a constant home, no matter where I am.

Publication History

"Good Girls," *Shimmer* 25, 2015.
"A Cup of Salt Tears," Tor.com, 2014.
"Milagroso," Tor.com, 2015.
"A Spell for Foolish Hearts" appears here for the first time.
"Have You Heard the One About Anamaria Marquez?" *Nightmare Magazine*, 2014.
"Syringe" appears here for the first time.
"Asphalt, River, Mother, Child," *Strange Horizons*, 2018.
"Hurricane Heels (We Go Down Dancing)," *Book Smugglers Publishing*, 2016.
"Only Unclench Your Hand," *What the #@&% Is That?*, 2016.
"How to Swallow the Moon," *Uncanny Magazine*, 2018.
"All the Best of Dark and Bright," *Philippine Speculative Fiction* Volume VII, 2012.
"Misty," *Horror: Filipino Fiction for Young Adults*, 2013.
"A Canticle for Lost Girls" appears here for the first time.

About the Author

Isabel Yap writes fiction and poetry, works in the tech industry, and drinks tea. Born and raised in Manila, she has also lived in California, Boston, and London. She holds a BS in Marketing from Santa Clara University and an MBA from Harvard Business School; she is also a graduate of the 2013 Clarion Writers Workshop. Her work has appeared in venues including Tor.com, *Uncanny Magazine, Lightspeed, Strange Horizons,* and *Year's Best Weird Fiction*. She is @visyap on Twitter and her website is isabelyap.com.

Also Available from Small Beer Press

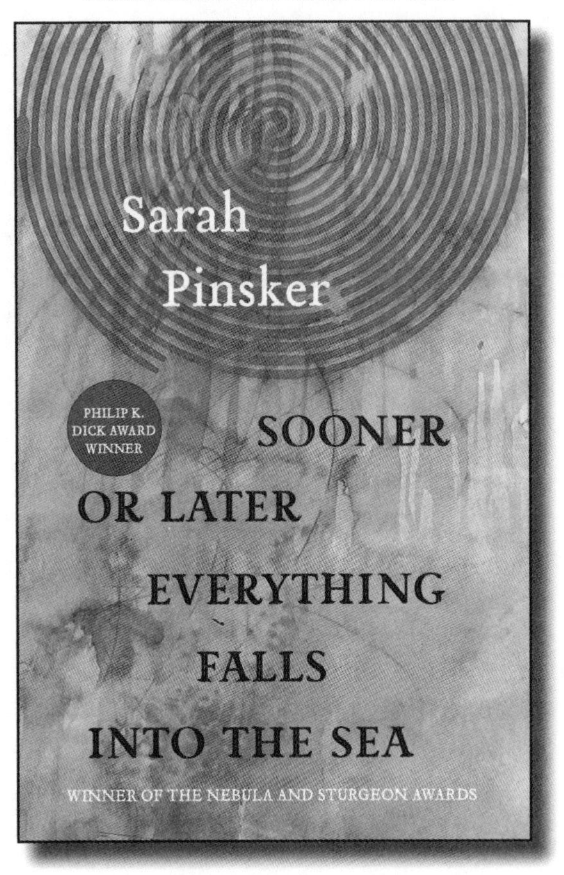

Winner of the Philip K. Dick Award
World Fantasy Award finalist · *Booklist* Top 10 Debut SF&F
Milwaukee Journal Sentinel Best Books of the Year

"Speculative and strange. . . . insightful, funny, and imaginative, diving into the ways humans might invite technology into their relationships." — Arianna Rebolini, *BuzzFeed*

trade paper · 320 pages · $17 · 9781618731555 | ebook · 9781618731562